Black Magick

Volume I

13 Tales of Darkness, Horror & the Occult

Black Magick

Volume I

13 Tales of Darkness, Horror & the Occult

Edited by Raven Digitalis

London, UK
Washington, DC, USA

First published by Moon Books, 2025
Moon Books is an imprint of Collective Ink Ltd.,
Unit 11, Shepperton House, 89 Shepperton Road, London, N1 3DF
office@collectiveinkbooks.com
www.collectiveinkbooks.com
www.moon-books.net

For distributor details and how to order please visit the 'Ordering' section on our website.

ISBN: 978 1 80341 825 4
978 1 80341 842 1 (ebook)
Library of Congress Control Number: 2024936456

A CIP catalogue record for this book is available from the British Library.

Design: Lapiz Digital Services
Associate editing by Miranda S. Hewlett
Selected proofreading by S.M. Lomas

UK: Printed and bound by CPI Group (UK) Ltd, Croydon, CR0 4YY
Printed in North America by CPI GPS partners

Contents

Dedicated to
Storm Constantine
(1956–2021)

Introduction

> *"I think people do kind of gravitate towards horror stories when times are tough, and times are scary — and that's certainly true now... And when you finish, you close the book and you've had a place to put your fears for a little while. You've been able to say, 'These problems are much worse than my problems.' And then you close the book, and you can go to bed and sleep like a baby. At least that's the theory."*
>
> — Stephen King

Hail and welcome!

Shortly after signing the contract for this anthology, I had a vivid dream. In the dream, I was leading a group of fellow dancers down the suffocating confines of a darkened stairwell to the backdrop of an upbeat and random musical number. The dancers were the authors included in this anthology, as well as many characters from their stories, unanimously grooving our way toward the ground floor exit.

Choreographing the moves of twelve independent authors (Poe was especially cooperative) has been both a personal challenge and a joy. I extend deepest gratitude to the fabulous folks at Moon Books for taking a stab at such an unconventional project. This is my first venture into the realm of fiction. I'm best known for my two triptychs of metaphysical guidebooks and Oracle cards: my "empath's trilogy" and my "shadow trilogy" – please see Meet the Authors toward the end of this book for more information.

Any occultist worth their salt understands that magick, just like reality itself, is a rainbow prism without absolutes. The title *Black Magick* is intentionally sarcastic, but harkens to a prevalent concept of "black" magick in reference to castings that decidedly interfere with another's freewill, generally in an effort to cause harm, madness, bad luck, or otherwise propagate crappy conditions. This term and others similar have been sources of fear and superstition for as long as humankind has been aware of their ability to influence change by nonphysical means, and this general concept is the thematic thread that connects the stories in this anthology.

The diversity of this collection is truly exceptional. Styles explored within the tales include folk horror, dark fantasy, mystery, erotica, sci-fi, cryptism, the supernatural, abstract storytelling, queer themes, period pieces, and so much more, all carrying that common theme of baneful magick – a theme that is sometimes apparent and at other times covert. Through fiction, one may explore the "darkness" of humanity, of the unknown, and of fear itself. Consider yourself forewarned.

Please note that nothing here is written by artificial intelligence. AI is taking over creative fields at alarming rates – a horror story in itself – and readers can rest assured that everything contained herein is the creation of the human mind alone. Additionally, I've structured the stories in a way to make for an excellent cover-to-cover read, but all stories are standalone, so feel free to hop around!

This is the culmination of an anthological compilation launched in 2007, now alchemically refined through blood, sweat, and tears – and just the right amount of laughter. Now, a remarkable and humbling 17 years since we set foot on the dancefloor, the *Black Magick* anthology is born, and I couldn't be happier with the result. It's no longer my awkward problem child, but a strong, independent, blossoming bloodflower. It has been an incredible experience watching this project take shape and come to life. I hope it is one of many volumes to come.

Thanks for reviewing (or "starring") this book online if the mood takes you, and for sharing it with others. I'm relying on you, beloved readers, to spread the word!

Happy reading, thanks for your support, and welcome to the spooky soirée.

Jai Sri Ganesha, Jai Mata Di, Aum Namah Shivaya,

Raven Digitalis

Holi Lunar Eclipse, March 2024

Candle Magic

Storm Constantine

The candle was already lit when Felicia came home with the intention of enjoying her Friday afternoon off in peace. She hadn't realised her flat-mate, Emma, was off work as well. A scorching day, too hot for May, and Emma was sitting on the floor lighting candles.

"Oh, you're here," Emma said, looking up. She sounded as disappointed as Felicia to find she'd have company for the day. The air in the room was thick with pungent fruity incense.

"Hmm. Had time in lieu. What are you doing?" Felicia went to open the windows.

Emma glanced at the candle. "Thinking..."

"Thinking..." Felicia nodded. There was a suppressed excitement in Emma's expression she was familiar with. "Anyone I know?"

Emma smiled secretively. "You know what's going on..."

Felicia shook her head and dragged her handbag, which was more like a satchel, over to the sofa. She slumped down and delved for her cigarettes in the depths of the bag. "I don't think either of us know what's going on," she said, lighting up and inhaling with gusto.

Emma laughed again. "Poor Fliss, you're just too practical!"

Felicia disliked the implication in Emma's words. She knew Emma often thought her a dull, unimaginative creature. She took a deep breath. "Look, Em, I'm a friend, so I have to say it: you're obsessed!" She waved her arm emphatically, scattering cigarette ash over the sofa and Emma's lap.

Emma brushed the grey powder from her curled legs as if without thinking. Her expression had soured. "So grateful for your support!"

"Em, *please*!" Felicia groped behind the sofa for an ashtray. "What am I supposed to think?" She laughed nervously. "Next, it'll be eye of newt and wing of bat; you're crazy!"

Emma drew up her knees gracefully, pushing back her auburn hair. She reached towards the single dark green candle standing in a congealing pool of wax on the coffee-table. Her fingers were a fan against the flame. "It can be done," she murmured.

A week previously, Emma had announced that she was in love. Felicia had known Emma for a long time and recognised immediately that her friend had fallen victim to yet another of the intense romantic fantasies, to which she seemed particularly vulnerable in the spring. Outside the window, even in the heart of the city, there was a thrumming vitality to the air. It was possible to feel the thrust of growth, and to be carried with it. Emma's imagination certainly seemed drawn to greater extravagances. Felicia was used to this ritual behaviour. Sometimes she became impatient with it, at other times she was prepared to be understanding. For all Emma's peculiar habits, she and Felicia got on together well, and Felicia had shared accommodation with too many people to undervalue that fact. Still, she and Emma were very different. Felicia had been in love three times in her life, and had once been engaged, but all her affairs had ended in infidelities and unpleasant scenes. Now, she was being cautious, and kept her few suitors at arm's length, allowing them the occasional privilege of her company in a restaurant or club, and even more rarely the odd night of sex in the flat. To Emma, however, love seemed to mean spending endless hours alone, locked in desperate reverie, a condition encouraged by periodic sightings of the object of her desires. It seemed almost like a sickness, a ravaging fever that burned her out. Actual relationships had occasionally sprung from her obsessions, but they had possessed the life-span of a plucked poppy. Felicia doubted Emma had ever been out with anyone that she wasn't obsessed with. Any other man who had the temerity to approach her was rebuffed instantly. Since Felicia and Emma had lived together in the flat – nearly four years now – Felicia had seen several beautiful young men go in and out of Emma's room, and a couple of those had wanted to become permanent fixtures. It had always been Emma who'd sent them packing. Felicia had even been out for a drink with one of them afterwards, to listen to his woeful rantings of unrequited love. Once Emma had decided she no longer liked them, they might as well not exist for her. Still, until the moment they cut their own throats with an unwise remark or behaviour Emma found disappointing, her regard for them was merciless in its intensity. No wonder they felt so bewildered once they'd been rejected. Felicia often felt very sorry for them, but she stood by her friend's determination not to stick with a relationship she was not happy with.

"You'll never learn, will you!" Felicia said, shaking her head, the remark softened by a smile.

Emma refused to be drawn into a sisterly spirit. She frowned. "I know what you're thinking. 'Not this again.' I don't expect you to understand, but..." She hesitated. "This time, it's different." Before Felicia could respond, Emma uncurled from the floor and began to prowl about the room.

Felicia didn't know what to say, wary of encouraging Emma's fixations, but nervous of upsetting her too much. Emma was touching things in a slow, deliberate manner; her beads hanging across the mirror, her crystal in its nest of velvet on the sideboard, her own throat. She and Felicia were the same age – twenty-seven – although Felicia always felt so much older than Emma.

"Perhaps we should talk about it," Felicia said, aware that her voice sounded too shrill. Even though she'd opened the windows, the air in the room was hot; hot and damp and dark. The flat only got the sun in the morning. Later, there might be thunder.

"Talk? There's little to say. I know what I want." Emma turned and smiled a cat's smile, lifting her thick hair in both hands. It appeared to be a studied pose, but Felicia had never quite convinced herself that Emma struck her regular dramatic postures consciously.

"Then, why bother telling me about it at all?"

Emma shrugged. "I thought it best to, in case anything happened."

"What do you mean by that?" Felicia became aware of tension across her forehead, a frown forming. Perhaps it was caused by the humid atmosphere. "Sometimes you frighten me, Em." She stubbed out her cigarette with swift, sharp prods. "What you need is a good time. Less mooning around, more real life."

Emma ignored the advice. "There's nothing to be afraid of. I *will* have him, Fliss..."

Felicia shook her head and gestured at the candle. "And is that what this is all about? Sitting here being witchy and dreaming dreams? Oh, Em, I can't decide whether you want to be the Lady of Shalott or Cleopatra!"

"You always laugh," Emma said nonchalantly, apparently unembarrassed. She came back to squat before the coffee table, her pale hand hovering over the candle flame, her eyes intent. 'This candle, it is exactly the right colour...' Her voice sounded portentous and full of intent.

Felicia sighed. Emma's mystical leanings occasionally bothered her; mostly, they could be ignored. "It's just a candle," she said, and then jumped up too quickly from the sofa. Emma's image seemed to vibrate before her eyes. She rubbed her face, finding her upper lip wet. "Can't bear this heat! Want a drink?"

Emma shook her head. "I'm ok, thanks."

Left alone in the room, Emma cupped her hands around the flame. She took a deep breath, held it, breathed out slowly. "Listen to me...," she said to the flame. "Help me..." She closed her eyes and threw back her head, clasping her crossed ankles. The image of The Man was difficult to conjure, because she was distracted by the sound of Felicia humming loudly to herself in the small kitchen off the sitting-room. She couldn't visualise his face properly. Traffic outside, the sound of children across the street as they played in the school playground; the clatter from builders working on the house next door: all mundane intrusions.

"I believe in what I want," she whispered fervently, "And to believe is to *make* it true."

"What did you say?" Felicia's voice asked from the doorway.

At night, alone with the moon, it was easier for Emma to direct her thoughts. Arms by her side or across her breast, it didn't matter; she visualised. Felicia had argued: "Okay, so he's good-looking, but that doesn't mean he's a nice person." Felicia *would* say something like that. She was attracted to men who were like herself; dependable and direct, scrubbed and neatly dressed.

Emma undressed in the dark and spread out her Tarot cards face down on the rugs in the pale light that came in through the shivering, gauzy curtains. Silvery incense smoke filled the room with the scent of jasmine. She picked a card and held it to her chest for a while, without looking at it. Then, she examined the picture. It was The Moon; signifying secrecy and delusion. *No,* Emma thought. *It is mystery and magic.* She scooped the cards up into their silk wrap and lit a cigarette, leaning back against the end of her bed. She felt the flat was aware of her, its walls listening to the beat of her heart, her thoughts. Felicia was out with all her secretary friends, drinking in wine bars, no doubt being chatted up by dull men. Emma always felt the flat manifested a different personality when she was in it alone. In her opinion, people like Felicia, for all their good intentions, killed any subtle atmosphere that did not fit into their narrow view of reality. Their presence suffocated mystery. They were like rotor-scythes ploughing through an overgrown garden, restoring order to something that had been precious and beautiful in its wilderness.

Tonight, Emma felt powerful and it burned within her like hate. If she stood up, her head would brush the ceiling. Her heart was projecting a net of luminous beams, each of which pulsed like a star at its tip.

She couldn't remember where she had first seen The Man. She was aware Felicia privately scorned what she saw as Emma's regular crushes on people, but Emma couldn't convey to her friend how, this time, the invasion of her thoughts had been not only unwelcome, but somehow threatening. She was torn two ways by the yelping dogs of Resentment and Yearning. The last time she'd fallen in love had been devastating. The man had shattered all her dreams by being not only insensitive and coarse, but unintelligent. He'd confessed he'd not read a book since childhood, and the mirror of Emma's hopes had cracked from side to side. He had been beautiful, but the beauty had been a scale on his skin, easily scratched off. Since then, Emma had vowed not to fall into the same emotional state again. She would retain her common sense and snuff out any mad desires before they took hold of her. She was too old now for childish passions. Felicia was always saying she should go for personality rather than looks in a man, but for Emma the two had to be intertwined. She had very precise standards. Still, this did not mean the right person wasn't waiting for her somewhere. She must not make another mistake. Surely the intensity of her feelings now meant she might have found her soulmate at last?

Felicia did not know to what extent the current infatuation had affected Emma, because Emma had kept the details quiet.

She could not confess to how she had become a fevered, feral thing; spending whole evenings following The Man from bar to bar, skulking in shadows, awed and sickened by what she saw as his unbearable loveliness. His face looked intelligent, his bearing was aloof yet intriguing. He was like a well-bred animal; graceful and aware of his own beauty without seeming arrogant. All this, Emma had discerned from a distance. For some reason, she could not employ her usual tactics and approach him. It was not fear of rejection exactly, but perhaps a fear of being disappointed again. She'd seen him looking at her sometimes.

"Where have you been?" Felicia would say when Emma came in late alone.

"Out." A shrug.

"Who with?"

Emma would lie. "Pat, Alison... you know." She didn't want Felicia to know she'd been on her own. Solitude was part of the condition. The pain conjured by the aching desire for The Man was companioned by an exquisite melancholy. She had to be alone, in order to surrender herself to the daydreams that filled her mind. At work, it was easy, because she could fantasise as she was hunched over her drawing-board. Nobody would bother her because she seemed so busy. In her mind, she lived out a hundred scenarios of actually speaking to The Man, different ways in which they could meet. She knew the best nights for locating him: Saturdays, Sundays, and occasionally on Wednesdays. He always seemed to be with people, but she couldn't remember their faces. She didn't know any of them. They were nobodies, eclipsed by his flame. At night, she dreamed of cards falling like leaves, twisting before her face, but she could never see their symbols. During the day, she would sometimes get angry with herself and say aloud, beneath her breath, "This is stupid! I'm gonna forget it. It's pathetic!" And she would straighten her spine, empty her mind of wandering thoughts, apply herself to a mundane task, and imagine the yearning had gone. But then the night would come again and that strange magic would start stirring within her and she would say to herself, "I have to see him," and find herself on the street, pulling on her jacket, her face hot, walking quickly.

Sometimes she couldn't find him, and then she'd become a demented thing, knocking back drinks too swiftly, going into places that normally, she'd never dare enter alone. It was as if he *knew*. At the end of the evening, almost out of her mind, she would catch a glimpse of him; his tawny hair, his dark eyes, and that would be enough. Then she could go home again and light the candles. Sometimes, she wondered whether she really had seen him or not.

On Saturday, Felicia thought Emma looked listless and depressed. The fizzing euphoria, so typical of her infatuations, was absent. Could it really be different this time? She knew so little about Emma's latest crush. She resolved to be sympathetic, and made them a pot of tea so they could sit down to a chat. "How many times have you spoken to this man?" she began, intent on building a dossier of facts about him.

Emma's eyes skittered away from Felicia's own. Felicia made a mental note.

"Well.... Once. He passed me in the pub. Put his hand on my arm."

"Is that all?" Felicia tried to keep her voice low. "What did he say?"

"He said 'excuse me'."

Felicia took a sip of tea to smother an involuntary smile. Then she put down her mug. "Emma... how can I say this? You can't be in love with someone you don't know."

Emma jumped up angrily. "Then it isn't love! Something else!" She clawed her hair.

The outburst surprised Felicia. "What else?"

Emma stared at her fiercely with eyes that seemed to burn within. "I've been looking for something," she said quickly, "looking for years. Now I think I've found it. I have to have him, Fliss. We have to have each other. I know it's right. I feel it. I..."

"Hold on!" Felicia held up her hands. "Does he ever look at you, make any signal he's interested in you?"

Emma swung around and began to play with her beads hanging over the mirror. "Of course he does."

"Then perhaps you should simply make the first move. Go up to him. Speak. It can't be that difficult. Pat or Ally would be with you."

Emma was silent.

"Shall we go out together tonight?" Felicia suggested brightly. "We haven't been out together for weeks! You've been seeing so much of Pat and..."

"I need some of his hair!" Emma interrupted hotly. "Then it would work better. I'd have a focus. I need to bring him to me."

"Emma," Felicia began carefully, "if you got close enough to him to pull his hair out, you could also say hello..."

Emma suddenly threw back her head and laughed loudly, causing Felicia to visibly wince. She saw something ancient standing there, something primeval yet essentially female. Emma thought Felicia lacked imagination, but she did not.

Although Felicia hadn't seen The Man, Emma had described him in such detail, she felt she'd recognise him if she saw him. Tall, long hair, and, like Emma, a lover of the colours black and purple. Emma had found paintings in books with which to illustrate her descriptions. "His nose is like this, his mouth like this..." Felicia indulgently paid attention, inwardly rather appalled that a woman of Emma's age could act so immaturely. This man might as well be a famous musician or a film star, seeing as Emma had built up her love for him on appearances alone. Still, Felicia comforted herself that Emma would soon tire of this paragon, once she got to know him. So far, all her infatuations had burned themselves out quickly, once the object of desire proved themselves to be disappointingly human and therefore unworthy of Emma's attention. Therefore, in Felicia's opinion, Emma must introduce herself to this new idol as soon as possible. What Emma expected from a man was, in Felicia's opinion, virtually supernatural, and nobody could live up to that.

"Emma, tonight, you are going to speak to your fancy man, even if I have to drag you over to him myself!"

"Perhaps you're right," said Emma.

Felicia sighed. How could a grown woman be such a child?

Emma dressed herself in a long black dress that swirled like smoke around her ankles, and wore her rich, dark red hair loose down her back, almost as if it was a symbol of her own power. Felicia dressed in a short dress that hugged her figure and shouted at the night in tropical colours. Both wore jackets – Emma, leather, and Felicia something expensive in cashmere she'd picked up in town. She and Emma walked along an avenue that was fragrant with spring, an unlikely-looking pair of companions. Above them, the moon rose full and heavy. Felicia chattered on aimlessly about people at work, mostly because she could think of nothing else to say. Inside, she felt quite nervous.

Emma appeared serene, nodding vaguely at Felicia's remarks, a slight smile on her face. She was imagining that a black panther walked on either side of her, and her hands were touching each one lightly between the ears.

They went from bar to bar, drinking, Felicia talking, an occasional friend pausing to chat; the evening stretched before them. Emma looked feverish, as if she was about to go into battle, and her eyes were never still, scanning faces. Looking at her friend's strained expression and darting eyes, Felicia thought, *I don't really know this woman; she is a stranger*. And bought them both another drink.

Emma raised her glass, smiled. "The elixir of life!" she said.

It was late, nearly closing time in the bar that had an extension until two, when Emma eventually spotted The Man. She hissed and grabbed Felicia's arm savagely. "There!"

Bodies milled around them, obstructing sight. There was high laughter, the offence of conflicting perfumes.

Felicia peered. "Where?" Her face had gone shiny. She was beginning to grin back at the shaved-neck office boys lurking at the boundary of her and Emma's space.

"Over there."

Felicia giggled, and stood up. "Right, this is it. Come on!"

Emma pulled her back down onto her stool. "No!" For a moment, she sat silent, her head bowed, and then she looked. up. "I'll go alone. I have to." She swallowed the last of her drink, stood up and smiled shakily. "Well, this is it! Now or never!"

Felicia raised her glass. "Good hunting, then!"

Felicia let herself into the flat alone. All the rooms were in darkness. Felicia didn't like the way the flat felt when it was dark. She turned on lights everywhere, and picked up the remains of Emma's candle, which was nothing more than a green puddle in an old saucer on the coffee-table. Kicking off her shoes, Felicia padded into the kitchen and turned on the kettle. She felt light-headed, but not drunk. The night had been fun. Pity Emma had walked out on her. Hardly a sensible thing to do. No woman should walk the streets alone in the early hours of the morning. Luckily, Felicia had had enough cash left to get a cab.

The kettle thumped and groaned to itself. Felicia put instant coffee and sugar into a mug. There was a click, followed by a disgruntled whine as the kettle switched itself off. As she picked it up, Felicia became aware of the intense silence of the flat beyond the kitchen. It seemed as if time had stopped.

Then the sounds came.

It was like flapping, something huge and dark, flapping. Felicia ran out into the living-room, convinced an owl, or some other large bird, had got in and was rampaging round the flat. The noises stopped the instant she walked into the room. For a moment, there was silence, and then she heard a muffled crash from the hallway, followed by an abrupt mew or stifled cry. Felicia stood in the living-room doorway, perplexed, the kettle still held in one hand. The hall beyond looked endless. Emma's door was closed.

"Em!" Felicia called. The silence had come back, that thick silence she hated. The walls seemed vigilant, waiting. Felicia crept forward.

Suddenly, a great sound, a trumpeting, like a siren going off, blasted right through her. She realised it was a scream. Rapid, frantic sounds, like something beating itself against the door, came from Emma's room. Then, again, silence.

"Em!" Felicia ran to the door, but was reluctant to open it, afraid. She knocked on it loudly. "Em, are you all right?" She put her ear against the door. She thought she could hear Emma's voice. No words, just inarticulate sound; distress.

Are you brave? Felicia asked herself. *Is someone in there with her*? *Is someone hurting her*? She gripped the kettle more firmly, and put her hand upon the door handle. She expected the door to be locked, but it wasn't.

Emma was alone, sitting awkwardly on the floor beneath the window, which was slightly open. The lamps were off, but the street-lights outside shone right into the room. Emma's possessions, which she treasured so highly, had been strewn about the room, as if in fury. And over everything were shining droplets of a dark liquid; the walls, the floor, the bed. Near

Emma, by the window, a large, dark puddle covered the carpet. Felicia's gorge rose; at first she thought it was blood. But the smell in the room, the overwhelming stink of burnt wax, of a hundred candles recently extinguished, quickly advised her sensible mind otherwise. Still, she was aghast. "Em, what's happened?" She glanced around herself, afraid some man would leap from the shadows.

Emma stared at her without expression. Her feet were bare; spattered with droplets of wax. It looked as if she'd been scratched.

Felicia advanced cautiously into the room, stepping over the mess. Emma owned over a dozen Tarot packs, and they seemed to have been scattered at random around the room. Many of the cards were torn. "What the hell have you done? Em... Em?" Felicia put down the kettle and squatted beside her friend. She attempted to pull Emma into a comforting embrace, but Emma struggled away.

"Get off me!" Her voice was unnaturally gruff. She seemed to have no whites to her eyes.

Felicia felt nauseous. The smell rising from the huge puddle of congealing wax at Emma's feet was too cloying; sweet, but somehow meaty as well. Some cheap scented candles? No, surely not. How many would Emma have had to burn to produce such a pool? There were feathers stuck in it; feathers and unidentifiable dark lumps. Felicia looked away. She didn't want to think about it. "Emma, where did you get to? You shouldn't have come home alone. Why are you upset? What did he say? Wasn't he interested?"

Emma blinked slowly and crawled along the floor on hands and knees. Then she squatted with her knees up by her ears, her mouth stretched into a grin. There was a dark oily crust around her nostrils, as if she'd been bleeding wax. "I went to him. I spoke..."

"What did he say?"

Emma sighed, her head rolling from side to side. "Everything. Everything that I wanted to hear."

"Then why did you walk out like that?"

"We walked out together..."

Felicia stood up, brushed down her dress. "Emma, don't lie! I saw you. You went out of that place like a hurricane! In fact, you knocked one girl's drink all over her. I thought he'd told you where to go!"

Emma threw back her head. It looked as if she was laughing, but there was no sound. "We were together," she said, in the same dull, low voice. "We are together now, and he is with me always."

"Emma... Emma!"

Emma had clasped her knees, and began to rock gently. She sang an insistent refrain: "Together, forever, together, forever..."

Outside, the moon hung low in the sky like a bag of blood, mottled with cloud. A full moon, a lunatic's moon. Felicia heard a dog whine in the yard next door.

Look into the candle flame, Emma. Make a wish...

Spanish Jones

Adele Cosgrove-Bray

Oxton Village was once one of the most affluent areas in England. Many merchants whose fortunes were made in the bustling port of Liverpool – which rivalled London in the bid to become Britain's capital city – built their homes in Oxton on the Wirral peninsula, divided from Liverpool by the boundary of the ancient Kingdom of Mercia, more usually known as the River Mersey.

Charles and Amelia Porter were popular guests at musical soirées and summer balls, being generous hosts themselves. They were lively and charming, and always the glass of fashion; and their beautiful daughter, Annabelle, was presumed likely to win a fine husband from amongst the sons of Oxton's wealthy elite.

Not all wealth is gained legally or fairly, and such was the case for Charles Porter, who earned a steady sum from the manufacturing of ships' sails. Much more lucrative, however, was Mr. Porter's illicit importation of fine wines and spirits.

Any illegal trade will inevitably bring a person into contact with strange and dubious souls, and so it came about that Charles Porter found himself shaking hands on a deal with Spanish Jones.

Tall and muscular was Spanish Jones, with a thick mass of curling black hair tumbling over his brown velvet jacket. His eyes were unusually large and dark, and he wore gold earrings and a heavy sword. His gnarled, scarred hands showed he was no stranger to the harsh rigours of a mariner's life.

Charles Porter and Spanish Jones were sat in Seagull Inn on Hilbre Island in the Dee Estuary. They supped tankards of foaming ale, having closed their business agreement with a gentleman's handshake.

"Unload the cargo at the rear of Hilbre, out of sight of the mainland," said Charles Porter. He took another swig of ale. "There'll be a light to guide you."

"The goods will be delivered at midnight," said Captain Spanish Jones, keeping his voice low. "And I'll take full payment in gold then".

"I am always as good as my word," Charles Porter replied.

Spanish Jones scowled as he rose to his feet and prepared to leave. "You'd better be. I always take payment one way or another."

Charles Porter was accustomed to such threats and took them in his stride. He had been in this line of business for far too long to react with concern. Besides, he was handy with a knife himself, and he had several loyal men stationed close by inside the little inn.

Midnight was almost upon Porter and his men as they carefully picked their way to the far end of Hilbre Island, where the Irish Sea crashed ceaselessly against ancient sandstone rocks. The curved sickle of a slender moon would keep their business veiled from prying eyes, and certainly the landlord of Seagull Inn would say nothing, his pockets being well-lined from similar trade.

The faint sound of oars slicing through choppy waters reached the ears of Porter and his men, and a lantern was raised to guide Spanish Jones's crew – not in to land, as those sailors supposed, but directly onto spikes of jagged rock.

Terrible sounds of grinding, splintering wood rent the night air, sending seagulls screeching into flight. The heavily-laden rowing boat swiftly took in water. The sailors struggled in the dark surging waves, thrashing their way towards the safety of

Hilbre only to be met by Porter's men, who ensured not one sailor surfaced to tell their tale.

Then Porter's men formed a human chain and lifted the barrels from the sea, and hurried them away to Seagull Inn where the landlord waited with bowls of hot broth and a jug of mulled wine.

"Three cheers for Charlie Porter! A toast to Charlie the Knife!" And the men raised their tankards in praise of the smiling Mr. Porter and another night's illicit profit.

The door of the inn smashed open as Spanish Jones strode in, one hand on his sword and a pistol in the other.

Charlie and his men laughed, and several mocking taunts were flung towards the furious captain.

"Well, you've got courage; I'll say that much for you," smirked Charlie. "Coming in here on your own..."

"Who says I'm on my own?"

Into Seagull Inn filed the very same black-eyed crew which Charlie Porter's men had supposedly drowned.

Spanish Jones grinned. "A drop of sea water won't harm my crew. You don't know who you're dealing with."

The innkeeper's face turned ashen. Only now did he guess the true nature of these resilient men.

Spanish Jones said, "Do it," and instantly mayhem broke lose as the drenched men unsheathed a brutal array of knives and quickly slaughtered all but the innkeeper and Charlie Porter.

"Tie them up," said the Captain.

"What are you going to do?" Beads of sweat were running off Porter's face. His knees were shaking, all trappings of dignity obliterated.

Spanish Jones walked towards the bar and poured himself a tankard of ale. "We're not going to kill you. Not yet, anyway. My crew are going to enjoy a well-earned drink in this worthy inn, and then they'll be on their way with the property you tried to steal from me, plus any interest earned – which means anything else they take a liking to which might furnish their fine homes around West Hoyle Bank."

A horrified cry escaped from the innkeeper. His worst fears had been confirmed.

"Gag him," said Spanish Jones, grinning. "And now I've some business on the mainland. Didn't I warn you that I always take payment one way or another? You've brought no gold to pay me with, so I'm off to Oxton, where there's a fine girl named Annabelle."

"You leave my daughter alone! Don't you dare touch her! I'll have your life for this!"

Spanish Jones chuckled. "You tried that once already. And as you can see, my crew are hard to drown."

Spanish Jones laughed and turned on his heel, and strode out of Seagull Inn.

Charlie Porter tried to bargain with Jones's crew, but they mocked his efforts and tied him and the innkeeper securely to chairs before rifling their pockets.

The trembling innkeeper was silent behind his gag. He kept his eyes on the floor as Spanish Jones's crew systematically stripped the place of every valuable possession.

The two bound captives only managed to free themselves long after the sailors had gone.

The innkeeper, once freed of the gag, began babbling about selkies; about seals which can turn into men and walk upon dry land before returning to the ocean as seals. Porter thought him overwrought, or perhaps a little insane.

And, of course, neither man could complain to the authorities without confessing themselves as smugglers.

As for Porter's slaughtered crew, well, the muddy bed of the River Dee has offered a soft resting place for many a corpse.

Charlie waited impatiently for the tide to turn and leave the vast expanse of sand exposed before he could hurry back to the mainland. The innkeeper's ravings about selkies kept ringing in his ears as he desperately tried to hitch a carriage ride to Oxton, but fate seemed set against him and he had to walk most of the way.

He was too late. His daughter was gone.

A damp trail of briny water led along the hall and up the stairs into Annabelle's bedroom, right to the side of her bed. Even the sheets were wet and smelled of the sea.

There was no trace of Annabelle – other than her voice which Charlie sometimes heard on the wind from beyond Hilbre Island, from the large sandbank known as West Hoyle Bank where seals lounge in the sun.

Charlie Porter took to rowing out there, until a sudden storm took his life. It's said that his ghost is still looking for her, rowing a spectral boat around Hilbre Island and calling her name.

But it isn't Charlie's ghost that this tale warns of.

Indeed not.

"Come on, keep up!" Barbara pushed her curly brown hair out of her eyes.

"I'm doing my best," said Ceri, "but it's hard walking on sand in these heels."

"Well, I *did* warn you. Just take them off and walk in your bare feet. You're gonna break an ankle otherwise." Barbara sighed and looked back towards mainland Wirral, where red and white sails glided along West Kirby marina. The car park beside it twinkled with reflected light, and the beach was thickly dotted with sunbathers and dog-walkers or kids queuing for donkey rides. The people looked so small from out here.

"That's easier," said Ceri, walking to Barbara's side. Her perfectly made-up eyes looked out from behind expensive Italian sunglasses. Her thin cotton summer dress billowed around her tanned bare legs. "How much further is it?"

Barbara turned away and continued walking over the exposed sands towards the small island. "Not much further," she lied. She knew that if she described the distance from the mainland to Little Eye, Ceri would start up with her usual whining.

"Those people are walking straight across the sands. You said we couldn't do that." Ceri began lagging behind again.

Barbara said, "Look, you read the information board yourself. You saw the map of the designated safe route. You've lived here all your life. Surely the words 'quicksand' and 'estuary mud' and 'tidal channels' mean something to you by now."

Ceri pointed towards the three hikers taking a shortcut over the sands. "Well, it seems perfectly safe to me."

"That's what every idiot says before they drown." Barbara tried to keep her temper. Perhaps persuading Ceri to join her on the trip out to the islands had been a mistake. Certainly Ceri's mother would be furious if she ever found out, but then she always had been neurotically protective of her precious blonde daughter.

And anyway, they weren't even walking the entire two miles to Hilbre, the furthest of the three islands. They were only going as far as Middle Eye, and Barbara had carefully checked the tide times so she knew they would be perfectly safe.

Well, they'd be safe now that Ceri had taken off those stupid high heels. Barbara had told her to wear something sensible. The problem was that Ceri didn't own anything sensible. Most of her wardrobe comprised of micro-dresses, summer tops, and revealing bikinis. Even her jeans bore expensive European designer labels. The closest thing to Barbara's recommendation of hiking boots was apparently a pair of strappy white sandals with four-inch spike heels.

"Oh, I've got sand under my toenails," moaned Ceri, tip-toeing some distance behind Barbara.

Barbara waited while Ceri caught up with her again. "There will be some rock pools further along. You can wash your feet in those."

"But the water will be all salty!"

"Well, yeah. The sea has that effect." Barbara thrust one hand into her jacket pocket and pulled out a can of cider. That was something else for Ceri's mother to disapprove of.

"The view is nice though, isn't it," said Ceri, looking wistfully back towards the mainland. The familiar coastal buildings looked like a miniature village from here.

"I can't believe you've never been out to the islands before," said Barbara.

"You know how Mum is." Ceri gazed curiously at the immense sky arching overhead. The pattern of small white clouds seemed to mirror the ripples left across the sand by the retreating ocean. Three black-headed gulls pounded overhead.

Barbara opted not to reply. Ceri's mother was one of those tedious people who had been born with a silver spoon in her mouth and pomposity infused through her brain. She thought Barbara a bad influence, mostly because Barbara's parents lived in a council house and they both worked in factories. Interestingly, Barbara was a university student while Ceri had dropped out of college and was now unemployed.

They reached the first of the rock pools which surrounded Middle Eye. Ceri hesitated, still holding her sandals in one carefully manicured hand. The jagged rocks were strewn with dark green seaweed which might hide crabs or squelchy creatures, and the sharp barnacles and cockle shells would easily lacerate her bare feet.

"Just stay on the sand and walk round the rocks," said Barbara. "We're going round the back of the island anyway. There aren't quite as many rocks on that side."

Ceri was not convinced that this was altogether true but, short of walking back over the sands to Little Eye and then to the mainland all by herself, there seemed little choice but to proceed carefully.

The rock pools were fascinating, like tiny underwater cities cupped by red sandstone. The water was perfectly clear. She could see fragile shrimps flee from her shadow. She wanted to stay and look at them for longer but Barbara quickly grew impatient.

The grass-topped bulk of Middle Eye loomed closer. As Barbara had promised, the boys were waiting. They must have been here for an hour already at least, because Ceri certainly hadn't seen them crossing the flat, open sands.

The two young men were sunbathing on the rocks at the base of Middle Eye. They barely glanced up as the girls approached them. They were probably a few years older than Ceri or Barbara. They were wearing old, badly faded jeans. They didn't seem to have brought shirts with them. They were deeply tanned, lean and wiry, with shoulder-length black hair and dark eyes to match. They might have been twins. Certainly they looked like brothers.

"Hi," smiled Barbara as she climbed over the fallen rocks to join them.

Ceri hung back, wondering how to navigate the rough ground without injuring her feet. Besides, she felt increasingly uncertain of the wisdom of meeting these two strangers out here, in the middle of nowhere. Barbara had been singing their praises for days to persuade her to come, but now that she was actually here, Ceri felt nervous and awkward as if she was doing something which she knew to be wrong. It was okay for Barbara; her expectations were different due to coming from a lower social class. Or at least that's what Ceri's mother frequently vocalised.

Barbara sat down next to one of the boys. "Come on, Ceri! Just watch where you put your feet."

One of the dark-haired strangers said, "What's up? You shy?"

"It's her shoes," said Barbara. "She came out in high heels and now she can't walk in them."

They laughed and watched as Ceri tentatively picked her way through the rocks, hissing under her breath as her feet became bruised and scratched. The seaweed against her skin felt revolting; cold and wet and slimy. She tried not to think about it.

She sat down on a flat rock a short distance from them. Barbara had already offered them sips from her open can of cider, which they readily accepted. It didn't look as if they'd brought anything of their own to offer in return, which seemed a bit tight-fisted. There was clearly no hope of chocolates and flowers.

One of them said, "What's your name?"

"Ceri."

"Barbara said you'd never been out to the islands before. Is that true?"

"Yes."

He leaned up to watch her more closely. "Why's that, then? You sound local."

"I am; I've always lived here. Mum says I'm not to come out here because of the tides."

A slow smile warmed his face. "So you're not supposed to be here now?"

"No." From the corner of her eye, she could see Barbara allow the other boy to put his arm around her shoulder. Their heads moved closer together.

"And yet you came out here to be with us?"

Ceri blushed and nervously fiddled with the hem of her dress. "No."

"So you walked all this way in your pretty summer dress and your high heels just for the scenery? Even though your parents forbade it?" His wide grin showed he was teasing her.

"Parent, actually. My father died."

"How?"

"A sailing accident. He drowned."

"Here, in these waters?" He ran one hand through his floppy black hair.

"Further up the River Dee. He was sailing his yacht. No one knows exactly what happened. Missing presumed drowned."

"When was that?"

"Three years ago. You ask a lot of questions." Ceri noticed how the ridges of his ribs showed through his tanned skin. He was lean, like an athlete. His arms were long and well-toned without looking heavy.

He shrugged and glanced towards his look-alike and Barbara. They were now stretched out side-by-side on the rocks, locked in intense kisses.

Ceri looked away from them, shocked by Barbara's behaviour. Or was she really shocked? Her mother would have said she ought to have been. She leaned forwards and brushed the drying sand from her feet, while trying to work out how she truly felt.

"Do you always paint your toenails?"

"Yes. Usually. Why?"

"It looks nice; very feminine. I like that in a girl. I'm a bit old-fashioned at heart."

Ceri smiled, feeling a little more relaxed. "It's just a matter of taking pride in yourself."

"I quite agree," he said, from beside her.

Ceri gasped. "How did you…? I mean, you were sat over there and now you're here."

He leaned back on the rock next to her. "Perhaps you were too busy with your feet to notice me move."

That seemed unlikely but she wasn't going to argue the point and make herself looked foolish. "What's your name? You didn't say."

"Joe."

"Joe what?"

He shrugged. "Joe Jones." He smelled of the sea and of dry sand warmed by the summer sun. Fragments of broken shells were in his hair and on his smooth skin but it didn't seem to trouble him.

Ceri watched as the island ranger's Land Rover sped along the sands behind Middle Eye, heading towards Hilbre. The ranger lived alone in Telegraph House, which the Victorians had built on the remaining foundations of long-gone Seagull Inn.

"Do you come from Wirral, Joe? Your accent sounds more Welsh somehow."

He laughed slightly, leaning back and closing his eyes against the sun's fiery rays. "I travel around a lot."

"What do you do for a living?"

He smiled. "You could say I'm a fisherman."

Ceri frowned, puzzled. "There isn't a fishing industry around here. Anyway, your hands look too soft for someone who works on a trawler." She glanced over to Barbara then hurriedly looked away again, her face flushing crimson.

Joe watched them too, but he seemed merely amused. "Yeah, my hands are soft. See," he said, sliding his palm over her calf, "no calluses at all."

"Keep your hands to yourself," snapped Ceri, nervously pulling her leg away.

"Relax; I won't bite." He smiled enticingly.

"Your breath smells like raw fish." She wrinkled her nose in disgust.

"Yeah, but my kisses are like fire."

"Oh, get lost! Back off, will you? I'm not like Barbara."

He laughed but didn't move away. "No? How come she's your friend, then?"

Ceri refused to reply. She was angry with herself for having been talked into meeting these boys. Perhaps her mother had been correct about Barbara after all. Right now, Barbara was half naked. Ceri ignored her small tinge of envy at Barbara's confidence.

"I say, that's a splendid barnacle next to your ankle! The sand is spiffing at this time of the year! And the kelp is simply divine!" His camp mockery grated on Ceri's nerves.

"Oh, shut up."

He laughed again and sat up, turning to face her. He quickly slipped one arm across her waist and with his other hand he pushed her shoulder backwards. He used his weight to force her down. Ceri struggled but he just laughed and tightened his grip.

"You know this is what you came out here for. If you were so bloody pure you wouldn't be here. Or do you like playing hard to get?"

The fragrance of cold fish forced her to quickly turn her head away. She grabbed his ear and a fistful of hair and tugged hard. Joe swore angrily and tightened his grip.

"Get off me!" She struggled and shouted, "Get off me now!"

"Are you ok, dear?"

A woman's voice rang out from the grassy summit of Middle Eye.

Joe sighed and let Ceri scramble to her feet. She shouted, "Get away from me! No means no!"

"Hello down there?" The voice called out again.

Ceri looked up to see three women in hiking gear staring down at them from the cliff top. Ceri shouted, "Hello!" She backed away from Joe as quickly as she could, ignoring the pain in her feet.

Barbara was entwined with the other boy. She seemed totally oblivious of their unexpected audience. Joe sat calmly on the rocks and smiled charmingly at the women high on the cliff top. His expression revealed no embarrassment or alarm.

One of the women called out, "Would you like to join us? We're heading back to the mainland. You can walk with us if you like."

"Yes, please," replied Ceri, shaking and thanking her lucky stars that these three women had arrived when they had.

"Alright! Walk onto the sand and we'll meet you by the steps which lead down from the summit."

"Thank you; I will," Ceri called out. Then she turned to Barbara and said, "Are you ready to leave?"

Barbara didn't even seem to hear her. She was totally naked now, her thighs wrapped tightly round her lover's grinding hips. Ceri repeated her question but got no reply. She snorted in contempt and walked proudly away from the three of them.

"I'll see you again, Ceri," said Joe. He was leaning casually against the rock and smiling as if amused by some private joke.

"Like hell you will," she said, as she walked away.

The three women were hurrying over the rock pools towards her. Once they saw that she was safe, they slowed their pace. They asked if her friend was ok, and Ceri told them Barbara had chosen to remain behind and that she was no longer any friend of hers. They expressed no judgement on this.

"What's your name?" asked one of the women, who had introduced herself as Lizzy.

"Ceri; Ceri Porter."

Lizzy's eyes widened slightly, but Ceri was used to this reaction. After all, the Porter family name was well-known among the Wirral social elite.

Ceri was absolutely frozen in her light cotton dress. No wonder hikers usually wore several layers plus waterproofs. The changeable sea breezes had stolen the heat of this languid summer's day, and Ceri was shivering.

The three women, however, didn't lecture her about safety. Ceri was relieved. She felt foolish enough as it was. They talked about easy things, like bird watching and recipes and quilting, until they reached the mainland. Ceri's feet were badly blistered by the time they walked up the concrete ramp leading onto West Kirby promenade, despite one of the women having given her a spare pair of socks from inside her backpack. They even kindly phoned for a taxi for her, to ensure she would arrive safely home. She thanked them profusely, of course, and then hurried back to the security of her comfortable life.

Ceri did not phone Barbara that evening, or the next day or the next. In fact, she only saw Barbara again when her face peered out from page four of the *Wirral Globe*. The small headline screamed, "Local Girl Drowned!"

Lizzy Porter frowned at the darkness shrouding Middle Eye. The full moon cast spectral light over mercurial waters which lapped the necklace of rugged sandstone rocks encircling the island.

Everyone was pulling full-length black robes over their ordinary clothes. Jenna had sewn these, her spiky burgundy hair bowed over an old-fashioned treadle machine for hour after hour.

Gerry lifted the ceremonial sword from his guitar case, which had proved an ingenious way of transporting the weapon without attracting unwanted attention. The blade glinted in the low light as he took a compass from his pocket and began checking cardinal points.

Gale was hunched over a thurible, trying to ignite the charcoal. By her feet lay a pile of sage wands for cleansing the area of negative influences. The sage had been grown in her own garden, and she had tightly bound the harvested bunches with silver thread. She wasn't confident of how effective they would be on this airy, windy island, but their use would be symbolic at least.

Hefin stood looking out to sea, sharp breezes tugging at his short, white hair. His robe only reached to his calves. He considered such garments to be superfluous but the others were keen on them. His eyes searched the waters as if trying to penetrate their inky mass. He felt uneasy. He had been against attempting this ritual but had been outvoted. And they were probably breaking a local bylaw by remaining on Middle Eye overnight.

Lizzy asked, "Are we all ready?"

"Not quite," said Gale, still coaxing the incense into life. The rushing sea breezes were not making this any easier. Suz knelt down beside her to lend a hand, her shoulder-length black hair blowing across her heart-shaped face.

The rest began to take positions to form a circle, the tough grass brushing their calves.

"I think we're gonna have to watch our footing," said Gerry. "The ground is very uneven. We don't want any twisted ankles."

"I've brought a First Aid kit," said Anne. "Still, it's something to be aware of, especially in the dark."

"We have company," said Hefin, still looking out to sea. "Some seals."

Suz asked, "Are they seals or selkies?"

"We'll know soon enough," said Jenna, rising to her feet and carrying the thurible into the circle.

Lizzy said, "Ok, everyone take your places, please."

Reluctantly, Hefin joined the circle. He wished his late wife were here to advise them. Margred's style of leadership had been very different from Lizzy's. Margred had always insisted that the Craft was a way of learning, but these younger witches had brought in many ideas which were no more than religious dogma. In protest he had resigned as the group's chosen High Priest, a role which Gerry had eagerly accepted despite his insufficient experience. As Hefin took his place in the circle, he spontaneously decided that as soon as this ritual was over he would announce his retirement from the coven.

The circle of seven witches faced each other.

Lizzy breathed deeply and concentrated on the task ahead. She had found no precedent for this ritual, so she would have to improvise. The prospect did not sit easily upon her shoulders yet she felt responsible for the protection of her relatives, even if she had been excluded as the embarrassing oddball of the Porter family.

Lizzy raised her arms and cried, "Guardians of the land and sea, our sacred circle calls to thee; join us beneath this starry night, and help our magic to take flight! Guardians of ancient Mercia, to work our magic here we are; help us cleanse this sacred land, of the murderous selkie band!"

Hefin raised an eyebrow, and silently confirmed his retirement decision. He was tempted to point out that Wirral had originally been considered part of Wales and not of Mercia, but this could wait. He set aside his inherent scepticism and tried to focus on the intent of the ritual.

Gale carried the smoking thurible slowly round the outside of their circle. The frisky wind quickly dissipated any fragrance other than that of powerfully pungent briny seaweed.

Gerry then followed in Gale's footsteps, holding the sword above his head and visualising a vibrant ribbon of protective white fire flowing from the blade as he walked slowly around them all.

Lizzy then raised her arms again and cried, "Guardians of the four quarters, grant our sacred circle your protection!"

Muffled laughter caused Anne to scowl, and she wondered who the culprit might be. She ran her gaze around the circle but nobody was smiling.

Lizzy called out, "Spirits of this sacred land, witness this; our moonlit rite! Spirits of the ancient sea, help us cleanse this place tonight!"

Gerry turned his head to one side. He had definitely heard quiet voices below the summit of the island. He had made absolutely certain that their group was alone on Middle Eye before the tide had cut them off from the mainland.

Jenna and Suz peered into the darkness surrounding them, but they could see nothing other than the silhouettes of rocks and the heaving mass of the silver-flecked charcoal sea.

Gerry said, "Stay inside the circle, everyone. No selkie will be able to pass through it."

Mocking laughter erupted from several points around Middle Eye.

Lizzy firmly said, "Ignore the selkies completely. Come on, everyone, focus on our work. Gale, the sage bundles if you please."

"Oh, well, actually," replied Gale, "they're over there." She pointed towards her backpack, which lay several feet outside of the protective circle.

There was a slight pause, then Gerry said, "Well, there are no selkies on the summit with us, so it'll probably be ok. I'll come with you just in case, and then we'll have to cast the circle a second time."

Hefin sighed and calmly left the circle. He collected the bundles of sage and handed them to Gale, then returned to his place without saying anything. Gerry felt annoyed. The trouble with Hefin was that he just didn't do things by the book.

"Won't we have to re-cast the circle now?" asked Gale.

Hefin replied, "The circle is as good as it ever was." He knew no one would argue with him over this issue, at least.

Gale quickly handed around the smouldering wands. Now each witch held one, and the sharp scent of burning sage filled the air.

"I prefer it with a spot of roast lamb, myself."

More disembodied laughter echoed through the shadows.

Lizzy said, "Don't be drawn into conversation with them. We're not here to make friends. We're here to cleanse this coast of selkies. Remember how many people have drowned in the Dee Estuary! Remember the selkies' curse on my family!"

Lizzy gathered her strength, then raised her arms and cried, "Spirits of this sacred land, witness this; our moonlit rite! Spirits of the ancient sea, help us cleanse this place tonight!"

"Didn't she do that bit before?"

"Yeah, I think so. Why does she keep waving her arms about?"

"Guardians of the Wirral coast," cried Lizzy, "banish now the selkie host!"

"What a cheek."

"I know. We were here first."

The witches concentrated on holding the visualised image of their protective circle foremost in their minds. Lizzy scowled with effort, feeling small beads of perspiration sting along her back. She called, "Leave this place of land and sea! Selkie host I banish thee!"

"Are you banished yet?"

"Nope. Still here."

"Me too," said a third voice.

"She's a rotten poet."

"Don't you know it."

"Oh, don't you start. One naff poet's enough, surely," said a sixth selkie.

"Maybe if we drowned her she'd shut up."

"I like the gurgling noises they make."

"I like the mad struggles, then how they go all limp when they accept what's happening."

"I like that look in their eye; the pleading and the sorrow."

"I like...."

"Yeah, we all know what you like!"

The vivacious laugher sounded much closer to the coven now.

The seven witches stared at the darkness around them, clutching the remains of their smoking sage bundles. Gerry strode forwards, wielding his ceremonial sword.

"Oow, what's he got there, then?"

"Didn't that bloke off *Star Trek* have one of those?"

"You mean *Lord of the Rings*, surely."

"He doesn't look much like Aragorn. Too short and fat." This was a girl's voice.

Selkies climbed up the steps which led up to the summit of Middle Eye. More selkies approached from the opposite end of the small island, up the rocky cliff face where a metal post hammered into the ground marked the route from the sands. The naked selkies were pale skinned, with thick dark hair. They seemed perfectly comfortable with their nakedness, and they looked entirely human – though their eyes were unusually large and dark and glowing, as if illumined by a strange black inner fire.

Lizzy declared, "Stand fast! They cannot break our sacred circle."

"No?" A broad-shouldered selkie stepped around Lizzy and walked steadily towards Gerry.

"He's broken the circle!" gasped Anne.

Gale cried, "How can that be? It's not possible!"

A young male selkie smiled at Gale and moved closer. She held out her stick of sage to ward him off but he sharply knocked it from her hand. As he walked towards her, she instinctively began to back away.

Gerry gripped the ceremonial sword with both hands. He had absolutely no training in the use of any weapon, but he most certainly intended to do his best if he had to. "Don't come any closer! I will use this sword!"

The powerfully-built selkie grinned and moved forwards. "Will you, now?"

Gerry stepped back and stumbled slightly on an uneven clump of thick grass. The selkie moved faster than Gerry could think. He felt blinding pain shoot up his forearm as the selkie struck with a vicious kick. Gerry's arm instantly numbed and he dropped the sword, which was scooped up by the selkie and hurled far out into deep water.

Anne found herself facing two male selkies. She tried to back away from them but was soon at the cliff edge. She looked around desperately but there was nowhere to run to, and the other witches were also surrounded by selkies.

"Leave me alone!" Anne stared at the two naked selkies who were moving closer to her. Her foot slipped and for split second she lost her balance.

One of them said, "Why should we leave you alone? You're in our territory. And you don't mean us well."

"But that's different!" Anne was frantic. She was very aware of the open space directly behind her. "You drown people!"

"Not straight away," said the other selkie, smiling.

And then she fell, and the two selkies dived into the waters and began their games.

Jenna screamed as she saw Anne plunge over the cliff and she instinctively ran forwards, but three selkies moved with her and before she could save herself she was hurled from Middle Eye and into the bitterly cold water.

Gerry clutched at his broken arm, swearing loudly and kicking out at the selkie who had effortlessly flung him to the ground. The selkie stood over him, grinning coldly. Gerry tried to scramble backwards on the grass, despite the jolts of pain shooting along his arm and into his shoulder. Two more selkies joined them, and they hurled Gerry into the swirling sea then dived in after him.

Gale had backed up right to the cliff edge. Tears streamed down her face. She could hear the screams of the coven members who were already in the water. The selkies were playing with them, like cats with captive mice, enjoying their terror and despair as they slowly began to die.

The young male selkie smiled warmly at Gale. "Well, you're a pretty thing."

"Let me go! Please, I don't want to die!"

He laughed very quietly. "Who ever does, really?"

"This was all a terrible mistake! We should never have started this!"

"Indeed not. Your spells are worthless but my family objects to the insult." His fishy breath was brushing her face now.

Gale wept, "What can I do? I don't want to die! I'm so sorry!"

"Ah, an apology. That's more like it."

Another selkie approached them and said, "You could offer her Spanish Jones's deal. If you like her."

The younger selkie looked thoughtful.

Gale's heel was over the cliff edge now. One more step backwards and she would plummet into the cold water. Her eyes were huge and bright with tears. She stared at the two selkies and waited.

Suz screamed as she plunged into the icy water. Four selkies dived in, and one of them pulled her to the surface. She gasped for air, her limbs already shocked rigid by the cold. The selkie suddenly released her and dived beneath the waves. Suz began frantically swimming towards the rocks around the base of Middle Eye, her long robe and heavy clothing weighing her down in the surging, bitter water. Her ankles were grabbed and she was abruptly pulled backwards, further out to sea. She thrashed with her arms and desperately tried to struggle for the surface. It was so dark under the water she might as well have been blind. Her lungs were screaming for air when her ankles were released and another pair of hands hauled her back to the surface then freed her. She gulped in air, panic blazing through her, and again she began swimming for Middle Eye. The selkies allowed her to place one hand on a rock before dragging her out to sea again.

"What exactly did you mean," said a young male selkie to Lizzy, "when you said we had placed a curse on your family?"

Lizzy's heart hammered in her chest as she recognised him as Ceri's would-be assailant. Her troubled suspicions about the dark-eyed boys' natures had been proven correct.

The night air was filled with screams, despairing cries, and cruel laughter. She could not understand how things had gone so terribly wrong. "Spanish Jones began it, when he murdered Charles Porter."

"Charlie the Knife Porter, hey? An ancestor of yours?"

Lizzy drew herself up to her full height. "You wretched selkies have murdered so many of my family!"

"And how many of us have you humans killed, with your yacht's keels and speed boats, with your fishermen's nets, with the pollution you soil everything with?"

Lizzy said, "That is not my doing!"

"Oh, right; it's everyone else's fault," sneered Joe. "How typically human to blame anyone or anything other than yourselves." He moved closer.

Lizzy backed away. From the corner of her eye she saw two selkies hurl Hefin into the water. There was only Gale and herself left on Middle Eye now.

Joe was just inches away from Lizzy. "So you're a Porter, hey? How amusing. Actually, we haven't placed a curse on your family. That your family still exists demonstrates that. But we are rather fond of playing with any Porter who comes our way."

"Well, I saved one from you last week!"

Joe smiled. "The girl? She isn't saved. She won a reprieve, that's all. Can you swim?"

Lizzy screamed as she was flung from Middle Eye. Time seemed to slow as the jagged rocks grew closer. There was hideous pain, then nothing.

"What is Spanish Jones's deal?" Gale was shaking in terror. The island was now deserted, save her herself and the two selkies before her. All the others were in the sea. The night echoed with frantic cries and ribald laughter.

The younger selkie said, "It's an idea my ancestor took from the Vikings who once lived here. I'll spare your life if you lie with me."

Gale was horrified. She turned to the black waters.

"But if you'd sooner drown, that's okay too."

The older selkie laughed harshly then dived into the ocean.

Only the two of them were left on Middle Eye.

The selkie held out his hand. Gale reached for it. She supposed he wasn't bad looking. In any other circumstance she may have been attracted to him. But her ears could still hear the fading cries of her dying friends. She was shivering from cold and shock. Her cheeks were wet with tears.

"Stop snivelling. And make your choice."

Gale sank down upon the grass.

"Undress."

Later, when it was over, Gale realised that there were no more voices on the wind. Her emotions were in turmoil. She felt like she wanted to scrape her own skin off. She wanted to weep but was too exhausted. Her bones were so cold they ached.

The selkie watched her curiously, then rose to his feet. He walked to the edge of Middle Eye, and stood looking down at the stygian waves. The cold didn't seem to trouble him. Then he gracefully dived into the water.

Gale turned to reach for her jumper and saw the older selkie, who had originally raised the subject of Spanish Jones's vile deal. He was walking purposefully over the grass towards her.

She babbled, "I made a deal! You witnessed it."

"I did. And my son didn't drown you. But I will. You've seen too much of my family. And surely you didn't seriously imagine that your childish interpretations of the laws of magic were any match for us?"

Then he grabbed Gale's arms and plunged with her from Middle Eye into the treacherous waters of the Dee Estuary.

And soon all was silent – save for the ceaseless lapping of water on rock and the susurrant whistling of dry sand through the rugged grasses on Middle Eye.

3:33

Rhea Troutman

My husband called it a sabbatical for the winter.

I would write a novel and soak in the mineral water that bubbled up from the earth in the tiny, isolated town of Medicine Waters, Montana.

It was really a trial separation before a divorce.

We drove the three hours to my new home in separate vehicles. He helped unload my things and drove away. I watched his truck turn a corner and disappear, then I shut the front door and locked it tight.

The little house was different from the pictures online: in reality it was small, dirty, and filled with stuff as if one could not be bothered to remove a trend or holiday before adding another. Shabby chic, country western, Christmas, Easter, Halloween, and glamping all fought to take center stage.

I sat at the kitchen table and pushed aside a figurine of Santa and gold glitter placemats to watch a deer on an afternoon stroll through a dirty window framed with ruffled curtains grayed from kitchen grease. The deer eyed me back with interest, like a nosey neighbor.

My phone chimed a call; it was my daughter.

"Mom, be careful. Women get roofied at that bar, Boone's. It happened to a friend; she still can't remember that night."

Wondering if I was a prime candidate for such a thing at age fifty, I thought not. I carry myself with dignity and have an air of "mature witch," wearing mostly black in elegant and modest cuts. Casual sex encounters at bars are not my style, and I'm certainly not the type to be slipped a date rape drug in my Grey Goose vodka and tonic with lemon.

"Am I even roofie-able?" I asked my daughter, "I suppose I do have wild gray hair that frames my face and lays on my matronly bosom just so," laughing to make the point.

"You're beautiful, Mom. Besides, it's more about opportunity than looks."

"I suppose you're right, I'll be careful. Love you, talk soon."

For the moment, at least, I was staying inside the house, shut away from small-town dangers at the local bar. I had a new home to make my own.

For three days, I wore the same white cotton nightgown. I loaded layer after layer of dusty clutter into boxes and stored them in the back room. Beneath it all, I uncovered a country chicken and cranberry motif in shades of barn red and creamy yellow. It's not what I would have done with the house, but I could live with it.

I scrubbed away grime accumulated from previous renters. Most would stay for a day or two to soak in the famous healing waters, then eat and drink at the local bars and restaurants, Boone's Pub on Main Street being the most popular choice.

As I worked, I burned bay leaves and placed star anise in the corners of each room, whispering love and peace into the air. Simple spells to help make the place light and livable.

Halfway through the third day, I peeled off the grungy nightgown, showered, dressed, and turned up the thermostat so I would return to a warm house. Leaving Pandora on the classical music station, which was playing Bach's "Air on the G String," I opened the front door for the first time in days.

Buttoning my wool sweater against the October chill, I set out on a walk. Leaves swirled in the wind and crunched under my boots on the empty streets. Looking back, I am struck with my first memories of Medicine Waters.

The town appeared to be dying on the one hand and coming back to life on the other. Shed-like hovels that had been built behind bigger houses, or in alleys and along dead-end streets, had become either low-income rentals or were left empty to rot where they stood. These structures gave the town an unnerving quality. It was hopeful to see the occasional remodel, as well as the discerning resident deer that roam the streets and sleep on the statelier porches and lawns.

Overgrown pine trees that had been planted as seedlings a hundred years ago or more, now stood in front of homes empty and dilapidated. Missing doors and porches rotted in on themselves from the inside out. Glassless holes that were once windows reminded me of eye sockets in skulls.

Residents of the town let trees take over lawns. Massive roots ruined foundations and forced paved walks and driveways to crack and be pushed upward, then tossed aside as if the earth were taking back what was hers. No one had thought of the future sixty years ago and now the trees stood seventy feet tall.

All sway my memory toward death.

I stopped to consider an abandoned structure made from concrete bricks. The yard hosted at least a dozen picnic tables and benches sinking into a hole as if the earth were swallowing them up.

Then I saw him. Watching me. He was a striking, tall figure with long dark hair, wearing a black pea coat. He was pale and handsome with angular features; probably forty years in age.

I froze while he lit a cigarette, took a drag, and spit as if ridding his lips of tobacco, never taking his piercing eyes off mine. I felt I couldn't tear my eyes from his as he took another long drag, flicked the cigarette in the gutter, and walked away. Adrenaline pumped through my veins as I watched him turn down another street and out of sight.

This little town is so weird.

Hurrying in the direction of home, I hoped my pounding heart was only surprise at his sudden appearance. My front yard was littered with pinecones and large exposed roots from a giant tree that overshadowed the little house, much like many of the houses in Medicine Waters. I walked the broken concrete path that led from the sidewalk in a downward slope through the yard to the decaying front porch.

I put the key in the lock and rattled the knob. The door flew open with a bitter cold blast. My breath caught with the shock of it.

"Hello!" A woman's voice: sweet, hopeful, and disembodied.

"Hello," I answered, noticing my breath vaporize sideways in the frigid air.

In the background, Patsy Cline crooned her early hit song "Always."

I would spend the winter with a ghost. A ghost that preferred Patsy Cline to Bach, it seemed.

It made sense; the house was old and had history, having been built in the mid-nineteen-hundreds. It stood across the street from the Rose Hotel, a legendary local hot spring, whose geysers had seeped through the earth's crust far longer than human beings had roamed it.

The resident ghost didn't concern me. I decided to call her Martha.

I boiled water for tea, then sat in the living room to watch late afternoon turn to twilight as it steeped. Through the warbled glass in the top half of the front door, the neon sign on The Rose flickered, "HOTEL," "–TEL," "HOTEL," "–TEL."

Something desperate and lost stirred. Echoes down a lonely canyon of blackness, a long stretch of highway to nowhere, empty, and dark.

As I stared at the flickering sign, my eyes filled with tears. My estranged husband had grown cold, and far more distant than the miles between us. My daughter, though well-meaning, had a life of her own.

Stop, you will fill your life with magick. You will find the beauty here. You have been through much worse; this is a piece of cake.

Pulling myself together, I put on a sophisticated black one-piece bathing suit and a long cozy robe, left the lights on for a welcoming return, and walked across the street to soak.

Scrunching my nose at the rotten egg smell of sulfur in the water, I passed the outdoor soaking pools filled with tourists and entered the lobby of the Rose.

The Rose had seen better days.

A friend who had recommended the place described it as "charming" and "reminiscent of times past." I chuckled to myself, wondering where one might draw the line between "vintage" and "run-down." Adorning the lobby walls were paintings of American Indian "princesses" that looked more like angelic white girls tinted brown. I took note of threadbare shag carpet in shades of avocado, and large glass ashtrays on mid-century end-tables. The original 1930s and '40s were mostly hidden under decades of aged repairs. I wondered what days past were reflected in this musty lobby and the rust-stained iron tubs in the adjacent spa room.

I walked past the front desk and out the lobby doors. I would soak in the pools outside and take my chances with the tourists.

It really was crowded, and I couldn't visualize myself squeezing in with all those bodies. Deciding to go home, I cinched the belt of my robe for the chilly walk back across the street, and then noticed three young women coming toward me with what looked like intent.

"Ma'am, come with us. We'll take you to where the locals go." I hesitated, but these three girls seemed to be townies, surely not any older than my own daughter, and friendly enough. I followed them across the hotel grounds to a tall wooden fence hidden behind pine trees. The girl that spoke opened a seamless gate and we entered a secluded area. A small circular pool with steam rising from the surface was surrounded by cracked pavement and wooden benches. It was perfect for a peaceful evening soak.

"Jesus Christ it's hot!" I laughed, sinking into the scalding water.

"It's the hottest water. It comes straight from the earth into this pool, then filters down to the other pools. Tourists and hotel guests complain about the temperature, so the locals built this fence. For the most part it's only people that live in town that come to this one." Digging around in her bag, she produced four tall plastic cups – the red ones that get used at a kegger or frat party – and a large box of Merlot.

"Bartender by trade and by choice," she snickered. "Drink with us?" she asked and swept her hand toward the other two. "Consider us your welcoming committee."

Prickles climbed my neck. An odd sensation, as I was sure I was boiling alive. She must have noticed because she went on to explain.

"It's a small town. We knew when you moved in, and today is your first time out. Welcome to Medicine Waters," handing me a cup of wine filled to the brim. She sat on the built-in seat next to me in the steaming water. "What do you do? Are you living here permanently?"

Trying to share as little as possible, and just enough to remain friendly, I answered with caution, "I'm here to write a book and not sure when I'll be leaving."

"This is the perfect place to write."

"So far I have not written one word," I chuckled as angst crept across my shoulders. *Why am I here?* The young women were silent and staring, maybe waiting for me to share more. Uncomfortable with how personal the conversation had become, I reminded myself to make the best of things and smiled back at them.

"You three seem college-aged; are you on a break?" I was making assumptions but wanted the conversation to shift toward other topics.

"No, we live here. We grew up in Medicine." For the sake of keeping things light, I decided not to ask why young women would stay in this weird and limited town.

"I'm Sarah, and this is Melody and Jinx." Tattoos covered Jinx from neck to heels. She kept her head bent and turned away, hiding beautiful moody green eyes behind a shield of long black hair while she listened to the conversation. I liked her.

"Maeve. Nice to meet the three of you."

"What do you think of our town now that you had a walkabout?" Certain I had not mentioned going for a walk, I shivered as another prickle climbed my neck.

"It's interesting. I noticed an odd building with a pile of picnic tables in a huge hole in the yard."

"That used to be a restaurant. Someone with a lot of money bought the old laundry building and remodeled it into a restaurant and bar. It wasn't successful. No one liked the owner. He took advantage of the people in town that worked for him. The earth didn't like him either and a big hole opened in the middle of the outdoor bar area."

I took a drink of wine, thinking about the earth not liking an underhanded person to the point of swallowing a restaurant, and decided I respected it.

"What you see is all that is left, just the building and some sinking tables." Sarah paused to twist her light brown hair into a knot on top of her head and refill her cup from the box of wine that sat on the edge of the pool. "Did you meet anyone while you were out?" Another prickle raised the hair on my arms. The question struck me as unusual coming from a stranger. Plastering the smile back on my face, I answered, taking care to keep my tone neutral.

"Well, no, but a man watched me from across the street. Long dark hair, tall, odd really… I mean, different. He didn't speak, just watched me." Jinx shot her head in my direction and spoke for the first time.

"You're a witch." I took a drink of wine and considered her for a moment, searching her statement for a clue of what her point might be.

"It was Wulf. That's Wulf with a U. He does not like witches." I took another drink, letting the musky flavor stay on my tongue a moment before swallowing. *Not bad for boxed wine.*

"How would Wulf know if I'm a witch or not?" I didn't bother hiding the hint of sarcasm in my voice because it all seemed ridiculous. Jinx narrowed her eyes at me.

"You must have done spellwork. He senses your presence." A wave of dizziness overtook me. I climbed out of the pool and laid down on a bench to cool off. "Are you okay?" Jinx asked with genuine concern in her voice.

"I'm fine. Just overheated." Sarah and Melody nodded their understanding and went back to drinking, talking, and soaking. Jinx got out of the pool. I noticed a barbed crescent-shaped scar on her thigh, shown raised and pearlescent. She had clearly tried to disguise it with a tattoo, but it was unmistakable in the moonlight. Fear flickered in her intense stare as our eyes locked. I looked away, not wanting to make her more uncomfortable. Jinx sat on the pavement next to me and drew her legs up to her chest, hiding the scar from view. I stretched out in the cold and watched the stars sparkle in the black night sky as heat dissipated in waves from my core.

"Wulf won't let you stay. He hates witches." I detected apprehension in her whisper before her tone turned cold and flat. "Medicine is full of war vets with PTSD and crazy people, all here for the water, but there are no witches because he chases them out, or else they go missing."

They go missing? I rubbed at the knot that had begun to tighten between my brows.

"Is that a threat? I'm staying. Mr. Wulf will just have to live and let live, as the saying goes." Jinx tilted her head to the night sky and took a deep breath, letting it out in a soft whistle.

"You seem nice, I hope you make it." *You hope I make it?*

I sat up, suddenly feeling vulnerable with my heart and belly exposed to the cold.

"It's been nice meeting you, Jinx. I'm headed home." She nodded and kept her gaze to the stars. I thanked Sarah and Melody for the conversation and wine, wrapped my robe over my wet, shivering body, and walked back to the house that glowed warmth from across the street.

That night, I awoke to a flood of light filling my room and the silhouette of a man pressed against the window next to the brass bed I laid in, his arms overhead and fingers splayed. I sat frozen with a racing heart and wide eyes, waiting for what might happen next.

The silhouette slid down the window and out of sight, followed by a scraping sound as if someone was clawing the ground and dragging themselves down the alley and away from the house.

The light went out, leaving the room dark again. I checked the time on my phone; it was 3:33 AM.

Sinking under the quilt and covering my head, I tried to reason away what just happened. Nothing made sense.

Just before dawn, I briefly fell asleep, then woke with a terrible headache. I almost didn't hear the click-click-click of the front doorknob. Someone was trying to open it from the outside.

Pain intensified behind my eyes as I swept the quilt aside and stood on the cold wooden floor. I crept to the living room. Breath caught in my throat as a shadow crossed the moonlight that poured in through the front door's window. For several minutes I stood out of sight from anyone possibly looking in, waiting on edge before nausea gripped my stomach. I ran to the bathroom to puke.

I faced the morning exhausted and not feeling well, telling myself it was the wine and hot water at the soaking pool. Too tired to write, I went for a walk instead, discovering Merc Wellness Co. on Main Street.

I was greeted by the smell of spice and geranium essential oil, comforting and familiar.

Employees and customers seemed happy, healthy, and somewhat normal. Dreadlocks, dirty Carhartt pants, Birkenstocks, and only the slightest hint of body odor. *Everyone here soaks in the evenings like ancient Romans in bathhouses.*

I ordered a panini sandwich from the café in the back of the store and walked around while waiting for it to be ready. The supplement aisle called to me. I hoped to find an effective herbal sleep aid. A well-muscled arm in a plaid flannel sleeve reached around me, and a large, work-worn man's hand took one of the sleep aid options off the shelf. I turned to look into deep blue eyes and got lost in them for a moment too long.

"Hi, Maeve, I'm Rome." He held his hand out to shake mine with a beautiful boyish smile that made a seductive contrast to his dark hair with gray at the temples.

"Rome, as in the capital of Italy?" I winced as soon as I said it. Wrinkles deepened between his brows.

"Well, probably, I mean, I don't know that my parents gave it much thought." He had taken my heedless quip as a genuine question. I liked him – oh, was I in trouble. I gave him a slow and flirty smile, noticing his jaw clench a little as he took it in.

"How do you know my name?" I asked, hoping I wouldn't get the answer he gave.

"It's a small town." He handed me the sleep aid he had taken off the shelf. "This works," he said with sober conviction.

"What's keeping you up?" Somehow I trusted him, and the words tumbled out.

"I awoke last night to my bedroom flooded with light and a man pressing against my window. I would like to sleep through it if it happens again." Rome seemed thoughtful, and then raised his eyebrows.

"Crazy Dan. He was probably trying to avoid being seen when the motion detecting light came on; the one your landlord installed. Crazy Dan walks the alleys at night." Tension lifted from my shoulders, and I could have kissed him.

"Is Crazy Dan dangerous? What's his story?" Rome gave a slight shrug of his shoulders.

"No, not dangerous, and I don't know his story. Some say he's a war vet who lost his mind and was sent home. Been here wandering the alleys as long as I can remember, and I moved here as a kid when my father bought Boone's."

A woman in the deli caught my eye and put a foil-wrapped sandwich on the counter. I thanked Rome for his help, taking my sandwich and herbal sleep aid to the register. As I headed down Main, Rome caught up with me.

"Hey, come to Boone's tonight and I'll buy you dinner and drinks; I'll be working." Before even realizing it, I smiled and said I would.

Home again, I unlocked and opened the front door. A cold blast, and Martha almost appeared. I say "almost" because it was like a shimmer in the air that felt as if she might materialize, but didn't.

"Hello, Martha." My breath vaporized and blew away with another blast of cold as if she had rushed toward me.

"Oh dear, he is coming!" Her concerned, hushed whisper recalled to me a grandmother wringing her hands with worry.

"Who is coming?" I asked and walked in to hang my coat in the entryway. The front door slammed shut behind me.

"The wolf!"

My stomach lurched and I stopped breathing. It was several seconds before I pulled myself together and asked Martha to tell me more. There was no answer, and the cold room began to warm as the thermostat kicked on.

In the kitchen, I unwrapped the sandwich and stared at it a moment, then wrapped it back up and tossed it into the refrigerator. I hadn't eaten since the morning before but wasn't hungry.

Irritated that this Wulf person had the power to scare me, I decided to fight. Not even sure what I was fighting, I lit a black candle and gathered items for a witch bottle: the rust-spotted blade from my shaving razor, bent stick pins, shards of glass, and a few rusty nails gathered from the alley. After putting the items in a small, empty spice jar, adding three drops of blood from a self-inflicted knife prick, and topping it with my own urine, I sealed the jar with puddled wax from the burning candle. A clink and ting sounded with each shake while I chanted a shield of protection around myself and the house.

Blood, urine, and rust residue mixed to create a bright brick-colored liquid.

The spell complete, I found a shovel in the tool shed and located a spot in the flowerbed a few yards from the front porch. Digging as deep as possible before hitting frozen earth, I put the witch bottle in the hole and covered it with the freshly dug dirt, stamping to pack it down.

"All is well, Martha, there's nothing to worry about," I called out as I stepped back inside.

Feeling empowered again, I put on a simple black dress, boots, and dark red lipstick.

With Samhain only two days away, the few blocks to Boone's was a fun walk in the dark.

Observing the neighborhood decorated for Halloween and trick-or-treaters brought a boost of spirit and a bounce to my step. October is my favorite time of year, and the little town seemed to suddenly come alive with jack-o-lanterns, headless huntsmen, and antique tractors with scarecrow drivers.

Entering the rustic atmosphere of the pub was like crossing a threshold to another world. By the look, it may have been the town's original watering hole. The place, buzzing with talk and laughter, went silent as I walked across loose floorboards creaking with each step. I sat on the only empty stool, and the noise resumed as before.

A combination of hippies, ranchers, kids, old folks, and everyone in between, all seemed happy to gather, eat, drink, and talk to each other. I liked it and wondered if I hadn't discovered why people stay in Medicine Waters.

Rome looked up from his work and made eye contact, handed a customer a mug of beer on tap from behind the bar, and came over to me.

"You look beautiful. What may I get you? At your service! Remember, dinner and drinks are on me." I beamed at the compliment and, for the first time in years, my cheeks flushed.

"Grey Goose and tonic with a wedge of lemon. Make it a double." I winked at him in hopes of appearing cool and confident despite blushing.

"Coming right up! Something to eat? The beer cheese and chips are much better than they sound." His smile won me over again.

"Sure, I'll have that, and a salad with balsamic."

"Done!" Rome moved down the bar to take orders from customers and mix drinks with two shakers overhead at a time. With a smooth swivel of his hips, he moved from task to task, sliding mugs down the length of the worn wood counter. A few minutes later he returned with my drink, all without missing a beat or spilling a drop.

"Here you go; enjoy." Then he was off to serve customers. The vodka and tonic tasted different; it was probably an unfamiliar tonic, but it went down easily. The warm buzz brought relaxed comfort that I had not felt in a while. My dinner was soon brought by Jinx.

"Hey, Maeve! I saw you come in, so I thought I'd bring this out myself. I work here, obviously." She chuckled and smiled with gleaming white teeth and sparkling green eyes.

"Oh! Thanks, Jinx. The booze seems to be particularly strong in these parts! I need to watch myself."

"It's the ice; our water is weird here." She smiled, nodding at my glass. I waved my hand dismissively.

"All good! Thought it was time to check out Boone's and take a break from staring at the blank page on my computer."

Jinx laughed and bounced off to socialize while she served food and drinks. Her demeanor was so different from the quiet, pensive Jinx I met at the Rose.

The beer cheese and chips were surprisingly good. I sampled several and pushed away the plate to try the salad. After a few bites, I wasn't interested in eating. Rome swept the uneaten food away and put another vodka and tonic in front of me. His charm was as intoxicating as the alcohol. My daughter's warning surfaced in my mind, but I pushed it away.

"It's karaoke night. Drink up!" I smiled at him through a warm haze, realizing another drink was probably not the best idea. I hadn't eaten much or slept well in days.

Two ranchers with high and tight haircuts, wearing clean white western shirts, boot-cut jeans, and work-worn cowboy boots, and a younger man with his hair in a bun, earrings, and baggy pants with rips at the knees, sang Queen's "We Will Rock You" well enough that I was sure they practiced together often. Enjoying the odd threesome as much as the performance, I yelled and clapped appreciation with everyone else.

Waiting for the next singer, I marveled at how euphoric and free I felt.

The lights went out.

A spotlight turned on. Jinx stood with the microphone clasped to her chest. Everyone stopped talking. The opening to Sia's "Breathe Me" filled the place. She brought the microphone to her lips and with the first notes she sang, it was clear she was special.

Tears slid down my face as I lived and died on each beautifully sung word. She finished the song and looked down, clasping the microphone to her chest again. There was meaning in the moment of silence that followed, then an explosion of appreciation and love.

Jinx put the microphone in its stand and went back to work.

Why is she here and not somewhere with more opportunity?

Boone's resumed buzzing with talking and laughter. I wiped away tears and felt bliss as a tingle all over my body. Rome leaned in and spoke close to my ear, sending a delicious shiver up my spine.

"Sarah will take over for me soon, then I will join you."

I watched him walk away, wondering what it would feel like to be fucked hard and senseless while I held on to his broad back and shoulders. The reality that I was still married... well, that's easily pushed aside.

He hasn't even called you, Maeve; it's over.

The noise level went down as several tables cleared and half the people at the bar left.

Jinx had a break in her busy shift and came to chat.

"What do you think of my singing? It's my hobby. I practice with the karaoke player whenever I have time, and sometimes I write my own songs."

"You're extremely talented, Jinx. I keep thinking you should be somewhere bigger where you will be discovered, or something like that. Take singing lessons and get yourself out there!" She shrugged her shoulders, the light in her eyes dimming a little. She looked both sad and wise beyond her years.

"I don't know, Maeve. Life is too complicated to have such big dreams. But I'll leave as soon as I find a way."

"Life is always complicated," I agreed. "But yours has just begun. I know it can be hard to leave your hometown, but I truly think the world needs your gift, and would want to hear you sing." I thought I saw a glimmer of hope in her shy smile.

"Maeve –" she said, glancing around, her voice almost inaudible. "Sorry, I'm just – look, I need to get back to work, okay? But I want to talk to you. It's important. You need to leave Medicine before it's too late. I know it sounds dramatic but it's not." Her voice became even quieter. "You're right, I need to get outta here too." She gave a quick glance around the bar, then shrugged as if to lighten her tone. "I'll explain soon."

Her urgency reached me through my euphoric haze, and I sensed she was truly scared for some reason. The memory of the scar on her leg flashed through my mind.

"Halloween's the day after tomorrow," I mentioned, "and I'm sure you're busy. I'll buy you lunch at the Merc on the 1st, okay? Meet you there at noon?" Jinx agreed and went back to serving drinks. Her intensity stayed with me for a few minutes until Sarah showed up and took over tending the bar. I hadn't realized Sarah also worked at Boone's, but it was a small town. Rome left her to it and came to sit with me. He smelled of soap and salty sweat. I took a sip of my untouched drink and looked at him from under my lashes, over the rim of the glass, and licked condensation off the side. The sound of his hard swallow and release of breath was satisfying. I had his attention; we would be dehydrated and spent before morning.

"Finish that." Rome nodded toward the drink and traced a finger up my inner thigh to the crease of my leg. Warmth flooded my lower abdomen, and it was my turn to release breath. I slid the glass away and stood up. He stood up too. With his hand on the small of my back, we walked out of the pub together.

A gentle snow greeted us outside. We laughed and stuck out our tongues to catch snowflakes. I shivered in the crisp air. Rome took off his flannel shirt and put it around my shoulders. Only wearing a T-shirt, he wrapped his bare arms around me and drew me close, lowering his lips to mine. I tingled with the chemistry of the kiss and melted against him. I couldn't wait to get to my house and feel his hands on my body.

"Stay with me tonight?" I asked. Rome nodded and tightened his arms around me, pressing his desire against my pelvis. We took the few blocks to my place at a near run. Giddy and alive, I laughed with the sensation of cold air blowing through my hair.

He stopped on the sidewalk in front of my house with an awkward stumble, crossed his bare arms with a shiver, and grimaced as if remembering something.

"On second thought, Maeve, maybe it's not the best idea tonight," squeezing my hand in a reassuring way. "I'm suddenly not feeling well. I don't know why... it just hit me. I'm sorry, beautiful. Let's get together soon. Keep my shirt for now; I know where you live." He kissed my forehead and gave me a gentle nudge toward the porch.

At the door, I turned to ask what had changed his mind, but he was already walking away at a fast clip.

Disoriented and suddenly overcome with exhaustion, I went inside, took off my clothes, and went to bed.

My dream had a smell... of burning rubber and stagnant water ripe with decay.

The soft black loam of the flowerbed a few yards from the front door began to mound. Crumbles of dirt fell away as the earth pushed the witch bottle out of the hole.

It rolled uphill alongside the cracked pavement of the path, then veered off to the tree, and disappeared into the shadows under a full moon's silver brilliance.

I awoke to light flooding my room and Crazy Dan pressed against the window.

Long after the light went out and Crazy Dan scraped down the alley, I lay in the dark and listened to the nighttime creaks and thumps of the old house, waiting for the eerie sensation that "nothing was as it seemed" to dissipate and allow my troubled mind some much-needed rest. Relief never came. Sometime around 3:30, I got up and crept in the dark to the front door's window.

The neon sign on The Rose flickered, "HOTEL," "–TEL," "HOTEL," "–TEL." A long shadow from the tree in the yard spread across the street, as if reaching for something unseen. The light of the full moon trickled through the branches and illuminated Wulf's face. He leaned against the massive trunk and stared back at me, the red glow of a cigarette in his mouth intensifying with each drag.

I put water on the stove for a cup of tea. Wulf would see the flames from the gas burner in the kitchen window, but it didn't matter. There was nothing I could do about him, anyway. Resigned, I went about steeping tea and tried to keep calm.

I sat on the couch and held my cup with trembling hands, sometimes checking to see if Wulf was still there, and each time I looked, there he was.

I awoke with a start at the first glimmer of dawn. Wulf was gone.

Come on, Maeve; maybe you imagined him under the tree. It was dark. Moonlight and shadows can play tricks on the mind.

I went out to the flowerbed. The hole gaped empty, and a pile of black soil lay next to it. The witch bottle wasn't there.

Scattered cigarette butts under the tree brought reality crashing in. The sky lightened with the rising sun as I fought to keep fear from taking over my thoughts. I went inside, made strong coffee, and called my husband. It went to voicemail.

It was another day I couldn't bring myself to write. I cleaned the house and did laundry instead, then went for a walk to clear my mind. I reached the primary school at the edge of town. Children were playing at the playground. Something about it caught my attention as I stood at the fence and watched. There was no shrieking and yelling. They ran and climbed, flew high on the swings, and played together in groups, but there was not the typical racket of a school recess. I walked away, unnerved by the silence.

Thankfully, the private soaking pool at the Rose was empty that evening. Hot water relaxed my exhausted mind and body while I stared at the stars and tried not to think. A man opened the gate and said hello. I nodded, hoping he wouldn't talk to me.

He mumbled to himself inaudibly, then coughed deep; hacking as if he stood at death's door. Apparently I could find no peace in this place.

"You see a woman with blonde hair? I'm supposed to meet a friend here." He gasped for air, followed by more hacking.

"Nope, just me."

"Nice to meet you, Maeve, I'm Henry." His addled smile revealed several missing teeth.

"You as well." I rolled my eyes and closed them, hoping Henry would get the hint and be quiet, or better yet, go away. Instead, he lowered himself into the pool, taking a seat across from me.

"Ever think about all the people that share this water? This is the best pool because the water in it comes straight out of the ground. Then it goes through a pipe to the next pool, then goes through another pipe to the big swimming pool." I nodded and kept my eyes closed. "It's disgusting," he remarked.

I opened one eye. The poor man looked genuinely appalled. I laughed before I could stop myself.

"The same minerals in this water are in our drinking water, too. I saw you watching the kids on the playground at the school today," he stated. My breath caught in my throat.

"Excuse me?"

"It's the lithium," he explained. "It keeps the kids calm. You noticed it, right? They're docile. We don't have much crime here either, just the occasional missing person or unexplained murder." I was getting used to strangers knowing my every move and tired of being told people went missing in Medicine Waters, even if there wasn't that much crime. I didn't even want to think about the occasional murder.

Natural lithium in the town's water keeping kids calm and quiet? Well, it reminded me of jokes with other mothers when our children where young. We laughed together, fantasizing of drugging our infants to sleep, and our two-year-olds into submission, then our teenagers. Dark humor got us through the hard times.

"Wulf said we shouldn't talk to you." Stunned, I snapped my eyes open to investigate Henry's half-crazed glare. We stared at one another for a moment before he pulled his gaze away and shot a quick glance at the gate.

"Are you nervous, Henry? I'm not going to tell anyone you talked to me." He was agitated, and I wanted more information before he bolted. He was silent for a few moments, then cleared his throat.

"Wulf said you're not one of us and you're not staying, so you don't need to know anything."

"Everyone here does whatever Wulf says?" Henry's dark eyes turned to unreadable black pools.

"Everyone who wants to live." My skin prickled as the hair on my arms raised.

"How does he hurt you, Henry?" He got out of the pool, hacking and coughing, and staggered to the gate. On his lower back, just above the waist of his shorts, I could make out the half-circle of a faded scar. Henry turned around to face me, shoulders slumped, and anguish etched on his haggard face.

"He has my blood, and if he doesn't already have yours, he will soon enough." Then he opened the gate and made haste into the dark. I stared after, turning what he said over in my mind, my stomach churning as fear crept down my spine.

What in the hell is *Wulf?*

The gentle snowfall turned to blizzard.

I went home to make dinner. Exhaustion and lingering nausea made it impossible to eat more than a few bites. To help myself out of the downward spiral since arriving in Medicine Waters, I nailed a folded bedsheet over the window next to my bed, made chamomile tea, swallowed double the recommended dose of herbal sleep aids, checked that the doors were locked, made sure the windows were latched, and went to bed.

From the depths of sleep, I heard the pounding of running feet, intensifying as it grew nearer.

I sat up, jolted awake. A shadow crossed the bedroom doorway.

"Get out! Enough!" I screamed to the dark with every ounce of power I could summon, the force of my voice splitting my already aching skull. No chance of falling back to sleep with my heart and head pounding, I got out of bed, wincing at the cold of the floorboards on my bare feet, and went to the kitchen to make tea. It was still snowing and the world outside the kitchen window had turned soft and white.

The time on my phone read 3:33.

At least I slept a few hours. Happy Samhain.

The morning wore on. I eventually called my husband. It went to voicemail. I paced the floor, watching the snow pile up on the sidewalk and street. My whole body ached as I made passes by the kitchen window. I decided to get candy for trick-or-treaters at Wally's, the town's only official grocery store.

I tromped through snow the few blocks to Wally's and wandered the isles looking for the candy section and ran into Rome, who was apparently doing the same thing.

"Maeve! I've been thinking about you!" I smiled, my worries fading into the background, and wiped frozen snot from my face, hoping he hadn't noticed.

"Have you?" He chuckled and took a step toward me.

"How about I come over and cook dinner for you, and we both give candy to trick-or-treaters together?" His deep blue eyes gleamed with confidence and warmth.

"I would like that... it's a great idea!" I felt safe with him and for a moment everything seemed better. Rome gave me his boyish grin and leaned in close.

"How about we drink wine, eat, take care of the trick-or-treaters' sugar highs, and then I will take care of you?" Heat rose to my cheeks, and I couldn't stop smiling. Rome raised his eyebrows and nodded, making my cheeks burn even more. "You get the candy. I'll take care of the rest. Meet at your place around 6:30?" I looked down at a puddle of melting snow from my boots and nodded.

"It's a date!" Rome went on his way, leaving me in the candy section to stare at the shelves for several minutes before I got my head out of the clouds and figured out what to buy.

The confident knock on the front door was startling, even though I was expecting it.

I took one last look in the mirror and bit my lips, bruising them berry red, and went to the door with an air of calm I didn't feel.

"You're beautiful, Maeve." Rome had his arms full of grocery bags but still pushed me gently to the wall with a kiss, his tongue tracing my lips and trailing down my neck. He stopped, leaving me breathless. "Wine and dinner, then?" I nodded and put cold hands to my burning cheeks. Rome raised an eyebrow.

"Oh, it's *going* to happen, but I want you fed and ready. You can cut the lemons and grate parmesan."

After answering the door to give candy to trick-or-treaters, pretending to be interested in their costumes, I turned my attention to what Rome asked of me, and he poured the deep red wine. I sipped while he made lemon butter bucatini. My mouth watered as the smell of browned butter and lemon filled the kitchen. Rome tossed a small salad, and we sat down to eat. The food was delicious. For the first time in days, I ate every bite.

"Here's to new relationships," he declared, with a clink of his glass against mine.

My lips buzzed and I tingled with giddy desire while washing the dishes. Rome cleaned the counters and poured more wine. His chatter about Boone's and other local businesses was lost on me as I finished in a floating haze of aroused euphoria.

Another knock on the door, and Rome followed me to help hand out candy. After the last trick-or-treater left, he turned out the porch light and pushed me to the wall, not as gently this time. His breath was hot on my neck as he pulled up my dress and unsnapped my bra to free my breasts. His fingers brushed my nipples, sending heat between my legs. Already half-crazed with desire, I pulled the dress over my head and removed my bra, tossing both aside. Rome stepped back, his eyes wandering over me standing in only black panties and boots.

"You have two choices: I carry you to your bed and take you right now, or you hold it together while I lick you where you stand." His voice was thick and deep. I tingled everywhere.

Is it the wine? Oh gods! I don't care!

I slid my hands down my ribs and stomach, squeezing my breasts together, slipped a finger into my panties and swirled it between my legs long enough to make my breath catch, then wiped my finger back up my body, leaving a wet trail to my mouth.

"Lick me."

Rome pressed me against the wall and lowered his head to my breast, teasing with his teeth, went to his knees, licked the trail of juice down my belly and pushed aside the crotch of my panties. I shivered when his tongue found my clit, moaning with each circular sweep. Twining my fingers in his hair and laying my head back against the wall, I panted with mounting pleasure.

As if suddenly remembering something, he stopped, stood up, and went to the kitchen. Catching my breath and regaining control of myself, I looked out the window of the front door. A couple of kids in costume walked in front of the house and kept going. Across the street I saw a shadow. The embers at the end of a cigarette deepened, then turned into a shower of sparks as it was tossed to the gutter.

"Let's drink this wine and then take it to your bed." I tore my eyes from the window and joined Rome in the kitchen. He took his coat off the back of a chair, draped it on my shoulders, and handed me the glass he had poured earlier. I drank in gulps as if taking medicine given by a parent, marveling at the potency of this town's liquor.

"Why did you stop?"

"We have the whole night ahead of us, Maeve." He put his glass down and went to the front door and rattled the knob, then clicked the lock.

He must be checking the lock, with trick-or-treaters still roaming around.

Rome returned; his body haloed in a radiant aura, and brushed his coat off my shoulders to the floor and led me to the bedroom.

He pushed me down on the bed with power, sending a buzz of excitement shooting through my abdomen and downward, making me wet. Taking his time to remove my boots, and lingering to kiss my toes, he brushed his lips up my thighs and slid my panties down to my ankles and tossed them to the floor. I wanted him to keep going, but instead he sat against the brass bars at the head of the bed and guided me to his erection. I understood what he wanted and put him in my mouth, brushing my fingers behind his balls, feeling skin contract and quiver. He became harder as I licked, sucked, and swirled my tongue. With a groan, he pulled me up to straddle his body. In that moment I was mesmerized, watching Rome's masculine Adam's apple rise and fall while he caught his breath. I held the brass bars on either side for leverage, moving fast and rhythmic, pulling forward and pushing back, panting harder as I approached release. Rome held my hips still, not allowing me to orgasm.

We stayed still like this for several tormenting minutes. My heaving sighs from the heightened tension calmed. Then he licked my nipples and teased with gentle bites, moving my hips in small circles, grinding me down on his erection, making me swell and throb even more. I held onto the brass bars and moaned as the taut escalation to climax began. Every delicious rotation brought me toward ecstasy. I nearly screamed from the intensity. He held my hips still again, and I cried out in exquisite frustration.

"Why won't you let me orgasm?!" I wanted to beg for his permission to release. I would have sold my soul.

The room suddenly went cold. Rome's breath hung between us as the sound of running came close.

"Run!" Martha's spectral warning sounded in the air.

"Rome won't let you climax because he's my servant," a husky voice sounded behind me. Frozen in terror, I searched Rome's eyes. He gave a reassuring nod and turned me around to face Wulf.

"Leave, spirit!" Wulf growled to the air.

"Oh no!" Martha's sigh swept past and out of the room.

Rome lifted me off his hips and onto the bed, wrapping his legs inside mine, holding them apart. Wulf stood in front of me, eyeing my exposed vagina. I shivered even as warmth returned to the room.

"Hold still, Maeve, this part will be over soon." My breath caught in my throat as Wulf climbed onto the bed and crept toward my open thighs as a predator stalking its prey. I heard my own scream, piercing and distant. Panic pounded in my chest, making me kick and claw to get away. Rome regained his hold, tightening his legs over mine, and I couldn't struggle against his strength. I sucked in air to scream again, but I choked as heaving breath and spit from my muffled scream pushed against the hand that he clamped over my mouth.

Wulf lowered his face to my spread lips and sniffed, his coarse hair brushing my thighs as he raised his head again and spoke to Rome.

"Hold her still." Rome tightened his clasp even more, forcing my head back against his chest. Terror seared my mind as Wulf flashed jagged, pointed teeth, and sank them into my flesh. I heard the crunch of his bite tearing into my skin and thrust my hips upward, straining against Rome as sharp pain shot through my body.

Wulf sat in a crouch between my legs and displayed a terrible blood-smeared grin. Reaching into the pocket of his pants and producing a small vial, he then collected my blood as it flowed down my leg and soaked into the quilt. Thankfully, my thigh went numb, and I relaxed in Rome's vicelike grip.

"I'm going to take my hand off your mouth. The worst is over. Sorry, beautiful. Now it'll just be you and me. I'll get something to stop the bleeding." He released his hold and went into the bathroom. Wulf watched in silence as I scrambled to cover myself with the bedsheet. Then he left without a word.

Rome returned and uncovered my bleeding leg, shaking his head as he wiped at the fresh bite wound. I watched him make a compression bandage with a hand towel and his T-shirt tied around my thigh. Then he covered me with the quilt and left to lock the front door.

When he returned, he handed me a glass of wine. I drank it, grateful for the effect I knew it would have. Rome took the empty glass from my hands and set it on the bedside table, then slid under the quilt, and wrapped me in his arms. Buoyant and free, I drifted in and out of consciousness, avoiding my confusion and questions, before falling into a deep slumber.

I dreamt of Jinx.

She sat with her head slumped forward, hair matted to her sunken and lifeless face. Steam rose from the surface of the water in the hottest pool as her body boiled, turning blood to brown debris that surfaced around her, then churned under again with the roiling bubbles. Cooked gray meat fell from her bones and was sucked into the pipe that supplied water to the next pool, making way through another pipe that filled the public swimming pool.

I awoke to muted light shining through the sheet I had nailed up, and the shadow of Crazy Dan pressed against the window. Rome slept peacefully next to me. I glanced at my phone; the time was 3:33.

It's the witching hour, and you have wandered down a path you cannot return from, Maeve.

I laid awake for a while after Crazy Dan disappeared from the window and the light went out, then snuggled against Rome and fell back to sleep.

I awoke in the early morning to Rome propped up on an elbow, watching me. He smiled and kissed me, brushing his hand down my body. I moaned as he touched my clit.

"Listen, you must never do spellwork, Maeve, and he won't think of you often." With a gentle touch, he untied his T-shirt from my leg and removed the hand towel.

Dried blood covered the jagged bite wound on my thigh. Rome traced the fresh scab with his finger.

"Look, I have one too." I followed his gaze to a raised and barbed crescent-shaped scar on his own inner thigh. Our eyes met for a moment before I looked away, not ready to hear the answers to the questions that plagued me. As if to change the subject, he lowered his head to lick my sex, slow and sweet until nothing hurt, and I cried out in delicious climax. I opened my legs wide for him, holding onto his muscled back while he moved to his own release, comforted by his kind lovemaking.

Afterward, I lay in his arms and accepted that nothing was the same as it was when I arrived in Medicine Waters. And yet, the nagging thought that I should leave still haunted my mind.

Rome went to the kitchen and started coffee. My phone chimed a call. It was my husband.

"Hey, I got a couple of messages from you, but all I heard was static with a weird voice in the background saying nothing, really, or nothing I understood. What's up?" He sounded like a stranger, or someone I had known long ago in another lifetime.

"I think I need to come home." I heard his sharp intake of breath at the other end.

"It's too soon, Maeve. You haven't been gone very long. Besides, you're probably not going anywhere for a while; the road from Medicine Waters to Missoula is closed. There has been a *lot* of snowfall and it's still coming down." I closed my eyes, sadness washing over me as what he said sunk in.

It really is over; he doesn't want you back.

I hung up and got in the shower. Hot water reopened my wound. I watched blood and water mix, run down my leg, and down the drain, and remembered I had to meet Jinx at noon.

I finished showering, put a couple of bandages over the reopened wound, and got dressed.

Rome handed me a cup of coffee and we sat together in silence for a bit. When he spoke, I was taken aback with the difference in his tone.

"You are never leaving, Maeve. Wulf has your blood. He gave you to me and you agreed." Tears stung my eyes at his sharp words. With the effort it took to keep from crying, my voice wavered and cracked.

"I know."

Rome took a sip of his coffee and looked out the kitchen window.

It was still snowing when I left the house. Several police vehicles and an ambulance were parked at the Rose as I walked the path from my porch to the sidewalk. No motors running, no lights flashing. Things looked calm.

Maybe a guest had a health scare.

The Merc was quiet. I read product pamphlets and wandered the aisles for several hours. Jinx never showed. Chill seeped through my wool sweater as I stood outside the health food store and watched the snow fall. I decided I would go to Boone's.

I'm not a day-drinker, but taking the edge off seemed like my best option. Boone's was empty except for Sarah behind the bar. I ordered a Grey Goose and tonic with lemon, watched her make it, and took a long drink.

The door opened and Wulf appeared in a flurry of snow. He entered and sat to my left. Energized fear buzzed at the base of my spine, reminding me of the night before. He was flawless in the light of day. Smooth, ageless skin, his movements clean and fast.

"You're only a young man," I joked with him, trying to hide the nervous tension I felt. Wulf chuckled and picked up my drink, sniffed it, flared his nostrils, and put it down.

"For hundreds of years I have been mystified by alcohol. Why do humans drink it?" The gravel in his low, growling voice intensified with each word as he stared at me, unblinking. I sat rooted, watching his eyes dilate and shrink, sure there was no point in answering. With nothing left to lose, I asked Wulf a question of my own.

"What do you want with me?"

"I do not want you. I was in the process of starving you, making you uncomfortable and afraid so you would leave. I don't like witches. Cocky, arrogant, always thinking you can throw power around to get what you want. Rome wants you. He serves me well; I gave him what he wanted, and you agreed to it." A phone chimed a call from behind the bar. I glanced at Sarah as she answered it.

"What will happen to me? Why did you gather my blood last night?" Sarah talked in the background, giving her name, and saying things I couldn't make out.

Wulf reached into his pocket, pulled out my witch bottle, and shook it with a clink, turning its contents a bright brick-red.

"I already have *this*. Your blood in my hands. Last night was for entertainment. Dream your dreams, witch, but do as you're told. And don't try to leave."

Sarah suddenly cried out. "Oh Jinx! Sweet Jinx! No! No! No!" A dark shadow crossed over me, leaving a lump in my throat. I tore my eyes from Sarah, who had crumpled to the floor behind the bar, still clutching her phone, and turned to Wulf.

"It's true, isn't it? I'll never be able to leave this town. Jinx found the only way out." Nonhuman eyes gazed back at me. His lips curled in a smile, revealing jagged, pointed teeth.

Entombed

Corvis Nocturnum

Gale-force winds blew across the desert sands, causing the cantina to shudder. Patrons swathed in cloaks and long robes murmured in their native tongues, and the clinking of glassware could be heard through the tavern.

The door swung open and a stranger stood on the threshold, squinting into the dim interior. The dull hum of conversation ceased.

The American shook the sand out of his hat and jacket, allowing the door to close behind him. He did not acknowledge the gazes that followed him to the bar. Eyes slowly adjusting to the lighting, he pulled up a stool and waited for the barkeep.

"What'll you be having, sir?" a short and shifty-eyed fellow asked at last, wiping his hands on a rag. The long night had clearly worn him.

"Anything cold and bottled," he replied.

"Sure."

Bending slightly, the barkeep retrieved a bottle from beneath the bar, popped the cap, and set it before the newcomer alongside an empty glass. After sliding a few bills across the bar, the man took a long swig from the bottle, ignoring the glass. Behind him, a pair of men stood and approached the bar.

"You lost?" one man asked suspiciously.

"Not lost, exactly," the American answered, turning to face the men, a cocky grin on his face. "But I could use a guide familiar with the valley over the ridge," he replied.

The men exchanged a glance.

"That'd be Sayid," the other man offered. With curt nods, they turned and walked away.

"Hey. Hey! Where do I find this Sayid guy?" he called after them, but they'd gone. He let out an exasperated grunt.

"Goddamn sand nig—" a hand on his arm halted his speech.

"I am Sayid," spoke the cloaked figure beside him. "What do you seek in the valley? It holds nothing but caverns full of wild animals seeking shelter from the sands."

"Sayid!" the American clapped a hand on the stranger's shoulder. "I'm Clyde. I need a local who knows the route to the remains of the buried citadel."

Sayid's face remained hidden in shadow. Clyde pulled his hand back from the man's shoulder and swallowed the dregs of his bottle. "I'm an archeologist."

"I see," Sayid replied.

"You know, like Indiana Jones," he chortled. "I'm conducting some contract work for a major museum in the states." He paused. "I can pay you well."

"Clyde… the money is irrelevant. We do not venture to this place."

"Oh, come *on*!" Clyde pressed. "Look at this rathole of a city! You mean to tell me you don't want out of here?"

Sayid turned slowly to face him.

"Many have tried to find the lost city and failed. All were motivated by greed. They had no respect for the ancient ones."

"Bah!" Clyde batted a hand dismissively. "We're talking about archaeology, man. Study. Education. The 'ancient ones,'" he formed air quotes with his fingers, "will be admired and respected by thousands, and their works stored under glass, lock, key, and armed security for all the world to see!"

He emitted a shrill whistle.

"Hey!" He called down the length of the bar. "Another round over here!"

Sayid remained silent.

The archeologist laughed and shook his head. "Look, I've been cleared by your government to do the dig, and my representatives are well compensated. Whatever ancient gods or mummies or what-have-you will be unearthed eventually. Why not be a part of progress? If I lead the dig, I can build up this city – put it on the map!"

Clyde pulled an envelope out of the inner breast pocket of his jacket. He placed it on the bar, and slid it toward his companion. After a few moments, Sayid sighed heavily. Without a glance, he slid the envelope toward the barkeep who was placing fresh bottles in front of the two men. He whispered something. The little man nodded and shuffled off, the envelope in hand.

"Not gonna count it?" Clyde asked.

Sayid shook his head, "No. If something happens, it will go to my family."

Clyde laughed and took a deep gulp from the fresh bottle, shaking his head. "Well, if you people don't have a sense of the dramatic! I'll be damned."

"Meet me here in the morning, nine o' clock," Sayid said. He left a bill under his untouched beer and departed.

As Clyde approached the following morning, a rifle strapped diagonally across his back and a pack slung over one shoulder, he spotted Sayid standing between two horses laden with saddle bags. Clyde blinked in the desert morning sunlight, his head pounding with hangover. He had slammed beers and thrown money at the ladies who brought his food, trying to entice them to bed, until the barkeep had shooed him out at closing time.

"This godforsaken place needs a casino and five-star hotel. And an airport. Think I'll build it all when we're done here," he laughed.

Sayid pointed toward the horizon, mounted his horse, and departed.

"What, no camel?" Clyde called out. When Sayid did not respond, Clyde pulled himself onto the second horse with far less grace than his companion had exhibited, then took off at a trot to catch up. It was going to be a long day, Clyde groused sourly, made worse by his humorless guide.

For hours, Sayid remained silent. He stopped riding only to rest the horses and allow them to drink from the water packs they carried.

Long into the day they traveled. To Clyde, the desert seemed to stretch on forever and he grew more and more impatient, voicing his frustration in seemingly endless streams of slurs and insults against the land and her people.

"Are you listening to me? How far are we?" Clyde demanded.

Sayid looked at him, then pointed into the growing dusk. In the distance, one could just make out a rocky ravine.

"There," he responded grimly. "That is the gateway to your rewards."

"Well, it's about time!" Clyde slapped his horse's weary flank to quicken the pace. Sayid's brow furrowed. His voice was sage.

"It is not too late to turn back."

"Turn back?" Clyde yelled incredulously over his shoulder. "Are you out of your mind?"

Sayid coaxed his bay gently until the horses trotted astride.

Clyde smiled and shook his head.

"The heat must have gotten to you," he chuckled. "I didn't come all the way out here just to turn around empty-handed." Clyde kicked the horse roughly, urging her into a gallop. Sayid silently followed, head bowed.

They reached the cave entrance by nightfall. The temperature was dropping rapidly. Sayid swiftly secured the horses, removing their saddles and patting down their heaving, weary bodies. He shook out their saddle blankets, then unfolded them and laid them across their broad backs to ward off cold and prevent cramping. He ignored Clyde's impatient clucking. He lit a torch and placed it nearby to ward off jackals.

When satisfied, he turned to face the cave entrance once more. In one pocket, he felt for his medallion and clenched it tightly, muttering a quick prayer under his breath. Clyde was clicking a flashlight on and off again, testing its battery, grinning, bouncing on the balls of his eager feet. He handed a second flashlight to Sayid and the two men entered the cave.

They began their descent beside walls gritty with sandblasting. Ancient desert debris littered the steep stone steps. Clyde pushed his way past Sayid, leading their modest band along the route for nearly an hour until they reached a landing. Three archways lay before them.

"Which one?" Clyde asked. Sweat glistened along his hairline and the nape of his neck as he swung his flashlight beam from one entrance to the next. Sayid stepped forward, shining his own beam on the inscriptions above each doorway. After some consideration, he pointed to the entryway on the far left. Clyde grunted his acknowledgement and led the way through.

They emerged in a narrow corridor, ending in another single archway, this one blocked by a large boulder. Gold coins littered the dusty earth. Clyde stooped to retrieve a coin. Holding the light in one hand, he turned the coin over in the other. He opened his mouth and bit the coin, then chuckled.

"They're gold," he said, holding the coin between his thumb and forefinger, grinning at Sayid. Without waiting for a response, Clyde squatted, sweeping his hands along the floor and gathering the coins in the upturned hem of his shirt. When the floor was bare, he shrugged off his pack and poured the coins into a zippered pocket, securing them inside. He looked up at Sayid who watched his actions without comment.

"Travel expenses," he chuckled and winked. Sayid remained stone-faced. Still on his knees, snickering at his own cleverness, Clyde replaced his pack. Something caught his eye, something protruding from beneath the boulder. He crawled forward, wrapping a bandana around his hand and brushing at the ancient sediment gathered in the doorframe. He peered more closely.

"Bone fragments," he clicked his tongue, gesturing as he looked back at the guide. "Human metatarsals, by the look of them." When Sayid did not respond, he added, "Pieces of a human hand. I'd put money on it."

Sayid's lips tightened in a firm line and he lowered his head in a slight bow, eyes closed, before looking up again.

"Poor fool," Clyde wheezed with a laugh. "Should have placed the doorstop, eh, Sayid?" Clyde chuckled again, swinging his pack off for the second time. He began to loosen the bindings of his pickaxe until he could slide it free, seeming to test the weight of it in his hands.

"It looks like it sustained some damage when it fell or slammed on this fella," Clyde explained. "See the cracking? I think I can get through it."

He braced himself and swung. The clank of metal on stone reverberated through the narrow space. He swung again and again. The cracks were widening, the stone separating. He shoved with his shoulder and the sound of the shifting rocks was audible within. Again he swung the pickaxe. A large wedge of stone dislodged and slid toward them. Clyde hopped out of the way, allowing it to tumble unhindered and come to rest. He began to kick and stomp against the remaining stone. It crumbled away in a cloud of heavy dust. He emitted a triumphant roar and scurried over the rubble, displacing stone shards as he went. Sayid muttered a prayer before climbing over the buried remains.

They'd entered a vast chamber. Their light sources reflected back the glimmer of metal. Drawn nearer, Clyde saw more of the unusual gold coins beside artifacts he could not immediately identify.

Clyde turned to gauge Sayid's reaction. The man stood silently in the entranceway, clasping his medallion.

"This was easy. *Too easy*! How come you never –" Clyde's words died in his throat. Above his guide, towering in the dark, stood a carved stone figure. It was approximately nine feet high, decorated with carvings of varied symbols. Clyde stowed his pickaxe and raised his light, drawing nearer.

Sayid stepped deeper into the chamber in order to follow Clyde's gaze. As he took in the sight, he nodded soberly.

"The guardian of the tomb of the king," His voice was gruff, low. "'All who enter seeking knowledge for the betterment of man will be at peace,' so reads the inscription that led us to this place."

"The king –" Clyde began, but stopped. Through their boots, the men felt a low vibration, rapidly rising in intensity. The chamber filled with a grinding, then a rumble that shook the ground upon which they stood. Sayid spread his legs and bent his knees, extending his arms to either side for balance. Clyde emulated, glancing around nervously.

The walls around the gargantuan figure began to crack. It had begun to pull away from the wall.

"Christ!" Clyde hissed. Rocks tumbled from their former frames, smashing and rolling along the floor, ever nearer the trespassers. They skirted backward, watching as the looming figure freed itself.

Its hollowed eyes peered lifelessly. Sayid had resumed his muttered prayers, working his medallion between calloused fingers. In the flickering light, Clyde caught a glimpse of the mark of the architects from the ancient days of King Solomon. "King," indeed. This discovery would be worth a fortune.

The stone guardian took a lumbering step toward Clyde.

Clyde snapped out of his stupor and reached for his rifle. He fumbled for the safety and raised it to his shoulder. The first shot sparked and ricocheted, leaving a shallow crater in the center of the creature's forehead. Unfazed, it advanced another step. Another. The space between them was rapidly diminishing. The rifle fired again. This time, the ricochet buried in the rock inches from Sayid's shoulder. The doorway through which they'd entered now lay in the wake of the advancing guardian. Sayid ran.

Scrambling over the rubble, Sayid heard Clyde cry out, then a hauntingly loud snapping sound, ending in a wet, gurgling sob. The vibrations of falling rock intensified. Using his hands to improve purchase, Sayid scurried as quickly as he could manage, the ground rumbling beneath him.

Once again at the landing at the base of the stairs, he dared to look back. The third entryway was no more, having collapsed upon itself, sealing the great chamber. With the exception of the settling dust, all was still once more.

He climbed the steep stairs he'd descended so recently, reaching the entrance of the cavern on legs that seemed to have aged a decade. As he breathed his first intake of cool desert air, he tripped, sprawling onto the ground. His heart caught in his throat, certain he'd been pursued as he rolled, prone body facing the cavern entrance and scrambling to his feet. He was alone. In the dust, he spotted the object that had tripped him. It was a small leather pouch cinched with twine. He stood, took two cautious steps toward the cave, and bent to retrieve the satchel. Its contents clinked faintly in his hands. Eyes still upon the cavern entrance, he slid the satchel into his pocket, raising his eyebrows in silent inquiry. There were no rumbles of disapproval. All was still.

Silently he untied the horses, readying them for the return journey. He took his time patting the dust from their short fur, holding dried fruit for their gentle lips to lift from his palms. No sound, no movement emitted from the cavern.

Content in their preparations for departure, Sayid paused before mounting his mare. He retrieved the satchel from his pocket and extended both hands, holding it like an offering toward the cavern's gaping mouth. When still no objection arose, he bowed his head in gratitude and departed, holding the lead of the riderless horse across his lap.

They arrived home shortly after sunrise. Sayid led his horses into two vacant stable bays, ensuring the troughs were clean and fresh hay laid.

In the cantina, his fellow patrons acknowledged him with knowing looks. A woman in a thin shroud caught his wrist as he passed, murmuring gentle gratitudes. Others offered subtle salutes.

Sayid slid into a corner booth. The waitress placed a heavy mug on his table and poured coffee. He pulled the small leather pouch from his pocket once again, turning it over and over in his hands. It was simple, unremarkable, and unmarked. He loosened the twine and carefully tipped the contents upon the table's surface. Gold coins glinted in the dim light, followed by a gaudy ring. The inscription bore Sayid's initials alongside the Seal of Solomon. Sayid lifted a coin gingerly, turning it over in his fingers. Along the edge of one coin were the indentations of teeth marks.

Fata Morgana

S.M. Lomas

Oily mirages crowded the highway in the late August heat as Troy drove southeast toward the border. His tired blue eyes fixed on a particularly vast one filling the next dip in the hot dry road like an inviting pool of water, reminding him once again of his own parched throat. He clutched the sweat-sticky steering wheel and tried not to think about how much the sunlight streaming through the windshield was already baking the exposed skin of his office-pale fingers. He decided right then and there that he really did not care for summer, and it promised to linger well into September this year.

Troy cast a mournful glance at his center console where his coffee thermos sat in its holder, half empty but still hot and entirely unappealing. Stopping for a bottle of water hadn't even crossed his mind as he hurried to get out of his apartment door to join the throngs of commuters on Highway 417 that morning. Then again, he realized, as his stomach gurgled unhappily, neither had the prospect of food. He should probably stop at the next gas station. Get some cold water, a tasteless and overpriced sandwich, and a blessed hit of indoor air conditioning.

He checked the LCD display on the dashboard: ten minutes after eleven already. Gas level still well above the midway mark; it was a good thing he had filled his tank after his shift the day before.

The blank daze he had put himself into as he drove toward the US border from Ottawa had got him through the last ninety minutes fairly well, but now the effects of a nearly sleepless night and nothing but cheap coffee in his gut were beginning to intrude upon his trance. He hadn't even wanted to make this trip in the first place, but his rash of poor sales over the last few months had left him little choice but to readily accept management's offer. Though in reality, it was less an offer than an unspoken ultimatum understood by both parties: get this firm in Concord as a client, signed and sealed, or pack up your desk and head straight to the nearest unemployment office.

As the border station and its inevitable queue of other waiting drivers loomed into view, Troy eyed the crumpled pack of cigarettes sitting in the dusty crevice of the passenger seat, trying to muster up a thread of resistance and relenting just as quickly. To hell with it, he decided, he could finally quit after this damned trip. Grabbing the mostly empty pack and fishing one out, he eased the cigarette between his dry lips before pushing the dash lighter home. As he waited for it to heat, he mused on the day ahead of him.

New Hampshire. He knew absolutely nothing about the place except that somewhere in the capitol a cheap hotel room reserved under his name and his last chance at securing his job just a convenient walk away the following morning awaited him. Apart from that, he didn't much care.

The lighter popped and he twisted it out of its socket to sear the dangling end of his cigarette. Acrid smoke filled his lungs and he immediately felt both a little better and a little guilty, but what the insurance agency didn't know about his unhealthy habits wouldn't hurt either of them.

While idling behind a silver minivan with a plethora of bumper stickers nearly obscuring its entire rear window, he smoked and roved his eyes over their slogans. *Eat, Sleep, Hockey. I Love Old People…As Long As I'm Not Driving Behind Them. If You Sleepwalk, Wear Pajamas!* The last one held Troy's eye as a dim memory flickered in his mind. The oddest sensation that he had been doing something weird last night in his sleep, partially awake but still under the thrall of whatever had gripped his now-forgotten dreams, arose with it. It was a feeling not unlike déjà vu. Something about sensing the cold linoleum under his bare feet, the metal of the front door's knob in his hand. Just standing there for a moment, hearing from somewhere behind him a disembodied, muffled whispering that seemed to be urging him on. The deadbolt had been thrown home, so he hadn't opened the door, but whether it was the lock or his mind faltering that had stopped him, he was unsure. Everything after that had been a haze, and he had woken up in his bed when the alarm on his night table chimed at six o'clock. Still, he clearly remembered lying awake well into the small hours despite retiring at a reasonable time. He had obviously nodded off at some point, though he couldn't have gotten more than two hours' sleep, which was the chief reason he felt so miserable at this moment.

As he smoked, his mind drifted back to his childhood, when sleepwalking and sleep-talking occurred frequently, or so his mother had claimed. Troy could hardly recall much about those incidents, but apparently he used to wander with closed eyes into the sitting room on the nights that she had chosen to stay up late. He would stand beside her recliner until she looked away from the television, startled at his presence. What he said in those nocturnal ramblings, she would never disclose. Just silly little nothings, she would assure him, but the lines that only appeared around her eyes when she was troubled bespoke the lie. Strange, he thought as he stabbed his cigarette out in the portable ashtray, he hadn't been the victim of such a childish action in nearly twenty of his thirty-five years.

Half an hour later, clearance-checked and free to glide back onto the interstate, Troy wondered if he should just plow nonstop through the remainder of his journey. He could probably make it. Get to his hotel room as soon as possible, grab the least offensive snack from the nearest vending machine, rinse off the sweat in a cool shower and crawl into bed. It was only a couple more hours, at any rate. Just a couple more hours under the already blazing sun.

Troy groaned and turned the AC up to its highest setting, knowing it wouldn't do much good. The old Impala could barely sneeze out enough cool air as it was, but crossing into Vermont had seemed to usher in a new intensity of heat.

Hardly forty minutes had passed before the vents gave a sputtering cough and began to blast hot air into the cabin and Troy's face. Cursing, he fiddled with the switches and buttons before smacking the dash vents, not realizing he had drifted onto the road's shoulder until the rumble strips vibrated his attention back up. As he jerked the wheel to correct himself, a dull but heavy *whump* exploded to his right and the car veered back toward the shoulder, sending him straight off the road's edge and down into an abandoned irrigation ditch. His head collided hard with the wheel's deployed airbag as the car's hood connected with the far wall of the trench, bringing the car to an abrupt and creaking stop.

Troy sat stunned for a few minutes, his head stinging, breathing the smell of the airbag's powdery dust and absently watching the tall yellow weeds sway in the light breeze over the car's buckled hood. The windshield, amazingly, had not shattered. Slowly, reality crept in and he unfastened his seat belt before shoving his door open. Stumbling out onto the sun-crisp vegetation, he assessed the steepness of the ditch and immediately knew without a doubt that nothing but a tow truck equipped with a hook would be able to haul his car back out.

Even in those few seconds outside, his white dress shirt did little to stop the intense sunshine from pricking his skin beneath. Sweat already began to manifest on his neck and under his arms while the buzz of passing vehicles, none of which seemed to have noticed or held the least bit of interest in what had just happened, swept up and down the interstate behind and just above him. He rounded to the other side of the car and saw his blown rear tire, suddenly recalling the spare sitting long unserviced in his trunk. Great, he thought, just absolutely, perfectly *great*.

Troy retrieved his keys from the ignition and slammed the door shut. Opening the trunk, he pulled out his briefcase and the duffle bag he had at least had the foresight to pack the night before. After slamming that too, he pulled open the rear door and grabbed his dark gray suit jacket, which had been whipped off its hanger hook and into the footwell. With a sigh, Troy slung the duffle bag over his shoulder and used his jacket as a makeshift visor with his free arm before scrambling up out of the ditch. He fervently hoped there was a town – and with any luck a service station – no further than a few miles down the road.

As he began to walk along the shoulder, cars passing from both directions at intervals, his hope of someone stopping to offer him a lift gradually evaporated. When one motorist graced him with an obscene yell and a blast of diesel exhaust, Troy's fatigue swelled to new heights. The sound of a revving engine approaching behind him a few minutes later did nothing to improve his mood. Expecting another unpleasant encounter, Troy walked closer to the shoulder's furthest edge and its grasshopper-choked weeds. The vehicle audibly downshifted before pulling over to block his path several yards ahead. Troy approached the old brick-red pickup truck's passenger side as the driver leaned over to unroll the dusty window.

"That your Impala back there?" a male voice yelled through the opening. "You okay?"

Troy reached the truck's window, his blazer still held above his head, and squinted inside. A young man, roughly eighteen, certainly no older than twenty-two, with suntanned skin and short, jet-black hair wearing a grease-stained white T-shirt sat holding onto the massive steering wheel in one hand while looking back at him with expectant hazel eyes. A slow, unfamiliar song floated softly and tinnily from the speakers over the heavy rumble of the engine.

"Yeah, that's me. Had a bit of a blowout," Troy explained.

The young man pointed at Troy's forehead. "Looks like you banged your head up."

Troy touched his forehead and felt the warm wetness high over his left eyebrow. Bright red came away on his fingers. "Shit."

"It doesn't look too bad though. Head wounds usually bleed a lot; might just be a scrape. But you do look a little like you're about to pass out. This heat alone'll do that."

A passing car honked as it roared by, kicking up dust and bits of chaff in its wake.

"You got a place you can go?" the kid continued. "I can give you a ride."

"If you could get me to a garage or a payphone that would be great."

The kid smiled (a very nice smile, Troy noted absently). "I think that can be arranged."

Troy opened the door to heft himself inside. He set his bags at his feet and crumpled his jacket in his lap with an expansive sigh before pulling the door back shut, relieved to feel proper air conditioning streaming from the truck's vents. He rolled the window back up.

The young man extended a hand. "I'm Ashley Valentine. Or Ash, to my friends."

Troy looked at the proffered hand and the black grime under its fingernails. He grabbed it and pumped it once, firmly, the way he always did with his clients. "Troy Monroe."

Pulling his arm back, Troy noticed he had transferred some of his blood onto that dirty hand. Ashley noticed it too.

"Sorry," Troy offered lamely.

Ashley shrugged and yanked what was once a clean blue handkerchief in its former life from his back pocket. "Just another stain for the wash to take care of." He began to offer it to Troy before thinking better of it and stuffing it back into his jeans. He gestured at the glove box. "There might be something in there you can use."

As Troy extracted a small packet of tissues from the various knickknacks and tools jumbled in the glove compartment, Ashley checked over his shoulder and eased back onto the road. "So you're down from Canada?"

"My driving skills gave that away?"

Ashley laughed (a nice sound, too, Troy thought). "No, no. Just your plates."

"Oh, right." Troy leaned to catch his reflection as best he could in the dirty side mirror and began dabbing the blood from his face. All things considered, the cut hadn't bled too much, but the sting was beginning to take a more pronounced effect as the adrenaline wore off.

"You picked a hell of a day for a road trip." Ashley threw another glance at him. "But something tells me you didn't declare 'pleasure' at the border."

"I suppose the briefcase and blazer gave that one away." He hoped that hadn't come out sarcastically, but Ashley only smiled again.

"Bingo."

After a brief silence, Troy asked, "You live around here?"

"Not far. In Fairhale. We'll be there in another twenty minutes or so."

"Is that on the highway?"

"Just off."

"If you don't mind me asking, what are you doing all the way out here? Isn't it a school day?"

Ashley chuckled good-naturedly. "I had to come out to help a buddy of mine replace his Mustang's timing chain. Plus a flat tire, which he decided to spring on me only after I showed up. But I'm still on company time, so he'll be billed for that too alright." He paused. "And I graduated two years ago, so I'll take that as a compliment."

All the dirt and grime suddenly clicked into place, and Troy gave his driver a closer look. "You telling me you're a mechanic?"

Ashley reached over the steering wheel and plucked a sun-bleached business card off the dashboard to hand to his passenger. "Your luck might just be turning around today, Mr. Monroe."

Troy eyed the card. *Phil's Auto Service, Fairhale, VT* it announced. "Well I'll be damned."

After a bit of mundane conversation about their work lives and that region of Vermont for the remainder of the trip, and Troy's insistence that a doctor was unnecessary since a concussion was unlikely with how lucid he felt, Ashley stopped in front of a motel with the assurance that it was the best out of the two operating in Fairhale. The young man had promised to head back north with the company tow truck to collect Troy's car and give him a call later that evening with any news of potential repairs (and their costs, of course). Ashley was a nice kid, though, so Troy hoped the outfit he worked for wouldn't see fit to take him to the cleaners. Considering his rather desperate situation, they could easily get away with it.

With a final farewell of thanks, his things gathered and the truck door open, Troy reached into his pocket and extracted his car keys to hand over. Ashley reached out both hands: one to pluck the keys up and the other to gently hold the back of Troy's upturned hand steady so that he might gaze into it. Bewildered, Troy didn't move, wondering what on earth the kid was doing.

"Sorry," Ashley said after a brief moment and shifted his grip around Troy's hand to give it a professional pump. "Force of habit. I'll be in touch later. Have a good afternoon, Mr. Monroe."

After watching Ashley drive off, the engine's growling still audible for some time even as the distance between them increased, Troy made his way into the squat motel office. Once a key was procured, he unlocked and shoved open the designated door. It was a single queen smoking room; the ghostly aroma of its former occupants made Troy wish he'd had another cigarette now. He had spotted a convenience store just across the street, however, right now his first order of business was a shower, which he saw to with more relief than he had felt in some time. His own apartment's water pressure was a drizzle compared to this place, and the pressure felt wonderful on his skin and muscles. He'd washed his short brown hair carefully, doing his best to keep the water from directly hitting his stinging wound. He felt much improved as he toweled off, though his head still ached. An ugly bruise would probably blossom by tomorrow morning, which wouldn't do him any favors if by some miracle he was still able to make his appointment.

Sitting on the bed's edge with a towel wrapped around his waist, his hair still damp, Troy looked at the age-yellowed telephone sitting on the bedside table. He ought to call his boss. Tell her what had happened. And while he was at it, he mused bitterly, just go ahead and concede that he was a total failure and not meant for this job after all.

With a weary sigh, Troy laid himself out on his back over the duvet and closed his eyes. He'd only meant to rest them for a few minutes, but when the phone rang at his ear, jarring him up, the room had already begun to darken.

He fumbled at the receiver and held it to his ear. "Hello?" His voice came out haggard even to himself.

"Hi, Mr. Monroe? It's Ashley from Phil's. Sorry, did I wake you up?"

"No, yeah, sort of. It's fine." He covered his mouth to stifle a jaw-cracking yawn. "And can you please just call me Troy? That 'Mister' stuff makes me feel old."

"Alright, Troy. How are you feeling?"

Troy thought he could hear that nice smile on the other end of the line. "Better, thanks. Just a killer headache."

"That's good to hear. Oh hey, there's a store just across the street from you. They should stock painkillers if you don't have any."

"I did take note of that. I'll probably be heading over there in a few minutes."

"Well, I won't keep you. I've got both good news and bad news about your car."

"Let's hear it."

"The good news is your tire was an easy fix. We got that finished today. The damage to your front end is mostly cosmetic, so the hood should be easy to straighten out and the broken headlight fixed up for now until you can get to a body shop. But the bad news is your fuel injection pump is busted and has to be replaced. It won't be cheap."

"Shit. Can you do that by tomorrow morning?"

"It's not likely. We didn't have the part in stock so I had to put the order out to our supplier after hours in Burlington. And since tomorrow is a Friday it might not show up until Monday."

Troy rubbed at his eyes with his free hand.

"You still there?" Ashley asked.

"Yeah, sorry. I'm just thinking about how I'll be spending all my free time now that I'm as good as fired."

"You said you have to get to Concord tomorrow morning, right? Well, I mean, I know we just met and all, but I'd be happy to give you a ride so you don't miss your appointment."

"Ash, that's mighty generous of you, but I can't ask you to do that. You already did me more favors today than I can repay."

"It's really no trouble. We don't have any car rentals here, so just consider it a courtesy service while your repairs are underway."

When Troy finally agreed to meet Ashley in front of his motel room bright and early the following morning it was on the condition that he be the one to pay for both gas and the day's meals. It might have been his imagination, but Troy could have sworn that Ashley sounded a bit excited when they'd hung up. What an odd kid, he thought. But then again he must've been bored out of his mind living in a two-horse town like this at his age, so Troy supposed he couldn't fault him too much.

Deep blue dusk had fallen over the sky to a symphony of crickets when Troy left his motel room and started toward the garish lights of the convenience store on the corner ten minutes later. The air remained quite warm and still, and the underlying country quiet of everything made it a combination of relaxing and slightly off-putting. He had only seen one vehicle pass by as he set out, making the road easy to cross, and just two populated the store's parking lot: a pickup truck with a rusted fender and a sleek, spotless, champagne-colored coupe. The latter struck him as being quite out of place as he passed it on the way to the store's entrance.

A metallic chime greeted him as the door slid open, and the heavyset, dark-skinned man sitting behind the counter merely cast a damp glance at him from beneath a battered Patriots cap before returning his attention to the tiny television bleating out statistics on the counter. Troy picked up a hand basket and wandered inside. Now that he had options before him for what to eat, he had no idea what he even wanted; the grocery shelves were surprisingly amply stocked, at least. As he browsed, locating and grabbing the aspirin first, he noticed an older man sporting worn overalls and a deep sunburn with a case of beer tucked under one arm approaching the cashier – most likely the pickup driver. The two men started up a desultory conversation at the counter as Troy perused the drinks coolers at the back of the store. He eyed the beers. Probably not a good idea with his plans for tomorrow, but he supposed just one couldn't hurt.

Opening the fogged glass door, he bent and pulled the last forty of Molson's from the bottom rack and was surprised to hear a man's voice at his elbow as he straightened to let the door clang back shut.

"Excuse me, I hate to insinuate myself into business that doesn't concern me, but I feel I must warn you out of a sense of human compassion that that bottle of Molson's has been expired for several years now."

Troy turned and examined the source of the smooth, cultured voice. A tall man of middling but indeterminate age stood regarding him as Troy quickly took in his straight blond hair pulled back into a short tail at the nape, pale skin, and casual but clearly expensive and tailor-fitting clothes: black polo unbuttoned at the top and impeccably pressed, close-fitting black slacks. In short, very good-looking and every bit the type Troy would peg as the coupe's driver.

"Uh, I'm sorry?" Troy practically stammered.

The man smiled, revealing a set of teeth that had probably cost a small fortune to perfect. "It's a nasty little joke of the proprietor's. You see, he's not terribly fond of Canadians for some highly personal and frankly senseless reason. He feels it his sworn duty to punish them in his own ridiculous manner. As such, he never rotates the stock of goods made by our northern friends. If one buys the product, an equally expired replacement is brought out from a special corner of the stockroom reserved for the purpose. A petty form of revenge that doubles as a means to expose his perceived enemies."

Troy examined the bottle and confirmed the old date stamped onto the glass. "But if he hates Canada so much, why go to the trouble stocking it at all?"

"That, I'm afraid, is the million dollar question. He refuses to tell me, as I was one of his victims some time back. Before I convinced one of his friends to let me in on his dirty secret. Here," the man said and extracted a bottle of small craft instead, "try this. Perhaps not quite as light, but I think you'll be pleasantly surprised."

Troy allowed the man to rather presumptuously place the bottle into his basket. "Alright, well uh, thanks for the tip. You're from Canada then?"

"Oh no. I just spend a considerable amount of time there on business. But even sympathizers are not immune from our friend's disgruntlement."

They both looked toward the front of the store to see the man at the counter frowning at them under dark eyes narrowed in suspicion.

The stranger chuckled and turned back to Troy. "It's not too often we see tourists around here, off the interstate as we are."

Troy placed the Molson's back in the cooler and replied, "I was actually on my way to a business meeting in New Hampshire earlier, but I got a bit waylaid."

He watched the man's pale gray eyes flicker to the wound on his forehead, reminding him that he should pick up some bandages as well before he left.

"Oh dear, nothing serious I hope?"

"Just some car trouble. I was lucky enough to find the means to make my appointment tomorrow, but I may be stuck around here for the rest of the weekend. Still," Troy shrugged and began to move away, "could be worse. Now that I know what to avoid buying while I'm here. Thanks again." He offered a weak smile and wandered off toward the snack aisle.

After a moment, the cooler doors banged behind him and the man approached again, holding a case of mineral water and looking a bit contrite. "Listen, I know this is terribly forward, but to continue in the spirit of human compassion I thought I would extend the offer." He handed Troy a dark business card edged in blue and waited until it was taken to resume. "Fairhale is not without its little charms, but sadly lacking in any sort of nightlife. My humble establishment just outside of town may appeal to you if you find yourself a bit tired of all the peace and quiet. We have valets upon request, so no car necessary."

The words *The Blue Seal* were emblazoned in metallic silver above a phone number. There was no address.

"Feel free to ring any time you like, should it please you, mister…"

"Monroe. Troy."

"Dmitri."

The man reached out a hand and Troy's eye was immediately drawn to the antiquated silver ring set with a large yellow sapphire on the manicured forefinger as he returned the gesture in a handshake. The skin there was cool, but Troy had no time to muse on that before a pang of sudden nausea stabbed from his stomach straight into his bowels, and for a moment he was dizzy with what felt like a sudden high fever. His head began to pound with pain again and cold sweat broke out across his skin, his blood thrumming loud and hard in his ears in time with his quickened pulse as his vision tunneled. An image suddenly swelled at the end of that tunnel as Troy swayed, and he hurtled headlong into it.

Opening his eyes, the dizziness immediately gone. His left arm, now encased in an expensive, navy blue suit jacket, extending to rest across the perspiring man's shoulders, conciliatory but firm. His long, pale fingers with their perfectly shaped and buffed fingernails digging into the fabric beneath them. Leaning in close to that balding head to whisper in a voice not his own as his other hand presses a small plastic bag into the man's waiting palm, clammy and trembling. "Remember well what we discussed about your extracurricular activities today, Mr. Palmer. I'd hate to have to remind you through the medium of your wife." The man snorting back a wet half-sob as the small bag is placed into one pocket and a thick fold of cash extracted from the other. His hand taking the green parcel from those podgy fingers and a smile lifting his lips against his will. "Always a pleasure, Mr. Palmer. We appreciate your continued patronage."

The episode ended nearly the moment it had begun as the vision dissolved, and Dmitri pulled his hand away from Troy's with a jerk. He stuffed it into the dark of his slacks' front pocket, but not before Troy caught a glimpse of the bright, eerily golden glow the old ring emitted. As Troy blinked back into the present, his wooziness suddenly evaporated.

"Well, it's been a real pleasure, Troy Monroe," Dmitri said after a brief silence, during which he had been studying Troy more closely. "I hope very much to see you again soon." He carved a smile into an expression that Troy could not decipher before striding to the front of the store to pay for his water. Then, without a second glance back, he left.

Troy stood for a minute breathing steadily and willing his heart to stop thudding so hard as he wondered what the hell had just happened. He tried to recall the images he had seen, but they disappeared into a haze of obscurity like the remnants of a quickly fading dream. He wiped the sweat from his brow with the back of his hand and considered the possibility that he might have been concussed after all. He suddenly wanted to get back to his room to sit down. Deciding not to be choosy, he tossed a random selection of snacks into his basket and headed back to the first aid section to grab some adhesive bandages before making his way to the register.

The parking lot was empty when he left, but he couldn't shake the feeling of eyes upon his back as he strode across the deserted street back toward the motel.

Troy awoke the following morning feeling a bit better, though he had again slept rather fitfully. Lying in the motel bed with the blankets flung off and the sheet pooled about his waist while staring at the ceiling, the air conditioner still rattling its gentle song from the window, he mused over the rapidly fading images from his nightmare. In it had been some kind of large, white, equine creature with enormous emaciated wings. Dark eyes, black sclera, with no visible irises. A lipless mouth, unmoving as a strange hissing issued forth from between massive flat teeth. Deep within the upper shadows, sitting astride this beast appeared to be a man, but its face and body were too obscured to make out. Only the lower legs were clearly visible, and these were just as sickly white as the horse. The three toes on those otherwise shapely human feet had long, sharp black nails like the talons of an eagle. As Troy watched, they had flexed apart as if to stretch, and as they came back together one slowly scraped against the horse's flank, drawing out a thin line of red liquid in its wake. The horse shuddered as the substance slid down over its hairless skin and dripped silently to the stone floor. And Troy, standing there naked and shivering before it in that dark place, unable to move or tear his eyes away from the thing that spoke to him so softly in a language he did not understand until he did. *"Go on,"* it had whispered before the shrill motel alarm had abruptly wakened him, *"try it!"*

A headache suddenly swarmed in to commandeer the whole of his attention, and Troy got up to take another dose of aspirin and get ready for the day ahead.

After donning his second set of dress clothes from his duffle bag (thanking whatever was holy for wrinkle-resistant fabrics), he realized he might have to find a dry cleaner if he was to be stuck in Fairhale all weekend. He leafed through his briefcase documents one final time to ensure all was in order and checked his appearance in the dingy bathroom mirror. He had almost forgotten to cover the wound on his forehead.

As he peeled the backing off one of the adhesive bandages, he heard the telltale rumble of Ashley's truck approaching. With a deep breath and a vague wish to whatever might be listening for good luck that day, Troy straightened his tie, grabbed his briefcase, and headed out the door to see the dusty red hulk idling in the parking space in front of his room. Ashley raised a hand in greeting behind the windshield.

Troy mirrored the gesture and headed around to the other side to let himself in. A bakery box lay on the bench seat between them and, to his surprise, the smell of coffee and cinnamon instantly greeted his nose. Ashley handed him a lidded Styrofoam cup.

"Hey, I thought we agreed that I'd be taking care of all this," Troy protested, but took the cup anyway.

"I know, I just wanted to intercept you in case you decided to run across the street for coffee. Trust me, you do not want that stuff anywhere near your mouth."

Troy took a sip of the strong hot brew, very lightly sweetened and creamed, exactly as he liked it. Weird. "Alright, noted. Thanks, Ash. And thanks again for today. I'm sure you had better things to do than play chauffeur."

Ashley put the truck into reverse. "Not exactly. The boss gave me the day off, so I'd just be hanging around the garage otherwise. Not a whole lot to do in Fairhale beyond that."

"I had wondered about that. It doesn't seem like a very fun place for a young guy. You grow up around here?"

"Yep, lived here my whole life." Ashley turned onto the old rutted road that led to the interstate and opened the bakery box with one hand, nudging it toward his passenger. Troy obliged and plucked out a fat cinnamon roll glazed with translucent vanilla icing.

"Still with your parents?"

"No. Not for a long time. I never knew my dad and my mom's been out of the picture for years. She's been down south in correctional for about five of them. I had a twin brother, too, but he died."

Troy's appetite swiftly diminished. "Jesus, Ash. I'm so sorry."

Ashley shook his head. "It's alright. Sam and I had plenty of practice taking care of ourselves for a good part our lives. We always got by. Having decent neighbors willing to lend a hand when we asked helped. But I guess it's not really any easier." His voice had taken on a softer tone, brooding. "With him gone."

"Listen, you certainly don't have to talk about any of this on my account. The last thing I want to do is dredge up painful memories."

Ashley remained silent for a moment before taking the second cinnamon bun for himself.

"So what about you?" he asked around a mouthful of pastry, his tone conversational once more. "Are you married?"

"Nope. I had a long-term partner, but that's been over for a couple years now. Not that he and I ever could, legally speaking, but I don't think married life was ever in the cards for me anyway."

Ashley shot him a brief, pointed glance before returning his eyes to the road. "No kids either I take it?"

"You got that right. Never been much of a one for them. No offense."

Ashley gave Troy a narrow look and smiled, and Troy returned it with one of his own.

They arrived in Concord with twenty minutes to spare, and decided to stop at a gas station at the city's edge, where Troy paid the attendant inside while Ashley filled up the truck. Stepping into the restroom to use the toilet and wash whatever frosting the paper napkins couldn't remove from under his fingernails, Troy immediately encountered a stooped elderly man dressed in a threadbare tank top and rolled-cuff chinos making his way out.

"Pardon me," Troy said, attempting to move to the side, but the man had brushed against him as he passed through the doorway. Whatever he had replied with was lost to Troy's ears as the world around him suddenly darkened and a brief but clear vision of this stranger filled his mind's eye.

Behind the wheel of the retired old Crown Vic he'd won at auction, still painted in its signature police black and white, gnarled hands gripping that wheel hard as he stares from the side window at the screeching children in the small park. Watching them dash around the base of the slide to climb back up for another turn. Waiting, tongue occasionally wetting chapped lips, as the sun slowly continues its inexorable creep toward the bloodying orange horizon. Eyes continuously straying to one little girl in a pink sweatshirt and green corduroys, sandy brown hair flying out behind her like a pretty kite tail as she runs shrieking gleefully from an older boy holding his hands up in mock curled claws. His own hand straying to the dashboard for the well-handled photograph of a golden Labrador puppy, now long dead. Waiting for the dusk, for the last straggler unwilling to return home just yet, hoping it will be her this time. Morphing in his mind the last happy screams of the evening into the ones of pain that he prefers.

The old man had already hobbled halfway to the store's exit by the time Troy blinked like someone just waking, and his mind cleared to let the bright fluorescents of reality back in. He had been standing there at the men's room threshold, the door propped open against his shoulder, staring after the man's back. A woman came out of the neighboring restroom and gave Troy an inquisitive look before he hurried inside to take care of his business, wondering what had just come over him. He glanced at the tan bandage affixed to his forehead in the mirror while washing his hands. It really was only a small cut and a bruise; aside from a persistent mild ache he didn't really *feel* any different. He probably just hadn't gotten enough sleep.

Ashley must have noticed something off in his expression when he got back into the truck. "Everything alright?"

"Everything's fine," Troy replied, and was surprised to hear the slight quaver in his voice, but Ashley didn't remark on it.

A quick and somewhat quiet drive later, outside the firm, Ashley insisted he'd be fine waiting right there despite Troy's protestations that his meeting might take an hour or more.

"I brought this to kill time," Ashley explained, pulling a dog-eared copy of Crime and Punishment out from under the bakery box, which Troy had failed to notice.

"A Dostoevsky fan, huh? You continue to surprise and impress me."

To Troy's utter amazement, Ashley blushed before opening the book to its notepaper marker and turning his attention away. "You better get going. Good luck, Troy."

His was a wish seemingly heard and well received. An hour later, they celebrated Troy's success and the resolution of nearly a month's worth of stress with lunch at a downtown Chinese restaurant. At Ashley's insistence, Troy expounded upon his travels as an insurance representative on the few occasions when he was able to leave his desk at the office.

"So where was your favorite place to visit?" Ashley asked over a plate of shrimp lo mein.

"Oh, just about everywhere and anywhere on the coast, really. Charming towns, with ocean and skyline for miles. Being in a place where there's nothing manmade in any part of your peripheral vision whenever you choose. The kind of place that makes you feel very small but completely free."

Ashley sat back in his chair and crossed his arms as he chewed, studying Troy intently.

"And Fairhale, Vermont, too, of course," Troy quickly amended and stabbed at a broccoli spear with his fork.

Ashley huffed an abrupt laugh. "Please. I was just thinking how interesting it is that I would answer almost the exact same thing."

"You're an ocean child at heart, too?"

"I suppose. But I haven't been there in years. The last trip I took was with Sam and Mom. That was a long time ago, but we used to go every year when we were kids. I think that was the last really good time we all ever had together." Ashley paused, gazing at an indistinct spot on the table. "We used to collect seashells, as mementos. We loved taking them home in a box to clean up and polish until they gleamed. Sam knew every type by heart by the time we were eight. And I mean all of them. I think he had the bigger brain of the two of us, but he tried his best to teach me. He loved doing that, and he was so patient. I think he would've made a great teacher."

"Well, the ocean's not too far away. Sounds like you're due for another trip soon," Troy offered, not without sympathy.

Ashley hummed thoughtfully and met Troy's eyes for several lingering seconds before Troy cleared his throat and reached for the bill the waiter had chosen that moment to set upon the table.

"Right then. Almost ready to go?" Troy asked, wondering if his face betrayed the sudden heat he felt behind it.

Ashley dabbed his mouth one last time and set his napkin on the table before standing up. "I'll just go to the restroom first."

"Ok, I'll see you outside." Troy picked up the bill folder and started toward the cashier at the entrance. As he waited for his credit card to clear, he mentally reminded himself that he was Ashley's senior by about fifteen years. That nothing good could possibly come from getting mixed up with whatever was forming at an alarming rate between the two of them. Unless he was much mistaken, and he was fairly certain now that he wasn't. Sure Ashley was attractive, and no doubt just as lonely as he himself, but it wasn't a good option. He wouldn't allow it to become an option at all, god help him.

They arrived back in Fairhale by mid-afternoon, and Ashley pulled up outside Troy's motel.

"I can't thank you enough for doing this, Ash. You may have just saved my life today," Troy said, and meant it.

"Nah, it was fun. I like to have an excuse to get away once in a while." He retrieved his novel and held it out. "Feel like reading it? There's a pretty good chance you'll go crazy from boredom out here with nothing but the local TV channels to distract you. Unless Maggie finally caved and had satellite cable installed, which I doubt."

Troy took the book reluctantly. "You sure?"

"I've read it before. You can give it back to me the next time I see you."

"Monday?"

"Or sooner, if you'd prefer. Maybe dinner on Sunday? I'd ask you out tomorrow but I have my weekend job to deal with until then. I should probably be getting ready for my shift tonight soon, actually."

Ask me out, the lizard portion of Troy's brain echoed, but the second part of Ashley's admission grabbed his foremost attention with concern. "A weekday and a weekend night job? You're not working yourself to death out here, are you?"

"No, it's nothing major. I barely have to do anything at all, really. It's...just to save up a little extra cash."

Troy wondered what that second job could be in a town that went to sleep with the chickens, but Ashley seemed to be deliberately evasive about it, so he didn't press the issue.

"Well, just don't wear yourself out," Troy said, avoiding what he'd assumed was a date invitation as he opened the truck door. "The last thing I need is my one and only hope of ever getting back home up and keeling over on me."

"Always the comedian." Ashley smiled at him, upper teeth on display, and Troy chided himself for the way that smile was beginning to make him feel.

"Goodnight, Ash. Be safe."

As it turned out, Troy didn't need an entire weekend to grow weary with boredom. By the time the sun began its sluggish descent on Saturday evening after yet another hot day, he had already run the gamut of available options for distraction. Nothing good was on any of the three TV channels, so he'd abandoned that pastime quickly. He had sat in the underpadded chair at the small round table and tried to read Ashley's book, but found himself unable to concentrate when his eyes began to slide over the same paragraph four times. He had already taken a constitutional around the neighborhood the night before just to wear himself out, but there was little in the way of sights outside of a few buildings, junked-out cars, and scores of trees in the earliest stages of transforming into fiery autumn hues.

Earlier that morning, he had spoken with the motel proprietor; the woman, Maggie, was pleasant, completely unselfconscious in the pink bathrobe cinched over her pajamas and the curlers still rolled in her graying hair, and even boisterously conversational as she recommended the nearest diner within walking distance where the fare was decent for the price. After another ten minutes of mostly one-sided chatter, she finally let Troy escape and make his way there.

But now it was far too early to turn in. He didn't much want to sleep anyway; he'd had that unpleasant dream again, causing Troy to wake up in a heavy sweat as dawn broke against the window.

He considered going back to the convenience store to buy a pack of cigarettes. He knew he shouldn't; he was doing so well with his attempt to finally quit, but the temptation was strong. Come to think of it, he realized he hadn't craved a cigarette all day while in Ashley's company. It had been far too long since he'd had such an enjoyable time with anyone, normally preferring instead to stay cooped up at home when not at work. Despite Ottawa's size, he didn't have many friends, and his coworkers were at best relegated to acquaintances on account of their lack of common interests and rather droll topics of office conversation: family and dating life, mostly. Troy had no close family of his own to speak of, his parents having divorced when he was still a child and both essentially estranged from him in his adult life, and he never felt the need to crow about his love life (or lack thereof) either, so he felt it best to just keep to himself whenever possible.

A pack of cigarettes and a beer or two sounded better and better as he got up to peer through the crack between the heavy window curtains. Troy thought about the bottle of beer that strange tall man had recommended-cum-foisted onto him the other night; it really had been as delicious and refreshing as promised. What was that guy's name again? Something Russian, he recalled, as he glanced at the book on the table.

It suddenly dawned on Troy that the mysterious business card was still tucked away in the back pocket of his other pair of trousers. He went to the small closet where they were currently hanging and retrieved it. He held its glossy surface up to the lamplight to give the silver embossing a closer look.

The Blue Seal. The eccentric man – Dmitri, that's right – had mentioned it was outside of town, and that drivers were available upon request. Judging by the obvious reek of money that he had exuded, it was surely a luxurious place. The kind of joint in which Troy would no doubt look, feel, and be completely out of place. Why someone in that social class had extended an invitation to a lower-tier, white collar salary man in readymade clothes like himself Troy could not imagine.

Troy set the card on the nightstand and wandered around the room, wondering what he should do. It might be worth a try if for no other reason than to alleviate his boredom. What could yet one more diversion outside his carefully crafted norm hurt?

Sitting on the bed's edge, Troy picked up the telephone receiver and punched out the card's number, resisting the urge to hang up as soon as the line rang. A smoky female voice presently answered the line by stating the name of the business, and for a moment Troy had no idea what to say.

"Hello?" the voice prompted politely.

"Oh, um, hi. My name is Troy Monroe and I'm not really sure what the protocol is with this sort of thing, but I was just wondering if I could get a driver for the night?"

A brief pause before: "Yes, you're on our list, Mr. Monroe. Can you please tell me where you're staying and when you would like me to dispatch someone out to you?"

I'm on their *list*, Troy thought with a detached sense of fascination. He gave the receptionist his details and hung up, wondering if he was alright in his current attire. As he didn't have much in the way of choice, he tried not to dwell on it. Instead, he went into the bathroom to put on his black necktie, brush his teeth, and comb his hair into something approximating style. His driver would be arriving shortly.

The evening sky was a violent explosion of orange and mauve beneath the weight a deep navy blue already spotted with stars as the car navigated through the dense woods outside Fairhale. Troy had taken to relaxing in the luxuriously soft backseat and just quietly watching the scenery flash by for the last twenty minutes or so, as his initial attempts to engage the reticent driver in small talk had proved too awkward to continue.

Troy had hesitated earlier when the black sedan with windows tinted so darkly one could not so much as see the driver's outline within had pulled up to the motel lobby's door as he loitered about outside, but the driver, rigidly straight-backed, black-suited and with a face seemingly chiseled out of stone, had stepped out of the car and opened its back door before Troy could flee back to the safety of his room and call the whole thing off.

When the foliage began to take on a neater, more orderly appearance as they rolled up a gently winding incline, Troy shifted his gaze to the front of the car. A large mansion loomed into view, its white façade practically glowing in the dusk. Four large, colonial-style pillars adorned its anterior between the roof's lower arches where several round Chinese lanterns hung, glowing a soft blue against the growing dark.

As the car pulled around the circular driveway, where several other cars were neatly parked along the outer edge, Troy examined the round marble fountain squatting in its center. Its centerpiece at the top of the bowled column appeared to be a grinning, well-endowed satyr holding a jug that tipped a continuous stream of water into the overflowing receptacles below. The car windows and the night were too dark to make out its details, but just the glimpse afforded of this grotesquery rekindled his uneasiness.

The driver stopped in front of the building, where a pair of indigo doors carved with swirling motifs stood like regal sentries above a short set of stairs. Troy waited for the man to wordlessly open his door before exiting the car and standing in a state of sheer awe at the beautiful architecture before him. The night air was dense with the cloying scent of lilies, which grew in long patches along the sides of the building. No sign indicated either the name or the purpose of the establishment anywhere.

The valet ushered Troy through the glossy doors, where a large saloon positioned just off to the left of a grand staircase immediately caught his eye. Clustered about the bar and tables were several men dressed in expensive suits and elaborate foreign robes, talking and laughing with each other while nursing cocktails in glasses that winked in the warm white lights overhead. Cigar smoke and woodsy incense tinged the air.

Troy stood dumb for a moment or two after the driver had left, breathing in the air and trying to identify its scent while looking about him in an effort to take it all in. Several of the men lounging at the tables nearby fixed their attention on the newcomer with undisguised curiosity. Not one of these men, Troy quickly realized, seemed like the typical small town New Englanders he had seen.

To his right was an equally large space filled with black leather lounge chairs and round wooden tables, each of which was topped with a flickering candle ensconced in a red glass votive holder. A stage weakly illuminated in dimmed red lights stood at the back of this room and completed its rather sinister aesthetic. A few scattered patrons sat at these tables, their heads tilted back to rest on the tops of the lounge seats. The couches lining the walls perpendicular to the stage held one or two others, who lay as if asleep. Troy couldn't help staring at one of these men, whose mouth yawned open as the candlelight caught a trail of wet running down his chin. He had only just begun to entertain the notion that these people were drugged when a hand smoothed over and gripped his shoulder. The glint of yellow betrayed the man's identity before his distinct voice could.

"Well well, my waylaid Canadian friend, so glad you've decided to come!"

Troy turned to his host, who wore a light gray mock neck shirt beneath a slim black blazer and a pair of finely tailored black trousers. His blond hair lay unbound around his shoulders like a flaxen curtain. Dmitri smiled and immediately began to lead him toward the bar.

"This place is amazing," Troy offered and allowed himself to be guided through the throng.

"Thank you. I had it built some years ago, according to my own schemata. I am myself quite satisfied with it."

A group of men noticed their approach and cleared a space for the pair at the black marble bar, where the barwoman immediately stationed herself to accept her boss's order.

"Now," that entrepreneur said in a silky voice close to Troy's ear so that he wouldn't have to shout to be heard over the chatter and laughter of the group, "I know you enjoy Molson's. Are you a wine drinker as well? We get our vintage special."

Though he rarely ever did imbibe wine, Troy did not want to appear uncultured. "Oh, absolutely."

Dmitri gave some nonverbal signal to the barwoman that Troy could not see, and she quickly turned and disappeared through a narrow door built into the back wall behind the bar. When she returned she held a dark bottle and two glasses. As she set these upon the highly polished marble, Troy's eye was drawn to the glass stems, which were crafted in the shape of two entwined serpents. The barwoman uncorked the bottle and poured out a small measure into each glass before stowing the remainder somewhere beneath the bar.

Dmitri took up both glasses and handed one to Troy. "To prosperous new acquaintanceships."

They toasted with a ringing clink and Troy brought his glass to his nose to inhale the wine's scent, though he could not identify any notes aside from the alcohol itself. He studied the liquid so deep red it was practically black in the low lighting and tilted the glass a bit. Though he knew nothing about wine, he could see this was thicker than most.

Dmitri observed his hesitation with amusement. "Go on," he encouraged, "try it!"

The words acted as nails pinning Troy to the spot, his mind reeling in an attempt to remember why those words had sounded so familiar. Like he had heard and done all of this before, but how could that have been? The sensation quickly passed, however, and he mentally shook it off as he raised the glass to his mouth.

The taste wasn't exactly terrible, but it was unusual for its being more viscous than expected, and certainly nothing Troy would ever want to order again. But Dmitri had been carefully watching him while taking a sip of his own wine, so he schooled his face into an expression of approval.

"Would you like the tour?" Dmitri asked and began to move off even before Troy could answer in the affirmative.

Troy could feel nearly every eye in the room on them as they moved back toward the main staircase, but he tried to ignore the exposed sensation it gave him. Dmitri continued in a conversational manner away from the noise of the crowd as they crossed toward the darkened lounge.

"Here is our parlor, where we entertain our guests with occasional live shows." He gestured toward the stage with its deep red lights. "As I'm sure you've gathered."

"What sort of shows?" Troy braved another taste of the wine, whose effect he could already feel both warming and numbing his stomach. In fact it had already begun to taste better than his initial sip.

Dmitri smiled in a way that didn't reveal his teeth.

"Many of my clients enjoy the baser things in life. They like to see flesh and pretty lights above all else. There is nothing inherently wrong with that, of course, though I myself prefer a more authentic spectacle. But come. There's more to see upstairs."

They returned to the staircase and began to ascend.

"So tell me what it is you do, Troy. May I call you Troy?"

"Oh, yes, of course. And I don't do anything very interesting, actually. I deal in insurance. Mostly the life variety."

"I see. Well perhaps it isn't the most glamorous career, as you say, but is it not the type of work that attracts a persuasive type of man? Someone who knows what he's about and can convince others to agree?"

Troy had never considered his job from such an angle before. "I'm not so sure, to be honest."

"You underestimate yourself. I could sense that tendency the moment we met. But I also sensed something special in you. Something of which you yourself appear to be largely unaware."

They reached the top of the stairs and Troy followed as Dmitri turned to the landing on the right, where a series of closed doors dotted the passage between tall potted palms.

"I'm not sure I follow your meaning," Troy answered.

Dmitri suddenly stopped at the third door and turned toward him.

"Are you a believer in fate, Troy?"

"Not...as such."

"What would you say if I told you that you were destined to be in this exact place at this exact time? And that you were owed something greater than the pittance you're currently eking out of life?"

Troy wasn't sure whether to be insulted or confused. "I'd probably say you're talking to the wrong guy."

Dmitri reached toward the doorknob. "I'd like you to meet one of my very special staff talents."

He pushed the door open to a dimly lit room beyond. Diaphanous loops of red and gold fabric hung about the walls and ceiling, creating a mysterious yet cozy environment. Behind these, Troy could see several candles lighting a space containing a small table and two chairs, one of which was occupied by a still form. The open window at the opposite end of the room allowed the fragrance of lilies to permeate the air.

Dmitri led him toward the room's inner portion and pulled the thin curtain aside to reveal a young man dressed in equally sheer, dark garments studded with glass beading that reflected the candlelight in a dazzling array of colors. Black eyeliner framed a pair of bright hazel eyes that lifted to acknowledge the visitors, but those eyes widened in astonishment when they landed on Troy, whose mouth fell open in wordless surprise. After a series of quick blinks and a very slight shake of the head, the young man's mien faded into indifference. Dmitri did not seem to notice this exchange as he launched into introductions.

"Troy, this is my house diviner, Sam Valentine. I think you will find a session with him both beneficial and convincing. Complimentary for first-timers, and I insist. Please take a seat."

He gestured to the empty chair across from Sam. Or was it Ashley? But Ashley had said that his brother was dead. He was about to voice his confusion when the young man shot him a look of such unmistakable pleading and another tiny shake of the head that Troy silently sat down and placed his wineglass near the table's edge, never taking his eyes off the ones that carried a trace of fear as they gazed back at him. Yet none of that fear touched the voice he recognized as the diviner spoke.

"A pleasure to meet you, sir. Will you allow me to reveal your fortune?"

Troy glanced up at Dmitri, who nodded and respectfully withdrew.

Once the door clicked shut, Ashley brought an emphatic finger to his lips. When Troy, still visibly confused, nodded, he spoke again.

"Have you ever had your palm read, sir?"

"No, I haven't," Troy said carefully. Whatever was going on, Ashley clearly wanted him to pretend they had never met before.

"Please give me your left hand." Ashley reached out and took hold of the proffered hand, turning it over to examine its palm. He traced one line delicately with a dark, painted nail. Troy's eyes followed the gesture, but when he looked up Ashley was gazing at his face.

"These lines signify your past," Ashley said and dropped his eyes again. "The life line. The head line. The heart line." He demonstrated each by running a finger along their length in such a manner that made Troy shiver. The process felt strangely intimate as, he was slightly ashamed to realize, he hadn't been touched by anyone apart from professional necessity in far too long.

"Your childhood was marked by something uncommon." Ashley began to concentrate in earnest on whatever he had found in Troy's hand. "A child more at home in his dreams than his waking life. A fractured social and family life. Lots of misunderstandings, and buried trauma. His place in this world unknown. A burden he did not ask for."

Troy felt something foreign to the wine's pleasant effects gradually seize his gut. An old familiar sense of despair whose source he could never quite put a finger on came over him. He swallowed, realizing he didn't want to hear any of this, but he couldn't resist asking: "And my right?"

"Your future," Ashley said, and took up the other hand.

For a while neither of them said anything as Ashley studied the lines.

"What do you see?" Troy finally murmured.

Ashley looked at him again with those beautiful eyes made all the more stunning for their smudged black outlines and Troy was shocked to see the start of tears in them. "There's a great challenge ahead of you. This is something you cannot avoid. You must face it head on, using your own god-given gifts, or you'll never hope to overcome it. It will end your life as you know it if you fail."

A memory of himself as a child suddenly flared to life in Troy's mind.

It was cold, nearing Christmas, and he was crying as his mother scolded him in front of a crowd of onlookers. She was explaining to them all in a placating tone that he was just suffering from a fever. And that strange woman whose arm he had accidentally touched in the jostle of the crowd kept glaring at him with open hatred and a touch of fear.

"But she killed him, Mama. She put the powder in his food and she killed him!" he insists. His arm being tugged hard in the opposite direction as his mother loses her patience and simply wants to escape all those staring eyes. He'd promised her that he won't say anything anymore when he sees those things. Not around other people. Don't ever tell, because it made Mama and Dada sad. Did he want to make Mama and Dada sad? Did he want people to think he was different?

For nobody to ever love him? But he just can't help it this time out there on the street so cheerily decorated with string lights and fragrant pine wreaths. That poor old man hadn't done anything wrong and it just wasn't fair!

He remembered it all clearly now. The visions. The glimpses into people's lives, their ugliest secrets laid bare for his undeveloped mind to cope with. No, he didn't want that. He never asked for that ability, or curse, or whatever it was. It had made him an outcast, a freak, and he certainly didn't want it coming back now. Not again.

Feeling sick, Troy tried to pull his hand away, but Ashley held firm and lightly kneaded it in a soothing gesture. It conjured a calm clarity that stole over him, like a returning to home, and his queasiness eased.

Ashley looked steadily into Troy's eyes. "But someone out there genuinely cares about you. You might not know this person very well, but they will help you. You only have to trust them and know that you're not alone."

Troy was startled to feel the pricks of tears starting in his own eyes, but he could think of nothing to say. He only wanted to bask in this feeling for as long as possible. Ashley smiled at him briefly before resuming nonchalance.

I hope this has been illuminating to you, sir. Is there anything you would like to ask about our session?" Ashley said in his most vacant and professional voice.

"I –"

"Then enjoy the remainder of your stay at The Blue Seal," Ashley interrupted. "And please return soon."

Troy stood and suppressed the urge to pull Ashley out of that chair and out of that house before demanding an explanation, but something told him to think better of it. Whatever was going on here, Ashley wanted him to play along, to trust him, so Troy would do so. He reached for his wine glass but was stopped from lifting it when Ashley's hand suddenly lashed out and knocked it over, spilling its remaining contents in a dark gash across the carpeted floor. At Troy's look of incredulity, Ashley only covered his own mouth and shook his head before pointing toward the door. With one last baffled glance backward, Troy left the room and rejoined Dmitri, who patiently awaited him in the passage.

"Well? What did you think?" Dmitri asked as he began to guide Troy further down the hallway.

Troy realized Dmitri was looking at his empty hand. "Oh, I must've forgotten my glass in there after I finished it."

Dmitri nodded, seemingly satisfied.

"But to be honest I think there was something funny in that wine."

"Nothing 'funny' I assure you. Just a little something to stimulate the pineal gland. I'm not convinced someone with your talents needs such a motivator, but it never hurts."

Troy stopped, unable to believe the flippancy of what he had just heard. "You, you drugged me?!"

"It's not at all what you're thinking, Troy. Every ingredient of my ceremonial wine exists for a purpose. They are all parts of the one whole, without any one of which it would cease to be as intended."

"Intended for what?" Troy demanded, indignant. "Am I going to end up like those men drooling downstairs?"

Dmitri laughed, apparently genuinely amused, and Troy did not like the sound of it.

"Oh my dear friend, no. Those are the ones who really have been drugged. Only by their own volition, however, I assure you."

"I think I made a mistake coming here."

Dmitri sighed and placed his hands on his hips, studying the carpet as if for inspiration. Troy looked down at the carpet as well, and was stunned to discover that it appeared to be alive and moving like the scales of a snake. No, he was surely just imagining it. He looked up quickly and for a split second swore he saw the shadow of bony wings behind Dmitri.

Suddenly woozy, Troy stumbled over to the railing and made the mistake of looking over the side at the waxed parquet floor gleaming and swirling far below. He gripped the banister hard as a sheen of sweat dampened his forehead and vertigo uncoiled through him. Dmitri approached and placed a steadying arm around Troy's shoulders.

"Are you alright?" he asked softly and, it seemed to Troy, without any real concern.

Troy glanced at the form beside him, amazed to discover he could see the man's aura. It shifted from dark to brilliant red in a slow, bleeding pulse.

"I think I need to sit down," Troy said and swallowed uselessly. The strange wine had parched his throat.

"Of course. I have a private room just here," Dmitri said and gestured to the door at the end of the hallway.

Troy did not resist being led there. Inside it was cool and sparsely lit by faux electric candles: a small anteroom with several plush chairs and ornate loveseats arranged along the walls. Dmitri helped Troy down into one of these before striding off through one of the two opaquely curtained doorways leading into what Troy presumed was the main room. He returned with a glass of clear liquid, which Troy hesitated to take.

"It's only water," Dmitri gently assured him.

Troy gave its contents a cautious sniff and, feeling too thirsty to second guess his host's claim, drained half the glass in two swallows.

Dmitri took the glass out of Troy's hand as a parent would a child, and set it on the floor at his feet where he kneeled and touched the back of Troy's hand. "Now, tell me truthfully. Is any of it coming back to you yet? What did you see when you shook my hand the other night?"

In an instant, the memory of what he had seen through Dmitri's eyes flared up in Troy's mind: the terrified man, the money, Dmitri's coolly unaffected demeanor. He recoiled from Dmitri's touch.

"How did you know about that?"

Dmitri held up his right hand, the forefinger encircled by the same silver ring as before. In the warm glow of the room, it seemed to contain a slow burning fire within its yellow gem.

"The ring?" Troy asked.

"An heirloom, so to speak. It belonged to my father, and to his. And so back for many generations. From where the first in my line acquired it is unknown, but the story goes that it was bestowed upon him from an angel of Hell."

"And you believe that?"

The blond man chuckled lowly. "What's to believe? The proof is evident. It tells me things, or rather, indicates them. The night we met it showed to me that you are a man with exceptional psychic abilities. A rare gift. Not quite unlike that delicious young thing to whom you've just been introduced. That is the reason he works for me, and that is the reason I now propose for you to do the same." He gestured with a sweep of the arm at the room. "Look around. You can have wealth like this too, and more. Work for me, and I'll give you anything you want. You have only to name it."

The nature of what he had seen finally dawned on Troy. "You're a blackmailer."

"A businessman," Dmitri corrected him. "And a very good one."

Dmitri stood suddenly, his aura again shifting between shades of dark and light red as he paced a few steps in apparent excitement. "Think of it, Troy! Forget days, weeks, months even.

You could read my clients in mere *seconds*. A straight vein to their darkest secrets." Dmitri grinned and tapped a finger against his temple. "The two of us could be very powerful men indeed."

"You want me to help you to..." Troy faltered.

Dmitri sat at Troy's side, his previous enthusiasm replaced by a paternal concern. "Let me ask you this. What are you getting out of life right now? Can you proclaim with any truthfulness that you're satisfied with the way things are? That you're happy?"

Troy shifted uneasily. "I'm not sure I'd like to have this conversation with someone I barely know."

Dmitri nodded. "I quite understand. However, though you might not like it, your response just now has only confirmed my suspicions." He sighed. "Listen, Troy. I'm not a villain, and I'm certainly not out to play one. I simply get what I want. Is that so wrong? These people come to me for a service, and I provide it in a secure and, I think you'll agree, rather sumptuous manner. If not for me they would go to someone else, someone potentially far less lenient when it comes to dues owed. I've seen men with mutilated hands, missing feet, eyes gouged out. I would never stoop to such barbarity, believe me. Many of these men are miscreants, deviants of the worst order, animals in human guise, and the burden of their sins far outweighs the sum of the things I've done. By keeping these poor fools under my thumb I'm doing them – and society – a favor, if you want the honest truth."

After a moment of studying Troy's dubious expression, Dmitri stood and held out a hand. "Will you trust me, if only for an hour more? I can show you why partnering with me would be in your best interest. Think of it as a sort of reverse job interview. Of course, you're free to decline if you choose, and you can return to your motel with no fuss whatsoever, but I'm confident I can convince you. Just one hour."

"You'd let me just walk out of here, knowing what I do?"

"My friend, you have absolutely no evidence that any of what I've told you is the truth. No one would listen to your wild stories. You of all people should know that."

Hesitating, musing on the lack of justice he sorely craved in his childhood, on his empty one-bedroom apartment back in Ottawa, and the dull, thankless job he'd be going home to, Troy reluctantly took the proffered hand.

"One hour," Troy stated.

The room seemed to seethe around him as he stood, and for a second the shadowed grin on his companion's face appeared positively demonic before it turned away and they started toward the second curtained doorway separating the rooms. Dmitri flung this barrier aside, and the sight of that obscured room met Troy with staggering force. It was not at all what he had imagined.

The room was large, spacious to the point of being nearly empty. The floor was bare stone and dark like slate, as were the walls and ceiling. Only several scattered candelabra and sconces full of real candlelight illuminated the room; there didn't seem to be any electric fittings anywhere. These candles guttered in the draft as they entered, and Troy imagined the play of shadows they produced to be tricks of the eye. But no, what he thought he'd only imagined remained before him.

A huge circle with several rings within one another lay painted in luminous green and yellow in the center of the room. Inside of this were four hexagrams surrounding an empty square positioned at dead center. At evenly spaced intervals were curious words, or names, that meant nothing to him. At the head of this strange circle was a large equilateral triangle with a single plain circle etched within. It too had ornate letters scrawled about it, but Troy could not piece them together in the brief glimpse afforded as he was drawn over to a podium, upon which sat a book of some visible antiquity and a stick of half-burnt incense in a simple metal holder.

"What is all this?" Troy asked, looking about in confusion.

"The secret to my success," was all Dmitri offered as he pulled open a small door set in the podium's side. From within the dark recess he extracted a bundle wrapped in sea blue cloth. This proved to be a thin hooded robe as it was unwound. A short rod the color and texture of old bone and a circular, bluish-tinged metal amulet on a chain lay revealed within.

Dmitri placed these objects on the podium before donning the robe, which slithered down over his slim form like a supple wet skin. Taking the amulet next, he lowered it over his head until it hung about his neck and glistened dully in the candlelight. Troy squinted at its design: two concentric circles with a pair of what appeared to be stylized wings within. The letters S E E R E, crafted in delicate filigree, formed a pentagram in distance between the two outer circles. Though intricate and clearly made with expert craftsmanship, the amulet looked cheap, like it was made of tin.

"Wait here," Dmitri commanded and strode off toward a door set in the wall near the anteroom, which was so seamlessly set it would have remained invisible until it opened. He returned in short order, carrying another bundle with him.

"Please, put this on," he said as he unfurled the cloth and handed Troy what turned out to be a black hooded robe. His fingers lingered on Troy's for a moment longer than necessary during this exchange, his thumb running over the back of Troy's hand. "I'm afraid I must insist."

Partially paralyzed by disorientation, Troy allowed himself to be helped into the garment.

"Perfect," Dmitri breathed as he pulled the generous hood up over Troy's head, obscuring half his face. "Now, listen very carefully to what I am about to tell you, Troy. We will enter the circle. No matter what you see or hear, you must remain within its borders. It may become frightening at some point, but I promise that no harm will come to you so long as you do this one vital thing. Do you understand?"

"I…I think so."

"Good." Dmitri maneuvered Troy into said circle and over one of its inner hexagrams. "Now, until you receive word from me, do not move from that spot. Do not speak, only watch and listen."

Dmitri crossed back to the podium and lit the incense before taking up the strange bonelike rod. The rich smell of frankincense and that same unidentifiable something from downstairs immediately began to fill the room. The smoke was strangely intoxicating, and so deeply pleasant that for a time Troy lost himself in its scent, closing his eyes and enjoying the gradual feeling of lightness it imparted to his senses. He was so entranced that he hadn't registered when Dmitri had entered the circle and stood before him, facing away toward the triangle, with arms uplifted and the rod in his right hand pointing down toward it.

"I invocate and conjure thee, oh Seer, Prince of the East, in the name of Him in whose supreme and divine likeness I am formed, to come forth now and obey my commands and desires. Come thou now in thy most pleasant, familiar shape and receive my Word without fail."

As the incense continued to fill the air, Troy shivered and his eyelids drooped closed again. The sensation of lightness in his head began to trickle down through his neck and over his shoulders like a sensuous touch before spreading ever downward into his toes. Soon his whole being was enveloped in a sensation he had never felt in an awakened state before, like his body was deeply asleep and his mind was free to roam at will. His flesh eyes now closed, Troy continued to see from somewhere above his own head. What he saw was a pale white light in the form of a pulsing ball hovering above the circle within the triangle. Gradually, the ball stretched and grew appendages, like a creature shifting about to break free from some weird elastic egg.

As Troy watched, spellbound, the shape manifested into a white horse with folded wings so thin they seemed to be made entirely of skin stretched across sharp bones. Its vacant eyes were completely black above a snorting nose and lipless mouth in a head nodding up and down. A pale, nude man with long white hair and the lower legs of a raptor sat upon its unsaddled back.

From the vicinity below, Troy could still hear Dmitri's invocations, though the words all seemed to run together until it sounded like nothing more than static in the background. He could not tear his eyes off the beautiful manlike creature before him, whose face now turned in his direction. Its eyes, black like the horse's, met Troy's and a smile crept over its impossibly symmetrical face. The light in the room dimmed as that smile broadened, and Troy felt himself suddenly alone in the dark with the thing before him.

An incomprehensible susurration issued from both the man's and the horse's mouths for a moment before the words finally morphed into a language Troy could comprehend.

"What is thy name, Summoner?" it asked, and the liquid double-voice seemed to echo both within the room and the confines of his skull.

Troy replied, dismayed to discover that the voice coming from his mouth, while still his own, also was not. It was as though he were sitting in a corner of his own mind, watching a part of himself over which he had little conscious control take over.

"What dost thou ask of us, Summoner?"

"I did not summon you."

"We answer to the one with power."

"Is that not the man before you?"

"Two sons of Man stand before us, but that one is as shadow beneath thy light. Yea, we know him well. It is he whose flesh intones, the instrument, but that is all. Command us as thou wilt."

"I have no request of you."

The humanoid creature and horse chuckled in unison, its sound like the rustling of dead leaves in a light breeze. *"We can see into thy heart, a fog of confusion. It is there all the same. Thy desires are bare to us."*

"What do you see?"

"Many things. They twist about, vying for release. At thy word, we might select on thy behalf."

"Yes," Troy sighed, and with it came a feeling like a long pent-up breath of stale air finally freed from his lungs.

The pale rider pointed a black-tipped finger to where Dmitri had been standing in the real world, but was now occluded from Troy's view. *"This son of Man desires thee. Both thy flesh and mind. He doth take all that he requests; we oblige his wishes. Thou must overcome him, or take a position in that shadow where thy desires reside and may be fulfilled. It remains up to thee which to choose."*

An image of Ashley dressed in the diviner's costume of sheer, sparkling rags on the garish stage downstairs suddenly materialized before Troy's eyes. As he watched from the audience's perspective, that likeness split into two identical twins, side by side, each of which had strings bound to their wrists. Between them their arms were lashed together as one limb, while their outer arms were held out straight to the sides, the strings pulled taut by some invisible source above. As the strings guided their movements upon the stage, the twin on the right slowly began to rot. His eyes became sunken, his flesh livid, then pale, thin and desiccated, before the skull-like head fell forward, lifeless upon his chest. Yet the dance continued, the living twin supporting his dead brother through the steps.

"What is this?" Troy asked, appalled.

"The truth thou seeketh. It shall inform thy choice."

The living twin – Ash? – looked toward him from the stage, picking him out from the crowd of shapeless black masses around him, and called out his name.

"Troy!"

It sounded close, panicked, and echoed in what sounded like a large empty room. Troy's heart clenched in sudden, unnamable fear.

"Thy time narrows. The Summoner must make our efforts to manifest worthwhile."

From seemingly far away, Troy heard Dmitri's voice, high and sharp. Angry words he could not quite make out.

"What will I need to sacrifice in exchange?"

The pale rider smiled again, a sight so beautiful in its unearthliness it was terrifying. *"Perception is keen within thee. The choice of Sacrifice is thine. Choose not, and we shall. But choose wisely."*

A loud crash to his right brought Troy back down into his body, and he opened his eyes. The horse and rider were nowhere in sight. Dmitri stood before him within the summoner's square, his expression enraged as he shouted at the source of the crash.

Troy looked over and saw a heavy candelabrum lying on the floor, half its candles extinguished while the others guttered in pools of wax. Ashley's transparent, wavering image stood above it, fists clenched and staring back at him through the haze of smoke filling the room before it faded away completely. The room had grown significantly darker.

"Ash..." Troy started toward the edge of the circle, but Dmitri seized his wrist and yanked him back.

"Stop, you fool! Do not cross the circle's barrier!"

Troy pushed his hood back from his head and turned to face Dmitri. The anger on the other man's face dissolved into fear and dismay as pale gray eyes widened in astonishment.

"What the hell have you done," Dmitri stated more than asked. Whether this was aimed at himself or Troy, Troy could not say.

The bonelike rod fell from Dmitri's slack hand and clattered to the floor before rolling toward the circle's edge.

"No!" Dmitri shouted, releasing Troy's arm and lunging for it.

Troy acted swiftly, letting his body react before he could second-guess himself. He crouched slightly and heaved against Dmitri, pushing the man out of the circle to sprawl on the hard stone floor. The impact just barely stopped Troy himself from falling out, but he collapsed to his knees at the circle's edge, his head suddenly enveloped in a fiery pain that seemed to emanate from its center. As the room's remaining light seemed to burn his retinas, he squeezed his eyes closed and clutched at his head in an effort to quell the sensation that his brain was trying to explode out from it. A single prolonged scream echoed around the room for one terrible moment, but whether it came from himself or Dmitri he could not say. His entire existence funneled into one immense spark of agony.

How long he sat there like that after all fell silent, he could not be sure. It felt like both hours and seconds as the tears slowly leaked from his eyes and the terrible pain began to ebb away. He could not take his hands from his face, could not look, terrified he would see that thing again, that beautiful, awful shape of death, smiling knowingly at him. And at whatever he had done.

The curtain swished open behind him and released a ray of light into the room.

A moment's silence followed before footsteps softly approached, stopping near him. A pair of hands gently pulled his arms from his face and Ashley was there, safe from harm, kneeling before him and looking at his tear-streaked face with such naked concern that Troy couldn't stop himself. He fell forward and pulled the kid into his chest, wrapping his arms tight around his back and letting out a sob against his neck. Trembling, Ashley returned the hug.

"I couldn't let him hurt you anymore," Troy said in a broken voice. "He's the one responsible for your brother's death, isn't he?"

Ashley stiffened. He carefully extricated himself from Troy's arms and cupped the man's face to look into his eyes. "We can talk later. Right now we need to get out of here. My truck's out back. Alright?"

Troy wiped clumsily at his face and nodded. "Yeah."

They stood, and Troy couldn't help but glance toward the heap of blue cloth lying unmoving on the floor near the podium. "Is he…dead?"

Ashley moved toward the body and crouched to feel for a pulse. Even in the low light of the remaining candles Troy could make out the facial features twisted in terror, the mouth open in a last silent scream. Ashley looked back at him and nodded.

"It looks like his heart just stopped. Scared to death of his own monsters," he said as he rejoined Troy and took his hand. "Never mind. They'll find him soon enough. Let's go."

Somewhere between the house, with the carousing laughter still echoing at full force from the ground floor into the quiet of the night, and the massive garage situated behind it, Troy had torn the black robe up over his head in disgust and discarded it on the lawn. Inside the cab of Ashley's pickup, the growl of the motor might have been the sweetest sound Troy had heard all night. They pulled around onto the circular driveway and out toward the incline that led to the road. He had half expected a rabble of angry occultists to screech out in their cars behind them, but the night remained quiet and dark as they left the mansion behind.

After a little while, Ashley spoke. "Are you okay?"

"I don't know. I feel strange, like I'm stuck in some horrible dream. I don't know how much of tonight was even real."

"It's that damned drug," Ashley spat. "It can be laced into anything there. The incense, the wine." He reached over and fumbled to take Troy's hand, squeezing. "I'm sorry. I wanted so badly to warn you, but I couldn't. Except for that ritual room, all the rooms in the house are bugged with microphones, and I was scared. I didn't want anything to happen to you, but I couldn't blow my cover. And when you walked into that room...I just couldn't believe that you were there. That he'd *already* scoped you out."

You were posing as your brother," Troy stated.

"Yeah. Dmitri didn't even know Sam had a twin. Didn't care about him at all as a person. Just a pretty piece of meat with an exploitable talent or two. I tried to get Sam to stop going there, to make him see that it was turning him into a different person, someone I was starting to not recognize anymore, but he liked the money and the attention too much. And then one night Sam came home late, probably already high as a kite, and overdosed on more of that bastard's stock. I was asleep, and used to Sam coming and going at all hours, so when I found him on the floor the next morning it was already too late to save him. After that I swore I'd get the evidence I needed to take that son of a bitch down. The law couldn't help; they turn a blind eye because they're either paid off or a part of it."

"And what you said before. In that room. Did you really see all that just in my palm lines?"

"Sam taught me how, but back then I wasn't really into it. Divination, I mean. Until I took his place up there, doing what he was being paid to do, it wasn't important. But nobody even knew the difference between us. Not even the man who claimed to be in league with higher powers. Small town folk are just disposable insects to the likes of him and his moneyed cronies. To use and crush however and whenever they like with no consequences."

"Ash, I think I saw his ghost tonight. Your brother's. I think somehow he saved my life."

Ashley sighed. It was too dark to see one another properly, but in the soft glow of the dash light their eyes met.

"I don't know what happened to you in that room, Troy, but I think I believe you."

It was nearing two in the morning when they pulled into the short driveway at Ashley's house back in Fairhale. The stars overhead burned like living fire to Troy's eyes as the crickets sang their ancient, eternal song in the nearby weeds. Once inside, at Ashley's behest, Troy kicked off his shoes and lay down on the soft bed, sitting up only to drink the nearly overflowing glass of water Ashley had insisted he finish to the last drop. Then, weary and tired of watching the textures on the ceiling swarming into grotesque images, Troy lay on his side and shut his eyes. The lights in the house audibly clicked off before Ashley's weight settled down behind him.

"Reading palms wasn't the only thing you had to do for him, was it?" Troy asked softly. "That stage..."

Ashley remained quiet for a moment. "I did what I had to do."

"Aren't you afraid they'll come after us?"

"No," Ashley answered at once. "Nobody in that place would dare to admit their connections to Dmitri. Not if it meant a closer eye turned on their own activities."

"I'm sorry, Ash. For everything you had to go through. You and your brother didn't deserve any of it."

Ashley reached out to hesitantly smooth a hand over Troy's arm. Troy reached up and squeezed that hand hard, scooting back a bit until they rested flush against one another with Ashley's forehead on the back of his neck.

"It's Sunday," Ashley said after a few moments.

"Yeah," Troy agreed.

Another silence stretched between them before Ashley broke it. "So, *will* you go out to dinner with me?"

Troy exhaled a weak laugh. "Just name the place and I'll be there."

"How does somewhere on the shoreline sound?"

"Like a dream come true."

Troy interlaced their fingers against his bicep. Ashley fell asleep like that before long, and Troy listened to his light and even breathing against the back of his neck with something bordering on satisfaction. But despite his best efforts to do otherwise, Troy could not help thinking back to what the creature had said. *Choose wisely.* Had Dmitri's life even been Troy's to offer up in the first place, or was his death really just some freak accident? Had his sacrifice been something else entirely? Or had the whole event merely been some elaborate hallucination?

Just as Troy finally began to quell these questions and doze off, a strange, empty sensation like some black hole slowly expanding through his mind overtook him. Then a light, dry, terrible laughter from the deepest corner of that darkness ushered him into a blessedly dreamless sleep.

Automatic Writing

Gabrielle Faust

Mary lowered herself to sit on the faded and frayed oriental rug in the attic where Vivian had once spent her days writing. Around the room, wide, pale pillar candles attempted weakly to ward off the night, their faintly flickering flames seemingly in time with the rain. Each droplet struck the tin roof like tiny steel nails, driving the relentless ache of sadness even further into Mary's heart.

It had been a month since Vivian's disappearance. She knew the detectives that had visited her were still working on the case, but something within Mary knew the cops would never find her, not where she had been *taken*.

There was a darkness that coiled at the center of the house Mary had owned with Vivian. They had both sensed it in the days after they had first moved in. Primal and filled with rage – it had never been mortal and had walked the earth long before humankind did. At first it had prowled through the attic and basement, stalking the halls at the witching hour, and hunkering down beside their bed to watch them, studying them like a serial killer.

In the weeks before she went missing, it had begun to visit Vivian and Mary in their dreams, taking turns tormenting one and then the other until they woke screaming and drenched in icy sweat. Its form and face eternally shifted from one nightmarish countenance to another, taking on the worst of humanity's nightmares as if it had absorbed all the pain and suffering over the eons it had roamed the earth; an escapee from Hell's darkest prison. It collected things – people, animals, trinkets of life it could pin down like butterflies in a realm where they could never be free. It took amusement in their terror, their tears as it dissected them, slicing away their flesh to expose every nerve which it plucked mercilessly, a torturous conductor devising an unimaginably brutal symphony of pain and destruction.

"Are you still here, Vivian?" Mary whispered into the shadows of the empty attic.

She turned to face a large trunk to her left, set beneath an octagonal window through which she could see the full moon, stark and cold and beautiful. Atop the trunk, in the upper left and right corners, she had placed white altar candles which she had rubbed with acacia oil. In the lower left corner was a personal candle coated in mercury oil, and on the lower right corner was a blue pyramid-shaped candle rubbed with primrose oil. In the center was a small black stone bowl holding a cone of myrrh incense. One by one, she lit the candles before lighting the incense.

Mary settled back into her cross-legged position on the floor, watching the stream of pale smoke snaking up toward the wood A-frame of the ceiling as the candle flames flickered, bending to and fro as if influenced by an unfelt breeze. The perfume of myrrh was intoxicating and heavy in the small space – she could feel her senses opening, her perception of the world, seen and unseen, becoming more acute with each passing second.

Mary whispered into the gloom. "Light the way toward my knowledge of all that is valid and factual. For I know that in truth, the way I need to direct my future actions will also be revealed. Let that which has not been spoken be told. Let all secrets be revealed. Spirit, guide me to the truth I seek. So Mote it Be."

The room temperature dropped swiftly. A heavy tightness formed in her chest as the feeling of being watched settled over her. She swallowed hard, steeling her nerves, and slowly repositioned herself so that she could see the entirety of the attic. To the human eye, she was still alone, but Mary knew better.

Drawing a deep breath to steady her nerves, Mary placed a pad of paper on her knee and pressed a pen to it. For a long moment, she stared at the blank page, beginning to wonder if automatic writing was the way she should attempt to reach out to the other side.

Any form of divination had disturbed Vivian – she would not allow spirit boards of any kind in the house and even went so far as to shy away from having her fortune told with Tarot cards. *You just don't know what could come through, what might be speaking to you through those things,* she would say, rubbing her upper arms as if overcome by a deep chill. But she knew full-well that Mary was a practicing witch and, for the most part, had come to respect and even appreciate her craft. If she realized Mary's deceit, she took that knowledge to her grave.

A sensation in the center of her being, like a mouse gnawing a hole through a wall's baseboard, now gave Mary pause about reaching out to the other side again, especially in this house with its many dark secrets. Her desperation to find Vivian, however, outweighed her hesitation. Before she could change her mind, she closed her eyes. Almost immediately, she felt her hand begin to move; the pen making whispering scratches across the page.

Words began to form in her mind.

Not here
Scared
So much pain
Help me, Mary!

Tears slid down her face as she channeled the words to the page.

It's here.
You need to leave.
Leave now!

The writing halted abruptly.

The atmosphere in the attic had changed. Not even the sound of the wind through the eaves or her own heartbeat could be heard. A stench creeped into the space – sulfur, coal, and the putrescence of rotting flesh.

Mary held her gorge, afraid to open her eyes, afraid to see what had slithered into the room on its belly, now hunched, hungry, and seething before her. It moved nearer. She breathed slowly, deliberately, praying silently to her spirit guides and the Great Mother for protection and forgiveness for once again opening the doorway to the unknown. She no longer wanted to know the truth, but this door could not be closed once opened. She had to proceed.

"Vivian? Where are you? Tell me how to find you," she asked aloud, her voice trembling with fear.

The presence in the room grew larger, its energy throbbing dully in and out of time and space as it forced itself into manifestation. Her eyes remained closed. The notepad slipped from her lap. The craven, eyeless, warped creature of her nightmares inched closer by the second, mutated and mutilated as if born of boiling tar pits and shaped for the sole purpose of torment by the claws of Beelzebub himself.

The demon hissed before her, its breath rank with icy ancient death, its voice the groan of an ancient hinge. "With me. Always and forever...with me."

It paused, inches away. Primal terror gripped her body. She began to shake uncontrollably, her teeth chattering.

The demon sniffed about her, drawing deep savoring breaths as it tasted the fear, enjoying the traumatizing anticipation its mere presence evoked in the human female before it.

Its taloned fingers, long and skeletal, deviously caressed the back of her forearm before slipping the pen from her hand.

Mary forced herself to open her eyes. A piercing scream trapped in her throat as she froze, unable to breathe. Where the demon's eyes should have been were pits of burning red hellfire, molten and churning gateways to the underworld. What was left of its charred mottled flesh clung to its misshapen insectile head like a frayed shroud. It grinned, baring long yellowed teeth that ended in needle points.

"Time to join your Vivian."

The scream that was trapped in Mary's throat broke free as a gust of wind extinguished the candles, plunging the world into utter darkness.

The Black Cat

Edgar Allan Poe

For the most wild, yet most homely narrative which I am about to pen, I neither expect nor solicit belief. Mad indeed would I be to expect it, in a case where my very senses reject their own evidence. Yet, mad am I not—and very surely do I not dream. But to-morrow I die, and to-day I would unburthen my soul. My immediate purpose is to place before the world, plainly, succinctly, and without comment, a series of mere household events. In their consequences, these events have terrified—have tortured—have destroyed me. Yet I will not attempt to expound them. To me, they have presented little but Horror—to many they will seem less terrible than barroques. Hereafter, perhaps, some intellect may be found which will reduce my phantasm to the common-place—some intellect more calm, more logical, and far less excitable than my own, which will perceive, in the circumstances I detail with awe, nothing more than an ordinary succession of very natural causes and effects.

From my infancy I was noted for the docility and humanity of my disposition. My tenderness of heart was even so conspicuous as to make me the jest of my companions. I was especially fond of animals, and was indulged by my parents with a great variety of pets. With these I spent most of my time, and never was so happy as when feeding and caressing them. This peculiarity of character grew with my growth, and in my manhood, I derived from it one of my principal sources of pleasure. To those who have cherished an affection for a faithful and sagacious dog, I need hardly be at the trouble of explaining the nature or the intensity of the gratification thus derivable. There is something in the unselfish and self-sacrificing love of a brute, which goes directly to the heart of him who has had frequent occasion to test the paltry friendship and gossamer fidelity of mere Man.

I married early, and was happy to find in my wife a disposition not uncongenial with my own. Observing my partiality for domestic pets, she lost no opportunity of procuring those of the most agreeable kind. We had birds, gold-fish, a fine dog, rabbits, a small monkey, and a cat.

This latter was a remarkably large and beautiful animal, entirely black, and sagacious to an astonishing degree. In speaking of his intelligence, my wife, who at heart was not a little tinctured with superstition, made frequent allusion to the ancient popular notion, which regarded all black cats as witches in disguise. Not that she was ever serious upon this point—and I mention the matter at all for no better reason than that it happens, just now, to be remembered.

Pluto—this was the cat's name—was my favorite pet and playmate. I alone fed him, and he attended me wherever I went about the house. It was even with difficulty that I could prevent him from following me through the streets.

Our friendship lasted, in this manner, for several years, during which my general temperament and character—through the instrumentality of the Fiend Intemperance—had (I blush to confess it) experienced a radical alteration for the worse. I grew, day by day, more moody, more irritable, more regardless of the feelings of others. I suffered myself to use intemperate language to my wife. At length, I even offered her personal violence. My pets, of course, were made to feel the change in my disposition. I not only neglected, but ill-used them. For Pluto, however, I still retained sufficient regard to restrain me from maltreating him, as I made no scruple of maltreating the rabbits, the monkey, or even the dog, when by accident, or through affection, they came in my way. But my disease grew upon me—for what disease is like Alcohol!—and at length even Pluto, who was now becoming old, and consequently somewhat peevish—even Pluto began to experience the effects of my ill temper.

One night, returning home, much intoxicated, from one of my haunts about town, I fancied that the cat avoided my presence. I seized him; when, in his fright at my violence, he inflicted a slight wound upon my hand with his teeth. The fury of a demon instantly possessed me. I knew myself no longer. My original soul seemed, at once, to take its flight from my body and a more than fiendish malevolence, gin–nurtured, thrilled every fibre of my frame. I took from my waistcoat–pocket a pen–knife, opened it, grasped the poor beast by the throat, and deliberately cut one of its eyes from the socket! I blush, I burn, I shudder, while I pen the damnable atrocity.

When reason returned with the morning—when I had slept off the fumes of the night's debauch—I experienced a sentiment half of horror, half of remorse, for the crime of which I had been guilty; but it was, at best, a feeble and equivocal feeling, and the soul remained untouched. I again plunged into excess, and soon drowned in wine all memory of the deed.

In the meantime the cat slowly recovered. The socket of the lost eye presented, it is true, a frightful appearance, but he no longer appeared to suffer any pain. He went about the house as usual, but, as might be expected, fled in extreme terror at my approach. I had so much of my old heart left, as to be at first grieved by this evident dislike on the part of a creature which had once so loved me. But this feeling soon gave place to irritation. And then came, as if to my final and irrevocable overthrow, the spirit of PERVERSENESS. Of this spirit philosophy takes no account. Yet I am not more sure that my soul lives, than I am that perverseness is one of the primitive impulses of the human heart—one of the indivisible primary faculties, or sentiments, which give direction to the character of Man. Who has not, a hundred times, found himself committing a vile or a silly action, for no other reason than because he knows he should not? Have we not a perpetual inclination, in the teeth of our best judgment, to violate that which is Law, merely because we understand it to be such? This spirit of perverseness, I say, came to my final overthrow. It was this unfathomable longing of the soul to vex itself—to offer violence to its own nature—to do wrong for the wrong's sake only—that urged me to continue and finally to consummate the injury I had inflicted upon the unoffending brute. One morning, in cool blood, I slipped a noose about its neck and hung it to the limb of a tree;—hung it with the tears streaming from my eyes, and with the bitterest remorse at my heart;—hung it because I knew that it had loved me, and because I felt it had given me no reason of offence;—hung it because I knew that in so doing I was committing a sin—a deadly sin that would so jeopardize my immortal soul as to place it—if such a thing wore possible—even beyond the reach of the infinite mercy of the Most Merciful and Most Terrible God.

On the night of the day on which this cruel deed was done, I was aroused from sleep by the cry of fire. The curtains of my bed were in flames. The whole house was blazing. It was with great difficulty that my wife, a servant, and myself, made our escape from the conflagration. The destruction was complete. My entire worldly wealth was swallowed up, and I resigned myself thenceforward to despair.

I am above the weakness of seeking to establish a sequence of cause and effect, between the disaster and the atrocity. But I am detailing a chain of facts—and wish not to leave even a possible link imperfect. On the day succeeding the fire, I visited the ruins. The walls, with one exception, had fallen in. This exception was found in a compartment wall, not very thick, which stood about the middle of the house, and against which had rested the head of my bed. The plastering had here, in great measure, resisted the action of the fire—a fact which I attributed to its having been recently spread. About this wall a dense crowd were collected, and many persons seemed to be examining a particular portion of it with very minute and eager attention. The words "strange!" "singular!" and other similar expressions, excited my curiosity. I approached and saw, as if graven in bas relief upon the white surface, the figure of a gigantic cat. The impression was given with an accuracy truly marvellous. There was a rope about the animal's neck.

When I first beheld this apparition—for I could scarcely regard it as less—my wonder and my terror were extreme. But at length reflection came to my aid. The cat, I remembered, had been hung in a garden adjacent to the house. Upon the alarm of fire, this garden had been immediately filled by the crowd—by some one of whom the animal must have been cut from the tree and thrown, through an open window, into my chamber. This had probably been done with the view of arousing me from sleep. The falling of other walls had compressed the victim of my cruelty into the substance of the freshly-spread plaster; the lime of which, with the flames, and the ammonia from the carcass, had then accomplished the portraiture as I saw it.

Although I thus readily accounted to my reason, if not altogether to my conscience, for the startling fact just detailed, it did not the less fail to make a deep impression upon my fancy. For months I could not rid myself of the phantasm of the cat; and, during this period, there came back into my spirit a half-sentiment that seemed, but was not, remorse. I went so far as to regret the loss of the animal, and to look about me, among the vile haunts which I now habitually frequented, for another pet of the same species, and of somewhat similar appearance, with which to supply its place.

One night as I sat, half stupefied, in a den of more than infamy, my attention was suddenly drawn to some black object, reposing upon the head of one of the immense hogsheads of Gin, or of Rum, which constituted the chief furniture of the apartment. I had been looking steadily at the top of this hogshead for some minutes, and what now caused me surprise was the fact that I had not sooner perceived the object thereupon. I approached it, and touched it with my hand. It was a black cat—a very large one—fully as large as Pluto, and closely resembling him in every respect but one. Pluto had not a white hair upon any portion of his body; but this cat had a large, although indefinite splotch of white, covering nearly the whole region of the breast. Upon my touching him, he immediately arose, purred loudly, rubbed against my hand, and appeared delighted with my notice. This, then, was the very creature of which I was in search. I at once offered to purchase it of the landlord; but this person made no claim to it—knew nothing of it—had never seen it before.

I continued my caresses, and, when I prepared to go home, the animal evinced a disposition to accompany me. I permitted it to do so; occasionally stooping and patting it as I proceeded. When it reached the house it domesticated itself at once, and became immediately a great favorite with my wife.

For my own part, I soon found a dislike to it arising within me. This was just the reverse of what I had anticipated; but—I know not how or why it was—its evident fondness for myself rather disgusted and annoyed. By slow degrees, these feelings of disgust and annoyance rose into the bitterness of hatred. I avoided the creature; a certain sense of shame, and the remembrance of my former deed of cruelty, preventing me from physically abusing it. I did not, for some weeks, strike, or otherwise violently ill use it; but gradually—very gradually—I came to look upon it with unutterable loathing, and to flee silently from its odious presence, as from the breath of a pestilence.

What added, no doubt, to my hatred of the beast, was the discovery, on the morning after I brought it home, that, like Pluto, it also had been deprived of one of its eyes. This circumstance, however, only endeared it to my wife, who, as I have already said, possessed, in a high degree, that humanity of feeling which had once been my distinguishing trait, and the source of many of my simplest and purest pleasures.

With my aversion to this cat, however, its partiality for myself seemed to increase. It followed my footsteps with a pertinacity which it would be difficult to make the reader comprehend. Whenever I sat, it would crouch beneath my chair, or spring upon my knees, covering me with its loathsome caresses. If I arose to walk it would get between my feet and thus nearly throw me down, or, fastening its long and sharp claws in my dress, clamber, in this manner, to my breast. At such times, although I longed to destroy it with a blow, I was yet withheld from so doing, partly by a memory of my former crime, but chiefly—let me confess it at once—by absolute dread of the beast.

This dread was not exactly a dread of physical evil—and yet I should be at a loss how otherwise to define it. I am almost ashamed to own—yes, even in this felon's cell, I am almost ashamed to own—that the terror and horror with which the animal inspired me, had been heightened by one of the merest chimaeras it would be possible to conceive. My wife had called my attention, more than once, to the character of the mark of white hair, of which I have spoken, and which constituted the sole visible difference between the strange beast and the one I had destroyed. The reader will remember that this mark, although large, had been originally very indefinite; but, by slow degrees—degrees nearly imperceptible, and which for a long time my Reason struggled to reject as fanciful—it had, at length, assumed a rigorous distinctness of outline. It was now the representation of an object that I shudder to name—and for this, above all, I loathed, and dreaded, and would have rid myself of the monster had I dared—it was now, I say, the image of a hideous—of a ghastly thing—of the GALLOWS!—oh, mournful and terrible engine of Horror and of Crime—of Agony and of Death!

And now was I indeed wretched beyond the wretchedness of mere Humanity. And a brute beast—whose fellow I had contemptuously destroyed—a brute beast to work out forme—for me a man, fashioned in the image of the High God—so much of insufferable wo! Alas! neither by day nor by night knew I the blessing of Rest any more! During the former the creature left me no moment alone; and, in the latter, I started, hourly, from dreams of unutterable fear, to find the hot breath of the thing upon my face, and its vast weight—an incarnate Night–Mare that I had no power to shake off—incumbent eternally upon my heart!

Beneath the pressure of torments such as these, the feeble remnant of the good within me succumbed. Evil thoughts became my sole intimates—the darkest and most evil of thoughts. The moodiness of my usual temper increased to hatred of all things and of all mankind; while, from the sudden, frequent, and ungovernable outbursts of a fury to which I now blindly abandoned myself, my uncomplaining wife, alas! was the most usual and the most patient of sufferers.

One day she accompanied me, upon some household errand, into the cellar of the old building which our poverty compelled us to inhabit. The cat followed me down the steep stairs, and, nearly throwing me headlong, exasperated me to madness. Uplifting an axe, and forgetting, in my wrath, the childish dread which had hitherto stayed my hand, I aimed a blow at the animal which, of course, would have proved instantly fatal had it descended as I wished. But this blow was arrested by the hand of my wife. Goaded, by the interference, into a rage more than demoniacal, I withdrew my arm from her grasp and buried the axe in her brain. She fell dead upon the spot, without a groan.

This hideous murder accomplished, I set myself forthwith, and with entire deliberation, to the task of concealing the body. I knew that I could not remove it from the house, either by day or by night, without the risk of being observed by the neighbors. Many projects entered my mind. At one period I thought of cutting the corpse into minute fragments, and destroying them by fire. At another, I resolved to dig a grave for it in the floor of the cellar. Again, I deliberated about casting it in the well in the yard—about packing it in a box, as if merchandize, with the usual arrangements, and so getting a porter to take it from the house. Finally I hit upon what I considered a far better expedient than either of these. I determined to wall it up in the cellar—as the monks of the middle ages are recorded to have walled up their victims.

For a purpose such as this the cellar was well adapted. Its walls were loosely constructed, and had lately been plastered throughout with a rough plaster, which the dampness of the atmosphere had prevented from hardening. Moreover, in one of the walls was a projection, caused by a false chimney, or fireplace, that had been filled up, and made to resemble the red of the cellar. I made no doubt that I could readily displace the bricks at this point, insert the corpse, and wall the whole up as before, so that no eye could detect any thing suspicious. And in this calculation I was not deceived. By means of a crow–bar I easily dislodged the bricks, and, having carefully deposited the body against the inner wall, I propped it in that position, while, with little trouble, I re–laid the whole structure as it originally stood. Having procured mortar, sand, and hair, with every possible precaution, I prepared a plaster which could not be distinguished from the old, and with this I very carefully went over the new brickwork. When I had finished, I felt satisfied that all was right. The wall did not present the slightest appearance of having been disturbed. The rubbish on the floor was picked up with the minutest care. I looked around triumphantly, and said to myself—"Here at least, then, my labor has not been in vain."

My next step was to look for the beast which had been the cause of so much wretchedness; for I had, at length, firmly resolved to put it to death. Had I been able to meet with it, at the moment, there could have been no doubt of its fate; but it appeared that the crafty animal had been alarmed at the violence of my previous anger, and forebore to present itself in my present mood. It is impossible to describe, or to imagine, the deep, the blissful sense of relief which the absence of the detested creature occasioned in my bosom. It did not make its appearance during the night—and thus for one night at least, since its introduction into the house, I soundly and tranquilly slept; aye, slept even with the burden of murder upon my soul!

The second and the third day passed, and still my tormentor came not. Once again I breathed as a freeman. The monster, in terror, had fled the premises forever! I should behold it no more! My happiness was supreme! The guilt of my dark deed disturbed me but little. Some few inquiries had been made, but these had been readily answered. Even a search had been instituted—but of course nothing was to be discovered. I looked upon my future felicity as secured.

Upon the fourth day of the assassination, a party of the police came, very unexpectedly, into the house, and proceeded again to make rigorous investigation of the premises. Secure, however, in the inscrutability of my place of concealment, I felt no embarrassment whatever. The officers bade me accompany them in their search. They left no nook or corner unexplored. At length, for the third or fourth time, they descended into the cellar. I quivered not in a muscle. My heart beat calmly as that of one who slumbers in innocence. I walked the cellar from end to end. I folded my arms upon my bosom, and roamed easily to and fro. The police were thoroughly satisfied and prepared to depart. The glee at my heart was too strong to be restrained. I burned to say if but one word, by way of triumph, and to render doubly sure their assurance of my guiltlessness.

"Gentlemen," I said at last, as the party ascended the steps, "I delight to have allayed your suspicions. I wish you all health, and a little more courtesy. By the bye, gentlemen, this—this is a very well constructed house." [In the rabid desire to say something easily, I scarcely knew what I uttered at all.]—"I may say an excellently well constructed house. These walls are you going, gentlemen?—these walls are solidly put together;" and here, through the mere frenzy of bravado, I rapped heavily, with a cane which I held in my hand, upon that very portion of the brick–work behind which stood the corpse of the wife of my bosom.

But may God shield and deliver me from the fangs of the Arch–Fiend! No sooner had the reverberation of my blows sunk into silence, than I was answered by a voice from within the tomb!—by a cry, at first muffled and broken, like the sobbing of a child, and then quickly swelling into one long, loud, and continuous scream, utterly anomalous and inhuman—a howl—a wailing shriek, half of horror and half of triumph, such as might have arisen only out of hell, conjointly from the throats of the dammed in their agony and of the demons that exult in the damnation.

Of my own thoughts it is folly to speak. Swooning, I staggered to the opposite wall. For one instant the party upon the stairs remained motionless, through extremity of terror and of awe. In the next, a dozen stout arms were toiling at the wall. It fell bodily. The corpse, already greatly decayed and clotted with gore, stood erect before the eyes of the spectators. Upon its head, with red extended mouth and solitary eye of fire, sat the hideous beast whose craft had seduced me into murder, and whose informing voice had consigned me to the hangman. I had walled the monster up within the tomb!

Don't Forget to Feed

Miranda S. Hewlett

When she awoke, she sat upright with a gasp, then immediately began to paw at her own eyes. It was as bleak with eyes open as closed. Her adrenaline spiked as her mind demanded –

Am I blind?

This panic temporarily staved off the next as, sightlessly, she recognized that she had absolutely no idea where she was. With tentative fingertips, she explored the floor upon which she sat. It was stone – gritty, damp, and cold.

Dread bathed her.

It was impossible to ascertain how long she'd been here or how much time was now passing. Cautiously, she raised herself to her knees in order to crawl forward along the stone floor, reaching outward into the inky blackness. Her fingertips connected with stone – a gently sloping wall. She stood, tracing the wall with her hands as she rose, then stretching to reach above her head as she found the low curve of a stone ceiling, measuring the space with her body.

Her mind raced through its files, attempting to compile these pieces into something familiar. A cave? The ignorance kept her silent, afraid of what could be waiting for her, or would soon come for her if she made it aware of her presence.

She stopped, one hand resting lightly on the damp stone wall for orientation.

What was the last thing she could remember?

Drinking coffee at her kitchen table. Morning. A cat stalking across the backyard through the window. Of course, afterward she'd left for the bus, right? She always did.

It felt hazy, uncertain.

The cat was specific. Beyond the image of the cat creeping across the lawn, her memory faded. And prior – nothing. It was a lone and unmoored photograph, floating in her memory.

The ominous dread remained. She had no memory of arriving in this place. She needed to get out.

She moved in a crouch to avoid scraping her scalp along the low ceiling, tracing her fingers along the wall to keep her bearings. The stones seemed to be the sluice for the groundwater beyond, which seeped imperceptibly through the worn spaces where molding had long ago given way to powder, seeping in grainy rivulets to the moist floor. Not a cave, then. At least not a natural one.

A tunnel?

Catacombs.

She felt exposed, as if she were being watched as she stumbled through the pressing darkness. A ghastly anxiety hovered over her shoulder, taunting her to turn around, insisting that her fingers would soon sink into something soft, forgiving, and gassy with decay. She would lose her balance as her hand slid into the depression in the wall, a small cubby – the eternal bunk of the deceased. Each time she whirled around, she was met with the blind nothingness of infinite possibilities. That was the inconvenient truth of corpses – they offered no source of illumination – resting and waiting. In darkness, one stumbled into or upon all that lay immobile ahead. The only scent was dank. She tried opening her eyes as wide as possible, coaxing light to make itself known, to illuminate *anything*. She turned, reaching then recoiling, shuffling both away and toward unknown threats, becoming disoriented. Her eyes processed nothing.

The certainty of reaching skeletal hands prodded her into a run. She gasped and gulped the humid, heavy air, whipping her hands back and forth in front of her as she batted at the phantom limbs scraping along the backs of her legs, driving forward. It was impossible to measure the distance she'd covered in the midst of panic and darkness, but her advancement stopped suddenly with a powerful smack against her forehead. Darkness disappeared into an explosion of featureless light within her own skull. She fell hard on the cobblestones, knees and palms catching her tumbling frame in painful bursts.

She was next aware that the knees of her jeans were soaking up the moisture of the cold, unforgiving floor. Her hands ached, but this was secondary to the throb in her head. She breathed slowly and deliberately, attempting to regain her senses around the pain. She gingerly touched her forehead. It was tender and she sucked in air sharply as she winced. As she raised her head, she felt the warm trickle of what could only be her blood slipping between her brows and down the side of her nose. She wiped at it, bringing her hand before her eyes for confirmation, but the darkness remained complete – red only a memory. She grimaced at the fact that she'd likely smeared the wet grime of the stones across her face as well. She rubbed her bloody hand against her thigh – the jeans were likely ruined anyway.

When she felt steady enough to stand, she did so, her head pounding in protest with the shift in her blood pressure. Despite the limitations of sightlessness, it felt imperative to keep moving. She could not shake the sensation that something lurked here – that motionlessness was suicide – that something was slowly pulling and crawling its diseased and rotting corpse toward her.

"Stop it," she hissed under her breath. She reached one arm tentatively above her head – her left hand. Her right, she kept at her side, not wanting to leave her torso vulnerable by exploring the ceiling with both hands. If someone was in fact lurking in the darkness, she'd have only her hands and arms as defense. With arms fully stretched out to either side, she could not touch both walls of the tunnel simultaneously – it was wider than her arm span. If there was a door, anywhere, or an opening – an outcropping in this maze – she had a 50% chance of finding it, if she focused on the right wall. It was orienting as well as exploratory, her only current method of escape.

She felt the same cobbled texture she had explored along the walls and floor when she reached up, trailing her left hand carefully along the low ceiling while anchoring to the right wall. It took a few minutes of backtracking before she found the outcropping protruding from the ceiling – the one responsible for her throbbing forehead gash. It was hard, cold, and moist much like the stones, and grimy as well – everything was seemingly coated in condensation and grit.

Keeping her right hand at her side as though she had a weapon to draw, she wrapped her left hand around this outcropping. It was curved – cylindrical, in fact. She followed it upward to where it seemed to grow from the cobbled ceiling itself. Slowly, laboriously, she explored this outcropping with fingers alone, her eyes unable to participate in the inky nothingness. The threat of toxic insects, or a sleeping bat, flitted across her consciousness.

Perhaps a bat would be useful. It would likely fly toward the exit.

As she traced her hand along this outcropping, she felt that it was not a solitary object penetrating into the tunnel, but that it curved and turned, leading to the right and left at 90-degree angles. A T-joint.

"A pipe," her voice was a raspy whisper, yet still it startled her heart into a gallop in her quaking chest. The cold, wet walls did not echo the sound, but instead seemed to inhale and devour it – muffling her words before she could be certain they'd existed at all. The separation from life, from reality, was surreal – a post-apocalyptic ancient subway system. What is sound, if nothing lives?

She continued to trace along the pipe until she reached the right wall where it exited into the stone with the same finality with which it had entered.

There had to be a room beyond that wall.

There had to be an entrance to that room.

She'd retraced her steps for 20 paces, searching along the wall in the direction from whence she'd come. She stooped and traced near the floor, midway near her hip, then tracing near the ceiling, searching fruitlessly for any change in the stony surface. Each stone felt like the next – rough and grimy, unforgiving and unyielding. Carefully counting her paces, she located the pipe again. With muffled grunts of effort, she'd attempted to loosen the stones around the pipe, digging her fingernails into the stone, the grout – vibrating her grip as she pulled, hoping she might somehow dig her way through the wall and follow the pipe to freedom – to... light. But the stones, despite their apparent age and the ever-present moisture, remained firmly nestled in their formations.

Crestfallen and weary, she wiped her soiled hands on her jeans. She felt the crescents of filth beneath her fingernails and attempted to dig out each nail with that of her thumb, dissatisfied with the sensation of full nail beds, then shivering with the sensation of rough, sandy grime grinding against her nails. She could not see whether her efforts were effective, and she gained only minimal relief. With a chill she realized that she was, with the mark across the top of her head, the moist dirt of her knees, the grime beneath her nails – becoming much like the stones themselves. Were these stones the deceased, in fact? Was the crypt-like aura of this tunnel cave a result of petrified and shrunken oblivion? Perhaps the stones were not stones at all, but the rear curvature of human skulls, stacked in endless rows, cemented together with the bond of endless centuries in the dark.

There was no sense of time without light. She assumed that, given enough ... *time* ... she'd begin to comprehend the passage of time through the rhythmic sound of footfalls, much like the ticking minute hand of a clock. Perhaps it would be the rhythm of breath. If and when she had to stop to sleep, she would lie with her legs pointing forward in the direction in which she currently walked. This way, when she awoke, disoriented and frightened initially at the lack of differentiation visually between sleep and wake, and the lack of a sense of direction in utter darkness, she would know which direction to continue walking when she regained full consciousness.

She hoped it wouldn't come to that. The cool moisture of the endless stones would lend an uncomfortable but also incredibly cold bed that would leech the remaining warmth from her tissues. It wasn't dreadfully cold in the tunnel – merely cool and even pleasantly so, if one were taking a leisurely stroll without a light jacket, as she currently was. But the coolness of the tunnel would morph into the frigidness of hypothermia if she could not retain body heat through cover nor movement. The thought made her nervous and she shoved it aside, concentrating instead on the path ahead, her fingertips still collecting their tedious data of stone surface.

She'd begun counting steps, but found that her whipping mind was still too agile for that type of distraction which grew tedious when kept mutely in the mind. She supposed counting aloud would be more... *real*. Somehow mentally counting became meaningless quickly, as she could not ascertain whether she was actually counting at all, or simply believing in the concept of advancing numbers at whatever pace at which her mind could comprehend the concept. She was hesitant to count aloud. Something about this place seemed to frown upon noise. This was a space of silent advancement. Her footfalls and her breathing were the only sounds, and these seemed deafening in the tunnel.

Had she screamed as she ran? She thought she recalled that. Screaming and crying and calling for help, wasn't it? She had no method for answering when that had been, nor whether it had actually happened. Her tactile senses were dull and nearly useless compared to those of her eyes and ears. She'd once played a game in a Sunday School class in which she'd reached her hand into a brown paper bag to seize an object within. As instructed, she'd held the object, squeezed it, slid her fingers along its surface – attempting to determine its identity. The teacher had an anticipatory grin as each child attempted this feat and failed miserably. She'd been young – perhaps six or seven years old. She did not recall any of the other items, but she did recall her own. When finally the teacher had asked whether she "gave up" and she'd admitted that she must, she had extracted from the bag a swatch of carpeting. It was a dull beige square of carpet. The rear side was a crisscross of very rough threads. She'd stared at that square dubiously and felt anger rising up her neck, burning her small ears, folding her brows into a frown. The teacher had cheated. It was a dirty cheat. No child in normal circumstances had held carpet in this fashion, nor imagined it in this compact display. First graders don't pore over carpet swatches. It had felt like a betrayal. Why not a rubber ball? An apple? A string of beads? A toothbrush? There were so many tactile objects she could have chosen. The teacher advised the students that they could keep their objects and take them home as prizes. She'd left her carpet swatch on her chair at dismissal.

The memory concerned her. She relied heavily on her vision, as the Sunday School game had intended to point out. The stones were black, grimy, wet rounded bricks because she believed them to be. She'd never seen them. For as far back as she could remember, there had been blackness. This segment of her life, this travel in the cavernous tunnel, had always been without vision.

She wondered if she was dreaming.

This wonder caused a flicker of hope.

A dream. A dream can be controlled. A dream is virtually harmless. She could awaken – *would* awaken – eventually. A dream was a hazardless adventure.

She'd certainly awakened from dreams within which she'd been certain she was awake.

She tried to remember if she'd ever been without the sense of vision in a dream.

She could not recall that she ever had.

She wondered if the blind could see in their dreams.

Onward she continued at an awkward gait. The throbbing of her head discouraged speed. She could not stand fully upright due to the low ceiling and potential of additional low-hanging obstacles protruding from it. She walked bent at the waist. Her lower back ached slightly and she attempted to harden her abdominals to give it additional support.

Then, it ended.

The tunnel came to an end, and she was facing a wall of cobbled stone. Her right hand had traced along the right wall for all of the paces beyond the pipe. She traced further, her body otherwise still, until her hand came to the curvature in the wall and the slope into the wall which blocked her path currently. Slowly, carefully, she continued to trace her hand along the wall, moving to the left. She had the sinking sensation in her stomach that she'd discovered a dead end, that the pipe had been a distraction and she'd slowly passed a doorway or offshoot from the left wall. She traced her hand along the wall at the end of the tunnel, her heart pounding. It seemed to hold no door nor switch, no lever. She pressed firmly against the wall, using the full thrust of her body weight. The result was a small give and pinch in her spine, but the wall of rock remained steady.

She cursed.

The sound was odd – muffled still but seeming to... slide.

Again she spoke.

Yes.

Her prior words had been immediately muffled as though she spoke through cotton batting.

She whistled.

The faintest reverberation.

Careful not to allow eagerness to cause a misstep, she traced her fingertips to the far-left corner of the wall which had quite suddenly halted her pace. Here it met the left wall. She took a deep breath, reminding herself that she was "turning around." In a few moments, the wall would be behind her, and her sense of direction would once again be meaningless – she would still have her right hand extended at her side, still tracing along the "right" wall as she walked – but it would be the left wall. She tried to make a map in her mind, a mental "picture" of this tunnel, a "map," to which she might return. She stood still, forcing the imagery to take form and shape in her mind, convincing herself that she could *see* the map as though it were in front of her, in her invisible hands.

Her map was phallic.

She smiled. She'd remember that.

Slowly she turned, her right hand keeping her bearings as she did so. She walked forward tentatively, her fingertips on the "right" wall. She saw herself on her map, walking away from the head and down the left side of the shaft.

She stepped forward carefully, the tunnel feeling new and foreign though it had been her tightly enclosed personal throughway for the extent of this journey.

She was on the *left* side.

Again her anxious thoughts crept, allowing her mind to tease with the fears of tripping over a slumped and decaying corpse who had fallen against the left wall to rot. A traveler. Just. Like. You.

"Stop it," she hissed. There it was again, the sound that seemed to pull to her... right.

Then, she fell.

She fell to the right – or what had been the right – that which was actually the "left" – because the wall was suddenly gone. She fell and she landed hard, scraping the heel of her right hand against the tiny dirt grains and the wet cement roughness of the stone floor. She cried out, more in shock than the pain of scratching and reopening her prior scrapes. Cool wetness seeped into the right thigh and ass of her jeans.

She was disoriented. She attempted to retrace her steps mentally, her body unmoving as she desperately sought her bearings. She was on the ground. She knew this because of the seeping wetness and cold solidness against her hip and right leg and beneath her torn hand. She knew this because of the distinct sensation of falling and the resultant jarring smack of her softer body smashing against the cold, wet stone floor.

You fell to the right.

You scraped your right hand.

You fell to the *right.*

She'd been walking in the tunnel. She'd been walking on the left side of the shaft, away from the wall which blocked the path.

She gasped, connecting her experiences in the sightless void. She'd discovered something.

She "looked" at her map in her mind's eye. She saw the phallus now had a growth to the left side, its furthest edge faded because that part of the map had yet to be discovered.

Still seated, she extended her arms to both sides. Her right hand almost immediately felt the familiar stone wall. Her left hand hung in the air and she snatched it back with the sudden fear of something in the darkness seizing it.

She stood carefully, slowly, her right hand tracing along the wall, her fingertips acting as her eyes. She was quite certain she'd fallen straight down, into a surprising opening in the left wall. Again she visualized her map. She had gotten lost before – lost herself in video game mazes or paths in the woods. It was easy to become disoriented when one was distracted. She'd relied heavily all her life on landmarks. She was not an apt pupil of spatial thinking, or at least she'd always claimed this weakness. Tonight – Today? – that was a shadow of a former self, the same self that had grown angry over a carpet swatch.

She stood cautiously, slowly. Her right knee yelped out a protest but held her body weight. She carefully walked backward one pace, two, three – until she felt the corner where two walls met. She could feel the spacious vastness of the tunnel behind her – *her* tunnel – where she'd spent all of recent memory. She was now venturing into the unknown. She took a deep breath, feeling her diaphragm compress and rise, pushing the dank, chill air from her lungs.

For a moment, she thought she could see the illumination of the vertical columns of stone in the wall ahead. It took a fair amount of self-control to keep from sprinting toward what could be some trick of her mind, an oasis built of desperation. She willed this away, frustrated with her dependence on her vision and her eagerness to return to this ease with which to decipher the world.

It could be a trap.

She could easily brain herself on a low-lying obstruction and, this time, she may never stand again.

She had a distinct disinterest in becoming the slumped, decaying corpse of her anxious imagination.

She walked forward, realizing that she felt cold across her knees and right side. She knew the cloth was wet and stiff against her flesh, but this was different somehow. She stopped and planted her feet, feeling the wall on her right side inches from her shoulder, grounding herself. She felt the fabric of her jeans. It was damp, as she'd known, but why suddenly so cold?

She brought her hands together and rubbed them briskly, taking advantage of the heat of friction. She rubbed her fingers against the insides of her palms, wincing slightly at the raw heel of her right hand as she did so. She rubbed diligently until all fingers felt her normal body temperature once more.

She placed her left hand against her belly and traced downward until she found the hem of her shirt. This she pulled out from her body and used to encircle and roughly wipe her right index finger. She lifted this finger carefully to her chin, not wanting to gouge something vital with her fingernail with an overzealous movement. When she found her chin, she slid her finger upward to her lower lip, stuck out her tongue, and wet the pad of her index finger. She held her wet finger up, near the side of her face. As a control, she lifted her left index finger beside her left cheek as well. She stood motionless.

Within a few breaths, her right index finger pad felt cooler.

It wasn't an exact science, but she felt her heart skip with excitement as she extended her right hand to find the wall once more and continue her journey forward.

There was a breeze.

She realized she'd begun to wonder, though distantly, if perhaps she were in a sort of purgatory, cast away to wander for eternity between Heaven and Hell.

She'd understood – once – in the land of light and sounds and vision – above ground in warm dryness – that there was no Heaven or Hell.

But the cold, damp darkness of endless tunnels was not the place for theological argument. And, much as she'd discovered during airplane turbulence, there was nothing like the threat of one's own mortality to ignite the dogma of one's childhood.

She was uncertain which she noticed next – the change in the sound of her footfalls, or the recognition of a new texture beneath the soles of her shoes. She stopped and knelt, keeping her right hand on the wall as she touched the floor carefully with her left. Gone were the stones. Here the ground felt like earth – hard packed soil. She dug quickly with her nails, her fingers displacing the soil and digging narrow ruts she could feel as she traced across them. She felt first the saline burn and then the hot tracks of two tears – one from each eye – escape and travel down her dirty cheeks.

Quickly but carefully she ascertained that the walls and ceiling remained the familiar cobblestone. Focused on her map – now a capital "L" lying on its side, its spine her original tunnel; her new tunnel: its horizontal single leg. She "colored" the map, about halfway down the "L" leg, a brown, indicating the transition to a soil floor. If no exit could be located, she could return to this space and attempt to dig her way out beneath the stone wall. This seemed a distinct impossibility, but it was more direction than her hope had dared tempt since arriving in this place, and she marked the map confidently after crawling a few paces to measure the expanse of soil floor. It remained. She stood, invigorated, and continued her stooped and cautious gait.

The cold had grown noticeable. She knew that sliding a hand down the back of her jeans would yield an ass as cold as death to the touch. Her right thigh and the flesh beneath her knees were similarly chilled in their wet denim cocoon.

There was no way to explain, even to her own mind, when she'd begun to process some differentiation in the shadow. It was a gradual transition of the bleakness, so subtle that it was not unlike the adjustment of the pupils to one's nighttime bedroom. At first, the darkness swallowed all. Gradually, faint impressions seemed visible, or distinction of depth and shadow in the bleakness. As she walked forward, the sensation intensified. The tunnel grew brighter. She realized that she could make out the shadows on the lee of the stones, darker than the foreground facing the light source. A dozen quickened paces further, and she became visually aware of the black soil. The ceiling was still low, but with the advantage of limited sight, she ran toward the light, giddy with a newfound energy and the promise of – what?

Vision.

It was all that mattered presently.

As she progressed, trying not to run, the shadows seemed unsteady. The inconsistent flutter of it made it seem more and more like the flame at the end of a candlestick, stirred by the gentle breeze that chilled her wet clothes.

A sudden concern rippled through her and she quickened her pace – just slightly – holding her left hand ahead and above in hopes that, if there were another outcropping, the hand would take the brunt of the collision before her tender skull. The breeze could extinguish a flame – this was her first concern. Time, regardless of its present meaninglessness – was her second. Candles did not burn forever. Their incendiary matter was finite and therefore limited to wick and wax. If she arrived at the location of the candle beyond the life of its materials, she would lose the light and possibly advance beyond its stoop unawares in the darkness. Despite her intimacy with the darkness for all of recent memory, these pressing threats quickened her pace still more. She tried to ignore the growing liability of the fragile missile of her body moving through unknown space and time, instead focusing on the delicious sensation of soft, forgiving soil beneath her feet, and the possibility of digging a shallow cradle into this soil in which to sleep, its sides effectively capturing and retaining her body heat far more efficiently than the abyss of stone tunnels. The reassuring thought of a place to sleep, and a method with which to make markings for herself – arrows dug into the dirt with her nails to remind her of direction – drove her further onward at her quickened pace, the light dancing reassuringly just beyond her footfalls.

She removed her hand from the right wall, pumping her arms awkwardly as she ran in her stooped position. She was tempted to lower her head and barrel forward, facing the floor, for maximum speed. From what she could currently see, there were no obstacles in her path. The new tunnel extended indefinitely. The ceiling and walls appeared uniform and consistent – no low-hanging pipes or fallen stones to crack her skull or send her sprawling.

She stopped. The faint light was coming from an opening to the left. It looked like a doorway without a door, the stones arranged from the floor on either side of the opening, side-by-side, curving in an arched frame. The light appeared to be shining from within and beyond this doorway. She attempted to visualize her map and found it rather difficult – dim. She knew she should close her eyes – the interfering data from her vision was clouding her mind's eye. A flicker of superstition told her not to close her eyes, fearful that, once plunged into darkness, she would not be able to return to light.

The doorway's stone frame was rather narrow. She stepped toward it and placed a hand on either side as she might have at home – in a place far, far away – when she would lean on the door jamb and speak to her mother within the room, not daring to enter the sacred space without her permission, yet craving her intermittent attention. She took a deep breath, checking once over each shoulder. The tunnel extended in either direction seemingly without break or variance. The distance from which she'd newly traveled was already mostly lost to the pressing darkness. To her right, the tunnel continued along the long leg of the "L" of her map.

She was alone.

She closed her eyes quickly, facing downward toward the floor, frowning in concentration. She willed herself to see the original shape of her phallic map, then the outcropping which became the long leg of her capital "L." Now she stood at a new juncture, understanding that the long leg of the "L" continued onward without her company. She "drew" a new outcropping, parallel to the original tunnel. She now had a capital "U", lying on its side, like three sides of a square. She saw the map, saw the brown crayon smudges denoting the location in the center path where the floor became soil.

Her eyes shot open. Relief at the dimly lit hallway, the stone archway, and empty tunnels before and behind her, was poignant, but her attention was distracted by something immediately greater. She'd heard something. Something beyond the gradually slowing heartbeat in her own chest, something beyond the breathing which was settling from her runner's pace. She became keenly aware of her ears, felt as though she might be able to move and angle them toward the sound, as a cat might, if she focused diligently enough.

Nothing.

What had it been?

It had been so brief, so surprising and yet so commonplace – nothing drastic nor terrifying, something that in the world of sunlight would have gone completely unnoticed in the din of human existence. Yet, down here, in the crypt of endless sodden stone and chill, moldy air – it had been *something*.

She stood stone-still for several more breaths, willing the sound to return. Had it been ahead? Further down the tunnel? Back from whence she'd come? She was uncertain. It had distracted her from her cartography, that much was clear.

A sound down here may not be welcome. In her eagerness to locate the flickering flame, had she mistaken threat for friend? Was it not equally possible that the solitary source of light in this dim, dank labyrinth belonged not to salvation but annihilation? She had no prior experience on which to gauge the relevance of these stimuli, other than their uniqueness and familiarity – their connection to something that felt more homelike than her current state and place. Was it worth the risk of abandoning the cloak of darkness? She glanced back from whence she came, into the gloom, breathed deeply, and stepped out of the archway, and into the new tunnel, toward the light.

Steadily her vision expanded as she grew nearer the light source. The stones appeared black, but she could make out their individual shapes now. She walked confidently, able to avoid any obstacles.

Ahead, the walls met, forcing the tunnel into a right angle. As she drew nearer this juncture, she saw an object lying on the floor against one wall. It was about the height of her knee and constructed of sodden, decomposing wood. The surface was coated in a peeling paint. Faint light streamed from the hallway behind her, casting her shadow across the – box? – partially dimming her view. She would have been able to see more clearly – to discern the subtle shades – before the lighting had improved, and this frustrated her. Her eyes had already adjusted to the new illumination. She kicked herself for so readily abandoning her failsafe techniques of orientation and direction. Where was her mental map? Had she marked the earthen floor when she'd turned into the archway? Dependent upon her eyes, she was certain to become disoriented the moment they were unavailable.

She knelt before the wooden object, feeling it with her hands. The wood felt soft beneath her fingers, as though it would crumble easily. It appeared to be a chest. As she ran her fingers across the lid which had begun to cave in from decay, she felt an incongruence in its surface – deep, irregular grooves. She began to trace them with her fingertips. She stood and stepped back a few paces, allowing light to fall across the box once more. Now that she was searching for them, her eyes could just make out the slashes across the wood. They were haphazard and unclean, as though someone unfamiliar with carving or in a great hurry had cut these wounds into the wood. The slashes were lighter – almost white – in contrast with the dark paint that had covered the lid of this chest before the carvings were made. So they were new – newer than the paint, at least. Why would someone bother to carve into this old box? Her apprehension rose. Could it be directions? A map, perhaps – left by a prior traveler who'd reached this far? Some equally valuable instruction? The dim was too great for her sight and she returned to the box to revisit the markings physically. She traced the slashes again and again with her numbing fingers. It was useless. The wood was too old and the carving so juvenile, it was too difficult to ascertain grain from gouge.

Dejected, she turned toward the flickering light ahead. Perhaps she could retrieve the candle – she had to be near it now – and return with the light source. The necessity of this move vibrated under her skin. She stood, looking back at the chest once more, before entering the new passage.

It was far narrower than any she'd thus seen. In mere steps, she came upon a recess cut into the stone wall from floor to waist height. Within this impression grew eight peculiar plants directly from the soil floor on straight, rigid stalks. At the ends of these stalks were bulbous – heads? She thought they must be a type of flower, but they were alien to her, and somehow thriving in the dimness. The flowers resembled jowled human faces. The stamen flopped forward like a nose above the heavy chin, and the topmost portion of the "face" was comprised of a single wide and curved petal which overhung the rest as a palm frond might shade a sunbather. Like all else, they appeared obsidian hued in the dim light. An uneasiness crept over her and, despite a desire to see the details more clearly, she took a step backward, putting space between herself and the macabre garden.

The backs of her calves brushed against something and she startled, turning to see an open plastic tote or packing crate. It appeared empty. She leaned forward to inspect it and could only just see a dark substance at the bottom.

A sharp, squeak – high-pitched and insistent – pierced the silence. Her stomach lurched and she leaped as though stung. She placed a hand against her chest, willing her heart to still as she glanced around frantically. The collapsing wooden box remained where she had left it. The flowers stood like obedient sentinels. The dark muck at the bottom of the crate was unmoving and likely as ancient as the wooden chest. It looked like stagnant oil. The tunnel behind and beyond appeared unchanged.

The wavering quality of the light caused the shadows to move along the walls, behind the (*creepy*) flowers. She disliked the masking quality of her own shadow as it was, for the first time, a hindrance in this journey, leaving the space behind her – the space most suspicious – almost entirely imperceptible.

The sound did not return. She breathed deeply, steadying her nerves as best she could. She *must* be near the light source. The flowers, the plastic crate – these items indicated that *someone* had been here. in this space. She was quite certain that the plants had to be artificial, erected in a false garden in much the same manner that some people enjoyed keeping false bouquets around their homes. Regardless, someone had taken the time to display them in such a manner. Their positioning was too precise, too uniform. Perhaps that *someone* was nearby – or might soon return. Surely it was this person who had set the light source which led her to this very location. And surely, therefore, there must be an exit.

She considered calling out, imagining someone in an unseen room just beyond where she presently stood, startling and standing up out of a recliner to come investigate. Perhaps the light was cast by a cozy fire in a fireplace. Her frigid skin longed for the thawing warmth of a fire. She couldn't imagine why someone might choose to live down here – was this perhaps an old wastewater drainage system? Perhaps she'd happen upon a vagrant who might be kind enough to show her the way out.

Then again, she might startle or surprise them, catch them off-guard, cause suspicion and trigger the human instinct of self-preservation and retaliation. Perhaps this was some kind of hideout and drawing attention to herself could prove itself more fatal than discovering the exit on her own.

She bit her lower lip in solemn contemplation.

Several breaths later, she walked slowly, cautiously forward. She would discover the source of light, then re-evaluate her options.

Ahead, there appeared to be a small depression in the wall from which the light emitted. A few steps further, she saw something rather small, flat and white on the floor. It was the brightest object she'd seen in recent memory, yet it was also dotted with dark blotches. She studied it for a moment from afar. It appeared to be some discarded rag or soiled T-shirt. She slowly approached, giving it a wide berth.

She progressed toward the light, now quite certain that it was a large candle or torch set into the wall. She could see it – perhaps 15 feet ahead. The hallway was quite well illuminated here and she was about to pick up her pace to a jog when she heard the high-pitched squeal again and froze in her tracks. It was much closer now. Much, much closer. She placed her left hand against the wall and listened intently, turning to look behind her to ensure she wasn't followed. Nothing. Had she missed a doorway? The tunnel behind her was dim and mostly hidden in shadow. Ahead, she could only make out the continued stone corridor.

There it was again, three sharp squeaks in quick succession. She felt her arms prickle in painful gooseflesh. It sounded *alive*. This was not the rusty hinge of a heavy door or a mechanical part in need of oil. This was...

It sounded again, insistent and right behind her. She whirled, panting. Nothing was there. The dim, shadowy hallway looked just as it had when she'd walked through it… just as it continued to look. She sensed no movement – her eyes anxiously scanning all they could absorb. Shadowy, unchanged set. She craned her neck to look above, but the tunnel ceiling looked as it always had – dark cobbled stones without break or variance.

She continued at half pace toward the light, turning full-circle from time to time, listening for the faintest sound, the slightest movement. She reached the depression in the wall. The source of light was indeed a flame, but a wooden torch rather than a candle. Here, the light was brilliant, bright, and beautiful. Her eyes were streaming relieved tears as she held her fingers to the flame in want of its warmth.

Here she stood in contemplation. From the direction she'd come, she knew there were no other sources of illumination. She did not know the path beyond her current location, but felt confident that she must be nearer the exit than where she'd begun, as she had stumbled upon human artifacts for the first time. She felt certain that taking the torch would arouse suspicion quickly if there was, in fact, someone down here with her. The light was the most apparent and obvious target she could possibly carry in this dismal space. On the other hand, the light would afford her a faster exodus. Perhaps, if silent enough, she could locate the proper path and climb out of this crypt before the owner of the torch took notice. Were they asleep, perhaps? She had no idea how long a torch could burn.

With a determined breath, she lifted the torch carefully from its perch. It was heavier than she'd expected, and she had to hold it away from her face as the heat was immediately overpowering. It was clumsy and awkward compared to a battery-powered flashlight, but it was light.

Though it was agonizingly tempting to continue forward along the corridor toward where she felt rather confident an exit must lie, she decided that she must first return to the chest and see if she could make out the scrawls there with aid of illumination. Had they indeed been directions, or a map, she could be out of here in no time. It seemed a sensible message to carve into an ancient box in the center of a maze, after all.

She began walking back toward the chest, torch in hand. She was halfway to her destination when she heard the squeal again, and she jumped to her right, away from the sound which seemed to be directly beneath her. She looked down quickly, with aid of the light, and saw what she'd initially disregarded as an old rag or stained T-shirt.

Bending for closer inspection, she saw the delicate movement first, the small and spotted rag wiggled and shifted slightly in the light and emitted the shockingly high-pitched squeal she'd heard so many times before.

"Oh, my god," she gasped aloud.

It was a puppy – a tiny puppy, lying on its belly on the cold dirt floor, its eyes squinting against the shock of the torch light.

She looked around for a place to set the torch, fearful that lying it on the ground would extinguish its flame. Finding nothing of immediate use, she dug a narrow hole into the dirt against the far wall with her fingers and propped it momentarily in the soil, bent toward the stone wall. The light behind her once more, she scooped the spotted white puppy into her arms.

Its skin was cold but it burrowed against her warmth and squealed again at the welcome shock of a living thing. She rubbed her fingers gently against its skin, cooing in murmurs as she did so. She'd heard that, in cases of extreme cold, humans could best warm each other with skin-to-skin contact. She pulled her T-shirt out and placed the puppy carefully against the warm skin of her own belly, taking a sharp gasp of breath as the puppy's cold fur chilled her hot flesh. She felt the little mouth rooting against her skin and felt her lack of milk a miserable personal shortcoming. Her eyes welled with tears once more. Where did this tiny puppy come from? Where there is a puppy this young, there must be a mother.

She retrieved the torch in her right hand, cradling the puppy's bottom with her left hand. She'd tucked her T-shirt into her jeans as added security against the tiny body falling from within as she walked. The source of the sounds now discovered and torch in-hand, she felt quite more at-ease exploring what remained of these tunnels.

She returned to the end of the hallway, to the odd chest in the corner. It was indeed a rotting wooden box with a painted lid. The paint was buckling and peeling from the moist conditions, but she could make out the more recent desperate gashes across the box's surface more clearly in the torch light.

"DON'T FORGET TO FEED –" the final word was obliterated as the box had begun to cave in here.

"Feed?" she asked. She carefully knelt, resting the puppy's weight against her thighs so that she might use her left hand. With some effort, she lifted the lid of the box. As she did so, more of the lid collapsed into the interior, breaking apart with her efforts.

She leaned forward, shining her light into the box. Aside from the rotting strips of wood, she saw only a drawstring burlap sack. She withdrew the sack and turned it over in her hands. It lacked any label or identifying marks – it was simply a sack sewn of rough fabric, held closed with a cord. She loosened the cord easily and opened the sack, shaking its contents onto the portion of her lap that was not filled with swaddled puppy.

For a moment, she stared uncomprehendingly, as though something had short-circuited in her brain. She recognized what she was looking at – had seen this object countless times before, or its kin – but it was quite honestly the last item she would have expected to fall out of that sack.

The puppy's squeals and nosing toward the object through her shirt brought her back to her keen senses and she leaned the torch in the corner of the wall.

It was a chicken breast.

She lifted it, testing its weight and consistency in her hands, sniffing it. Little filaments of the burlap's rough hairs clung to it in several places, but it was indeed a simple, apparently boiled, chicken breast. She lifted it to her nose and inhaled. No scent of turned meat or rot. She pulled the meat apart in her hands and it separated along the grain as she had seen cooked chicken behave all her life. Again, she sniffed the meat, the mews of the puppy growing ever more insistent. She detected no rancidity.

She freed the puppy from the confines of her shirt. Its little nose rooted and burrowed along her arm in search of the pale meat. She tore a strip of the breast meat into smaller morsels and gently placed them against his waiting mouth. The puppy ate hungrily but, unaware of how long it had been since his last meal, she gave him only a few pieces, setting him on the floor to allow him to finish.

She lifted the lid of the chest once more.

"DON'T FORGET TO FEED" it read. The final "ED" of "FEED" had begun to break apart and there was a considerable hole in the box lid at this point. She lifted her torch and shone it deliberately and fully into the box, illuminating each nook. There were a few pieces of rotten wood, no more. She lifted these pieces until she found one with the remnants of carved scrawl. "CHAR" it read. These last four letters were carved heavily, deeply, apparently with such force that the carver had punctured through the lid itself with their aggressive message.

"DON'T FORGET TO FEED CHAR" she read aloud. At the sound of her voice in the silence, the puppy mewed and dragged himself on his belly in the direction of her voice. She scooped him up and under her shirt, tucking it and tying it at her side, forming a makeshift belly papoose for the dog.

"Char, char," she said to herself, rolling the word around in her mouth. She pronounced it with a hard "CH—" sound, like the word meaning "to burn."

She wondered if the note was about the puppy? Perhaps the puppy was a gift or a ward of someone who lived down here? Someone... forgetful?

"Is that your name – Char?" she whispered to the bundle against her belly. Perhaps it was Charles. She rubbed his head tenderly through the thin cotton of her shirt.

"Little Charlie," she mused.

She had retrieved her torch and made up her mind to find the exit, her efforts redoubled as the lives at stake had likewise doubled. She deposited the remaining chicken into the sack, tied it through a belt loop of her jeans, checked the security of Charlie's swaddling, and held her torch high to light her way. She had begun to walk once more past the odd garden. Now she could more clearly see the color of the petals – they were a deep black or perhaps a dark blue, with thin threads of red through the upper petal. They were rather striking, and unlike anything she could recall seeing before. She bent to examine them more closely and caught movement out of the corner of her eye. She turned her head. They were moving. Before her eyes, their massive heads turned and leaned toward her, their stalks bending as though with their will. She backed away quickly, aghast. The two flowers nearest her seemed to change shape slightly, their heavy chins sinking away from their stamens, revealing an open maw within.

They were leaning toward her, reaching for her, getting eerily near, and she instinctively pulled back against the far wall, bumping into the plastic crate.

She turned, shining her light upon what she'd bumped into, and felt the blood in her veins turn to ice as she cried out in horror. The puppy against her belly squirmed and cried, burrowing against her nude flesh.

It was a blue plastic tote. The bottom six inches or so had been filled with what appeared to be water. Small puppy corpses bobbed in their death bath, a putrid cereal in a murderer's basin. There were six of them, nearly identical to the one she currently cradled in her shirt. She saw the little curve of their tiny noses, their tiny paws and still sealed lids.

She'd heard stories of people drowning litters of puppies or kittens they could neither sell nor care for. An involuntary sob eked from her throat. She cradled Charlie and looked around nervously. He'd been spared, though it seemed likely that it had been accidental rather than intentional if these were, in fact, his siblings. Perhaps whoever had brought them here had dropped him.

She considered whether she should examine them – determine if they were all, in fact, deceased. She peered again into the bin. No signs of life in their shallow, watery grave.

She felt the slightest pressure against her pant leg and looked down to see one of the flowers. It had stretched a considerable distance from its original position. She realized that it was reaching, maw agape, for her leg and the burlap sack which hung there.

"Are you... *hungry?*" she asked, frowning at the final word.

Curious, she opened the bag and tore a chunk of the rubbery meat away, holding it out to the strange bloom. The remaining flowers responded with apparent savage interest. She was reminded of the singing flowers from the *Alice in Wonderland* film she'd watched as a child.

She held the chunk of chicken above the nearest bloom, wary of potential teeth in this odd species, and grateful for the distraction from the perished litter. She dropped the chicken and watched as the flower slowly, rhythmically swallowed it whole, the mass moving down that formerly rigid stem until it disappeared beneath the soil surface.

She fed the next two flowers in similar fashion, transfixed by their peculiar digestive tracts. Just as the third flower's meal had sunk beyond view, she noticed that the first flower she'd fed was now considerably shorter, its massive head having shrunk toward the ground to a height half of where it once stood. The remaining five flowers reached and stretched in apparent impatience, a hybrid of bird hatchlings and a sentient Venus flytrap. She fed each in turn, but was careful to reserve the bulk of the meat for her slumbering puppy.

The first flower to devour the chicken had sunk to the point that all that was visible was a bloom upon the soil. Then she realized that something was growing up and out of the soil – growing up around the bloom. It looked like a lotus flower opening around the sunken flower head, its petals thin and semi-transparent, a deep purple color. As she watched, the remaining flowers followed suit in short succession. As the lotus-like bloom grew from the ground, it rose and surrounded the original flower, curving and curling around it, engulfing it, until the original bloom was hidden within the purple casing, at which point it closed in a tight bundle over the top of its prize like a large purple onion.

"It's a bulb!" she cried. Each of the line of flowers ended this way, until what was once a single-file of exotic blooms was now a tidy row of encased pods.

Her mind flitted to a memory – her mother – planting tulip bulbs in the unkempt garden outside her childhood home, explaining to her curious and confused mind how a bulb, like a seed, could grow into a beautiful flower.

She reached out and touched the first bulb. It was warm. Cautiously, she wrapped her fingers around the pod and tested to see if she could lift it. It was much lighter than she'd expected, like a bulb of garlic. She imagined that morsel of chicken breast at the center of this elegant bulb, imagined the plant breaking down the proteins and absorbing them, readying for a subsequent blooming. She smiled and shook her head. A fully carnivorous plant which thrives in the complete absence of sunlight. Incredible.

She wasn't much of an artist and she had no camera, but she felt that she couldn't walk away from this discovery without evidence of these incredible flowers. She glanced around sheepishly, already ashamed of what she was about to do. What if it was some kind of amazing scientific discovery? What if there was some mad scientist living down here and –

She stopped short.

There clearly *was* someone, or something, staying down here.

Or visiting regularly.

The chicken breast was reasonably fresh.

As were the puppies.

She supposed it was possible that a pregnant dog had somehow wandered into these tunnels and had given birth to her litter, but it was human interference that had caused them to be drowned.

Someone – something – would return.

Someone had lit the torch and left the meat.

In a box.

Engraved with instructions.

Someone… had walked past a plastic tote full of drowned puppies to do so.

She needed to leave.

Again, she positioned the torch in the corner near the crumbling chest. She shook the remaining chicken breast from the burlap sack and slid it into a rear pocket of her jeans. She deposited the bulb into the sack and secured the leather cord tightly. She was familiar with *Little Shop of Horrors* and didn't want to realize too late that the damn plant was eating through her numb thigh as she walked. The burlap was measly armor, but as she'd glimpsed no teeth, she felt relatively satisfied with her choice.

An impatient voice buzzed at the back of her mind – at the base of her skull – insistent.

Leave.

Her anxiety was twisting through her nerves again. She patted the puppy against her belly, reassured by its warm presence and her maternal response. The desire to protect his delicate body – the one remaining soul from his litter – gave her journey a purpose and renewed motivation. Could he sense the deaths of his siblings so near?

Reluctantly she turned once more to peer into the tote. It was ghastly, really, the commonplace innocuous nature of the blue plastic crate in juxtaposition with what it held. She felt a minor betrayal here, but also a sense of absent justice. She imagined the tiny puppy bodies bloating and rotting, the water turning to the thick paste of decay... the stench. She felt a glimmer of gratitude that she'd discovered them now, dead likely a matter of days, rather than weeks. She'd have benefited, she supposed, from the guidance of her sense of smell in that instance, though she was uncertain if she'd have followed such a guide, familiar with the noxious stench of rotting flesh.

Charlie wiggled against her, rooting. Without a second thought, she tipped the tote over, dumping its contents upon the dirt floor. The water rushed in all directions, spreading infinitely further than its prior volume seemed capable of. She gasped and turned to eye the torch. It remained propped and cheerily burning, two feet above the spreading moisture.

She squatted and dug six shallow holes in the muddy earth, in a line much like the flowers. Six graves for six siblings. It seemed appropriate, beside the flower bed, as she had no proper object with which to mark their hasty graves. Carefully she lifted each frigid corpse and gently deposited them into their respective graves. Her fingers were numb and likely split with the effort of digging into soil, but she dismissed this, covering each tiny body with the disturbed soil until six tiny new graves lined the wall between the wooden chest and the unusual garden.

She admired her work solemnly. She could think of nothing to say. She kissed her fingertips – the index finger of her left hand and all the fingers of her right, and pressed each finger one by one into the soft earth that covered each tiny body.

"Rest in peace, little ones."

She stood, causing Charlie to squirm as his perch rotated and sank with her movement. She retrieved the torch. The cold of the dank space grew painful and she held the torch nearer her body, cautious of the damaging flame yet hungry for the warmth it carried.

She considered the blue tote, lying on its side. It was large. She imagined she could fashion a sort of sledge that she could pull behind her. It would slide easily on the packed earth and she could remove her T-shirt and make a little nest for Charlie. Anger welled up in her throat at the thought and she cursed herself bitterly. She wasn't going to make a bed from the basin in which his siblings had drowned. It was a cruelty to assume his ignorance. The damned plastic crate was a murder weapon, and here it would remain. She considered kicking it or throwing it into the tunnel behind her, but decided against the potential cacophony. If the puppy killer was near, she had no intent to draw them.

She walked, leaving the tiny cemetery and garden in her wake.

She passed the depression in the wall where she'd found the torch. With the illumination, she felt she was making better time than she'd made previously. There had to be an exit. It was near. She could feel it. She and Charlie would climb out – would feel the sunlight on their skin.

She walked. She walked. The tunnel extended on and on, much like all the tunnels before it. She realized that the light was only temporarily comforting. The further she walked, the more she felt she was on display, exposed and separated from the comforting blanket of the darkness. Here, as she carried the only light source, she was a moving beacon – a lighthouse for whatever lurked in the darkness beyond her flame. Whereas her sense of time had felt compressed and contained within the darkness, she began to feel the pressure of time as she walked – the – minutes? – seemed agonizingly long. She felt it was taking far too long. She should have been there already. She should have seen the exit. Surely no one would hike so far down these labyrinthine tunnels.

She noticed an almost imperceptible shaking in her body. It began first in her arms until she felt the cold begin fanning and radiating out from her lower back as well. She traded the torch back and forth between her hands in order to hold the free hand nearer the flame. It occasionally dropped hot ash or a smoking piece of charred fabric from its glowing head. The brightness of the flame prevented her from eyeing the torch too closely, but she had the distinct sense that it was growing shorter. It wouldn't last. She needed to locate an escape hatch – a door, a ladder, anything! – before the torch burned itself into a smoking stump, or she would once again be cloaked in absolute darkness. She shook savagely, her shoulders sending a ripple through her musculature all the way to her legs. Charlie mewed quietly.

The concept of time – once measured in steps and progression of stone beneath hand – was now measured in the gradual sinking into hypothermia, starvation or sleep deprivation. How long had she been awake?

What an odd turn of phrase. How *long* was an underground tunnel? It could be measured in paces, in thoughts, in finger lengths or hands, like the horses of yore. It could be measured in the illumination provided by a single torch.

How many torches does it take to reach the exit?

Where had she begun?

The concept of Purgatory again teased across her mind, the idea that she might spend eternity, ever frigid, ever shaking, ever walking in stooped, damp cold, ever desperate and longing.

She shook her head, willing the desperate thoughts away, feeling her body sinking into hopelessness.

She'd come so far.

She'd found *light*, she'd found *life*.

There was discernible progress here.

But *surely*, she was making progress.

The cold seemed to seep through her bare skin, through the cold wet of her jeans, a cruel osmosis.

How long had it been since she'd eaten or drunk anything?

How... *long*?

Time was not a length one could measure with any tool made by man.

Time was a collection of human experiences – comparisons, averages. How *long* it has been since one last ate is measured against one's prior meal and the sensation of emptiness in one's stomach or weakness in one's limbs. Minutes are meaningless in these equations.

She'd reached a "T" junction.

She slowed to a stop, eyeing the intersection reluctantly.

Left or right?

She turned and looked behind her at the tunnel through which she'd walked for all of recent memory. It extended as far as the illumination provided – into darkness. Nothing but an expanse of stone tunnel.

She shone the light left and to the right. The paths had no distinctive markings or objects, no further light sources.

She sighed wearily, her gumption rapidly evaporating.

She closed her eyes. She felt – could *see* – the soft glow of the torch light through her closed lids. This interference with her vision seemed to cloud her other senses. It was as if she could only truly focus each sense to the extent of its ability when the others were deprived.

She heard nothing.

Aside from Charlie's little cries, and her own sounds, the tunnels were auditory vacuums.

She opened her eyes.

She had a complete absence of information on which to make this decision.

With a set jaw, she turned right, unwilling to sacrifice momentum to indecision.

She walked. She walked.

Endless stone walls, coated in wet grime. The air tasted and smelled of stagnant water and lichen – like the chilled air seeping upward from an old well.

The skin of her forearms and calves had pulled taut in her body's desperate efforts to hold in her body heat. The hairs seemed to pierce out of her skin like fine needles. She was unable to determine whether her jeans were still wet as her hands and jeans were equally cold.

The exquisitely soft polyester blanket from her bed floated to her mind. She cursed the memory of her former self who would kick off that blanket as she lay sweaty in the night. Now, she wished her jeans were lined with the stuff, that she had enough plush polyester to wrap herself from head to toe until her body heat thawed her aching, frigid flesh.

She stopped suddenly, thinking. It was the evaporation of water that caused wet clothes to chill the body so completely. It was the reason one shivered sitting by the poolside, even in the summer heat. It was the reason sweating was effective.

She looked for a place to prop her torch but, finding none, realized the center of the hallway was best suited to her new purposes. She knelt and dug at the soil with her frigid fingers, no longer paying heed to the gritty crescent of grime beneath her nails, nor the cuts and scrapes she'd generated. She dug and dug, inserted the torch carefully approximately six inches deep, then packed the displaced earth tightly around the handle. The torch stood erect at the center of the tunnel casting shifting light upon the surrounding walls.

She removed the chicken breast from her back pocket and tore a few small pieces from it, then freed Charlie from her shirt and set him on the floor beside the torch. On second thought, as he carefully chewed a piece of chicken breast, she dug a depression into the floor – a shallow cradle with steep sides – and set the puppy into the depression with a few more pieces of meat. She didn't want him sneaking off as she worked.

She wore sneakers which were as grimy as the stone walls. She slipped one shoe off, exposing a damp socked foot within. Carefully, she removed her opposite foot from its shoe and then stood carefully upon her shoes so as not to stand directly on the moist soil. She unbuttoned her jeans and, with a final glance in either direction of the tunnel, she pulled off the jeans, careful to step back upon her shoes as she pulled each foot free of the denim casing.

The dank air was at first shocking on her exposed legs, but seemed warmer as she stood, the moisture evaporating from her bare flesh and leaving her skin dry. She untied the burlap sack from her belt loop and set it carefully just outside of Charlie's cradle, uncertain of what the heat of the torch might do to the nocturnal bulb.

She felt the air above the torch – the warmth of it – and held her jeans above the torch. The air, she knew, was humid, and the level of evaporation she might achieve was perhaps negligible, but all she could focus on now was the potential pleasure of slipping back into warm jeans.

Time passed, not in footsteps now but in the gradual warming of denim fibers, the clumsy chewing from a young puppy, the slowly decreasing height of a disintegrating torch flame.

When she slid her bare legs back into her jeans, the denim was exquisitely hot and she felt her full body shiver in orgasmic waves. She stood barefoot upon her shoes, toasting her socks in much the same manner before sliding warmed feet back into her sodden shoes. Her hands were warmed with her work. Finally, she leaned over the flame, eyes closed, feeling the waves of heat hit her face and her thin eyelids. She rubbed her cheeks, chin, forehead – coaxing the capillaries with friction. She rubbed the brittle cartilage of the cloves of her ears.

Content, she once again gathered her supplies to continue her journey.

Her blood seemed thinner, to flow more freely and fully through her thawed veins. She wanted to run, craving the lubrication of her stiff joints. She attempted a few quickened steps, warily eyeing the flickering of the torch. She attempted to hold it low, the flame shielded by her torso, but the onslaught of air rushing toward her body at her quickened pace threw the flames against her chest and throat painfully and she slowed once more. She could not risk the loss of the flame any sooner than its course prescribed. She realized with a dawning horror that she was "fanning the flames," and recalled how her father had once encouraged kindling to catch from burning balls of crumpled newspaper with powerful gusts blown from his mouth into the fireplace. She cursed her idiocy under her breath and slowed her pace, assured that Charlie appreciated the leisurely stroll as opposed to the jostling of her jogging anyway.

She stopped occasionally to stamp her feet against the packed earth, forcing the circulation through her cold feet. The heated socks had provided some comfort, but the cloth of her shoes was surely holding a fair amount of chilling moisture which it would continue to accumulate as she walked.

Presently, she came upon an "L" in the tunnel, forcing a right turn. They pressed onward, the unlikely pair, their torch ever dwindling. The tunnel stretched before her and behind her as it seemingly always had. Her optimism was renewed with her body heat, and she had essentially resigned herself to this fate for the foreseeable future, when she spied a stone archway ahead in the right wall of the tunnel. Her heart rate sped and, despite prior reservations to the contrary, she quickened her pace.

The doorway was much like the one she'd found previously, carved into the stone tunnel itself and lined in a curvature of stones outlining the arched doorway. Her heart was skittering with excitement and she heard Charlie emit a few mews in response, his tiny claws scraping the flesh of her belly as he shifted position.

"We're on the right track," she whispered, cradling the puppy in her free hand and casting the light of the torch into the tunnel that led into the darkness beyond.

"Hang on, little buddy," she whispered, recognizing that she was speaking to Charlie, the torch, and to herself. "We're going to make it."

She stepped across the threshold, holding the torch high. Once again, she faced a long and seemingly endless stone tunnel once more. Despite the threat to her light, she felt her legs moving more quickly, eagerly reducing the distance between herself and freedom. She could feel it. She could practically *taste* it. She laughed at the thought, wondering whether her sense of taste had heightened in the absence of sensory stimulation. Perhaps the adage had roots in human experience after all.

Ahead, she saw that the tunnel curved to the right once again.

"This must be it!" she spoke aloud again, wanting to run, her muscles poised with the adrenaline of anticipation – of release. Something dark lay on the floor ahead. It reflected no light. She slowed, approaching it carefully, knowing full well her light would already have been seen by anything waiting around the final bend of her journey. The nearness of her freedom, the electricity in her veins, boosted her confidence. She made up her mind, slumped corpse – whatever – she was pressing on. She was all-too-aware of the limited remaining light. Her adrenaline held each tendon and ligament in tense readiness to spring in flight or fight.

As she drew closer, her mind's eye seemed to distort her literal vision. The shape morphed into a crouched person, wearing a dark coat. Could it be? She slowed. The flickering light could play tricks on her eyes – her racing emotions –

It was not a hunched man. It was a box. A chest. Resting in the corner of the tunnel where it took a sharp turn to the right.

"Another –?" she started, then felt her breath collapse back into her lungs in an agonizing intake of realization.

Not another box. *The* box.

DON'T FORGET TO FEED

She tried to speak, to ask the word, "What?" into the cold, dark air, but she emitted no sound. She examined the lid, caved in in exactly the same place – same carving. She turned back from whence she came, lifting the torch until it nearly scraped along the low ceiling. The light cast behind her until it dissipated into darkness. Her challenging glare met no response.

She slumped to the ground and began to weep savagely, angrily – bitter tears burning tracks down her icy, grimy cheeks. She felt Charlie burrowing and shuffling against her belly.

"How? How?" She formed the words with her frozen lips, soundless and pleading. How. How. How.

She attempted to retrace her steps. Closed her eyes and tried to conjure her path. She could not. She could not recall the bends and twists she'd taken since leaving this landmark in the first place. Somehow, in her initial jubilant efforts to locate the exit she'd been confident was so near, she'd circled back, back to the carnivorous garden which lurked just around the next bend.

She tasted the salt of her misery as it reached her quivering lips, leaving itchy trails from her tragic eyes. She thought vaguely that she should not cry – that she should conserve water – that, despite the dankness of her current environment, she hadn't yet found a solitary source of potable water.

Her disappointment was a thick and angry cloud, crowding out efforts at resolution. She laid the torch against the trunk in the corner of the hallway as she had so many steps ago, noting dismally how much shorter it was – nearly hidden behind the trunk. Ignoring the cool press of moist earth beneath her, she pulled her knees into her chest and laid her head over her arms across the perch they made. Charlie squirmed into the space between her legs where his little body would not be compressed. She felt the delicate scratching of his tiny claws and the tip of his nose rooting into her belly button, ever searching for the milk her warm belly would never provide him. This made her weep harder, her ears alive with the gasping, snorting music of her weeping and the gentle *pat-pat* as her tears hit the dirt floor below.

Time was measured in stuttering breaths, in the percussion of fallen tears.

She felt the fatigued ache of her body. She felt the cold – cold and wet in all directions, on every surface. She knew with a sickness that whirled in the pit of her empty stomach that the light illuminated in a halo behind her would soon extinguish and she'd return to the utter blackness. She knew this knowledge should invigorate her forward. Surely this was lucky, returning to this space. This was the space that was the most *human*, after all. The chicken, the note, the flowers, the torch – surely someone would return to this space. Surely someone had a means of exiting and entering the tunnels that could not be too far away. She closed her eyes hard, pressing them shut with the muscles of her cheek and brow, squeezing until she saw sparks of illumination in her lids. She scoffed a bit at this, at her ability to "create light." She'd need that luminescence soon enough.

Her eyes closed, her forehead resting upon her folded wrists – she'd received a sharp jolting reminder of the injury there as she rested against her arm. In all the numb chill, she'd long forgotten her head injury.

In the utter darkness of closed lids, she conjured her original map. It was faint at first. Dull. First, she saw the phallus again – grateful she'd made the silly association, though she no longer respected the element of humor there. She saw the tunnel where she'd... begun?... and marked a red "X" at the base of that tunnel, watching a tiny dot (herself) ascend the shaft on the right side (fingers trailing the wall) until it reached the head, then turning and continuing down the left side of the shaft until she (fell) found the exit to her right. She recalled the original map – a capital letter "L" lying face-down. She'd followed the leg of that "L" until she'd found the stone archway to her left – the same stone archway she'd just passed through. She drew the archway into her map, and a leg parallel to the initial tunnel. At the end of that tunnel sat the chest with the carving (DON'T FORGET) and there was an immediate right turn. She drew the garden and the (tiny graves) depression further along where she'd discovered the torch. Just a bit further, she'd come to a T-junction in the tunnel and had taken a right.

She groaned. Of course. That right turn had led her around full-circle to the initial long-leg of the "L," back to the stone archway from the opposite side than she'd approached it previously, thus fooling herself into thinking she was making actual progress.

She formed the word "idiot" through gritted teeth.

So – left.

Left at the end of the next tunnel.

That was the answer.

It had to be.

She did not move. She studied her map, retracing her steps, adding the "circular" square she'd discovered in her series of right turns.

She'd stopped.

She'd planted the torch in the earth and warmed and dried her clothing.

She'd stood nearly naked in the tunnel, disrobing and dressing and drying her clothing.

Had she gotten turned around somehow?

She felt the anxiety snaking through her exhausted limbs, threatening to tear her mental map to shreds with the weapon of self-doubt. It began to fade, her images fading and warping.

"No…" she groaned weakly. Charlie squeaked lightly in reply, bringing her back to her present.

She hadn't gotten turned around, because if she had turned around, she would have turned left back into this hallway and would have seen the torch depression first, then the garden, and the trunk at the very end. No. She had come full-circle, had approached the trunk again just as she had originally – down the same path she'd traversed in the same manner – though better lit and far too presumptuous this go-around. She sighed deeply.

She'd just have to try it again. If her map was correct – and she felt quite certain she'd "drawn" it accurately – then she had a left turn up ahead that she had not yet explored.

She allowed herself a glimmer of hope then. When she'd discovered this nook the first time, she'd felt quite confident that she had to be near an exit, certain that no one would traverse (miles?) the tunnels for such great distances just to plant an exotic underground garden. It was too – inconvenient – to be realistic. Right?

Right?

There was no one to doubt or question her reasoning, so there it stood.

She lifted her head. The tunnel back to the stone archway was dim indeed, but her eyes, having been shut, were more sensitive than they'd been recently. The glimmer of the torch cast faintly behind her and she stood and turned to retrieve it. It looked rather pathetic, more of a weakly burning stick now than a torch. She lifted it, feeling the warm air above it, relishing it. Her ass was quite numb.

"Alright, Charlie," she said, "Let's..."

Her sentence perished in her throat, her mouth agape, the thought already forgotten.

Ahead, she saw the tiny burial ground for the deceased puppies. She'd intended not to dwell here, concerned for the strength of her own resolve, but she could not tear her gaze away.

One – two – three – four – five tiny mounds. The sixth had been disturbed. She saw the tiny body, white and spotted in the dim torchlight. She saw two tiny legs and the curl of a tail. The rest of the puppy's body was engulfed within the head of one of the ghastly flowers – its blossom separated and expanded like the unhinged jaw of a ravenous snake. The stem was stretched along the soil ground, its bulb askew as though the flower had dragged itself out of the earth itself in order to reach the fresh grave and devour its contents. She saw the shape – a massive lump – expanding into the flexible esophagus of the strange (creature) plant. The remaining flowers – now there were seven – were rapidly (crawling) growing along the ground toward the burial site as well, a few of them producing offshoots from their stems that resembled very thin arms – reaching and pulling themselves out of the soil.

Something rose in her – a venomous bile – a collection of all of the pain, the confusion, the loss and suffering, the crushing authority of darkness – cold and wet – of underground labyrinths where disorientation and self-doubt conquer all sense of accomplishment.

"No!" she cried out. She fell to her knees, digging at the dirt with her hands, desperately clawing at the rigid stems of the plants. The tiny puppy feet – the tiny pink pads of the tiny puppy feet – were too much to bear. Somewhere deep inside, she understood that there was a natural order to things. She comprehended decomposition and the roles of insects, fungi, and scavengers. She knew this. Some version of her from the past – some version that had worn clean and dry clothes, that cherished the cleanliness of water and could still feel her own fingertips – that version had adored birds of prey and vultures – had photographed them countless times and admired their grace.

But now, in darkness and cold, something snapped.

Something broke within her – the cord connecting reason to decision.

She'd dug those graves with her own hands.

She discovered those poor, murdered babies, forgotten and floating, and she'd buried them to leave them in peace. She'd vowed, at some level of her consciousness, to do all that she could to save their one surviving brother who'd somehow avoided the hangman's noose.

"You can't have her!" she screamed. The sound – the sheer volume of it – was like a blade through her eardrums – it sang and screeched and shook along the wet stone walls. The flowers that had not yet reached a grave shrunk back. She was dimly aware of the frantic digging of the puppy alive and terrified within her shirt, hanging loosely in the draping cloth. She felt him push out through the neck hole, felt him moving with a speed induced by panic.

"No," she gasped, reaching up to catch the puppy in her hands before he fell to the ground below. She felt his silky soft body squirm and wiggle, desperate to escape. "No, no, no," she was repeating again and again, trying to grasp his slippery body.

He wriggled free and hit the floor on his tiny tummy, stunned for a moment. She lurched forward, cupping her hands over his small body, shielding him.

It was then that the torch fell.

She heard it scrape along the stone wall.

She'd set it down – dropped it? – at some point in her distraction.

It hit the floor with a dull and unimpressive thump. Small cinders scattered around the remains of the wooden handle. It glowed dimly, the final coals at the bottom of a dying campfire.

Her mouth continued to form the "No" in involuntary spasm. She lifted her shirt, pressed the puppy against her stomach and lunged for the torch.

She blew against the cinders. They glowed more brightly, emitting a low crackling. She repeated this again and again, but knew it was fruitless. Everything in this cavern was moist, damp. She had no fuel for her remaining coals. Her eyes were tattooed with the brilliance of the glowing coals as she attempted to scan her surroundings.

She was blind again. The embers at the end of the stick she held were little more than ornamentation. They would serve as a heat source for an indeterminable time, but their light was minimal.

She stood carefully, reaching across the tunnel for the right wall, wanting to be as far from the savage plants as she could be. She needed her fingertips on the wall. Her night vision was returning, but in such sparse light, she registered only layers of darkness.

"Well, well."

She sucked in air and moved quickly, hitting something – the blue tote – with her blind feet and nearly falling to the ground once more.

A voice. A man's voice.

She fell against the wall, pressed both hands against it, pressed her body against it, trying to disappear into it. She breathed as quietly as she could, listening. She had dropped the torch. It thumped against the moist earth a final time and came to rest, extinguished.

Darkness.

Silence.

She willed her ears to pick up anything – the slightest shuffle of a shoe over earth – a breath. She was deafened by her own rushing blood and the engulfing silence.

"What have you done to my plants?"

She heard a sharp squeal of shock and couldn't be certain whether it had been her own voice or the dog's.

A voice. A man's voice.

She remained motionless.

She heard him again, not words but the "tsk tsk" or "tut tut" of disapproval through his teeth.

Her heart was screaming in her chest.

She wanted to feel relief – this was a fellow human, after all. How long had it been since she'd heard another human voice?

Steps and steps. Breaths and steps.

The darkness was complete. She could not get a sense of where the man stood. His voice seemed to come from further down the hallway, though she hadn't heard him arrive nor seen him before her light had been extinguished.

She'd been distracted.

Her mind flashed a photograph of the tiny puppy pads and she felt her eyes close, then couldn't be certain whether they were open or closed. She blinked deliberately. There was no distinction.

She heard him then – barely. The shuffle of clothing as one repositions oneself, the involuntary exhale of a bend, the crack of a knee.

"My sweet, sweet babies."

His voice was just behind her, though dimmer, as though he were facing away – facing the flower bed. Tentatively, she slid one foot backward, then the other, creeping her way backward, away from the man.

"Such a lovely treat today," he said. There was mirth in his voice, softness.

When he spoke, she moved, masking the sounds of her departure with the invasive decibel of his voice. With the darkness came clarity. She saw the map radiantly clear before her eyes. She could backtrack. She could run back down through the stone archway, take a left and follow the tunnels back around to the left pathway. The exit had to be down that final stretch – there was no other option. She knew the darkness; she knew the height of the tunnels. She could run, her hands now free of the cumbersome torch. If she could just get back into the tunnel before rousing his suspicion, she could disappear into the inky cloak. She knew these tunnels.

"Their growth will likely be incongruous now," the voice said. "It's too late to stop Doris now, she's nearly engulfed him. Did you see that extension? I'll have to cut one of them in half..." his voice trailed off, contemplative.

"I do love the poetic touch here, though – the tiny grave sites. It's so quaint." He paused. Her breathing was thunderous in her ears. She'd given up straining to see him – the bleakness was complete. His voice, however, allowed her to *feel* his essence and its approximate distance from her body as she continued to inch further from him.

"They're just incredible, aren't they? Just – gorgeous. I don't blame you in the least for wanting one."

A sudden hollow *thunkthunkthunk* echoed through the tunnel. She froze.

"You see, I keep the meat in there. It's cool enough down here to keep it fresh – though I have not yet tested whether my girls are at risk from consumption of, shall we say, *turned* flesh, but the tub is necessary also to keep them from overfeeding, you see." He chuckled. "My girls are quite overzealous with their feedings. I usually don't leave it out here. We've had an unexpected treat, haven't we, my lovelies?

"Plastic seems to be an effective barrier through which their delicate sprouts cannot penetrate. Also, the wood, but I think that might be more of a distance issue. So far, the longest growth recorded over a 24-hour period is just shy of 14 inches. In all actuality, you've inadvertently created an experimental atmosphere requiring each subsequent flower to grow *further* than her sister prior, in order to reach each grave in succession." He laughed again and she heard the slap of open palm on fabric, as though he'd slapped his own knee. "It's quite silly, really, that you buried them in earth. They are flowers, after all. It's their medium.

"My little Charlotte – she's the one on the end here – has always been the runt of the patch. The others get to the food before she does, returning to their hibernation state. They emerge stronger, faster. It is as though they actually *learn* with each subsequent feeding. As though they have *memory*."

She felt the heel of her foot extend into open space. The edge. Methodically, she lifted her remaining foot, turning her back toward the tunnel behind her, feeling the open space at her back with a combination of dread and invigoration.

"Just a bit of sibling rivalry, really, but it might be what she needs to maximize her potential."

She ran.

With her left hand, she held Charlie up and against the soft pouch of her stomach, attempting to shield his tiny body from the shudders of her rapid footfalls. If he cried out, she did not hear it. Her ears were keen on the space to her back, tuned for the heavy thuds of pursuing footfalls.

She hit the edge of the stone archway hard with her left elbow, seeing the false light dance in front of her eyes. She sucked in dank air through clenched teeth and turned left, not allowing her pace to slow.

This stretch of tunnel was longer and it ended in a forced left turn. She saw her map, alive, her tiny dot moving like a car in a digital GPS map. Her elbow throbbed and she dared not straighten the arm, just kept it cupped beneath the puppy's solid form as she ran, her right fingertips now tracing the stone wall as she progressed.

She reached the bend, sensed it – the change in the air – the sense of space before her suddenly short and stagnant. She stopped and turned left, her fingers tracing. This was the home stretch. The final tunnel. There would be an opening to her left soon which led into the hallway where the torch had once hung – the hallway of the gardener of horrors. She'd feel the opening expanding to her side and she'd allow it to pass, continuing onward into the final unexplored tunnel. The tunnel which held the means of escape. The final uncharted territory.

An explosion of pain erupted in her ankle and she pitched forward. The ankle – one moment a congruous grouping of tiny bones – shifted and snapped, curling beneath the weight of her body as she fell upon it.

She was on the ground. She could feel the cool damp earth beneath her knees. She heard the gentle whimpering of her puppy, knew her belly would be textured with the thatch pattern of a thousand tiny scratches.

A hole. She'd stepped into a hole and tripped.

But there had been no hole.

She'd traveled this tunnel with the torch – immediately after picking it up.

There'd been no hole in the ground – she'd certainly have seen it.

She felt the chill of self-doubt. She scanned her mental map.

Had she made an error?

Was she lost?

She shook her head roughly, knowing she could not allow herself the luxury of doubt. Not now. Her pursuer could be paces behind her. She had to rise. She had to get to the final tunnel before he reached her.

She checked that her shirt was still tucked tightly into her jeans, then pressed her hands into the cold earth on either side of her body and gingerly lifted herself to her feet. As she did so, her left hand felt the indentation of a round hole in the earth, just to the left of the shallow hold into which she'd fallen. She frowned, marking the impressions on her map (just in case), and attempted to put weight on her ankle. It felt as though the skin running across the top of her foot buckled and folded into a fat crease. Curious, she leaned and pressed her fingertips beneath her sock. The cold of her fingertips was shocking to her warm ankles, but the flesh itself felt normal. She stepped forward, and again, and again. It held her weight, though the sensation felt awkward and slightly unstable. She quickened her pace, favoring her right leg in a hobbled, bent sprint, her right hand grazing along the rock wall.

When she first saw the flicker of light, she felt excitement, confirmation – but this rapidly melted into dread.

When he stepped into the tunnel, he was a shadow in a dome of light.

She heard the "tsk, tsk, tsk" click of his tongue against the roof of his mouth again, disapproving, disappointed. She took a step backward. His hands were clasped at his waist rather than hanging at his sides, giving his silhouette the appearance of armlessness. He seemed to be advancing toward her, dissolving into the shadows which hid her. She stepped backward, not daring to turn around.

"They were rabid, you know," he stated. "The puppies. I had to put the bitch down myself. A raccoon bite, most likely."

He continued to advance, slowly, patiently. There was no malice in his voice, only the calm, informative tone of an instructor speaking to an irrationally defiant child.

"You see," he continued. "Rabies, it's a virus. A nasty thing, really. Neurological. It causes rapid destruction and degeneration of the neural pathways – the nerves – the transmitters sending messages through the body. First there is confusion, heightened emotion, increased aggression. The more obvious physical characteristics don't actually show up until near the end – you know, the foaming mouth." He chuckled good-naturedly.

"My beauties – they are my life's work. I create life, I foster and feed it – I don't *destroy* it." She could hear the smile in his voice, his *"this has all been just a crazy misunderstanding"* tone.

"The bitch – the *mother*, if you prefer – was rabid. It happens. It's a sad, sad sight, really. The virus does not spread through the placenta, typically, but as it is shared through bodily fluids, is most frequently transmitted during childbirth between mother and offspring – either through blood or, more commonly, saliva. Possible through the milk."

She froze. She felt the rooting infant against her skin.

As though reading her mind, he continued through his invisible grin.

"I doubt that little guy has teeth strong enough to bite through your skin yet, but a puppy that young is surely trying to nurse on every warm, fleshy surface. I don't suppose he's suckled your open flesh, has he?"

She felt a wad lodge in her throat – as though her heart were rising and attempting to escape her body. Her mind's eye cast aside the map, showing her a clear photograph of her torso, covered in tiny puppy scratches.

The rooting. The constant rooting.

Was she already infected? She exhaled a shuddering breath.

"Ah," he crooned. "There you are."

His silhouette was dim, hazy in the darkness. She had just processed the change in it, the raising of his right arm, the fact that it seemed much, much too long –

She heard the *crack!* first – a sharp, almost musical collision of wood and bone that sang through her piqued ears. She had the briefest sensation of gravity, of shifting light, of lying down, exhausted, for the first time in such a very long time.

He filleted her body with swift efficiency. A grimy copper pipe protruded from the ceiling above his head and extended briefly along the wall in front of him, ending in a large spigot. He turned the handle and a stream of frigid water flowed through the raw pipe end into a double industrial sink. He had balanced a large cutting board across one basin. He whistled while he worked, washing the blood into the drain, tossing portions of meat into the blue plastic bin at his feet. When he'd completed his work, he rinsed the larger bones and cutting board, leaving them in the sink to drip dry.

He had removed the clothing from the body before he'd begun the butchery, as one might pluck a goose. It was essentially clean, though the denim beneath the belt loop that held the burlap sack had been nearly eaten through, as had a considerable portion of the sack itself. He found no injury on that thigh, but the gash on the forehead was apparent. She'd likely wiped the blood on her pants. He carefully loosened the cord and extracted the bulb within, chuckling with adoration. She had begun to bloom, the head of a flower unfolding from within, nourished by the human blood. Fascinating.

He cut the remaining denim and cotton T-shirt into strips and arranged them in a tidy nest within an old wicker basket, then set the simpering puppy inside as he'd be comforted by the scent.

He bent over the blue tote and made his selection, inserting a bloody fillet into a fresh burlap sack and pulling the drawstring taut. He selected a second before covering and pushing the tote into a corner of cool, dark stone. It slid easily on the packed, moist soil.

Whistling to himself, he ducked through a low doorway and into the passageway where his garden grew. He gently set the temporarily misplaced bulb – Charlotte – from his hand into her empty spot in the procession, watching as she shivered and shifted, making herself comfortable. He set the fillet before her and watched eagerly as she immediately began to stretch toward her prize. Her sisters, content to digest their canine tartare, remained still.

A few feet away, he carefully lifted the lid of the wooden chest, running a hand over the collapsing lid as he did so, feeling his handiwork. The rusted hinges creaked. He dropped the burlap sack within and repositioned the lid, wiping his hands on a kitchen towel he kept tucked into his belt.

Whistling, he returned to the garden. The disturbed shallow graves stood vacant. He smiled benevolently down upon his girls. Young Charlotte was now fully outside of her bulb, her tendrils wrapped hungrily around the fresh flesh, drawing it toward her open mouth. He laughed and clapped his hands together, the sound triumphant and booming in the narrow space. The puppy whimpered from within the basket in the next room.

He watched her feed for several minutes, then retrieved a small trowel and began to fill and tamp down the graves the trespasser had left behind. When the dirt floor was once more uniform, Charlotte had retracted back to her concave space. Her lotus-like coat emerged, folding over her body, enveloping her in a protective dome once more. He sighed contentedly, admiring them in their slumber. He hadn't measured them today, but he estimated they had nearly doubled in size this week.

He crouched to pass through the low door. He laid the towel over the sink edge and performed a proper surgical hand scrub of his hands and forearms.

Once dry, he retrieved his blue blazer, slung over the back of a chair, and slid easily into the familiar sleeves. He lifted the wicker basket, extinguished the lights, and stooped to return to the hallway once more. A torch glowed and flickered a welcoming beacon from its depression in the stone wall as he approached. He patted his pockets, locating and extracting his keys. He tested the small LED flashlight he kept on his keyring. It shone an obedient purplish stream of luminescence. He doused the torch, returned it to its sconce, and walked to the T-junction at the end of his hallway.

He turned left. In less than a minute, he reached a ladder ascending into the darkness. He climbed one-handed with the ease of familiarity, exiting into the cool night air.

The Night Everything Changed

Raven Digitalis

I don't even know where to start.

Namaste. That's a good start.

My name is Bodhi Singh, and this is my first entry. My therapist said I should write down stuff that caused emotional trauma. She said that "journaling homework" would be helpful for the healing process. Handwriting takes forever, so she said it was okay to type it out on my computer.

Do we ever really heal, or do we just carry those scars and learn to cope? I try to look at things from a realistic perspective. I'll talk to her about this later. For now, I'll focus on the story.

It took a lot of reflecting on whether or not it was a good idea to even write about these things, but I've realized it actually is cathartic, so I'll just give it a shot. I've never written about myself, so some of this might sound annoying or melodramatic. But that's okay. People can think what they want, and come to their own conclusions. I've heard rumors that I'm pretentious or arrogant, but I'm actually just shy. I know myself.

I don't have anything to say about childhood trauma, although my heart goes out for survivors of abusive horrors. No, my survival skills were learned around this time last year. Finally I feel okay writing about it.

I was told to be "honest and unfiltered," so... yeah.

Now I'm worried that this story will sound like some type of admission of guilt. I don't think I have anything to actually feel guilty for, so maybe it's something closer to shame. I'm not sure what for, but that's what comes up. It's just that I find myself questioning the past over and over, what I could have done differently… all that typical stuff. But I strive to live in the "now moment," because that's all we have. Maybe that's why it's hard to dive into the past.

So. My mind is spinning and my heart is racing. It's hard to know where to begin.

I guess I'll start with the night that made it all sink in.

What do veterinarians inject to euthanize animals?

Top result: Pentobarbital

Where to buy pentobarbital

Top result: Help is available. Talk to someone now. 988 Suicide & Crisis Lifeline. Text or call 988 any time…

"Honey, I'm home!" I closed the tab, bringing back the tab for *Ancient Aliens*. "What's up, cunt? I am *literally* over this day; those guys can suck my rod." Jachin continued, "They want me to work the front but I'm literally prep. How the fuck do I run the registers? I don't fuggin' know; they never taught me! So it's like…"

"Jake, dude, just sit down and breathe, seriously."

"Whatever, man. Hah, it's just… whatever. I'll get over it. They know I'm unconquerable. Indisposable. Irrefutable. Irreconcilable. They won't fire me because I'm the best they've had. Way better than the Millennials they're potty-training."

"Well," I began, "they need someone like you to do hard work and teach new hires how to –"

"What, wash dishes? It's not rocket science. But anyway, I'm horny."

"Okay, okay, want some coconut oil?"

"Hey Bo, suck it!" was the best response he could come up with.

I never liked the pet-name Bo. He was the only one who called me that. Jake had all but forced it on me the previous year, saying something about it being the name of a Kabbalistic companion. He said it was destiny for someone whose name starts with "Bo" to be brought together with someone named Jake. I didn't like the nickname and never bothered to research its mystical alignments. And still, I never spoke up about it because I knew better than to question – much less refuse – Jachin's "spiritual epiphanies."

Anyway, he had assumed the esoteric name Jachin (pronounced *Jay-keen* or *Yaw-kin*) in retaliation of the Biblical name Jacob – and by extension a renunciation of his strict Christian upbringing. I knew he had those wounds, and I wanted to help him with them, but he only knew how to explore these things with anger. The last thing I wanted to do was trigger a trauma response.

We met two years ago in art class, exchanging glances for an hour before properly introducing ourselves between periods. He charmed me from the start with quick wit and an adorable, nonchalant giggle. He never shied away from eye contact, and had something to say about everything under the sun. I've always been more of a quiet type, so his boisterous energy proved a refreshing contrast. I admired his jovial outlook, and the way he convinced me not to obsess about the small stuff. He was very touchy-feely, especially at first, and his touch felt like medicine. It was a type of comfort I hadn't experienced. He wasn't afraid to brag to others about our developing relationship, and constantly tagged me on social media. It felt nice. Special.

Since we were both considered nontraditional UMN students, being in our late 20s, I was anticipating sharing mature conversations about life goals and aspirations. But last year, with both of us on the verge of a Saturn Return, it was slowly becoming clear that this would likely never be the case.

I was focused on empowerment, and he was focused on power.

"No, seriously, *suck it*! I'm not gonna be *Jachin* off tonight!" He thought the play-on-words with his "magickal" name was just as funny the millionth time as it was the first. To me, it was becoming more boring than entertainingly vulgar.

His shirt now removed, strong muscles supported the veins in his arms. His musculature was framed in violet in the dim blacklit room. I have a thing for veins. Especially in the forearms. I've never had a particularly high libido, but strong veiny features are a turn-on.

I don't know if it's connected to why I've always had a fear of blood and needles. I just cannot stomach the image of those precious life pathways being punctured. Even the sight of blood takes me out of the moment instantly. Jake had to learn early on that blood, especially in a sexual setting, was my biggest boundary, despite his wanting to push the issue.

"No, seriously, I was two seconds from stroking it in the bathroom at work. You know you want this load."

I didn't, actually. I felt ambivalence. I hadn't thought about sex all day, but understood that he "needed" release around sunset, and almost always after a shift at the diner. Because Twin City Karens are the worst, as he reiterated weekly. I "wouldn't know" because I work from home (as if he'd stumbled across some profound experience that only someone of his great intellect could fathom).

I slipped my hand along his abdomen and beneath his waistband. As my fingertips found his pubic hair, I paused to gently pet him. The sensation of his hair began to ease the tension of his grating words. I took comfort in the sensuality. Gentle and soft.

I enjoyed his balls, his armpits, the scant trail down the center of his chest. I admired his body, so different from my own. Muscular and solid. My body is thin and lanky, but he never seemed to mind.

Slacks unbuttoned, the veins of his impressively thick seven-inch lingam perfectly accented the muscles of his body.

He took off my T-shirt rather quickly, from the bottom up. The shirt was now inside-out, lying on the floor. I knew I'd eventually have to shake it out and flip it back properly. I thought about little things like that. When he was horny, he would "become" nothing but horniness. He yearned only for release.

"One sec," Jake muttered softly, running to the bathroom to grab facial concealer. He liked to dab a bit on my nipples to make them appear brighter, whiter. I thought it was odd, but I didn't really mind; it's what he liked.

At the time of our two-year relationship, I think my finding his physique so ridiculously attractive had become the main keeping point. I've never quite felt comfortable in my own skin, but it's not a big deal at the end of the day. Jake pretty much ignored any request to address me with gender-neutral pronouns. It took months upon months to build up the courage to even request such a thing. He just brushed it aside, pretending like I never said it. I tried a few times, but he would always scoff and change the subject. I wish that he would have at least made an attempt.

I had become accustomed to him brushing aside anything I thought was important. But even now, "he/him" is fine, even though I feel more comfortable with "they/them" … but I digress.

It's hard to say what caused his alluring personality shift into something abrasive over time. Condescending. Cynical. He wasn't always like that, or maybe I just didn't see it. But, he tolerated my occasional slumps – sometimes I would stay in bed for 12 hours or more – so the least I could do was put up with a flippant attitude. We had our own way of connecting, and we had our own habits and routines. Somehow we made it work, and that's not something I regret.

He was born here on the outskirts of Minneapolis. I was born closer to the city but was never quite as outgoing as him. Maybe it's because of the chill Yogic outlook on life instilled by my Sikh family. They were always okay with my choosing not to wear a turban, especially because they could see that I am, and always will be, Hindustani at heart. They're not hung up on orthopraxy, thank the gods.

Jake never liked the fact that I speak fluent English, Hindi, *and* Punjabi, with a bit of Sanskrit, Java, and C++ thrown in the mix. This was especially considering the fact that he struggled to read, write, and speak his one and only language, and I firmly believe this was borne of sheer laziness; not any type of learning disability.

We were good partners in many ways, especially at first. Some things, however, never really clicked. To be honest, we never really connected sexually. Maybe just a little, and it was mostly at first. I think it made him upset, and I wished every day that I could be more like his ideal. Even now, there's so much about myself that I wish was different. In hindsight, I don't think we ever truly connected on other levels, either.

I had high hopes. Hopes that we would grow together; not apart.

I felt bad for even talking. Not always, but most of the time. I don't know if it was the sound of my voice, but he seemed agitated when I would speak, and this agitation only increased with each passing day.

I had learned to nod in agreement to most of what he was saying at any given time. I hate conflict. Even if I learned something on my own that discounted or was contrary to what he had told me, I didn't really say it. I learned from experience. Any time I would say something that disagreed with his alleged occult wisdom, he would counter it with arguments that didn't even make sense. He didn't seem to value the fact that I've studied Western occultism and Eastern mysticism off-and-on for 15 years; he always "had" to know more than everyone else.

For example, I remember, about one year into our relationship, when he explained that the magick number 93 is a reference to the zodiac because 9 + 3 = 12. But I knew that wasn't true. I never studied much about Thelema or the OTO, and have only read a handful of quotes by Aleister Crowley, but I do remember specifically reading about 93 because I think language is fascinating.

I remembered that in Greek gematria, the numeric value for the actual *word* Thelema is 93. Thelema means "will," which is a concept similar to dharma or destiny. Also, 93 is the value of Agape, which is a type of unconditional universal love. I was excited to have remembered that.

I explained all this to Jachin and, like I said, was excited about it because it was something we could both connect on and philosophize about. I thought it would be cool for him to learn something from my own casual studies. I even told him that this is why the Book of the Law says, "Do what thou wilt shall be the whole of the law… Love is the law, love under will," *all* of which boils down to the number 93. Also, this concept of "will" is where the Wiccan Rede got the phrase "An' ye harm none, do what ye will."

The whole time I explained this, Jake was glaring with a furrowed brow. I was sitting naked on the side of the bed and he had just gotten up to get dressed for work. I was talking with my hands, animated while reciting what I had learned just months prior. He did, at least, let me finish the entire explanation.

"Yeah, I know, Bo," he responded, "Know-Bo. I also *know* that *your* name means knowledge, but that doesn't mean you literally know everything." I chuckled and put my head down, deflated. He put his hands to his head with a "psssshhh" sound, bringing his fingers outward as if to say "mind blown." His eyebrows were raised and his eyes were wider than usual. Otherwise, he was stone-faced. I chuckled again, lowering my gaze. That was the end of that conversation. I thought about it for months.

Back to the story: Jake only wanted to get off. I swear that he had already masturbated in the morning, though, when I was still half asleep. But it didn't matter; I was actively practicing present-moment awareness. He needed my touch and longed for my mouth. I had grown accustomed to him coming back to the apartment all horned up, and didn't want to bother him with details about how my day went.

Jake's pale northern skin illuminated violet from the blacklight's glow, and his veins took on a special hue under that light. I liked to run my finger along his forearms, barely touching skin, and do the same on the V-line running from his hips to his groin.

I worked the soft head of his dick with my tongue, stopping every few moments to give it a kiss. I actually loved feeling the thrust of his cock in my mouth, but wanted it to be natural; not contrived.

I surrendered to the moment, gently giving him pleasure while he let out an occasional grunt. He liked to close his eyes and thrust his hips with force. A *lot* of force. It felt strange that he was always so focused on the climax; not the buildup. I preferred the buildup.

As usual, he wanted me to go "faster! harder!" Sometimes he would even grab my hair and force it. He would usually forget that I didn't like that. One time he pulled out a bunch of my hair in the process. It wasn't noticeable, but it did cause a little bleeding, which was entirely unpleasant.

"Come on, come on!" It's what he said to prompt me to lower my pants so he could give a fondle while receiving pleasure. I didn't mind. I got hard pretty quickly (never had a problem with that), and he gave some comment about liking uncircumcised cocks, which he had already said a million times in the past.

After a few minutes, he ejaculated in my mouth and, like normal, I swallowed his thick, salty seed. It didn't bother me. I didn't think one way about it or another.

It was rare that he wanted me to reach climax *after* he did, and this was no exception. He hopped in the shower and I went back to surfing the web. No need to finish.

Okay, so now I'm getting some anxiety. My mind is all over the place, and I keep writing and deleting tangents. This is actually my first time writing about myself.

Anyway, I'll just do my best to write truthfully about stuff that happened. I don't want to trigger anyone or be anything negative in anyone's existence, okay? That's genuinely the way I feel. So I guess that's a disclaimer.

Drug use plays a big part in the trauma, for lack of better words. Not my own drug use, though; that's never been problematic. I actually don't really like drugs. Cannabis is cool and chill; I can do that sometimes, especially if it's indica. Besides, I always say a prayer before consuming. But I don't really consider it a drug; more of a sacrament. I suppose it's a drug in the long run, but it's more of a medicine when used correctly and sparingly. Jake couldn't smoke or eat weed because it caused paranoia, but for me, the occasional puff or edible was relaxing, even in the midst of his delusional episodes.

I don't know what it is with powders. Every time I've tried powders (which is only in the last few years), it creates an uncomfortable nasal drip. Aside from ketamine, I've never "met" a powder that does much for me. (Special K does hold a "special" place, but only occasionally and in moderation. And especially when watching Björk videos or listening to Aphex Twin or something downtempo.)

Hmm. I'm going off on tangents again. Well, tangents are natural for me because that's how my mind works. I'm writing this on an almost-full moon, so maybe that's why I'm a bit wound-up. It's supposedly a blue moon. I keep hearing people talk about the blue moon – and by that, I mean posting online. I don't really understand why people are going on about it being a blue moon. Personally, I think the only *real* blue moons occur during the second full moon *within the sun's same zodiac sign*, not in the same made-up Gregorian calendar month. I tried explaining this to Jake once, and all he said was, "Duh, there are two different types of blue moons." WeLL SoRrY, jAkE, hOw DaRe I sAy SoMeThiNG?!

Argh. I'm not being very nice. Honestly, I don't like talking smack about people. But I was instructed to face all the facts and feel all the feels. My therapist says I should accept the term "abusive," but I don't quite vibe with it yet. Not least because that puts me in a role of "victim," and that's not a frame of mind I want to be in, only to eventually break through it and dramatically rise like some prototypical phoenix from the ashes. It's just not my jam.

Jake was actually mean to me most of the time. Inconsiderate, demanding, sometimes threatening. Now that I reflect on it, Jake actually did make me feel like a tool; an object; a human dildo; some type of trophy. I didn't like it, but never really brought it up as an issue. I realized that a part of him always wanted to be straight, and I didn't want to hurt his feelings, so I refused to say anything that could possibly be interpreted as shameful. The last thing I'd ever want is to make someone feel bad for being themselves.

He was going all around the house all crazy like, which he sometimes did after getting off work. I didn't do my tech job on the weekends; only a little schoolwork. He had dropped out of school earlier in the year. He was texting people like usual (I didn't ask), while I surfed YouTube on the laptop. I remember him coming up to me suddenly.

"Hey, check it out!" he came up, holding his phone, "This little girl literally thinks this bear is a dog and she's trying to pet the bear but thinks it's a dog. Look."

I reluctantly watched the video, one hand over my mouth, and saw a young bear make its way to the girl. My heart rate intensified, recalling another time he showed me a video of a man accidentally getting eviscerated by farming equipment. His insides were on the outside. It's something I can never unsee. Sometimes I have dreams about it, and wake up gasping for breath. I was worried this video would be another one of the same. But, luckily, the little girl's family pulled her away while she screamed, "Can I pet that dawg?! Can I pet that dawg?!"

I guess he was amused just because it was a funny viral video; surprisingly it wasn't humor at anyone else's expense. I don't know why that stuck with me. Maybe it's because I was surprised that it was nothing more than a funny videoclip; nothing cruel, like I said. And now I'm surprised at *being* surprised, because I should have realized that normal people aren't entertained by real-life violence.

Some of his violent fixations make me wonder about his past lives. I don't think he had any real understanding of karma, which, from Sanskrit, translates to "action." I try to act like a decent human being as much as possible. Why is that *so* hard for so many people?!

Sometimes he would perform *tasseomancy*: reading my tea leaves. He did this with coffee grounds from our French press; not actual tea leaves. At least once a week, he insisted on reading my "fortune" from grounds left in my mug. I think he learned it from a movie. Everything he said in every reading was dark. Nothing positive.

He usually ended up gossiping about other people he would "see" in the coffee grounds instead of anything related to my own future. One time he told me that he "saw" one of our older professors getting "busted for kiddie porn," and another time he "saw" my cousin Rini, who het met only once, "becoming a lesbian." The thing is that nothing he predicted *actually* came true. I can see now that he was just projecting his own existential torment onto an alleged spiritual practice. It wasn't true and it wasn't genuine. These were his own demons. That sort of thing actually made me want to become an atheist more than anything.

I know he did meth behind my back. I heard him talking on the phone about "ice cubes," and I'm street-smart enough to know that "ice" means methamphetamine. Especially when he talked about "drinking some Coke on ice." I wish he would have just been honest with me about it. He felt like it was edgy and exciting to keep secrets.

Anyway, that night, Jake was insisting that I go out. Have a night on the town. He was expecting it. It was the weekend. A drizzly September Saturday.

He knew I didn't actually enjoy going out, but I agreed with him early-on that I'd make an exception for one night a month, because I knew he liked going to Goth clubs and gay clubs. I hadn't joined him for a few weeks. He went out every Saturday. Sometimes he'd go on Fridays or Sundays, too, but it would be someone else picking him up and dropping him off; some other friend from the club. He especially liked going on fetish nights, which I don't entirely understand.

That's when things took a turn. It was around 8:00 p.m. I was streaming a video about the multiverse theory. I couldn't get enough quantum physics, especially when it related back to spiritual concepts I was familiar with. Sometimes it felt like I had the ability to predict what someone was going to say, when someone was going to text, and even how the weather would behave. It was comforting to watch science videos; that's when I felt most in touch with the Universe.

Anyway, when the video ended, I realized that Jake had been in the bathroom for at least 20 minutes. It was hauntingly quiet, and the bathroom door was closed. He almost never shut that door.

"Jake! You good?" He didn't respond. I made way to the door, passing by a couple half-stitched black poppet dolls he had thrown in the corner for some reason. The little dolls felt ugly; I cringed in their direction.

"Jake! You okay?"

"Yeah, hey, yeah, hey... what's up?" The paranoia in his jagged voice was palpable.

"Just seeing if you're good."

"Fine, yeah, good." I didn't like how disjointed he sounded, so I opened the door. It wasn't locked.

I noticed a tiny spatter of blood on the white linoleum floor. Startled, I thought he must have gotten cut. Then I saw his legs. He was propped against a wall by the toilet, wearing only boxers. Five or ten rubber bands were taught on his skin above the elbow of his left arm. His right hand held a syringe.

My vision blurred. I stared wide-eyed, mouth agape. I stopped breathing for a moment.

"Bo, snap out of it," he demanded, "I'm fine. What's your deal?"

"Oh my God, wh— what's happening?" I finally mustered the strength to say something, stammering and stuttering, "You – you – you're okay? Oh my God. Wh— where the *fuck* did you get a needle? What are you doing? Wh— why are you doing this?"

"Dude, chill. I'm fine. It's not my first time. I haven't shot up forever, so just chill out."

"Jake! No! No, no, no! I won't chill out! I love you. Wh— why are you doing this? What even is it? Where did you—"

"It's just blow," he defensively retorted, "don't ya know? Bo? Ya know?" I was at a loss for words. He glanced around with frustration while I squatted near his feet.

"Please don't… no, don't do this." I could feel the weight of tears welling.

"Literally stop. I'm sorry… I'm sorry you don't like it. This is part of who I am, and I'm not gonna let *you* shame me. You're a fucking buzzkill. You're always judging me from your high horse. You always look down at everyone else and think you're so smart. Well, guess what, Bo, you're not."

"Jake, no, just please—"

"No, just stop. Literally shut up. I don't wanna hear it. You're a gaslighter. Always trying to make me feel like a worthless failure. Yeah, congratulations, you win! You made me feel like shit! Meanwhile you're supposedly perfect. Still going to school and kissing ass. Just a cog in the wheel. You're part of the system. You're part of the problem!"

"That's not fair! Look at yourself, it's just—"

"I already told you to stop! Now I'm getting pissed. Everything was fine, and then, like you do time and time again, you rain on the parade. I'm not working tomorrow and neither are you, so just shut up." I stared back at him, my mouth open in shock. I noticed a drop of blood beading at the injection site on his forearm. I glanced at the syringe, noticing it smeared with a streak of blood, and a small amount of blood retained in its otherwise empty chamber.

"Please, Jake, I've been really sad lately and sometimes I think about dying. Sometimes I want to… end it all… because I don't know what to do, and I don't want you to be unhappy with me, but this is not okay, so I need—"

"Now you're blaming me for making you sad? Not cool. You make *yourself* sad. So get some mental help. I am *done* with this conversation, and I'm *done* with your shit. You're not better than everyone else." He quickly rose to his feet, removed the rubber bands, and placed them in a plastic baggie along with the syringe.

"Jake, I cannot have you hurting yourself like this! Nothing about this is okay! And – and – I can't afford it! *We* can't afford it!" My breath was fast and shallow.

"You're a liar, Bo." His voice was guttural and frightening. "I know you get off on my pain. You like it when I'm stressed out and pissed off. You want me to feel like a waste of space. You're always plotting and scheming how to make me feel like a nobody. Well, guess what? I'm living my best life, and you don't get to tell me what to do!"

"No, that's not how it is. I love you. Don't hurt yourself. Don't—"

"*Don't* tell me what to do!" His voice became louder and his breath deepened, sounding almost nonhuman. His strong chest and stomach rose up and down while nostrils flared and his gaze intensified.

A shadow jumped across his face while the nightlight flickered. It never flickered. We had a large Himalayan salt lamp next to the bathroom sink. He took a few steps, unplugged it, and slammed the base down on the bag, breaking the plastic syringe in two. My muscled seized for a moment; what was next?

"There! Happy now?! Fuck!" He plugged the light back into the wall and tossed the baggie in the trash.

I took a deep breath, glanced at his arm, and offered a bundle of toilet paper torn from the roll. He grabbed it from my hand and held it to his arm, declaring, "This conversation is done. I'm fine. You're fine. Let's move on and hit the road. It's getting late. Come on. It'll be a good night. Don't worry about it. I'm not even mad at you. No worries. Let's get going. Okay, Bo? Okay? I'm not even mad." His voice softened; a total departure from seconds ago. He gently brushed my cheek with the back of his hand.

"Okay," I acquiesced, "Love you. I'm gonna lay down for a minute and then get ready."

"Cool."

I couldn't stop thinking about the shadow that was cast across his face moments ago. Was it because of the nightlight? Maybe an optical illusion from the blacklight? All I could think about was the alleged "spirit" that Jake would sometimes mention he "controlled," and whose name he said was Akash. I didn't know who or what Akash was, and I didn't want to know. As with most of his flights of fancy, I chalked it up to another delusion. It made him feel better to have an invisible servant.

I contemplated the whole exchange for five minutes or so and, upon hearing the rattle of his belt, forced myself to get up and prepare for the night out. I felt awkward applying eyeliner.

My hands were still shaking. The bedroom mirror gave an ugly, panicked reflection.

I asked Jake for a benzo, which I was in the habit of taking once or twice a month. He happily grabbed a green Klonopin from another baggie in his satchel. I broke the pill in half and we each chewed up our pieces. He showed off his makeup, having done up all sorts of liquid eyeliner streaming from his mouth and eyelids. He looked dark; more scary than spooky. I thought he was trying too hard. It didn't look attractive to me, but maybe it did to him. Or it would impress others at the club. I have no idea.

Like usual, I wasn't looking forward to going out, but wanted to support whatever adventure he needed after the workweek, especially after our argument. I agreed with him to have a good time and not "dwell on the past," as he put it.

We usually met his friend Vanessa at Ground Zero. She was never a good friend to me. She was more of a "fag hag" than an actual comrade. I hate that term. She loved the term. Jake was amused whenever she'd refer to our sexual preference and relationship status; I didn't think it mattered. Jake liked the attention. He liked any attention.

Anyway, I don't talk to her anymore. Toward the end, it seemed like he was always in an altered state, and I knew she preferred him that way. It was uncomfortable at first, but then I got used to it.

Vanessa came from a messed up home. Which is ironic because she's a pretty white girl that could make anyone of any gender swoon over her charismatic personality. She certainly acted privileged. She was barely 21, and saw no reason to change her "party girl" persona.

She was with us that night. At least at first. He wanted to party with her and do some dancing. I was just along for the ride, even though I was driving. Like usual.

Vanessa thought she was a psychic vampire. I don't know, she probably was. She met him at school before he and I met, so I don't know their sordid few-month history, but I do know that he was on the "vamp trip" himself before we met. It never sat well with me, but he shrugged it off as "ethical psychic vampirism," whatever that means. He didn't talk to me much about it.

They even wanted to get matching Satanic sigil tattoos, but it never came to fruition. I could forgive some of *her* frivolity of youth, but I couldn't look past his behavior. He should know better.

I've talked with people (at school or at the club or whatever) who have been through *far* worse abuse than he could ever imagine. Violations so sick and depraved I don't want to recite them here. But, guess what, they chose to be better people as a result, and even ended up helping others because of it. Not perpetual victims, and certainly not perpetrators themselves. They broke the cycle. Jake never broke the cycle.

Vanessa met up with us at Ground Zero. She was wearing a short velvet skirt with a corset she'd inaccurately laced herself. Flowing dyed-black hair accented mesh arm cuffs, and her makeup was uniquely pastel. I was wearing black slacks and a black button-down shirt (when in doubt, wear black), and Jake was sporting ripped-up black jeans and a short-sleeve pirate-style shirt that enhanced his muscular features. It was a regular night out. Maybe we'd get cheese fries or pizza afterward.

The two of them talked outside while a wide array of Goths filtered through the doors. I tried to smile to each person, but most of them insecurely glanced away.

Jake and Vanessa smoked their nasty menthols while gossiping about workweeks. Somewhere in the mix I could smell the faint scent of a clove.

A girl and her boyfriend walked past. We had all talked before, but I don't remember their names. She was wearing gossamer faery wings with glittery violet fishnets. She knew she looked great. Jake looked at her and interjected,

"Hey girl! Damn, you look fine. What you been up to?"

She smiled sheepishly and gave a moment of small talk. Her boyfriend, like me, looked around as if keeping guard.

We eventually made our way into the club. I remember Skinny Puppy playing... It was that song "Assimilate." I know that track. Anyway, the dancing bodies sported full regalia while the bar shone in striking neon colors with a snarling gargoyle perched atop.

After Jake and Van danced for a couple songs, we sat at a small rectangular table. I had bought all three of us cocktails. We sipped them while Jake's eyes eagerly darted around the nightclub. Vanessa rarely looked away from him, smiling in a way I could always tell was disingenuous. Why did she want to impress him so much? I didn't trust her and still don't.

After sucking down our drinks, Vanessa offered him a bump of something. They indulged, and I politely declined as the designated driver.

We all got up and danced a bit to a remix of something, I think it was Dead Can Dance, and the two of them kept whispering into each other's ears. I was used to this happening, and it was because they were "scouting the wicked," as they put it.

It's hard to put into words. Basically, they were looking for people in the club who they, for whatever reason, deemed to be "wicked," and who thereby deserved to be punished. Bound, to be specific. Binding spells.

The goal – and I don't know if it ever actually worked – was to make each "bound soul" into a "servitor," to use their terminology. They believed that they could control the thoughts and movements of people they bound, and would often convince themselves of this when they encountered someone at the club who they had previously cast upon. Phrases like, "see, I made him do that," became all too common. Not only that, but they would "suck the prana" from these poor souls by covertly looking in their direction and sucking air through gritted teeth, almost like a backwards hiss. It was discomforting, but I didn't see the harm in letting them play-pretend. Besides, I didn't dare make it an issue. I just chose not to participate.

They did this almost every time, looking for someone to bind. At that point, they must have bound a few dozen poor souls, probably more. I like talking to people and getting to know them, not "fixing" them by some sort of self-aggrandized decree. But I let them do their thing; I knew better than to ask questions.

"Fuck that guy," Jake said to her with a maniacal grin.

"Eww, *you* fuck him!" They both laughed.

"Let's get something." Jake brushed past the long-haired fellow as if making way to the bathroom. I knew his strategy. He'd explained it one drunken night when he'd first dreamt it up, and I'd witnessed it more times than I care to count. He had prepared a piece of double-sided tape on the palm of his right hand. The tape was wrapped up and around his middle finger in order to secure it. He gently bumped into the fellow with a "pardon me," meanwhile touching his back to secretly collect whatever debris would stick to the tape. He never got caught.

It didn't matter if it was dandruff, strands of fabric, stray hair, or anything else; they both felt that it was the key to grabbing the "essence" of a person. The club was always crowded and noisy enough to allow for a discreet grab.

After meandering for a moment, Jake made way back to Vanessa. They both went back to the table while I reluctantly danced to the next song. I really wished I had just stayed home, but tried to make the most of it. I did like looking at the cute DJ. I didn't mind dancing on my own; I would stand in place, waving my arms like slow-moving liquid.

Vanessa reached into her coffin-shaped handbag and pulled out a poppet: a little black doll she stitched herself. I glanced over every now and then. As usual, the lips and eyes of the poppet were made of red X's, and the outer stitching was also red. It was always red on black, and she would stuff the doll with "binding agents," as she called them, meaning herbs, leaves, and oils, and the body was stuffed with "wild-harvested cotton," whatever that was.

The top of the head was always open, later to be stapled (she literally carried a stapler for the purpose), awaiting the aforementioned "essence" of the target to be placed inside.

Jake secretively deposited his piece of tape into the cloth doll's head. She smiled and handed it to him for safekeeping. They didn't staple the poppet shut that night, at least not as far as I could tell.

He always carried a small bundle of twine in the back pocket of his jeans. It was jute twine from the hardware store. He went through it quickly, considering all the binding rituals he'd perform.

He would, without fail, call upon his "shadowy servant Akash" when he held or worked with a binding poppet. He had stated that the spirit was a thoughtform tasked with doing his bidding.

I never took part in the bindings. I didn't want anything to do with it.

It was approaching last-call, so folks were filtering out. The DJ started playing a slow track with typical droning sad-Goth-dude vocals.

After getting in the car to drive Vanessa home, since they decided against going to the pizza place, she offered him a bump of white powder, then another, which he sniffed up with glee.

I became concerned with the amount of uppers and downers he was mixing, but kept my mouth shut and started the car. He loudly exclaimed,

"I low-key wanna meet a cop so I can blow some blow in his face, and I'll say it's some kind of Voodoo powder, and whisper 'thinner' or something! Low-key like Loki." Vanessa responded with an unbearably fake giggle. I don't think he had ever researched the actual deity Loki before that Marvel movie came out, whatever it's called. "Anyway," he continued, "let's *blow* this popsicle stand." The puns were getting dumber by the day.

I remember something she said when I dropped her off that night. She locked eyes with us both and said, with an awkward grin, "Be careful!" She said it once Jake and then to me, melodramatically raising her sweat-smudged eyebrows. I wished her a good night and made way onward.

I was taking Jake to the Stone Arch Bridge, which is on Franklin and overlooks the Mississippi River, to finish his binding ritual. That's the place where he would speak an incantation, wrap Van's handmade poppet with twine, and throw it off the edge. (I thought it was littering, but learned to keep my mouth shut after questioning it a couple times.)

On the way to the familiar location, I offered to stop at a gas station for snacks. My stomach was growling.

"You don't need to eat when you're blowin'. You could take off a few pounds anyway, hooker!" Jake reached over from the passenger seat to smack my stomach. It was a way of showing affection. He looked at the road and back at me, again and again, wide-eyed, as if both required immediate attention. A slick black Tesla cruised in front of us in the other lane.

"Speed up, rich bitch," Jake carried on, "It's a 60, not a 40." Jake extended a middle finger. I noticed that it was a 45 zone but didn't comment. The driver couldn't see or hear us anyway.

"Hey Bo. You remember Ram Dass?"

"I like Bodhi better," I was quiet for a moment before continuing, "but yeah, I know Ram Dass. He wrote *Be Here Now*. Remember I said that I saw that documentary with—"

"Yeah, well, I bet you didn't know he was gay."

"What?"

"Yep. Total homo. Just learned that. I should have guessed."

"That's not nice to say."

"Well, it's true!"

"But, like, is that even relevant? He was one of the most amazing gurus the world has ever seen—"

"Dude, *gurl,*" Jake interrupted "just *say* that you didn't know it, and stop taking everything so seriously. You're way hotter when you're not being a bitch."

We'd arrived at the bridge and I decelerated. Jake released his seatbelt and raised himself on one hip to stretch between the seats, hunting for his black satchel of magick supplies. I felt his breath on my cheek as he turned to lean past me, the sudden closeness causing me to flush involuntarily. He grunted, his body contorted and lithe, part in the front seat and part in the back. Again he grunted with the effort of lifting the sack, but then he was returning, yanking it through the narrow gap between our seats. I was just rolling the car into a parking spot, wheels crunching over the gravelly surface, when I winced and cried out as a sudden, sharp, burning pain etched across the back of my hand that was preparing to shift into park. Shocked, I pounded my foot against the brake pedal, lurching us both forward.

"Aah! What the—"

"Bo, chill out, sorry. I didn't mean to stab you or whatever. It's just my athamé." I looked over and saw the tip of his ritual dagger piercing through the bottom of his fabric bag. I couldn't believe it was so sharp. "Here," he said. He dropped the bag onto the floor at his feet and leaned forward, opening the glove box and extracting a napkin. He held it against my bleeding hand. I wasn't actually in shock, but was instantly lightheaded. The whole ordeal echoed the sight of *his* blood six hours prior. I froze up, trying to process what happened. Then I spoke,

"Jake! If you weren't so high all the time, you'd notice a fucking blade sticking out of the bottom of your bag! Oh my..." I allowed my voice to trail off, thinking I may have been overreacting. I didn't want another confrontation.

I made myself come back to my senses rather quickly. Jake remained quiet while removing the napkin and handing over a fresh one, pressing his hands against mine. I liked the touch; it was warm and comforting. It felt like he was trying to be nice. It was rare for him to express compassion (that was supposedly a weakness, which I entirely disagree with). But, it was nice in the moment, and eased the pain pretty quickly. It wasn't too painful. Just surprising.

Jake would always feel better after visiting the bridge. He'd feel satisfied. The evenings would go well afterward, so if this is what it took to create a sense of peace, I was all for it. I would stay in the car while he'd go chuck the poppet into the cold river below.

It was a beautiful starry night. Clouds were coming and going at a quick speed, and I remember that Mercury and Venus were both retrograde. The cosmos blanketed the night sky; a welcome reprieve from city lights.

Sitting in the idling car with the windows rolled down, I inhaled cosmic energy with eyes cast upward, held my breath for a few seconds, and slowly exhaled through my mouth. I could have done this all night, contemplating the reality of infinity, and the curious manner by which life and consciousness sprang into being. I wanted to spend a while looking for UFOs – or UAPs, as they're now called.

Jachin walked ahead, the poppet dangling by a piece of twine. He stopped a little way ahead, under a streetlight, and gazed over the railing. It was a windy night, and the river was roaring. He didn't hear me get out of the vehicle to gaze at the sky. In an effort to get away from the glare of a streetlight, I moved closer to where he was standing, probably ten feet behind him. He was intently focused on the ritual, beginning a familiar incantation above the water,

"Akash, Akash, come to me. We now bind this soul and body," I recognized his go-to chant. But, this time, there was an unusual second line. "Boaz was my lover, now my prey; he is mine 'til the end of days."

Wait, what? What did he just say? He almost never called me Boaz; it was something he dreamed up when we first got together. I had never heard him recite a second verse during the chant, and certainly not one using that name. Although the howling wind made it difficult to make out every word, by the third time he repeated the chant, there was no doubt in my mind. Once his lover, now his prey? The sense of shock returned. I stared at his back, vulnerable and confused.

I suddenly understood what was happening. He tricked me. He was casting against me, not the guy at the club. But why?

At the time, I couldn't wrap my mind around his habit of binding people he deemed wicked, much less wanting to bind *me*, his loyal partner. What kind of narcissistic sociopath did I get involved with? Of course, at the time, I didn't have a frame of reference for those ideas because I had never met anyone who could possibly fit the description.

Listening to his words in disbelief, it finally made sense: he was dishonest from the start, and our relationship was all building up to *this*. I felt weak. I was frozen. My throat was numb and my feet were tingling. My mind raced between thinking that these sensations were a result of my own anxiety and thinking it was the result of his spellwork. I've come to believe that these things aren't mutually exclusive. Whatever the case, I was most definitely under his spell and *had been* all this time. I was just too naive to realize it.

I instinctively looked back up at the night sky. My eyes met the seven sisters; the Pleiades. Vision blurred, and the sky turned into ripples like an ocean. I blinked, and it was gone. It felt as though the Pleiades were singing, but I couldn't quite make it out. My energy shifted. Something powerful and good had entered my body, my aura. Something had my back. I closed my eyes, inhaled, held my breath for a few seconds, and exhaled. When I looked back over at Jake, he was holding the doll above his head. He was consecrating it "as above" before tossing it "so below," as he would say.

I made out the glow of the napkin he'd used to collect my blood moments earlier. There was also something more sinister in the periphery.

My eyes weren't playing tricks. Standing to his left was a shadow figure, clear as day. Slim, probably eight feet tall. It was featureless and black as night. It was difficult to see the silhouette, but it was there.

A single car drove past on the road behind us, its headlights momentarily bathing the scene. The shadow figure was lost to the illumination. As the light continued its journey and the shadows crept back in, I saw it return. It was there. The shadow vanished. Then it reappeared. I wondered if it was really happening, but the fact that it remained after I studied it quizzically was proof enough that it was real.

The figure stood still, as if waiting for a command. I didn't know Jake's relationship with the thing, and I probably should have paid better attention when he was rambling on about his this "spirit he controlled" over the past year. Turns out he wasn't entirely delusional after all. It took all my mental strength to stay anchored in the present moment; thoughts couldn't become a distraction. This was a matter of protection. I felt the entity's power, and remained frozen in fear at its manifestation.

Jake stared intently at the poppet, which he was now suspending above the river at arm's length. At that moment I felt something pull from my core. It felt like magnetic energy. I became weak for a moment. It was as though every muscle in my body quivered for a split second, then stopped. Despite being frozen, trying to process what was going on, my mind was racing.

It was then that Jake realized I was nearby. He must have sensed it. His head shot in my direction. His otherworldly, dark eyes were locked in gaze. I could see the mania, but also sensed panic. He looked like a rabid animal, but also looked frightened. I could sense the innocent, childlike part of his spirit that had become buried with chronic anger, abuse, and addiction.

I suddenly (and surprisingly) remembered a mantra I had learned five or six years ago. It popped in my head out of nowhere. I knew something had my back.

I had learned the mantra from an older friend of my parents, who was part of the local Indian community before passing away a few years ago.

Like any other language, I couldn't forget the words. I never even sang it to Jake because there was no reason to do so. This is mainly because it should not be overused, misspoken, or said nonchalantly. It's a call to Lord Shiva in his aspect called the Conqueror of Death. I was told that the *Maha Mrityunjaya* mantra should only be used in dire circumstances. This was the first time I had used the mantra since it was taught.

I recited it from memory. Three times. Each increasingly louder,

"Om Tryam-bakam Yajamahe, Sugandhim Pushti-Vardhanam. Urva-rukamiva Bandhanan, Mrityor-mukshiya Mamritata."

I blacked out for a few seconds at that point. I had never raised my voice anywhere near Jake, but everything instinctive within me (and outside of me, I suppose) said to bellow the chant to stay alive.

My third recitation of the mantra wasn't quite a full-on *yell*, but it was louder than I've vocalized in years. It was time to stand up to an imminent threat. I would no longer stand in helpless wait. The mantra was the only defense I had.

The first recitation was a whisper, the second one more like a command, and the third time felt like something took me over. I'm thinking it's something in the DNA; maybe cellular memory or spiritual instinct, or maybe something cosmic. Ancestral? Pleiadian? I suppose the source doesn't matter. It happened.

A wave of nausea forced my eyes closed again. I blacked out for another split-second, almost as if my brain was short-circuiting or receiving a "download," as they call it. I saw a kaleidoscope of colors on the back of my eyelids; a vision almost mechanical.

The wind picked up, rushing in a manner only comparable to the mighty Mississippi. My eyes startled open to Jachin's exclamation,

"Oh! Oh! No, no, no!" The poppet he was holding seemed to jump out of his hand, prematurely falling toward the river before he could complete his working. It happened so quickly, but I swear I saw a shadow rush against the doll, descending alongside it to the watery depths. But that's not all it took.

In an attempt to grab the flying poppet, Jake's body jolted with panic-stricken desperation. The top half of his body flung across the railing while he reached for the falling doll in a manner only comparable to Gollum jumping after his precious ring.

Jake was too far over the railing to steady himself on the pavement, even if he tried. He tumbled head over feet, the doll only inches away from his grasp, the whole scene drenched in a streak of shadow.

I ran to the railing and, looking over the edge, could barely see his black-clad body hit the river with an audible splash and a horrific scream that haunts my mind daily.

I gasped and shouted his name over and over. I tried to make out his location, but it was just too dark. There was no way he could have survived a fall like that, and certainly not so heavily under the influence.

An anxiety attack gave way to calling police. They would never recover a body.

Days of frantic searching resulted in nothing.

Sometimes I still visit the bridge, hoping for a sign, a clue, anything.

I will never forget the terror of his scream. The echoing splash. The intensely rushing wind and river. The crickets that graced the night.

I do miss him. Parts of him. But that doesn't erase the fact that every day was a struggle to tolerate his behavior. I loved him, I really did, and I told him that every day. Sometimes he said the same in return.

In hindsight, I loved him the same way I love everyone. I've come to believe that we are all reflections of each other. Each of us a different manifestation of the Divine, doing what we believe is best in the world. And despite the horrors of humanity, I still love everyone because I love the Divine. God. Goddess. The gods. Creator. The Universe. Ourselves. Nothingness. Everythingness. Same thing.

Maybe a part of me wants to make it known here that I really and actually did love my partner. But that doesn't mean I *liked* him.

It's just… it's not nice to speak ill of the dead.

Namaste.

ReBound

Tracy Cross

Not one part of the city was dark. There were no less than two lights per person, flooding alleys and lighting a million different pathways as Jai walked toward her hovel. Blue and red colors danced on her brown skin and shone in the small water puddles as she made her way through the street. The air smelled of a damp fusion of food, sweat, and an oncoming rainstorm. And yet, despite the continual protests of her mother, she liked living in the city. She fully enjoyed the city. It felt like a warm hug embracing her as she walked. Even though spontaneous holographic ads appeared from nowhere and blocked her path, she smiled and slithered past them, reminding herself to wear her adblocker holodot the next time she left her place.

She stopped off at Garcia's to pick up her Mexican-Chinese fusion; she'd saved time by ordering ahead, and made small talk with Mr. Garcia.

"You charging those *ratones* rent yet?" He bagged her flour tortillas along with a pack of ginger, chilis, and fresh cut garlic. "The wife thinks you're so thin that she made you some wonton elote soup for free."

"Yes, no charge, no charge. So skinny!" Mrs. Garcia-Deng smiled from further back in the kitchen area of the truck. Garcia's was an old semi-truck, retro fitted with rockets instead of tires. At night, they packed up and pulled into a quiet sky spot to sleep. But now was the dinner rush and she heard the distinct pat-pat of homemade tortillas being made in Mrs. Garcia-Deng's small hands.

"Drink all broth, good today. I use real chicken bones for you, skinny girl."

"Well, thanks, but it's just—"

"Aht!" Mrs. Garcia-Deng interrupted, "Just do, no talk."

A man sitting at the bar in front of her was crowded over a bowl of stew. "Ey, wot's this then? Cat?"

"Lloyd, eat up. You asked for cat soup! Meow meow!" Mrs. Garcia-Deng playfully smacked his hand.

"Don't make the missus leave her cooking station!" Mr. Garcia passed the stapled brown paper bag over the counter to Jai.

"My cue to leave. Did you add seven percent? It's not much, but I tip what I can." Jai held her Delphius watch over Mr. Garcia's watch to make the transaction.

"No tip. You student. Remind me of my idiot son," Mr. Garcia started.

Mrs. Deng came running from behind Mr. Garcia and swatted at him with a white dishrag that was previously laying on her shoulder. She yelled at him in Chinish, the bastard language of Mandarin Chinese and Spanish combined.

In the city, everything seemed to merge and nothing ever remained what it was.

"Thanks!" Jai dropped her head and backed out toward the street.

She weaved her way between the street urchins begging for change or a piece of fruit, past the first shift of streetwalkers and the cops that chased them down the block to their different spots.

A hologram stood in front of her and stopped.

"Jai, come see me baby. Come see me tonight. Fifty credits, which is cheap." Her ex, now "host boy," Charlie; he of the large brown eyes, porcelain skin, and pompadour black hair, bowed in front of her.

She walked through him. "Not tonight. I've got a lot of homework and this is my last class before my internship, then graduation. Not like you'd know, 'Mr. Never Finished School.' Besides, this is also putting me closer to my degree."

The lights around them combined and shone purple on her velvety smooth skin. She ran her fingers through her loose corkscrew curls as she sidestepped to avoid him.

"Remember us? How it used to be?" He kneeled in front of her and she kept walking.

"Charlie, you were never good for me. I'm not that idiot girl anymore. I'm in my 'grown responsible adult woman' stage of life now. Things to do." She made a flicking motion with her free hand.

"Oh Jai, your sense of self is so micromite-ish. C'mon, give me another chance." She stopped walking.

"Give you money so you can dab in the drugs again? Mandy saw you on A-Block last week with those diseased girls. Eyes all bloodshot from dropping 'glass.' Not a pretty picture. Don't think I don't know!"

Charlie's jaw opened and closed like a fish gasping for air as he stared at her walking through him. He grabbed his crotch and made a vulgar motion toward her. She mimicked him and yelled, "Later, gator!"

He watched her walk until another woman came along. He started up his spiel.

"Hey Miss, I'll treat ya special for fifty credits. Come see me in the G-Block Lover's Suite, that's 'G' for gigolo, and tell them Charlie sent you. First time's the charm and you get a little discount too."

Jai listened to her ex hustle as she crossed the street in front of one of the local hover buses to make it back to her rattrap hovel while her food was still hot.

Jai made her way down the hallway to her goshitel. The smell reminded her of the disinfectant they sprayed nightly in the streets to kill all the annoying little bugs that bite at the ankles and leave huge welts. The white walls glowed as she pressed her eye to the retinal scanner on her silver barrier of a door.

The locks clicked inside as she heard someone call her name, running from the opposite end of the hall.

"Jai! Wait!" Pepper had bright electric blue hair and dressed like she only read catalogs from the late 1990s, despite the year being 2134. She had ocular implants that changed her eye color. This week's color was a bright silver, which was a perfect contrast to her tanned skin.

"What is it, Pepper? I'm just getting home and I'm hungry." Jai held the door open with her hip.

"I wanted to talk to you about the assignment. Like how long before it's due?" Pepper squeezed past Jai and slipped inside Jai's goshitel, taking her package of food with her. "Don't just stand there, you lettin' all the stank out!" Jai rolled her eyes.

"One day, you'll speak like the rest of us in this world and not like some sitcom you watch on some bootleg channel you get by hanging an antenna out the window."

Jai's goshitel was in the Spirals of the worst part of the city. Everything inside the lobby looked new, but the actual rooms that were rented out were small and almost uninhabitable. Something was always broken or halfway fixed. If the sink wasn't shooting water across the room, the toilet wouldn't properly flush or the mailbox wouldn't open. Once, she had to reach inside for her mail before the box shut itself on her wrist.

She always thought her room was like a child's version of the future. First, it was only big enough to hold a sideways Murphy bed. Everything else was latched to the walls around it. A dropdown table was across from the bed. Behind the table was a black square where she could project movies she had on her laptop. Above that was a digital clock displaying the time in military hours.

The carpet on the floor was dark gray and skimpy. It seemed more like an afterthought than a real carpet. Luckily, the bald parts were hidden by cheap rugs she purchased in Koreatown. The walls were painted a soft gray with dot matrix prints of homework assignments and other things she printed out with her old printer. To the right, facing out over the street, several stories down, was a huge window. She managed to get this room cheap because the lights from across the street shone inside and tinted her room a bright reddish orange when she turned everything off.

She watched Pepper walk over to the small kitchen (a tiny sink, a smaller fridge, and a water hose dispenser) and pull out two small bowls from the transparent cabinet above it. The bright white light shone in their faces as Jai flipped it on, took the bowls, and grabbed some chopsticks.

"My dinner, not yours. You need to go." Jai didn't like being stern with Pepper, but this was her only meal of the day. She was going to eat it all, check her messages, and head to bed.

"But, I need help with my assignment," Pepper whined, trying to stick her finger into the bowl where Jai poured the delicious smelling cuisine.

"How are you paying for school, Pepper?" Jai asked, scooping up a large amount of noodles and scarfing them down while Pepper watched.

"My mom—"

"See, I work a million jobs. I'm paying out of pocket. That means no meal plan. I'm sure you can afford one, so leave." Jai pointed to the door.

"I'll let you eat, but I'm coming back." Pepper walked backwards toward the door, her ocular implants turning red as she did.

"Your red eyes mean nothing to me." Jai walked over, closed, and locked the door behind Pepper. She paused, then ran a heavy metal bar across the door that she used for extra protection.

She pulled down the Murphy bed and sat on it, cradling the bowl. After managing to kick off her shoes, and finishing off half the meal, she checked her Delphius phone for messages. She projected the typed-out messages on the silver speckled ceiling panels above her bed.

"Jai, this is Mom. I may have sent you something by mistake. Call me when you get it. I don't know what I was thinking, but send it back, okay? I'll pay you for the postage or delivery."

She closed her eyes and scrolled to the next message.

"Jai, hi, Mom again. Listen, I hope you got that package. I can't find it here and I really need it back. It's a family heirloom. Just… just send it back after you get it. Okay? Love you."

Jai rolled off the bed and walked over to the mailbox next to the door. She pressed her finger against the screen and a door slid up. Inside the mailbox were some letters (probably bills) and a small box. The box was addressed to her, from her mother.

"Why would she address it to me if it was a mistake?" Jai pulled it out to examine.

It was small; only big enough to fit in her hand. It was wrapped in brown paper with her name printed on it in her mother's flowy script. It almost looked fake, considering all the twentieth-century stickers her mom had covered the box with. She often chided her mother to use her money more wisely.

"Maybe I'm reliving part of my past that I never lived before," she'd say to Jai whenever she purchased something Jai considered useless.

Around the box was a piece of twine that Jai promptly cut with a knife she pulled from the side pocket of her gray leggings. She stuck the knife into the huge pocket of her sweatshirt with the picture of a cartoon character getting its brains blown out.

"Huh."

When she opened the box, she saw a small doll inside it. A small, strange-looking doll that smelled of dried rosebuds and jasmine. It wore some kind of flowered dress and had its arms tied around itself. It looked like someone literally wrapped the doll with string and put something over its eyes. Yet, the one weird thing about the doll was that the hair was clearly human. It was a dark reddish color with a red bow. It looked like a miniature braid.

"What in the name of—" Jai lifted the doll from the box and examined it more in the light. The more she flipped it around in her hands, the more the room filled with the smell of dried flowers and something she didn't know.

"Why would mom send this to me? I haven't had a doll in a long time," Jai mumbled as she pulled the knife from her pocket and started to cut the string off the doll.

"I'll fix you all up. This looks like some crazy stuff from the twentieth century or something." She cut off part of the thread, and the smell of honeysuckle strongly filled the room.

Her Delphius vibrated on her wrist. It was Pepper calling again.

"What, Pepper?" Jai tossed the doll onto the bed and picked up her bowl to finish eating.

"Okay, I won't bother you anymore. Just tell me when it's due."

"Do you even bother taking notes in class, or just rely on me because I'm not on scholarship? I'm just your poor stupid friend that needs to pay attention," Jai said between slurps.

"Well, at first, okay, I thought it was a partner project, but I *did* find my notes and saw that it wasn't. *Then* I thought that it was something else, but it wasn't. I thought it was for our psychology class, but, okay, I remembered that we don't take psych together anymore." Pepper's voice kept going and going, like something on a treadmill.

"The class that we are in together, right?"

"Uh, yeah, okay." Pepper sounded unsure.

"The class that has the paper due in a week or so," Jai said.

"Did you do it yet?"

"The class of 'The History of Africa in the Americas: A Study of the Influence of Africa on Native Southern Cultures?' Yeah, I did it. Why?"

"Can I just see it? Your paper?" Pepper asked, whispering the words into the Delphius on her wrist. "Just to get an idea."

Jai disconnected the call.

"She got some nerve, right? Tryin' ta copy ya work."

"I know! She always does that!" Jai looked around for the voice she heard whisper in her ear. "Who am I talking to?"

She laughed to herself and picked up the doll. She set it on the clear shelf above the sink, next to the photograph of her mother and a Snoopy-like toy that she carried with her as a child.

It was time to take her shower and wash off the day, only to do it all over again tomorrow. She flipped a switch on her Delphius, blocking the one window in her apartment with a room-darkening screen. She stripped out of her clothes and headed for the small shower stall across from the mailbox in her room. The smell of flowers seemed to linger wherever she went; she figured it was something from her mom's box.

Before showering, Jai picked up the empty box and tossed it into the trash chute, where it slid down to the lower levels to be destroyed.

Despite taking the hottest shower she could, the small stall was filled with ice cold air and the same smell of flowers. Jai kept adjusting the water settings until she checked the temperature and saw that it was over 100 degrees Fahrenheit. Yet, the water hit her skin like ice cold pellets until she couldn't stand it anymore. She turned off the water off switched on the in-shower dryer. It blew fiery hot air, drying her body almost instantly.

She stepped out of the shower stall and into the goshitel. Something felt off as she heard the phone ringing again.

"Who's calling?" She asked.

"Your mother is calling for you again, Jai." Suzy, her AI assistant answered. "Shall I put her on speaker or—"

"Speaker."

"Jai? Jai, it's Mom. Listen, I may have sent you something..." Her mother's high-pitched voice filled the room. It seemed like her mother never got used to talking on speakerphones and needed to speak twice as loud with the old models. She carried the same behaviors over to the newer models.

"Um, yeah, I got it, Ma. What's up?"

"I shouldn't have sent that to you. I'm on my way to get it. Please don't do anything to it. It's an old family heirloom. I was sending you something different but then the dog jumped up and the AI maid grabbed the wrong package and I started screaming..." Jai's mother spoke more stream of consciousness and less common sense. If Jai didn't stop her, she'd go all night.

"When are you gonna get here, Ma?"

"Tomorrow, honey, maybe sooner, if I can get a ticket on that new fast train from the countryside? Deltatrans? I hear those things go up to 300 miles an hour and I would get there in about twenty minutes or so. I mean, where would we be without... you know, this reminds me of when I was younger..."

"Mom, as the kids say, 'dock the boat at the pier.' You don't have to explain. I'll see you tomorrow. Just call me and I can meet you somewhere."

Jai walked over to the strange-looking doll and picked it up. She twirled it around in her hand, examining it, when there was a knock at the door. "Ma, I gotta go. There's someone here."

"...because in your great grandmother's time, there was a regular train, didn't go as fast, and she would say that they slept on the train. Can you believe it? *Sleeping* on the train, like a going on a trip and waking up on the train? I would tell my mother that I didn't believe it because..."

"Bye, Ma." Jai smiled and added, "Disconnect."

The knocking at the door was urgent and the area around the door was chilled. The pale blue tiles on the floor were practically icy. Jai exhaled and saw her breath before she looked through the peephole.

Pepper stood outside the door, but she didn't look like Pepper. She looked more like the doll that Jai pulled from the package. And if that wasn't strange enough, Pepper was chewing gum, popping it, and knocking on the door.

"Hurry up an' open this do'!" Pepper didn't sound like herself.

"Open it up so I can jump in her body." Jai heard a voice whisper behind her.

"I'm busy. Let me see you tomorrow, okay?" Jai stared through the peephole, watching Pepper place her hand on her hip in a hugely exaggerated motion.

"I'm gonna kick this do' in if'n you don't open it!" Pepper pressed her eye against the peephole, trying to look at Jai. "Don't think I cain't see ya in there, I sees ya front an' back!"

What the hell is this? It's like her train has left the station! This is not how Pepper talks to me.

"I'll see you tomorrow. I'm heading to bed."

Pepper stood for a few moments outside the door before her head snapped back, then rolled forward. She lay her hand flat on the door and pushed herself away. She shook her head again and looked around her, like she didn't know where she was. Then, she turned and walked away from the door.

Jai felt a chill run over her body as something moved through the door and to the other side of the room. She grabbed her school bag and pulled out some papers to study.

Jai awoke to the sound of Pepper banging at her door. She checked her wrist; her Delphius had been going off for twenty minutes and she hadn't heard it.

"Pepper, I'm coming!" She yelled as she whipped her legs around and out the bed.

"Hurry up! We're gonna have to use hover skates to get to class on time." She heard Pepper flop against the door, "I can't believe I waited for you. At least put on a pot for some mochaccinos."

"We can grab some on the way." Jai opened the door while she literally jumped into her jeans.

"Toothbrush in the mouth is a nice look." Pepper barged in and grabbed papers off her bed, shoving them into Jai's brown messenger bag.

"Skates are in the closet. Yours are too; you left them the last time you slept over." Jai rushed into the bathroom and rinsed her mouth out.

Oversleeping was a new experience for her, so she scrambled to get dressed as quickly as possible. Pepper handed her the roller blades as she hurriedly put them on, while Jai tied her shoelaces together and tossed her shoes over her shoulder before joining Pepper in their speedy journey down the hallway, hunched over to maintain balance.

Amidst the hustle and bustle of people on the streets, Jai couldn't shake off the image of the red-haired girl from earlier, constantly turning and reaching out for her. She stumbled a few times, feeling like the girl was somehow pulling her closer.

"Thanks for lettin' me out," the girl whispered in her ear.

"What? Who are you?" Jai stumbled, trying to move around what she thought was a hologram, and fell to the ground.

"Junior's mah name." The girl smiled.

Pepper turned and gaped at Jai on the ground, "You coming? We are already late!"

"I ran into a holo ad. Did you grab some holo blockers before we left?" Jai felt behind her ear only to feel the holoblocker in place.

How was she seeing this girl with the holoblocker on?

She pulled herself together and skated up to Pepper. "These might be defective. I keep seeing—"

"Save it! We still have to get to class!" Pepper grabbed Jai's arm and pulled her along, zipping through the crowd on campus to reach their destination.

The professor stood in front of the class, scribbling notes on the airscreen and discussing the significant impact that African culture had on American society during the era of slavery.

As the professor dimmed the lights, he explained, "The only thing the Africans could bring with them was their culture."

Jai and Pepper sat in the upper rows of the stadium-like seating, squinting at the presentation on the airscreen.

"Just pull up the mini screen in front of you." Pepper tapped Jai's desk and a small version of the screen popped up.

"I forgot." Jai scratched behind her ear. "This stupid holoblocker has just got me all—"

"Ssht!" Pepper held a finger to her mouth.

They both watched the onscreen presentation as the professor droned on about hoodoo traditions in the American South.

"The slaves had a strong belief that with the help of natural ingredients, they could defend themselves against anyone or anything. This powerful knowledge gave them hope and strength to stand up against their masters' abuse and even manipulate feelings of love in others. Typically, this miraculous feat was performed by a single expert in the village, a conjurer; someone who had mastered the art of conjure."

Jai watched the video on the screen and whispered, "What a shit time to be alive."

"I c'n tell you thas right. I don' even lak the way this man talk," a voice next to Jai spoke.

When she glanced to her right, she saw Pepper.

To her left was an empty aisle.

"I don't understand." Jai whispered.

"Well, I *can* let you borrow my notes but *you* gotta pay attention, okay?" Pepper said, snapping her gum.

Jai waved her hand in front of her. "No, I understand what he's saying—"

"You jus' don't know where I am," the voice whispered again.

"Right."

"Is there anything you'd like to contribute to the class, up there? Miss?" The professor turned the lights on, raised his hand and pointed toward Jai.

Her cheeks flushed bright red as she put her head down. "I'm sorry, I...I..."

"Yew may wanna be careful wit whatcha say." The voice whispered again.

"Junior?" Jai whispered.

Junior laughed and floated toward the front of the room. Jai couldn't help but watch as she stood behind the teacher, playfully mimicking his every move. He dimmed the lights and continued speaking, while Junior danced around behind him. Jai's heart raced as she bit her lip nervously and felt sweat forming on the back of her neck. Sweet scents of jasmine and honeysuckle filled the air as she watched Junior glide through the classroom.

"Pep, can you... ah... turn on the sensors on your watch? I'm trying to see something?" Jai stuttered as she blindly reached for Pepper.

"Sure, am I looking for something?" Pepper scrutinized Jai, her eyebrows furrowed.

"Just turn it on, would you?"

Junior swept down next to Jai and whispered, "I don't know what that is, but it ain't gonna catch me."

Now, Junior seemed to be *teasing* Jai. The way Junior drifted around the room while no one noticed; even when she pretended to stab the professor and hung next to him like her neck was broken.

The bell rang, dismissing the class. Jai kicked off her shoes and put on the skates. She ran out the classroom, leaving most of her things behind while she yelled for Pepper to grab her stuff for her.

"Where are you going?" Pepper yelled.

"I'll meet up with you later!" Jai glanced at the message blaring on the Delphius watch and saw her mother was waiting in front of her goshitel.

Junior did everything to keep Jai from reaching the goshitel. Fake trees fell in her path, Jai felt Junior swiping at her neck, trying to remove the holoblocker. Something pulled at one of her skates, tripping her up.

Jai stopped and stood in the middle of the busy sidewalk, surrounded by bustling crowds of students. Her favorite food stand was just a few steps away, the vendor manning the cart, cooking up delicious noodles with a variety of toppings. The neon lights of the city buildings illuminated the area, casting a fluorescent glow on Jai's face.

"What do you want? Really? What is it?" Jai yelled.

"I don' wanna go back in that dollbaby," Junior said.

To those nearby, it appeared that Jai was talking to herself. Only she could see Junior's mischievous presence as she knocked over objects and playfully swiped at unsuspecting individuals. The onlookers were baffled by her behavior, unaware of the invisible companion causing chaos around them.

A message blared over her Delphius messenger, "Hurry, please. Love, Mom."

"I have to go, Junior. You still haven't given me a reason for wanting to stay here." Jai glided over to Garcia's and requested two lunch specials. Mrs. Garcia-Deng carefully bagged the food, a friendly smile on her face as she handed them to Jai. But then, her gaze shifted past Jai's shoulder and landed on Junior. A sudden chill filled Mrs. Garcia-Deng's eyes as they darted back to Jai.

"*Espiritu!*" She pointed at Junior and screamed.

Mr. Garcia bolted toward the front bar, his body trembling as he grabbed his wife's shoulders and spoke frantically in a hushed tone, pleading for her to calm down. But Mrs. Deng's rage grew, her eyes ablaze as she ripped off her necklace and shoved it into Jai's hand.

"Protect." Her voice was strained, shaking with unbridled anger as she pushed against Mr. Garcia, the force propelling them backwards into the kitchen. She pointed an accusing finger at Junior. "*Mal espiritu*!"

"Ah used ta go ta church. What she mean 'protect.' Ain't nothin' gonna stop me." Junior ran toward the counter and reached over it.

Mrs. Deng screamed and swatted at Junior.

Speechless, Jai watched the interaction before apologizing to Mrs. Deng and racing away from the stand. Junior raced behind her.

"You're making life hard for me, you know." Breathless and skating, Jai tried to understand what was going on. "How could she see you and nobody else can?"

"She got some religion. She done put that cross in ya hand. Blessed by somebody important. I was baptized in the same place as ya kin, Pee Wee."

Ignoring Junior, Jai skated on. Her holoblocker did its job of blocking out the ads and holograms, except it didn't block out Junior. When she saw her mother sitting on the stoop in front of her building, she sighed.

Junior stopped. She stopped talking. She stopped moving. She stopped everything and stared at Jai's mother. She floated in the air as Jai skated over to Mom.

"Got here as soon as I could. I brought lunch," Jai said to her mother.

"So, ah guess we's meeting uh-gin, Junior." Jai's mother pushed Jai aside and stepped forward.

"Not you! No!"

"And ah still got what's yours. See I always likes to keep a little ah you wit' me, no matter where I am or where I go."

Jai's heart raced as she watched her mother approach, a shadow of her former self. Gone was the vibrant woman who stood tall and confident. In her place was a hunched figure with graying hair and a voice like treacle, moving slowly forward with something clenched tightly in her hands. Jai could see Junior's eyes widen in fear as her mother closed in, each step slow and purposeful. The air seemed to thicken with tension as the two faced each other, the weight of their past traumas hanging heavily between them.

"Don' try an' run, now. See, I gots this las' piece a yo hair an' I'm gonna getcha girl. Gonna bind you ag'in. Bind you from doin' harm to nobody, bind you from yo'self. Hell, I should bind you from ever escapin' this doll again." Jai's mom's laughter turned into a sadistic cackle, her shoulders hunching up to her ears. She stared hard at Junior, as though she stared through her while she made furious wrapping motions with the object in her hands, her fingers working faster and tighter as if possessed by some dark force.

Jai watched Junior drop to her knees, begging to be released. "Pee Wee, remember when we—"

"Shut up! When you gone, you s'posed ta stay gone. Not come back! I bound you once and I'm bindin' you fo the last damned time!" Jai's mother stopped and stood over Junior on the ground.

"Please!" Junior begged.

"Don't evah come back and don't evah let them wake me from mah sleep agin! You unda stand me, chile?" Jai's mom knelt and touched Junior before Junior disappeared.

"What the hell?"

Jai's eyes darted around, searching for any sign of attention from the bustling crowd. But it was as though she, her mother, and Junior were invisible, completely unnoticed despite being in plain sight: the people flowed past them without a second glance, as if they were a mere mirage or figment of imagination. People avoided getting too close to them, casting wary glances, and giving their corner of the street a wide berth, like a sun flare that could scorch anyone who got too close. It was a lonely feeling, standing on the fringes of society like an outcast.

"Jai, come help me up." Her mother stretched out an arm.

Jai ran over and helped her to stand.

"What just happened? What was all that?"

"There are things... things about our family you need to know."

"Like what?"

"Like how your great grandmother, they called her Pee Wee, was a real powerful conjure woman. Casting spells and such."

"She was a witch?"

"Not exactly..."

A smile crept across her mother's face. As Jai watched, her mother's transformation began. The once graying hair now shone with a deep, rich black hue, falling in a thick and luscious bob just above her shoulders. Her skin, once slightly dry and weathered, now glimmered with a youthful sheen, appearing softer and suppler than ever before. The years seemed to melt away, leaving behind a rejuvenated version of her beloved mother.

"Let's get inside. I'll tell you what happened."

Jai led her mother inside the goshitel and to her room. All the while her mother talked about how much she truly hated coming to the city, let alone this goshitel. She even invited Jai home to live with her.

"So, Ma comes in and she said that she used some old hoodoo spell her sister gave her to channel some relative that bound up Junior in the first place." Jai sat cross legged on the floor, reaching over with her chopsticks, grabbing some rabbit-flavored tofu from Pepper's container.

"Your brain is out of the station, girl. There is no way someone can take over another body! No way!" Pepper playfully swatted at Jai's chopsticks.

"But she did *and* she showed me. Anyway, I didn't think you'd believe me but there was definitely a ghost in here and I released it. I can't believe I was that stupid. But not anymore. No ghosts for me, thanks."

"So, like, did your mom take all the ghost stuff back? I mean how do you *know* you don't have any ghost stuff here?" Pepper asked as Jai picked up their containers to take them to the recycling.

"She promised!" Jai shouted over her shoulder.

Something beneath the bed caught Pepper's eye. She leaned over and reached for it. She pulled it forward and made a small sound, like a squeal, then swallowed it back down.

"Hey, what's this?"

Jai walked over and joined her on the floor again.

In Pepper's hand was a withered hand with three fingers. The ring finger and the pinky were gone, and black thread was sewn over the spots where they should have been.

"It was under your bed. I thought it was something fake from Halloween last year, when you went out like a dead man or something from our classes on the twentieth." Pepper dropped it to the floor. "Either way, looks gross."

"I don't remember wearing anything that looked like that." Jai picked it up and examined it carefully. "Maybe Mom left it or something. Well, I wish I knew what it was, but I gotta study. Did you get the notes from the Probability & Statistics class?"

Pepper's mouth opened and closed as she stared at the hand. She pointed and motioned for Jai to look at it until Jai said, "Oh, I know what this is now."

One of the fingers on the hand closed as the phone rang.

"Honey, it's Mom. I think something fell out of my purse at your place. Don't use it! I'm on my way tomorrow to pick it up!"

Captured

Jaclyn M. Ciminelli

She remembered their first date. He owned the secluded beach behind the Temple of Neptune. Here they had shared a small picnic before dancing in the moonlight.

"What are you... into?" she whispered.

He shrugged and softly smiled. He'd had many lovers over the centuries and didn't wish to intimidate her.

"What about you?" he asked, combing her long dark hair behind her ear. "How may I seduce you?"

He was indescribably beautiful.

"Dancing under this beautiful full moon is definitely a good start."

He drew her closer.

"I believe in treating my lovers with respect. If anything I do makes you uncomfortable, tell me."

"Same with you." she smiled and kissed him, slowly and gently, sliding her hands down his lower back to caress the taut curve of his ass before brushing her fingers over his hips, downward, feeling the fabric tight and straining over his growing bulge.

Lucius returned her kiss, sliding his tongue into her mouth. It was ecstasy. She explored his mouth hungrily, yearning for his touch. He smiled against her wanting mouth, expertly removing her neon pink panties from beneath her short black dress. The cool ocean air was delightful against her heated skin.

He nibbled along her throat, sucking deeply.

"Is this okay?" he asked.

"Gods, yes," she whined. "More."

She cried out when his fangs lightly penetrated her skin, his tongue savoring the quick taste of her blood.

"Barely a scratch, my love," he whispered, kissing her again as his hand cupped her shaved labia. She ached for him, unbuttoning his pants with vigor. One soft fingertip found her swollen clit and she hissed in breath, yanking down his pants and exposing him to the moonlight.

"Lie down," she panted, nibbling his earlobe, tasting the metallic flavor of his small sword-shaped earring.

Lucius removed his shirt as he lay on the blanket. His body sank into the swells of sand still warm from the sun's rays. He was glorious. She knelt and began massaging his erection. His eyes closed.

Soon, his hands were clenching handfuls of blanket and sand as she licked and sucked his balls before running her tongue along his shaft. She twisted her tongue around the tip before gently taking him into her mouth.

"Oh, oh, Andromeda."

When he climaxed, she climbed on top of him, pressing him inside of her body. She began to push, moaning his name like a mantra, loving the feel of him between her legs and inside her.

Lucius caressed her thighs and breasts. His moans and cries began mixing with her own until she could bear it no longer and released upon his undulating pelvis.

Gently, he lifted her and cradled her in the crook of his arm, their bodies bathed in the light of a million stars.

Andromeda Marcello paused at the entrance of Eros Boutique, absently fingering the amethyst crystal that hung from a silver pentacle between her breasts, lost in her memory. Her sundress was black velvet, and she wore a corset bodice. A striking strip of neon pink accented her otherwise black hair, which hung in long tresses.

These seven days of anxiety had left her muscles stiff and weary. She longed for her husband.

Perhaps I should've chosen a larger amethyst. Great Mother Goddess be with me.

The door opened with a chime. "Vampyre Erotica" by Inkubus Sukkubus played through speakers mounted near the ceiling. Walls and tables were crowded with a variety of sex toys, films, and lingerie. A young woman was ringing up items at a register in the center of the dark room while an eager couple looked on, giggling conspiratorially.

A marble statue of a Greek God, Eros himself, lounged across a black velvet Victorian-style chaise lounge.

A neon pink vibrator brought her from her ruminations and she smiled, lifting the package from its hook. There was something deliciously ironic about a forty-four-year-old Goth woman who loved pink. Even in the nude, it would match her attire.

"You'll kiss me, then miss me.

I'll laugh at your torment."

Andromeda blinked slowly at the lyrics, taking in a deliberate breath. The song brought an image of Lucius to the forefront of her mind once more; her ancient Roman vampire, her best friend and lover. Gods, how she missed him. The Temple of Neptune, nestled among the brightly-colored houses of Carolina Beach, had felt so empty without the High Priest.

She was overcome with longing for her husband. They had met four years prior on the Carolina Boardwalk when she and a friend took a mini-vacation after selling their homemade soaps, metaphysical wares, and spell kits at state fairs, festivals, and farmer's markets across the country. Lucius had been browsing the traveling shops at the North Carolina State Fair. She could visualize him clearly; he stood five feet tall with an average frame and striking features. Long black hair reached his waist. His preferred clothing was anything black. She could almost smell his otherworldly, aphrodisiacal scent.

She held back tears, glancing around the store. The chime sounded again as the door opened to allow the couple to depart with their newfound treasures. The man held the door ajar, speaking jovially in words she couldn't make out. An older man in a well-tailored suit slid past him and entered the store.

He was tall, in his mid-fifties, and looking terribly out-of-place in his pristine garb. His suspicious eyes swept across the shop, locked with Andromeda's for a moment, then away. She felt a shiver and busied herself with a large display stand. It held a random collection of oils, rose quartz crystals, statues of Aphrodite and Eros, red and pink candles in the forms of male and female reproductive organs, and other items utilized for sex magick. She sighed. It was useless, novelty stuff. She couldn't use any of it for the ritual they would conduct tonight. It was the off-season, however, and all the occult shops had closed hours earlier.

The gentleman approached the cashier, placing two magazines on the counter.

"Hey Iris," he spoke softly. "Any news?"

The girl smiled weakly. "Nothing good," she drawled. "There was another murder this afternoon, down by the pier."

Andromeda stepped behind a high shelf of adult films, moving closer.

Don't let it be Lucius, please, Goddess, don't let it be him, she thought, a sick feeling churning in her stomach.

"It's only been a week since the last one." The man shook his head morosely. "It's not right, being afraid to leave my own house at night. They don't have any leads?"

"Nothing Mom has shared with me," Iris sighed.

"Just – not right," the man mumbled. "I trust you have a police escort walking you to your car?"

"Nah, Enzo's here. He's in the back, working on the website." When the man didn't respond, she chuckled lightly. "Don't worry about me, Rick. I'll be alright."

He cleared his throat and they completed the transaction in silence. When the door chimed again, Andromeda stepped out from behind the shelf.

"Take care, Iris," the man called.

"Will do!" she replied to his departing back, hand raised.

Andromeda approached the checkout counter.

"Find everything alright?" Iris smiled. She was blonde, her nose speckled with the freckles of too much sunlight. Her shirt and matching shorts were tie-dyed.

No, but I hope to Gods Veronica did.

"Yes, thank you," Andromeda placed the vibrator on the counter. "I apologize for eavesdropping, but there's been another murder?"

"Yeah," Iris frowned. "Are you a tourist?"

"No, not technically. We moved here a few weeks ago from Ohio."

"Hell of a welcome party, huh? Welcome to North Carolina, home of the Boardwalk Killer," she scoffed.

"Yeah, it's been a bit of a shock," Andromeda admitted. She watched Iris slide her purchase into an anonymous paper bag, no doubt to preserve the privacy of their clientele. "It sounds like the town is looking out for each other, though," Andromeda gestured toward the door.

"Oh, Rick? Yeah, I mean, my mom is a detective, so he's been coming in to press me for *the scoop,* I guess," she chuckled. "I don't know anything, though. I mean, it's not like she can discuss an open case or anything." Iris shrugged. "But, it's a small town. People talk. They expect me to do the same." She continued, "But I'm fine; Enzo's husband offered to teach Karate and self-defense to me and the other girls that work here. Besides, I have my best friend, Smith & Wesson, right here under the counter!"

Andromeda nodded. "I'm sorry to press the issue, but do you happen to know anything at all about the victim?" she asked, taking her bag from the young woman's outstretched hand.

Iris smiled sadly. "No, the police haven't released anything about his identity yet. They think it's the same guy though, the same serial killer who started offing people here like ten years ago." She paused. "Maybe it's time I got out of this place. Where did you say you were from?"

Him? Is he even acting alone?

Andromeda waved a hand. "Oh, I've been all over the country. We're rather nomadic."

"I've always wanted to travel," Iris continued, looking into the distance. "Just to be the tourist for a change, you know?" She met Andromeda's eyes and laughed lightly. "I mean, I love it here. But, honestly, working in the only smut shop in a one-smut-shop town is about as risqué as it gets around here. I could tell you some wild stories!"

"It's always worthwhile to see the world," Andromeda agreed. She glanced at her phone. "Does your shift end soon? I can walk you to your car."

"Oh, no, I'm closing tonight," she paused. "Thank you, though. That's really nice of you to offer."

"Not at all. Apparently, we townies have to stick together," Andromeda offered a knowing smile. "I heard the gentleman say that your name is Iris. I'm Andromeda."

"Nice to meet you," Iris said. "I'm sure we'll run into each other. Small town and all." She handed the receipt to Andromeda who accepted it and slid it and her debit card into her purse.

"Take care, Iris." She walked toward the door and called back, "Be safe!"

"You as well," Iris agreed as the door chimed.

Andromeda said a silent prayer to the Gods for her protection as she exited the shop and headed for her car.

She drove with her windows down, breathing the salty air and trying to clear her mind. The beach was nearly empty. The restaurants, hotels, and beach houses had ocean-themed names and were painted in vibrant colors like the residential homes. Large aloe plants and palm trees grew plentifully amongst the buildings.

Tori Amos sang on the radio.

Her phone rang from the cup holder. Unknown number. She grabbed it, punching it to life as she skidded to a stop.

"Hello? Hello?" she asked frantically.

"Hello, Andromeda."

"Where the fuck is he? Let me speak with him."

"It's as though you've forgotten who has the upper hand here."

"Fuck you! Let me talk to Lucius."

"You can't. I staked him, right through the heart. His body is paralyzed. He can't move or speak until it's removed."

She gritted her teeth. Losing her cool was not helpful, but negotiating with this punk was the last thing she wanted to do.

"Who are you?" she asked.

There was silence for a beat.

"Listen to me carefully, bitch. You have something that belongs to me, a photo you did not have permission to take."

"What? What photo?"

"On the pier. Bring the camera and the photo. Once they are destroyed, I will release your husband."

"What are you talking about?" she yelled into the receiver. The knuckles of her left hand were white on the steering wheel. "I've met thousands of people. I've taken a million photos. Could you stop being so goddamn vague and fucking *elaborate,* you sadistic asshole?"

There was a faint chuckle on the other end of the line.

"'Sadistic', says the bitch married to a monster."

"Fuck you; he's perfect."

"You have until midnight, Andromeda," he stated and ended the call.

She sat in her car, watching dark waves caress the sand until her heart rate returned to normal. He *was* alive, but barely. They would find him. They had to find him.

Andromeda approached the bright turquoise building that housed the Temple of Neptune. She passed the ten-foot statue of its namesake, a trident-wielding merman, and entered the ritual room. Their modest living quarters stood at the end of a brightly lit hallway. The house and temple's décor carried an oceanic theme with wicker furniture, seashells, and an array of statues. Music from a passing car pumped Lady Gaga through the open windows and with that, memories of dancing beneath the stars. She breathed deeply.

She tried getting rid of the image of her beloved lying somewhere unable to move. In high school, it was chilling to learn how alleged scientists in the 1800s discovered that wooden stakes didn't kill *subhuman* vampires; they only locked them into a state of suspended animation. She shivered at the thought of all those premature burials prior to discovery.

Quit thinking about that. He may be fucking with me, and Lucius may not actually be staked. He's going to be okay. Everything will be okay.

Her hand touched the amethyst stone around her neck. Instantly she felt its healing and relaxing energy.

We'll find him.

A tall, dark-haired woman dressed in black shorts and a *Phantom of the Opera* T-shirt approached with empathetic eyes, placing a hand on Andromeda's shoulder.

Andromeda turned toward her friend, "Have you found anything?"

"I was able to get obsidian, amethyst, black tourmaline, and also some clear quartz to help amplify the spell."

Andromeda nodded, a sob rising in her chest. "I hate that we can't just go to the police."

They embraced. Veronica spoke near her ear, "We'll find the asshole, curse his ass, and then let the cops finish him off." Andromeda nodded tightly. Veronica pulled away, holding her friend's arms and looking into her face. "How did it go at the store? Did she know anything?"

"Nothing much. She mentioned that the cops think it's a serial, one from a decade ago." She swallowed. "He called again. On my way home."

Veronica placed her bag on a small table next to the main altar. Her jaw was set with determination. While she removed the candles and other supplies, she said, "Start casting wards at the entrance. After the ritual, tell me everything."

Andromeda agreed and opened a large wooden chest, withdrawing an abalone shell, a stick of sage mixed with dragon's blood resin, and an owl feather. Veronica gathered a silver chalice filled with seawater.

Andromeda flicked a lighter to life and walked toward the door, running smoke along the entrance as she chanted words of protection. After creating a shield to deflect negativity, she retrieved a broom and intently swept the space in an effort to cleanse and prepare the energy. Finally, she cast a circle with the saltwater.

An equal-armed cross, the length of the room, was etched into the black and turquoise marble floor. Four tall, thick candles – one for each terrestrial element – sat atop four marble pillars. She ignited one by one.

Vines wrapped around the northern pillar whose surface bore the images of red wolves, corn snakes, cottonmouths, and cougars. Sandpipers, seagulls, monarch butterflies, black swallowtails, and winged horses were etched in the marble on the eastern pillar. Dragons and fire ants decorated the red-orange southern candle's pillar.

The western pillar faced the ocean and was decorated with a garland of scallop shells. Seahorses, mermaids, and other oceanic creatures were etched into the surface.

The broom was stowed and replaced with an athamé. Andromeda walked the circle, pointing the ceremonial blade towards the sky while casting a circle around the main altar.

Veronica lit an orange candle for courage and strength. She brought out two black goblets, each depicting bright purple grapes framing a picture of Bacchus. Next, she extracted a small bottle of red wine, pouring a splash into each goblet. She withdrew a small package of wheat crackers. Normally, the bread would be freshly baked, but desperate times called for desperate measures. She laid two crackers on an antique saucer.

The two women began the ritual of protection side-by-side, first cleansing each other by sage and feather, then calling the quarters. They focused on the desired intent.

Andromeda declared, "We seek Hecate, Sekhmet, and Hera to protect Lucius and the town of Carolina Beach. We hereby ask Artemis, Diana, and other Gods and Goddesses of the Wild Hunt, to guide the police in capturing the person responsible for the killings throughout the beach towns. So Mote it Be."

"So Mote it Be," echoed Veronica. They closed their eyes and Andromeda led a meditation. Together, they visualized a white light covering Wilmington, Kure Beaches, and Fort Fisher. Next, they pictured Lucius engulfed in the protective light, safe, very much alive, and the police capturing the perpetrator.

Andromeda held the tip of the athamé over the crackers and wine, whispering a blessing. They each took a sip and bit into a cracker before pouring the remnants on the offering table.

They opened the circle, thanking the deities and elements for assisting.

Hand-in-hand, they silently departed the ritual room and entered Andromeda's study. Boxes still lined one wall. They hadn't had the time to unpack, and then, after Lucius' disappearance, they'd lacked the motivation.

"What exactly did he say?" Veronica asked.

Andromeda closed her eyes, willing the conversation to return.

"I should have written it down," she whispered. "I was just… so *furious*."

"It's alright, it's alright. It's only been an hour. Focus."

"He was just so fucking *vague,* there was nothing *to* remember!" She felt her rage returning, her nails digging into her palms.

"Try," Veronica insisted.

"He said something about a photo… a photo that I didn't have permission to take. He said he'd set Lucius free once the photo was destroyed, and that we have until midnight to find it."

"A photo?" Veronica wrinkled her nose. "Like, on your phone?"

"I don't know!" Andromeda threw up her hands with exasperation. "I told him that I have a *million* photos. How the hell am I supposed to know which *one* I didn't have 'permission to take'?"

Veronica frowned in thought.

"A photo. Well, it can't be anything on the shop's page. Those are public; anybody could see them. I mean, you can't destroy anything once it's been on the Internet."

Andromeda pulled out her phone and began flipping through her photo gallery. "Even most phones automatically back up to like a Google drive now," Veronica ruminated. "How could we 'destroy' a photo?"

"He said he'd destroy the photo and my camera."

"Your camera?"

"Yeah, I guess he wants my phone too," she widened her eyes with exasperation.

"Wait," Veronica said, placing her fingertips on Andromeda's wrist.

"What?"

"Did he say what was *in* the photo?"

"Just 'the pier,'" Andromeda huffed. "That could be anything. We had the table set up there for days. I took hundreds of photos!"

"Andromeda," Veronica breathed. "What about your Polaroid?"

The color drained from her face. That little pink plastic Polaroid. Lucius had purchased it from one of the tourist shops, returning to their table with a grin on his face, the little gift bag dangling from his index finger. It had been last year's Carolina Pagan Fest.

"You and Lucius were snapping selfies all day. Where is that camera?"

Andromeda's eyes darted from side to side, searching the files of her memory.

"In one of the totes from the shop?" she asked without conviction, looking at Veronica with pleading eyes. "Oh, you're right, that must be it. Where the fuck is that camera?"

Her mind had been so distracted with grief and fury. When had she last seen it?

"I'll go through our totes from the shop to see if you threw it in there. Can you remember which purse you took that day? You start there."

They searched high and low, Andromeda's hopes sinking with each passing moment. This was it. Of course it was. How could she have forgotten—

"Found it!" Veronica called out triumphantly from another room. They nearly collided in their rush to reach each other.

"Oh, thank the Gods," Andromeda exhaled. They powered on the camera and began shuffling through the photos visible on its tiny screen. The resolution was dreadful.

"Where are the pictures, though?" Veronica asked.

"What do you mean?"

"Isn't that the appeal of these things? They print out a little photo right when you snap the picture."

"Oh, they can, but we were just goofing around. I didn't print—" Andromeda stopped, her memory fluttering to life. "Kitchen."

She walked briskly to the refrigerator. Beside the handle, just at her eye-level, a small photo hung from a magnet. In the picture, Lucius stood beside Andromeda, his arm around her waist. His other arm was extended, holding the Polaroid in an awkward attempt to capture a selfie.

She pulled the photo from the fridge, Veronica leaning over her shoulder as they scoured the image. The angle was askew, the couple taking up the lower half of the photo. Behind them was an expanse of lake with a wooden bridge that stretched across the water.

There, in the background, on the trail leading into the thick forest, stood a blond man, staring directly into the camera.

"Oh, that's fucking creepy," Veronica whispered. "I can't believe I never noticed that before. Is that him?"

"I have no idea," Andromeda spoke in a low voice. "I mean, it has to be, right? This is the only photo I actually printed out that day."

"He's leaving the woods," Veronica stated.

"It's so tiny, though. Who could even tell who that is?" Andromeda argued. "He kidnapped my fucking husband for *this?*"

"Do you recognize him?" Veronica asked.

"Not really. I mean, we saw hundreds of people that week."

"He must have come closer. He knew it was a camera, that there was a photo."

"What do you mean?"

"I mean, he sees the photo being taken here," Veronica said, pointing her finger at the distant blond figure in the photo. "But he must have approached us in order to make out the details. He might have even tried to swipe the camera."

The blood drained from Andromeda's face for the second time that evening.

"He was that close. We might have even spoken to that bastard."

"It's how he knew to take Lucius." Veronica paused. "He wants this camera because it has some kind of memory card in it. That's how we were able to view the photos. It stores them. I'm going to plug the camera into my laptop and see if we can get a better look at that photo. If I can get a digital copy, we could send it to the Aberdeen Police Department and explain everything."

Andromeda glanced nervously toward the window.

"We can't go to the police. Not yet. We agreed not to involve the police." An involuntary sob slipped over her lips as she whispered, "Lucius."

In minutes, Veronica had the image pulled up on her laptop and zoomed to the maximum the pixels would allow.

"Didn't you say that the chick at the Eros store is the daughter of the detective working on the Boardwalk Murders case?" Veronica asked.

"Yes, that's what she said."

Veronica nodded as her fingers clicked across the laptop keyboard. "That Eros store is still open. And they have a website."

Andromeda watched the parade of brightly-colored dildos scrolling rhythmically across Veronica's screen.

"What's your point?"

Veronica did not answer, but opened her email browser and attached the digital image, including the zoomed screenshots she'd taken. She flipped back to the Eros website and clicked the "Contact Us" link at the bottom of the webpage, copied the email address, and pasted it into her "To" field. In the subject line, she wrote, "ATTN: IRIS."

"No," Andromeda said. "We can't. She's going to go right to the police."

"Patience, my pet," Veronica smiled. She typed out a quick explanation in the body of the email, then clicked the drop-down beneath the "Send" button, and chose "Schedule."

"It's on a delay for a couple hours. If we—" she stopped, looked to Andromeda, and smiled reassuringly. "If we run into trouble, at least the chief's daughter will have these breadcrumbs. Deal?"

"What are we going to do in these couple hours?" Andromeda asked.

"We're going to take a little hike in the woods," Veronica smiled, closing her laptop.

On the shore of Lake Aberdeen, the waters black under the moonless sky, Veronica unfolded the tourist brochure she'd plucked from the Information kiosk on their walk in. She turned to a map of the park and held it open on her upturned palms. Andromeda removed her amethyst pendant and held it above the map, allowing it to swing like a pendulum above the simple sketch. The buzz of insects halted in respectful anticipation.

"There!" she cried, capturing the pendant in her shaking first to halt its movement.

They followed the wooden trail beside the lake. Where the spirits had indicated, they found an abandoned stone concession stand. It was padlocked, but they'd anticipated this obstacle and made swift work with wire cutters.

Lucius lay supine without breath or sound, his eyes wide and unseeing. There was, in fact, a wooden stake driven through his heart. Planting her feet on either side of her beloved's petrified frame, Andromeda wrapped her fingers around the stake and yanked savagely with all her might. She fell into Veronica's waiting arms as it tore free. Before their eyes, his body began to mend.

Andromeda's phone rang at midnight. Safely home with their High Priest returned, the three welcomed the embrace of their sacred space. They sat in the warm glow of candles burning atop marble pillars.

Andromeda touched her phone's screen to accept the call.

"I have the camera and the photo, asshole" she growled. "How do we do this?"

She listened, Veronica and Lucius touching her knees and each other's hands, closing their inner circle in a chain of their connected energies.

"Fine," she agreed, and disconnected the call.

The only sound was the lapping of the ocean as a blond man crossed a deserted boardwalk, collar raised to hide all but his forehead and searching eyes. In his right hand, deep in the pocket of his long wool coat, he held his pistol at the ready.

He glanced at his watch. 3:30 AM.

The waves lapped. All else was still.

Where the fuck is she?

He ran his left hand across his forehead. He'd begun to sweat. He was weary of this meddlesome bitch.

"What seems to be the problem, sir?" A woman's stern voice sliced through the silent night. He whirled, pulling the pistol from his pocket, but the teeth of her taser darts were faster, penetrating his clothing and biting into his flesh. He collapsed, writhing, his feet thumping against the wooden planks of the boardwalk that had infamously become his namesake.

The detective had him cuffed and his useless pistol bagged even before he'd stopped convulsing.

Lucius emerged from the shower and entered their bedroom, wrapped in a long, black towel. His lovely wife was cuffed to their bedframe.

"I love you, Lucius," she whispered, a tear sliding down her cheek as she watched him draw nearer. He smiled and lifted the paper bag from the bedside table, raising his eyebrows inquisitively as he slid out the pink vibrator.

"A homecoming gift?" he chuckled.

He knelt between her thighs and she felt the stroke of his tongue, heavy against her clit. He moved the vibrator in and out of her until she climaxed again and again.

He raised his body, admiring hers with his caresses. He tenderly sucked each nipple into his mouth, then rose to suckle her throat. As she climaxed a final time, he sank his fangs into her flesh.

Andromeda cried out in ecstasy.

Red Gifts

Daniel Adam Rosser

The crows tell me things. I can hear the sound of one tapping on my window even now; they know I'm here. As much as I keep the shades drawn and curl up into a bedroom corner, they continue to tap. For some reason they are unable to leave me alone. I'm aware that the events of the last couple of months are my fault, and as I sit here reflecting, I can't help but wonder why I, of all the billions living on this planet, was fated to experience this living nightmare.

I'm from a small midwestern town of about 2,500 people. It's more of an island, really, surrounded by a sea of corn. Just like every other little town, it has a small downtown neighborhood, schools, and a local cinema. There isn't much opportunity for anyone who chooses to settle here, save for farming corn.

I live with my parents and attend the local high school that lights up on Friday nights so that everyone in town can indulge in the local favorite pastime: football. My mother and father are both hardworking farm folk, and though always loving to their only son, they are for the most part regularly ambivalent to my presence. They're rarely interested in my day or what extracurricular activities I have going; that is, unless I forget some chore or errand, and only then do they spontaneously decide my whereabouts are important. I'm not sure if it's because they suspect I'm gay – which I am, having at this point failed to find the right time to come out – and they prefer to live in the serene bliss of denial, or if they are genuinely too self-involved to even care. Whatever the reason, rarely do my comings and goings garner any notice. I don't have many friends; not too many of my peers are eager to befriend the town's suspected homosexual. I spend the majority of my free time with homework and helping my father grow and harvest corn.

My nightmare began during an excursion onto the land surrounding our house. It was an autumn afternoon in late September and I, having no homework, made for the makeshift garden I had planted for my mother near the edge of one of our cornfields. I had installed a wire mesh fence around the garden to keep out wild rabbits and rodents.

As I was entering the enclosure, something small and struggling caught my eye. A small crow was entangled in the fence. As I approached him cautiously, he became still and silent. Our eyes were fixed on each other, and in some odd way I could sense his thoughts; he was trying to judge whether I was friend or foe.

I took off my work gloves and knelt down. He didn't move. I studied him for a moment and was surprised to notice the peculiar markings on his body; markings I've never seen on your average run-of-the-mill crow. The tips of his wings were stark white. I lifted my hands to untangle his wing, slowly at first, as I was expecting him to start struggling at any moment. To my astonishment, he remained still and let me remove the wire mesh from around his wing.

As soon as he was free, he flapped his wings and perched carefully on my hand. I smiled toward him warmly, and again could almost sense thoughts of gratitude for his liberation. He lifted into the air, circled above a few times, and perched on the waiting branch of a nearby elm, where he continued to observe with curiosity. I went back to harvesting the last few vegetables of the season, and after a few hours decided to call it a day and gathered up my tools. As I began to leave, I turned to glance at the tree, and there still sitting on the branch was the same crow. He stared silently as I walked back to my house.

The next morning, I took my bike and set out on the dirt road leading toward school. I put on a beanie and zipped up my jacket to stave off the cold. As I was doing so, I spotted the shadow of outstretched wings. Looking up, I instantly recognized the same crow. He circled for a moment before rising to depart.

Nearing the school, I once again noticed a bird-shaped shadow. I knew crows were intelligent, and I figured he had followed out of appreciation for setting him free the day before. I decided I couldn't go on calling him "the crow" so I named him Tux, as his white wingtips reminded me of a little avian tuxedo.

I locked up my bike and headed to class. After twenty minutes of listening to the teacher drone on about the Civil War, I happened to glance out an open window to notice Tux. He was perched on the school's fence, quiet and still as stone, staring intently into the classroom. A small part of me began to feel somewhat unnerved by this attention, but in the end chalked it up to a grateful, harmless, and unassuming bird who had formed a bond with the human who set him free. But I was wrong. Dead wrong.

The following day, and the days that followed, Tux accompanied my rides to school. He would wait outside each classroom, disappear, and then reappear at some point outside a window. He would watch me sitting in class and then follow back home. He would perch on various branches and, when night came, would disappear completely. This routine continued for several weeks.

One night as I was studying, I heard a faint tapping on my windowpane. Tux was stationed on the windowsill with something white and silver in his beak. He let it drop onto the sill and flew off. I had heard that crows will sometime leave little gifts for humans they like, whether it be little pieces of glass, string, colorful pebbles, or whatnot. I smiled and thought this must be his way of saying "thank you."

I looked delightedly at my new gift through the glass, then opened the window to retrieve it. At first it appeared to be some small piece of porcelain inlaid with silver, but as I picked it up for closer inspection, I froze and dropped it from my hands. This couldn't be what it looked like, but there on my bedroom floor it lay. It was a human tooth with a silver filling in its center.

I stared, wondering how and where he could have found this. Most macabre of all was the blood still freshly clinging to its root. After a while I picked it up, brought it to my bathroom, and flushed the thing down the toilet. I decided it was all some sort of weird coincidence and put it out of my mind. That, however, would prove more difficult than I imagined.

The unsettling dreams began that night. I remember that one vividly; I was working in our cornfields. The sun was shining brightly, warming a cool morning into a pleasant afternoon. There were no clouds in the sky, and a comfortable breeze was my companion. As I worked, I noticed my shadow slowly starting to dim. Looking up, I saw what appeared to be dark storm clouds gathering overhead. These weren't storm clouds, however, as they looked to be descending toward our farm at an alarming rate. Millions of crows blocked out the sun and any hint of blue sky. They were heading toward an old scarecrow we had propped up in the middle of one of our fields, swirling and perching on anything strong enough to hold the weight of so many birds. I watched in horror as they kept descending. I ran back to my house and barricaded myself inside. I watched from my second-story bedroom as the sea of crows covered our cornfields.

At that point in the dream, it all went quiet; every bird landed and stood still. An actual storm had gathered, turning the dark atmosphere of the farm into a dreamscape of eerie terrain. Far afield there was movement. It was the scarecrow my father and I had erected several months ago. It had begun to move, somehow suddenly animated. I stood frozen while its form increased in size, first to five feet, then to ten feet, until at last it had grown to over forty feet tall. The crows stood silently watching.

The scarecrow began to move toward the house in labored, unsteady steps, like a toddler just learning to walk. Stuffing fell from its weathered trousers and shirt as it made its way in my direction. The hat it wore over a stuffed bag of straw bobbed side to side as it strode closer. It stopped at the edge of the cornfield and produced in its straw-stuffed gloved hand a large black reaper's sickle. In one swift stroke with the blade, it tore its makeshift head from his body, and there in its place was the head of a crow. This enormous, straw-stuffed, bird-headed monstrosity stared unflinching.

The creature glanced down at someone cowering on his knees. I couldn't make out who it was, as his back was turned to me. The frightened man was kneeling in front of the monster, nude and overcome. He appeared to be an older gentleman, thin with a farmer's tan and a head of red hair. He was staring up and looked to be pleading with this thing, his hands clasped over his head in some sort of appeal.

In one fell swoop, the crow-headed monster brought the sickle right through the middle of the man's head, splitting it perfectly in two. The crows burst into a terrible cacophonous cawing. The crow-beast lifted its sickle and, among the gore, hair, and teeth stuck to it, flung it in my direction, straight at my windowpane. Just as it was about to strike, I woke up, shooting upright in bed as beads of cold sweat dripped from my face.

At that moment, I heard something strike my window. After gathering myself and wiping away the copious amounts of sweat, I headed to my window and eyed an object sitting on the sill. It was another human tooth. I backed away, still terrorized from the dream, and sat on my bed. I stared at the tooth. After a while, I once again flushed it down my toilet. I pulled the shades and got back into bed. I don't think I slept the rest of the night.

Tux circled above as I rode to school. I didn't pay attention, not that it mattered to him. I suddenly stopped my bike, looked up, and began shouting, asking him to stop following. As expected, this did nothing. I made for school, and Tux again waited as silently and faithfully as ever.

That evening, local news was blaring from the living room. Normally I'm not very interested in anything local, but the words "tragic death" caught my attention. The county newscaster was doing a story on the death of a local farmer, Mr. Bill Hyde. I sat beside my parents to watch the broadcast. I had heard his name before; he had tried to patent an invention that netted and killed crows plaguing his farm. At one point he boasted that his invention had dispatched over a thousand crows, and because of it his crop yield had increased by fifty percent. He had even tried to sell one to my father when he was in town.

They showed his picture on the screen, and my heart started beating so fast I thought it would leave my chest. There was the thin, red-haired, farmer's-tanned man from my dream. He was found under mysterious circumstances with large deep lacerations across his chest, scratches covering his body, and both eyes removed. Shaking, I got up from the couch just as the newscaster added that Mr. Hyde was also missing several teeth. I bolted to my bedroom and reached for the blinds. Just as I was about to close them, there was Tux, sitting on a branch and staring into my room. I wrenched the shades closed and went to bed.

I was determined to have nothing to do with that damned bird anymore; there were too many horrible coincidences that I just couldn't shake.

As I biked onto the dirt road in the morning, Tux was nowhere to be found. It was as if he had heard my thoughts and stayed away. He wasn't around my school, and he wasn't waiting as I rode home. A certain level of relief came over me, and I was glad to be free of him.

One week turned into two, then three, and still there was no sign of Tux anywhere. I eventually forgot about this feathered pest and things began to go back to normal.

One day during gym, we were picking teams for flag football. Not being very athletic and somewhat of an outcast, I was naturally picked last. Anthony Gaines was the captain of the football team. Larger than most sixteen-year-olds and gifted with athletic prowess, he was the darling of the town during Friday night football games, often leading our team to victory. This increased his popularity as well as his ego. He was also gifted with a mean streak that could turn violent at the first sign of any kind of weakness on the part of his fellow classmates. I ended up on his team this particular day.

After I failed to catch any of several passes thrown my way, he decided after the game was over – and after the gym teacher was out of sight – to remind me of these failures. He stopped me as I left the locker room, threw me up against a wall, and threatened to rearrange my face should I ever end up on his team again.

After I mumbled some half-hearted apology, he threw me to the floor and spit in my direction, much to the entertainment of fellow jocks. I picked myself up and dusted off my clothes, which is when I noticed Tux out the window; he was perched in a tree, staring in silence. When he noticed me looking, he flew away.

A week later, a new kid started at my school. His name was Brandon Sawyer, a transplant from upstate, whose parents has purchased a farm on the east side of town. He had tried out for the school football team and made the cut, becoming friendly, unfortunately, with Anthony Gaines. Brandon was athletic, smart, and handsome with light sandy brown hair and green eyes, and he was pleasant with pretty much everyone he met. I, on the other hand, kept my distance – not out of spite, but because Brandon was probably the handsomest boy I had ever seen. I was so incredibly shy that I couldn't even bring myself to say hello. And I was quite sure I just blended into the background to him.

Every day, my thoughts began with what I needed to work on for school, but they would always slowly morph into thoughts about Brandon. Whether I was on my way to class, riding home, helping my father, or trying to concentrate on homework, he kept coming to mind.

I finally decided I needed a distraction, and made it a point to visit Mrs. Barnes, the theater instructor. We discussed having me join the theater group as part of the production crew, as I had no delusions about my ability to act or sing. She welcomed me with open arms, and with the blessing of my parents I was in. Mrs. Barnes had begun auditions for the school production of *Singing in the Rain,* and as I mused about who might try to step into Gene Kelly's shoes, I worked to have the scenery painted and the lighting just right.

I learned the ropes of a stagehand rather quickly. It was now time for student auditions.

As I was about to ascend a stage ladder, I heard a familiar voice warming up for his audition. Surprisingly, it was Brandon.

I peeked cautiously behind the scenery and witnessed in awe. Not only was he a talented athlete, but he could sing wonderfully.

When he was finished, I made my way into the audience just in time to hear Mrs. Barnes congratulate him on being cast as the lead. Everyone clapped, including myself. As he passed by, I uttered a shy "congratulations" that I thought he didn't hear. He actually turned toward me and thanked me! He smiled that radiant smile right in my direction, then turned and left the auditorium. I was so elated by Brandon's sudden acknowledgment of my existence that I almost didn't hear Mrs. Barnes calling to ask about some props.

Tux stayed away during this time and I rarely saw him, save for the occasional night vigils he would hold outside my bedroom window, and as always I would just close my shades. I stayed after school several times, feigning work on the theater set, but in reality I was just there to watch Brandon perform. He was incredible, and the more I watched him, the more of an infatuation developed. I was determined to talk to him again.

One afternoon during rehearsal, I found Brandon's script laying on a stool next to the stage. I looked around and spirited it away back to where we were working on scenery. After a while I could hear him asking the cast if they had found the script he had misplaced. After several nos, I slowly walked up to him and mentioned I had found a script backstage. He flashed me his smile and I led him back to the place where I had allegedly discovered it. He looked relieved and thanked me for my help. Before he could walk away, I asked how long he had been singing. This started a long conversation about how he grew up, about his old school, his parents, and how he tries to balance it all out with being a football player simultaneously. I hung onto his every word and shamelessly stared in admiration.

It was time to rehearse again. Thinking quickly, I asked if he'd like to hang out at my house and stay for dinner. Surprised by the invitation, he thought about it for a second. He agreed to meet me after rehearsal and we could both head over.

After a quick introduction to my parents, I took Brandon outside and showed him our farm. He was comparing it to his own farm when he suddenly stopped and glanced at one of the trees. He asked me if I could see the "weird looking crow with white markings" perched on one of the branches. I looked up, and there was Tux sitting still as a rock, watching our every move. I hurriedly changed the subject and quickly told him I had never seen the bird before, and we walked back to my house for dinner. As usual, my parents barely spoke a word as we ate, and most of the conversation was between Brandon and I. His smile, his laugh, everything about him was amazing.

After dinner, we walked outside to check out the sunset, at which point he asked if I ever spent time walking among the corn. I responded that I did frequently, and he explained that he would only explore his family's cornfield when necessary, finding it creepy. We both laughed and I ran toward the corn, disappearing into the field. Brandon ran after, and proceeded to sneak up playfully from behind. He grabbed my waist with surprise, and I turned around laughing nervously. He looked at me for a moment, then grabbed some debris that had lodged itself in my hair. He removed it slowly and I looked at him smiling. He brought his hand to my face and we just stared at each other. Slowly and gently, he pressed his soft lips to mine. Once again, I thought I must be dreaming, but that wasn't the case. He moved his body toward mine and increased the intensity of his kiss. I stood there savoring every moment, every move, every touch, and drifted into a bliss that up to that point in my life I had never felt before.

Just as soon as it began, it was suddenly over. A loud caw pierced the air overhead. As I looked up, there was Tux circling overhead. The sound had broken the atmosphere between the two of us, and Brandon stated that he had to get home. I walked him to the edge of our farm and he thanked me for dinner. We said our goodbyes and he headed home. I walked back toward the house, and there perched on the porch railing was Tux. I erupted in anger and shooed him away from the house. He noiselessly lifted into the air and disappeared into the night while I shouted at him once again to leave me alone.

We prepared for the play's opening night the following week. We went into overtime painting sets, helping with costumes, and making sure we had the stage lighting on point. Brandon was supposed to attend football practice that afternoon but apparently hadn't shown up yet. I could hear Anthony Gaines bellowing through the auditorium asking anyone and everyone if they had seen Brandon Sawyer.

As I was ascending a stage ladder, I heard him come backstage calling Brandon's name. As he came through, he tripped on some equipment and went flying into my ladder. The can I was holding toppled onto Anthony, covering his new football uniform in lime green paint. I fell backwards and caught myself just in time to see Anthony explode with wrath. I got onto my feet as he hurdled forward, determined, I surmised, to inflict as much bodily harm as possible. I ran out the back stage door and into the Senior parking lot with Anthony in hot pursuit.

Just as I was about to make it out of the lot, I felt Anthony's meaty hand grab the back of my neck and pull me toward the ground. He was on top in seconds, pummeling my face blow after blow. I could feel my face starting to swell and tasted the metallic tinge of my own blood. Just as he was about to land another punch, a hand grabbed his arm and pulled him off. It was Brandon. He faced Anthony, the two of them yelling and trading insults. Mrs. Barnes eventually reached them and quelled the fight. Anthony stormed away. Just before he was out of sight, he turned back to scream that I should watch my back from here on out.

Brandon pulled me to my feet. He and Mrs. Barnes asked if I was okay and if I needed anything. I said I was fine but should probably leave. Brandon went to fetch my things and asked if he could walk me home. Of course I agreed, and Mrs. Barnes returned to ensure the rehearsals were going smoothly.

As I waited for Brandon, I looked at the fence surrounding the parking lot, and lo and behold: there was Tux perched and staring silently. It was different this time, however, as there were at least a dozen other crows with him. Up until that point I had never seen Tux as part of a flock, but there he was, the others staring in equal silence.

Brandon's voice broke my trance, sending Tux and the other crows flying into the air, disappearing over the school. As he walked me home, he apologized for what had happened. I told him Anthony Gaines had it out for me way before he ever moved to town, and not to think on it anymore. He looked around cautiously as we walked, and then slowly took my hand in his own, holding it the rest of the way home. I thanked him and he headed back to school.

I walked past both my parents as I entered the house; neither one looked up or asked why my face was covered in blood. I skipped dinner, showered, and went straight to bed.

The dreams came again that night. I found myself on a football field on an overcast day surrounded in mist. I could hear heavy breathing in the distance, slowly progressing in my direction. Suddenly, out the mist, Anthony Gaines was running toward me in his football uniform in slow motion. Breathing heavily and carrying his helmet as he ran, he had a look of horror on his blood-soaked face, becoming more prominent the closer he came. I moved out of the way, and he ran right past me as if I wasn't there.

Suddenly, a knight clad in full medieval armor appeared out of the mist in his footsteps. The knight rode a strange-looking black horse that didn't appear to have a normal coat, but instead was covered in silky black feathery plumage. Its head was not equine, but that of a crow's.

He rode past in a slow dreamlike gait, stopping briefly to remove his metal helmet. In place of a man's head, the knight also had the head of a crow, complete with a long beak and silky feathers. With one quick movement of his hand, he manifested a black sickle. He raised and hurled it toward Anthony as he ran on ahead.

The blade struck and lodged into Anthony's back. He let out a sinister wail. He fell to the ground, a look of terror frozen on his face. I stared in silence, disbelieving the sight. As I stepped closer to his body, Anthony's eyes darted in my direction. I jumped back in surprise and the crow-headed knight turned to face my direction. I awoke again covered in a cold sweat. I didn't sleep the rest of the night.

I stayed home from school the next morning and holed up in my room. I don't think my parents even noticed I was there. I mentally played back the events and dreams of the last month, trying in my own adolescent way to make sense of them. I kept telling myself over and over again all was well, that everything that's happened is just coincidence.

That evening, I heard the familiar tap on my bedroom window. I opened the shades just in time to see a black streak fly away. Will that goddamned bird ever leave me alone? As I turned to leave, I noticed what appeared to be some sort of red lollipop on the sill. Another gift or trinket from the crows? If it was teeth again, I knew for sure I'd hunt that bird down. But it wasn't.

There, staring up at me, was an eyeball covered in blood, and next to it an index finger.

I backed away slowly, my heart beating a hundred miles an hour. I ran to the toilet, vomiting at the thought of the vileness on my windowsill – and the fear that ensued. I barricaded myself in the bathroom and curled up on the floor. What sort of demonic manifestation had come to this town in the shape of these crows? Why did I rescue that accursed bird? This, apparently, was my reward.

After several hours, I opened the bathroom door and made my way to the window, and still sitting there was that gore. I couldn't leave it there, so I grabbed a bunch of paper towels and, without looking, scooped it all up and ran to the bathroom to again flush it all away. I cleaned the remaining blood from the windowsill, noticing Tux perched on an adjacent tree. This miserable bird was silently taunting my living hell.

The opening night of *Singing in the Rain* was fast approaching, so I was prepared for a long Friday. After classes wrapped up, I made my way to the theater and noticed several police cars in front of the administration building. I saw Brandon talking with one of the police officers. He looked at me briefly with solemn eyes as I passed. When I saw him enter the auditorium, I slowly made my way toward him and he flashed that amazing smile he always wore. I asked if everything was okay, since I noticed he was talking with an officer. His smile faded and he said that Anthony Gaines had been found dead. The color faded from my face and I took a step back. The police wanted to question Brandon because it was known that the two of them had a fight. I asked if he was sure, and how he knew he was really dead.

The police had found Anthony face-down on the football field two nights before. He had deep lacerations on his back, his eyes were gone, and his entire body had been scratched up. I looked back at Brandon in shock. Just then, Mrs. Barnes called him over, but right before he turned to leave he added that Anthony's body was also missing a finger. I walked to the back of the auditorium and sat in silence, struggling to process the information. Mrs. Barnes had apparently been talking to me for several minutes but I hadn't heard a word she'd said. I stared at her for a moment, walked out of the auditorium, and headed home.

When I got back to my house, I overheard my father complaining to my mother how there were more crows visiting the farm than he could ever recall. The last thing I wanted to hear about were those damned crows, so I headed straight to my room.

That night, as I drifted off to sleep, the dreams slowly returned. This time I was amid thousands of people running and screaming, seemingly being rounded up by men on horseback, complete with cowboy hats, boots, and ropes at their sides. As they rode past, I noticed that these men had the faces of crows, and they were herding all the humans toward a giant pit that was two miles wide and at least a mile deep.

I peered over the edge as people tumbled down. Tall, wiry figures on what appeared to be stilts were walking over those unlucky enough to get in their way, but upon closer inspection, they were scarecrows moving on their own accord, not on stilts but on long, sharp metal swords that were impaling and piercing those maimed and broken who had survived the fall. I woke up suddenly and thought I heard the flap of wings in my bedroom.

It was Saturday. I couldn't bring myself to walk past my bedroom door, so I sealed myself inside with the shades drawn. I heard a small knock on my door several hours later. It was my mother informing me I had a visitor. A visitor, I thought, could only be one person. I dressed and walked to my front door, and there with his beautiful smile was Brandon. We went outside to walk around the property. I told him all was well, trying my hardest to blurt out this lie as convincingly as possible. He didn't buy it.

After gently pressing me to be honest, the truth came flowing out in a deluge of tears and despair. I told him about Tux, how I rescued him, how he follows me everywhere I go, and how he's not an ordinary crow but some sort of hellish creature. I told him about my dreams, about the deaths, about Mr. Hyde and Anthony Gaines, and about the gruesome gifts that were left outside my window. I explained my belief that everything must be connected somehow.

My first thought was, "well, this is it, he's going to think I'm genuinely insane and want nothing more to do with me." To my surprise, that wasn't the case. He listened carefully to the entire confession. I stopped sobbing and he put his arm carefully around my shoulders. He said that everything was going to be okay, and that he believed every word. At that moment, I felt the weight of the world lift from my shoulders. Amidst all of this terror, I had someone on my side.

Just as I was starting to feel things were beginning to make sense again, a large caw bellowed from above us. There in the branches of the tree near us was Tux. Brandon eyed him carefully and asked if that was, in fact, the crow from my confession. Brandon quickly flew into a rage, picking up any large rocks he could find and hurling them at Tux. He was screaming that he would end this monster right then and there. Rock after rock flew at Tux, and he darted above, lifting and descending through the air at various intervals. I latched onto Brandon and pleaded that he stop, telling him that nothing good would come of this. But, he continued throwing a barrage of stones at the circling crow.

Between my begging him to stop and his hurling curses at Tux, a loud high-pitched caw was heard and something fell to the ground. I ran to Tux's twitching body. A rock had broken his neck. I stared at the bird almost longingly, and Brandon came up from behind. I looked at Brandon, shaking my head, hearing the words "what have you done?" exit my lips. Brandon looked at me puzzled. He told me that it was over, that he had ended this nightmare. I took out a blue handkerchief that I kept in my pocket, and lifted Tux's broken body inside.

Brandon gasped. Surrounding us were hundreds of crows, silently observing. I turned to Brandon and told him he should go home. When he inquired why, I brusquely told him he needed to leave. I walked over near my mother's garden, Tux in hand, and stared at his lifeless body. I heard Brandon's footsteps fade as he left, and I knelt onto the grass, remaining there for what felt like hours.

I slowly dug a small hole and laid Tux, wrapped in my handkerchief, into the solemn earth. I touched his white markings for a moment and, little by little, covered his body with soil. I put a few stones over the grave to mark it and went inside. From my bedroom window, I could still see hundreds of crows, silent as the setting sun. I closed my shades. As I lay in my bed, I knew the dreams would be vivid. I was sure it wasn't going to be pleasant, but even so, I willed myself to sleep and drifted off.

I awoke that morning refreshed, never having dreamt a thing. Maybe Brandon was right – he had officially ended the nightmare. This relief was suddenly interrupted by my father slowly opening the bedroom door. The police were here, and they were wanting to talk. Of course they were. They had questioned everyone else about Anthony's death, so I supposed it was my turn. I dressed and walked downstairs to the officer in my living room. He greeted me rather indifferently and asked when I had last seen Brandon Sawyer. I felt my legs beginning to give out from under me, and steadied myself against the living room wall. I asked if he meant Anthony Gaines, but he looked at me curiously and reiterated that it was Brandon Sawyer he was asking about.

I immediately ran from the house, out into the yard, the officer and my father running after. I approached the small grave where I had buried Tux, and to my astonishment it was empty. Only the hole and the blue handkerchief remained. I told myself it was stray dogs or cats that dug up the grave, or some sort of scavenging animal. I turned white as a ghost and faced the officer. He repeated his question about the last time I had seen Brandon. I told him he had been here yesterday and had headed home around mid-afternoon. I asked what happened, but all the officer could say is that his parents had discovered him near their farm, deceased.

I fell to my knees and sobbed profusely. My father, surprised by this reaction, helped me to my feet and walked me back into the house. I heard him say something to the officer, at which point he turned and left. He helped me to my room, brought a glass of water, and left me there in silence. I laid down and cried myself to sleep. I decided this was all my fault – why didn't I just leave that bird in the fence to die?

I reluctantly went to school that Monday and met with Mrs. Barnes. She was sitting quietly in the auditorium staring at the scenery. She turned to look in my direction and bade me to come sit next to her. She asked if I knew, and I nodded with tears streaming down my face. She had decided to cancel the musical out of respect for Brandon's passing. She said that she would remember that beautiful voice of his as he sang the title's tune. As I got up to leave, she told me to be careful, that the twisted maniac who had left Brandon's body in the condition it was in was still at large.

Condition? I pressed her gently for more information. She lowered her head and explained that Brandon had been mutilated. His body had been eviscerated and beheaded. His head, apparently, was still missing. I left without saying a word and spent the rest of the school day hiding in the music room.

When I finally headed home, I began to hear a faint singing coming from elsewhere. There were no other houses on this route and no cars in sight. It became slightly louder, but still nearly inaudible. The tune felt familiar, and then my blood ran cold. Someone nearby was singing the title song to *Singing in the Rain*.

It became louder and louder as I ran. Approaching my house, I noticed storm clouds growing in the distance and raindrops slowly beginning to fall. I went into the house and called after my parents, but no one was home. I ran to the living room window and stared at the hundreds of crows gathering together on the farm. They were on the ground, in the trees, on the roof of my house – everywhere.

Thunder struck, and with it the sound of hundreds of crows cawing in unison. I locked the doors, closed the shades and ran to my bedroom. I barricaded the door, grabbed a pillow and blanket, and huddled in a corner of my room. I have been here ever since.

The Iconoclasts

Mona Fitzgerald-King

A shard of light slices through the crack of her open lids before she squeezes them shut in agony. There is a sickening feeling of liquid sloshing in her skull – an aquarium with crunching gravel. She clenches her jaw and concentrates on breathing slowly through her nostrils.

With great caution she begins again the feat of opening her eyes.

Slowly.

Slowly.

Her vision is dim waves through fog. Her own folded hands in her lap come into focus. She is wearing a white nightgown. She becomes aware of the gentle bounces of a moving vehicle. Her stomach lurches and she dry heaves, falling back against the leather seat. Again, her gorge rises, and she gags audibly, exhausted. Her mouth is bathed in sickly-quenching saliva she is afraid to swallow into her churning belly. There are two men and another woman in the car, all dressed in similar white night clothes. They appear asleep or comatose, staring at fixed points with faint smiles playing across their lips. Her heart pounds and she moves her tongue in her sour mouth. Her hands are frigid and clammy. Her feet are bare.

The car slows and turns, tires crunching over an uneven terrain. She turns to peer out the tinted window. They approach what appears to be a massive cathedral, towering in twin columns of pale, porous stone. The car – a black limousine – slips over metal runners embedded in the concrete drive as a wrought-iron gate creeps open with screeching mechanical hesitation. It's all unfamiliar, as are the staring passengers.

The limousine comes to a gradual stop at a stone porch before the cathedral, which is more of an institution than temple from this vantage. The driver turns off the car, invisible to his passengers through a tinted separating glass. She listlessly reaches for a door handle and realizes there are none. The interior is smooth and flawless.

Silence. The sloshing liquid of her skull has cascaded over her, and she moves slowly and deliberately as if attempting to run in the depths. She opens her mouth to speak but, as she takes in the visages of her colleagues once more, she closes it. Were it not for the gentle, simultaneous rise and fall of their chests, they'd be mistaken for dead. She studies a blond man who is slumped in a seat across from her, watching his eyes, willing them to blink, to dart, to flinch, to show some sign of consciousness. The minutes pass... the expressions remain unchanged, the eyes motionless. She feels the prickling of panic scratching down the length of her arms. Her throat is closing.

At last, the limo door opens, allowing a hideous, blinding light into the dim interior. Her eyes close again, and her hands slowly search for her face to shield her delicate vision from what feels like a spotlight's glare. The silence continues. No voices of greeting, no rustles of clothing, no efforts to disembark. Gradually, she allows the light to tighten her pupils, wincing as she looks out the door. A woman is standing there. Her bright red hair seems to burn on her scalp in the sunlight. She wears a nondescript white lab coat. Suddenly, the red-haired woman seizes her hand, pulling her to her feet with surprising force.

The drive is covered in jagged white rocks. She buckles and sways, frowning and looking around desperately for explanation as her legs seem foreign and weak. The red-haired woman is unresponsive, expressionless.

Two large men in white lab coats appear on either side of the woman. One man places a hand beneath each of her arms and lifts her as one might lift a small child. Her legs hang uselessly beneath her body, feet dangling and dragging. She is turned as he clamps an arm across her back and her toes scrape along the ground and over the threshold through the ajar double doors of the unmarked building.

Inside, the flooring is a deep green vinyl linoleum that continues down a seemingly endless hallway paralleled with numerous closed and unmarked doors. She is dropped unceremoniously into a waiting wheelchair, then feels her gorge rise again as the chair is maneuvered rapidly by an unseen driver behind her. She hears the soft footsteps and the creaking of more wheels behind her. Door after door is left in her wake. Her skin is sickly moist and the gown clutches to her otherwise nude body. She manages to lift one leg slightly and watches with horror as it begins to quake with dramatic tremors before she drops it. Her foot falls between the footrests and hits the linoleum below, causing the chair to veer. The chair halts and a white-coated individual stoops to lift her foot and place it back into the footrest, securing a strap around each of her ankles before resuming the wordless journey.

They arrive at a door that is standing open. The linoleum gives way to industrial Berber carpet. Four recliners face a projector screen and small folding table. With silent efficiency, her body is lifted from the wheelchair and dropped into a recliner. The men in coats disappear. The red-haired woman stands at the table, her hands held in a steeple before her chest. Her hair is held in a tight bun. Her face is clean and severe.

"Welcome," the woman says and feigns a smile which threatens to split her taut face. "I am pleased you have arrived. I trust you are all comfortable."

She holds a small electronic device in one hand and the projector screen flickers to life. She motions toward the screen with a small thrust of her head. The false smile remains on her thin lips.

"You are here because you have chosen to better yourselves. You are excited to be a part of the newest breakthrough in scientific research," she continues. The screen flashes forward, showing pictures of smiling adults, cradled babies, giggling children, parks, picnics, still photos of leaping dogs catching Frisbees, and an elderly gentleman strumming a guitar.

"You have completed the first phase of the program. All of the best amenities have been provided. You are all very pleased and eager to begin the next chapter of your new lives." Twin girls dunking cookies in overflowing mugs of milk, a woman in an apron kneading bread dough, a preening parakeet.

"Now is the time to prepare for peace. Your affairs are in order. You are doing a great service. Your lives have meaning."

The men in lab coats appear once more, wheeling a stainless-steel cart. A surgical saw lies in a silver tray on the lower shelf, reflecting the overhead fluorescent light. On the surface shelf are four syringes, side-by-side. One of the men lifts a syringe, tests it briefly, and swiftly sinks the large needle into the neck of the man seated closest to the door. The man's foot jerks, lifting several inches in the air for sickening seconds, before falling stiffly once more. Another man in a lab coat holds gauze to the gaping hole now oozing blood in the flesh below the still man's ear. The empty syringe clatters as it returns to the tray. The next is swiftly retrieved and the small team moves to the next silent passenger. The injected man slumps to one side, eyes open and glazed as ever.

Her heart threatens to beat out of her chest. Her adrenaline is surely at toxic levels. She hears the harsh rasping of her own quick breath as it flows through her throat and gaping mouth. She raises her arms and plants her hands in the soft arm rests, struggling to hoist herself to stand. Her bare feet hit the rough carpet and she fights every instinct to collapse weakly back to the chair. The red-haired woman watches her, hands in the peak of joined fingertips, still. The men are content to work, inserting the next syringe into the next colleague. This one did not jerk, merely slumped, tongue lolling from the corner of a flaccid smile.

Her legs rock and shake, and she fights against them, a battle of mind against weakened frame. On the projector, three ducklings waddle after their mother; a blonde girl with braided pigtails stretches her legs toward the sky on a tire swing.

She wills her legs forward with excruciating bursts of strength resulting in merely shuffling steps. She does not return the steady stare of the red-haired woman over her long, thin fingers.

Her breath claws through her lungs and throat, the dryness threatening to choke her. She attempts without success to ignore the mental image of herself curled in the fetal position on the floor, gasping for air and fighting against the resistance of her own muscles. The panic is boiling inside, causing her half-conscious muscles to buckle and shake even more as she jerkily moves with excruciating slowness. At any moment, she will feel hands clamp around her shoulders as she is forced back into her chair when it's time for the fourth syringe to be brought home.

She reaches the green linoleum. It is cold and provides little traction as she pulls herself along the hallway, clutching at each passing doorknob to maintain her balance. She hears voices behind some of the doors. Each step is paired with the flinch of anticipation. A pair of lab-coated men pushing a steel cart approach from behind and rush past her, casting a cursory glance from the corners of their eyes. She struggles forward, keenly focused on the natural light seeping in through the panes of the double door entrance. She is panting miserably as she braces for the pursuers who will drag her breathlessly screaming back to her own nameless injection.

Her knees buckle and she falls hard, slapping her chin against the tile and feeling a twist in one wrist as her teeth smash together. She rolls to her back, instinctively drawing her knees and elbows to her chest, shielding her body against what must surely be advancing upon her. The hall is empty. She turns and crawls toward the door, pulling and sliding with the aid of soft cotton beneath her knees against the smooth tile. Her heart feels too large and too heavy, seeming to gulp of her oxygen-deprived blood.

At the doorway, she pulls herself to her feet once more, holding the large, ornate, brass door handle. She is acutely conscious of the change beneath her feet as she steps over the threshold onto the cool concrete stoop. The gate is in sight at the base of the sloped drive, and she feels a shimmer of hope as she hobbles over the graveled drive.

Here stands an operator's hut which houses the controls for the gate and security system for the grounds. A young boy with a pocked face and greasy hair, manning the hut, looks up from his magazine and stares as she advances toward the street. She is unaware that her feet are bloodied and raw. The boy's face is distorted through the pane that faces the street and she forces herself into a trot to the sidewalk across the road.

She squats and collapses against her own thighs, breathing slowly and deliberately. A woman approaches swiftly in a pink jogging outfit with a tiny dog in tow on a pink leash. She casts a questioning glance and touches her wedding band nervously with the thumb of the same hand. Her pristine white sneakers continue beside the tick-tick-tick of tiny dog feet.

She knows neither the time nor day. As reality sinks slowly into her, she begins to lift her head. A light breeze creeps up the nightgown. Conscious of her nudity beneath, she pulls the gown firm toward her knees as she stands, glancing around for onlookers.

The operator hut is empty. The gate is closed. The cathedral grounds are still and quiet.

It is twilight and the breeze has begun to carry a chill. Cars flick on their headlights as they speed by.

Her feet ache and throb. She runs her tongue along the chipped surface of a front tooth and tastes the metallic presence of her own blood pooled inside her lower lip. She spits and watches the gob of pink land on the pavement, then winces as she wipes a string of saliva from her chin.

The sun has set and still she stands. No lights appear in the ghostly windows of the cathedral. No smoke rises from its sentinel chimney.

She turns in all directions, searching desperately for a familiar landmark. In the darkness down the street, she recognizes the glow of a city, of street lamps and convenience store signs challenging the oncoming darkness.

The cathedral looms. The yard is overgrown. She is utterly alone.

A car horn sounds, cutting the evening silence ferociously. She emits a screech and stumbles backward, realizing she had been standing in the middle of the road. A man behind the wheel of a brown sedan shakes his head and dramatically swerves into the oncoming lane.

"Trying to get killed?" he bellows, leaving her in a cloud of stinking exhaust.

Slowly she turns and begins to walk along the sidewalk. She turns, watching the building, unable to walk with her back to its ominous presence.

She hears the crunch of slow-moving tires and turns to view its source. Approaching her is a black limousine. The brakes squeak as it slows before the gate. The gate screeches and begins to slide open slowly, shaking mechanically. The car creeps forward to the drive. She sees the shadows of four passengers. The cathedral doors swing open and a woman, her hair the color of blood in the moonlight, stands waiting, her patient fingers steepled at her thin chest.

Meet the Authors

Storm Constantine was the author of over 30 books, both fiction and non-fiction. Her fiction titles included the two best-selling *Wraeththu* series, *Hermetech* and the *Grigori* Trilogy, and her esoteric nonfiction works include *Bast & Sekhmet: Eyes of Ra* and *Grimoire: Kaimana.*

In 2003, Storm set up her own publishing company, Immanion Press, in order to have more freedom over what work she released and to get back-catalogue titles back in print. This expanded to publish many other writers with similar desires. Storm later set up a nonfiction imprint of Immanion Press, Megalithica Books, which concentrates on cutting-edge books on magic and occultism.

www.immanion-press.com

Adele Cosgrove-Bray is a writer and artist based in Wirral, England. Her writing has been published traditionally in magazines and anthologies, and she has also explored self-publishing. Her *Artisan-Sorcerer* novels, which follow the lives of members of an occult order, have drawn an impressive cult following.

She has worked as an editor, a health promotion officer, a library assistant at Liverpool City Libraries, a photographer, a tarot card reader, and as a potter and tour guide for Pretty Ugly Pottery, and since 2010 she has been an Activity Coordinator in the care sector, working with vulnerable people who live with dementia and other mental health issues. Adele's paintings can be viewed on her website or on YouTube, where you can also hear her reading aloud some of her stories.

https://adelecosgrove-bray.blogspot.com

https://www.youtube.com/@ArtAndFiction

Rhea Troutman lives in Missoula, Montana, where she works as a professional Tarot card and psychic reader, both online and in person. She enjoys Yoga, strength training, meditation, writing, and the great outdoors. She is the founder of the metaphysical supply store Between the Worlds in Hamilton, Montana, which is known for bringing together individuals from a wide variety of lifestyles and spiritual practices. Rhea is currently working on her first full-length novel.

www.facebook.com/rhea-troutman
www.facebook.com/rhea-troutman-quartermoonreadings
www.instagram.com/quarter-moon-readings

Corvis Nocturnum (E.R. Vernor) is an author, publisher, and lecturer who has written over a dozen books on popular culture. His content ranges from vampires and zombies to the Devil and the occult. He has appeared as a guest speaker at DragonCon, Scarefest, Parafest, and has been interviewed on the BET Channel's The Lexi Show episode "The Church of Satan."

He is best known for his debut book *Embracing the Darkness: Understanding Dark Subcultures*. Other titles include *The World History of Vampires*, *Promethean Flame,* and most recently the self-help book *Limitless Getting to the Top After Hitting Rock Bottom*. He has also been a consultant for A&E Channel's *Paranormal State*. He has lectured at various events across Indiana, Michigan, Ohio, Illinois, and Georgia on the subjects in *Embracing the Darkness: Understanding Dark Subcultures,* work detailing the truth and crossover of alternative lifestyles, gaining the attention of readers all over the world. He belongs to the Church of Satan, where he holds the title of Media Representative and Reverend in the priesthood. Various writings of his have appeared in newsletters and online groups, and he has spoken out on thousands of Blog Talk online radio shows. He currently the publisher and CEO of Dark Moon Press.

S.M. Lomas is an ardent reader who has been writing short stories since she was old enough to wield a pencil, and has been a fan of the weird and macabre for just as long. She loves animals, horror and B-movies, and generally being a hermit. She holds a BA in creative writing/literature from the University of Montana and currently lives in Portland, Oregon.

Gabrielle Faust is an author, editor, entertainment journalist, and illustrator best known for her internationally renowned post-apocalyptic cyberpunk vampire series *Eternal Vigilance*. To date she has successfully released thirteen novels and anthologies in the horror and poetry genres. Her work has appeared in magazines and websites such as *Weird Tales Magazine, SciFi Wire, Girls & Corpses Magazine, Austin Food & Wine Magazine, Fatally Yours, Examiner, Doorways Magazine, Fear Zone,* and *Gothic Beauty Magazine,* as well as various anthologies. In addition, she has served as the lead editor on seven novels and two anthologies, including *Blood Games: A Vampire Anthology*. She is represented by the renowned New York literary agency the Knight Agency. In 2013 she was crowned "Vampire Royalty of New Orleans." Faust is currently at work on several new literary projects, as well as her first cookbook. When she is not writing, reporting, or painting, Faust is the owner of the Austin-based bakery Ice Pick's Pies.

gabriellefaust.com

Edgar Allan Poe was an American writer, poet, author, editor, and literary critic who is best known for his poetry and short stories, particularly his tales of mystery and the macabre. He is widely regarded as a central figure of Romanticism and Gothic fiction in the United States, and of American literature. Poe was one of the country's earliest practitioners of the short story, and is considered the inventor of the detective fiction genre, as well as a significant contributor to the emerging genre of science fiction. He is the first well-known American writer to earn a living through writing alone, resulting in a financially difficult life and career. (source: wikipedia.org)

Miranda S. Hewlett has worked in secondary and higher education in the fields of English Language Arts and Rhetoric since 2015. She is an Adjunct Professor and is passionate about increasing access and equity in education, particularly for marginalized groups who have not historically received equal access to quality educational opportunities. Part of this work includes supporting access for the deaf and hard-of-hearing population. She has worked as a freelance transcriptionist – creating captions for television, film, podcasts, corporate training materials, university lectures, and online streamed content since 2007. Though she began writing fiction for personal expression when she was in third grade, this anthology is her first formal fiction publication. She lives in Austin, Texas with her two incredible children and her loving life partner, Nina.

Raven Digitalis is the author of the "empath's trilogy" consisting of *The Empath's Oracle, Esoteric Empathy,* and *The Everyday Empath*, as well as the "shadow trilogy" of *A Gothic Witch's Oracle, A Witch's Shadow Magick Compendium*, and *Goth Craft*. Originally trained in Georgian Witchcraft, Raven has been an earth-based practitioner since 1999, a Priest since 2003, a Freemason since 2012, and an empath all of his life. He holds a degree in cultural anthropology from the University of Montana, co-operated a nonprofit Pagan Temple for 16 years, and is also a professional Tarot reader, editor, card-carrying magician, and animal rights advocate.

www.ravendigitalis.com

www.facebook.com/ravendigitalis

www.instagram.com/ravendigitalis

Tracy Cross has had her stories featured in several podcasts and compilations. Her debut novel, *Rootwork,* was released by Dark Hart Publishing in 2022. It delves into the power of family and her past experiences with hoodoo. Her next novel in the series, *A Gathering of Weapons,* was released in 2024. She resides in Washington, DC and is an active member of the Horror Writers Association. Additionally, she loves disco music and posts updates to her blog:
tracycrossonline.com

Jaclyn M. Ciminelli is the author of the dark fantasy/Gothic romance series *Witches & Black Roses* and the short story spinoff *Witch's Diaries*. Since middle school, she's loved Gothic romance novels of the 1960s and 1970s, the work of Anne Rice, and other tales of mystery, the paranormal, and the occult. She has been a witch since 2004 and is fond of bellydance, swimming, and travel.

Daniel Adam Rosser is a writer and artist from San Diego, CA and holds a degree in Social and Behavioral Sciences. He has been a healer and Holistic Health Practitioner for nearly 20 years. His lifetime interest in both history and metaphysics has led to an extensive study of the occult and the paranormal.

Mona Fitzgerald-King was raised by two loving adoptive fathers after she was discovered abandoned in a small-town funeral parlor. She is an avid (albeit mediocre) violinist who prefers the company of felines to humans. When she is not weaving tapestries of fiction from the fodder of fitful nightmares, she pines for a life of clarity in a country that truly respects women and taxes the wealthy appropriately.

MOON BOOKS

PAGANISM & SHAMANISM

What is Paganism? A religion, a spirituality, an alternative belief system, nature worship? You can find support for all these definitions (and many more) in dictionaries, encyclopedias, and text books of religion, but subscribe to any one and the truth will evade you. Above all Paganism is a creative pursuit, an encounter with reality, an exploration of meaning and an expression of the soul. Druids, Heathens, Wiccans and others, all contribute their insights and literary riches to the Pagan tradition. Moon Books invites you to begin or to deepen your own encounter, right here, right now.

If you have enjoyed this book, why not tell other readers by posting a review on your preferred book site.

Bestsellers from Moon Books
Pagan Portals Series

The Morrigan

Meeting the Great Queens

Morgan Daimler

Ancient and enigmatic, the Morrigan reaches out to us. On shadowed wings and in raven's call, meet the ancient Irish goddess of war, battle, prophecy, death, sovereignty, and magic.

Paperback: 978-1-78279-833-0 ebook: 978-1-78279-834-7

The Awen Alone

Walking the Path of the Solitary Druid

Joanna van der Hoeven

An introductory guide for the solitary Druid, The Awen Alone will accompany you as you explore, and seek out your own place within the natural world.

Paperback: 978-1-78279-547-6 ebook: 978-1-78279-546-9

Moon Magic

Rachel Patterson

An introduction to working with the phases of the Moon, what they are and how to live in harmony with the lunar year and to utilise all the magical powers it provides.

Paperback: 978-1-78279-281-9 ebook: 978-1-78279-282-6

Hekate

A Devotional

Vivienne Moss

Hekate, Queen of Witches and the Shadow-Lands, haunts the pages of this devotional bringing magic and enchantment into your lives.

Paperback: 978-1-78535-161-7 ebook: 978-1-78535-162-4

Bestsellers from Moon Books

Keeping Her Keys
An Introduction to Hekate's Modern Witchcraft
Cyndi Brannen
Blending Hekate, witchcraft and personal development together to create a powerful new magickal perspective.
Paperback: 978-1-78904-075-3 ebook 978-1-78904-076-0

Journey to the Dark Goddess
How to Return to Your Soul
Jane Meredith
Discover the powerful secrets of the Dark Goddess and transform your depression, grief and pain into healing and integration.
Paperback: 978-1-84694-677-6 ebook: 978-1-78099-223-5

Shamanic Reiki
Expanded Ways of Working with Universal Life Force Energy
Llyn Roberts, Robert Levy
Shamanism and Reiki are each powerful ways of healing; together, their power multiplies. Shamanic Reiki introduces techniques to help healers and Reiki practitioners tap ancient healing wisdom.
Paperback: 978-1-84694-037-8 ebook: 978-1-84694-650-9

Southern Cunning
Folkloric Witchcraft in the American South
Aaron Oberon
Modern witchcraft with a Southern flair, this book is a journey through the folklore of the American South and a look at the power these stories hold for modern witches.
Paperback: 978-1-78904-196-5 ebook: 978-1-78904-197-2

Readers of ebooks can buy or view any of these bestsellers by clicking on the live link in the title. Most titles are published in paperback and as an ebook. Paperbacks are available in traditional bookshops. Both print and ebook formats are available online.

Find more titles and sign up to our readers' newsletter
www.collectiveinkbooks.com/paganism

For video content, author interviews and more, please subscribe to our YouTube channel.

MoonBooksPublishing

Follow us on social media for book news, promotions and more:

Facebook: Moon Books

Instagram: @MoonBooksCI

X: @MoonBooksCI

TikTok: @MoonBooksCI